BLACK TIDE RISING

Dark Prophecies

Kelvin L. Singleton

Dedications

Sharrie Dionne Singleton, Richardine Lynnette Singleton-Brown, Marcella Theola Singleton, and Richard Mathew Singleton, Jr. Some of us are slow starters, but we do start and we finish stronger.

ACKNOWLEDGEMENT

Evangelist Veronica McCoy, the first person I sought out to read this novel to be certain that God Almighty would not damn my soul to hell for the sin of blasphemy. Thank you.

To Mrs. Virginia Bartels, formally an American English teacher, who once bridged the gap between the minds of my fellow students and the knowledge we learned to crave.

...likens teaching to gardening in that she could plant the seeds of the future, and watch the minds of her students grow. The analogy is a profoundly personal viewpoint that she shares with very few.

DISCLAIMER

B lack Tide Rising: Dark Prophecies is a work of fiction. Although some of the character names, herein, are real and existing people, the roles that they play for the sake of this dramatization is not meant as a reflection of their true personalities and actions in life. Nor is this work of fiction created to further the divide among the races or persons of differing religious beliefs in this great nation or any other of this world. It is written as a testament to the strengths of the human heart and spirit, for we often need to peer, unflinchingly, into the depths of utter darkness to recognize even a miniscule pinpoint of light that may lead to humankind's enlightened evolution. We are all the children of God, no matter whose name you may call out in the belly of despair. The author, Kelvin L. Singleton.

THE GENESIS PROLOGUE

Since a time long before the genesis of this world, there has always been the Lord God Damballah. Although he is all-powerful and the master of things both great and small, a vast emptiness flourishes within that is an unbearable loneliness.

Placing forth his left palm, he blows a raging inferno that becomes the companion, Lucifer, who is also known as The Satan; the soothsayer with a silken voice for the ages.

He now blows a mighty wind upon the right hand to create the twins, Marrassus and Dossa, who are pleasing to the eyes. Damballah grants powers unto them all, and they are free to rule this immense universe at his side. Again, Almighty God sweeps his hands forth to form a sanctuary and ten-thousand legions of angels, whom art the servants, hereof. All is good in this season of leisure and discovery, but Lucifer waxes a most envious god.

Coveting all that Damballah creates, Lucifer sets aside a place for himself in heaven. Although legions have been created from nothing, he forms angels of his own to rival the whole. Soon, hereafter, Marrassus and Dossa divine it prudent to create legions of their design. Soon to overflow the walls of heaven, much distress is wrought amongst the guardian entities. So great is the disquiet that angry spirits often flare where a forbidden war seems imminent. Weary of the petulance, Damballah journeys to a place of quiet serenity deep within the void where he is again inspired to create. Thusly, in the beginning, Damballah creates the heavenly firmament and then the earth. This world is without form and void, darkness is upon the face of the deep. Moving upon the face of the waters, the spirit of the Lord God Damballah decrees, "Let there be light." And there is light…

Upon the sixth millennium of creation, for unto Almighty God, two-thousand years is but an hour, Marrassus and Dossa join him and see that it is good.

Pleased to see them, Damballah says, "Let us make man in our image, after our own likeness. Let him have dominion over the foul of the air, over the cattle, and over every creeping thing that creeps upon the earth.

Of the dust from the ground, the Lord God forms man. Into his nostrils, Damballah blows the breath of life so that man becomes a living soul.

Damballah plants a garden eastward in Eden, where he places the newly formed man. Out of the ground, Damballah causes to grow every tree that is pleasant to the sight. The Tree of Life prospers in the garden, and so does The Tree of the Knowledge of Good and Evil.

Damballah places man in the Garden of Eden to dress and keep it well. He commands the primitive man, saying, "Of every tree of the garden, thou may freely eat, but thou shall not eat of The Tree of the Knowledge of Good and Evil. For on the day that thou hath eaten thereof—thou shall surely die."

The Lord God calls this man, Adam, whom he sends out to name all the creatures of the air and the earth. When Damballah sees in Adam the very seed of loneliness that once inspired the creation of his lesser companions, he says unto Marrassus and Dossa, "It is not good that the man should be alone. We will make a helpmate for him."

With a whisper, Damballah causes a deep sleep to fall upon Adam. He then takes one of Adam's ribs and closes up the flesh, thereof.

Of the rib, Dossa makes another, whom she brings unto man. And Adam says, "This is now bone of my bones and flesh of my flesh. She shall be called woman because she was taken out of man. Her name shall be Eve." Both are naked, the man and his wife, yet they are not ashamed.

Despising the new world that was formed without him, Lucifer scornfully watches from afar, abiding seething torments unto the moment of its undoing. Therefore, it is upon Dossa's day of rest that he comes unto her to whisper such venomous doubt into her ear that belief in what she hath created becomes tarnished and weak.

Lucifer, The Great Satan, now challenges Damballah, saying, "These creatures are all naught unto our mighty powers and they shall fail thee to utter misery. I shall now go among them, and they shall boldly abandon thy every commandment."

Damballah forbids The Satan to defile this world. Setting forth the angel La'am as guardian of the garden. Yet, Lucifer is cunning and full of deceit, causing La'am to abandon his post.

As a serpent upon its belly, The Satan approaches the woman Eve while alone. Because she fears not its subtle touch, the serpent pleasures the woman Eve, gently stroking her unto blindness. With great skill, his cunning tongue deceives her so that she eats the forbidden fruit from The Tree of the Knowledge of Good and Evil.

Having set her feet upon the path of wickedness, Eve soon tempts Adam's lips with the forbidden fruit. To his shameful failing, Adam tastes thereof.

Damballah is furious, raging against the firmament. Now overwhelmed by sorrow, Dossa weeps down upon the earth because the diminished faith in that which she conceived fails its very creation.

Into Damballah's ear, Marrassus speaks of mercy, for man surely faces destruction this day. Because of their sin, Adam and the woman Eve are punished and cast out of paradise.

Though he has succeeded in tainting the Garden of Eden, The Satan bellows angrily, for man still walks the earth. Having great dominion, he beguiles a multitude of the faithful servants, commanding his own army unto the very gates of heaven. Because of the one thing they lacked, an envy of the human soul, they lay siege upon the God of Creation.

Legions upon legions are destroyed to paint the firmament black. Blood-soaked and deeply saddened in the wake of great devastation, Damballah banishes The Satan.

Marrassus and Dossa beseech Damballah's mercy on behalf of the beguiled, who find themselves defeated at great cost. The fallen are driven from heaven. Once removed of their powers, many are doomed to join The Satan in a fiery realm within the heart of the sun, while others are cast down upon the earth as leviathans and behemoths. Many are the fallen, having chosen Damballah's only reprieve. Thus, by decree that they obey the laws of Eden and the sacred tree thereof, they form into creatures of the air; they form into denizens of the water, and of dry land. As the tree was once sown from the earth, mortal man became forbidden fruit because the fallen shall forever remain subject unto God in heaven.

As one-thousand years unto Damballah is merely a moment in time, humanity multiplies upon the earth. From her womb, in utter agony, the woman Eve bore twin sons. The eldest, Cain, is of ivory skin and most fair. The youngest is so named, Abel, whose skin is bronzed like copper and most comely.

The dark lord is unbound of his damnation by whispering false words of repentance, gaining the key to his freedom. For a time, The Satan resides within the void, far and away Damballah's loathsome creations. Yet, the day of his return is soon at hand.

When The Satan again murmurs his poison into the winking ear of mortal man, the eldest son of the woman Eve slays his brother, whose offering gains favor in the eyes of Damballah—for only Abel has sacrificed the most prized of his flock. For the hand of his sister, Arimaal, only Abel offers all because his love for her was true and good.

The Lord God so believes in humanity, he weeps for the young son taken by the first murder of the world. Even so, Lucifer still contrives evil upon the land, and within the hearts of Damballah's creations.

The time comes when he sweeps his dark, crimson wings down upon the distant desert sands of a barren land called Egypt to seek the dog beast, Ana`Anubis.

The Satan whispers words of envy and deceit into the winking ear of the fallen one of the burning dunes, for it would travel far to prey upon the daughters of Adam and the woman Eve. On frigid nights, whence the new moon rises, the beast takes them as a man takes his wife in carnal manners.

When the distant most child of the woman Eve does willingly lay with the beast, she is taken unto the talons of madness such that she leads the beast to the very abode of the first man.

The Satan writhes in his dark glory whilst Ana`Anubis of the desert ravages and devours the elder Adam and his wife in their poisoned slumber. Behold, once given to his mighty wrath, driven are the angry fists of the Lord God Damballah into the dry land to crack the earth that separates the troubled waters.

Dossa and Marrassus weep down upon the firmament days thrice, for they foolishly released The Satan from his damnation. They cower from Damballah's sight as many are punished for the sins of the jackal. Even the fallen are doomed to perish upon the earth amongst God's furious cataclysms. Swallowed up, their essence is trapped within a black teardrop that falls from Damballah's eye. He casts it into the air and disassembles its hardness with a bolt of angry lightning. Equally shattered unto seven parts, they are scattered throughout space or about the earth to remain forever hidden.

By the loving mercy of Damballah, the soul of Adam is resurrected. He is given form and purpose anew, while the soul of the woman Eve draws nigh unto the bosom of Dossa as a remembrance of both their failures to Eden.

The Lord God sets Adam's feet upon the land and bids him well. The first son is blessed with another helpmate, who is commanded to work at his side until called unto the glory of heaven.

The Lord God commands that his legions bind Lucifer with heavy chains and cast him into the sun where the fiery pit burns, eternally. Damballah blesses the earth with a living oracle, whose charge records the triumphs and woes of humanity. Through Adam, Damballah imparts his laws and wisdom unto the hearts of his children upon the earth. He then travels once more into the great void to rest from his weary toils and violent battles. Although all seems good upon the earth and in the heavens, sadly, in all things, Lucifer has sown a seed inherent of evil to taint the land and its inhabitants.

CHAPTER 1

FLIGHT INTO MADNESS

Suitland, Maryland. April 5, 2001

The balanced, rhythmic tick of the grandfather clock, which always imposes its presence upon any room when it chimes, now fades into obscurity like an echo from the distant past. While sitting with her legs curled up on the couch, Melissa Parker eagerly turns the page to read on because time is getting short.

Humankind creates towering monuments with great veins of gold borne from the bowels of the earth on the backs of the enslaved. They foolishly honor themselves, creating false gods, false prophets, and pillars of stone that boast of arrogance. Such are grave abominations of vanity—now and forever. Gone by the wayside are our children in assuming the roles of gods upon the earth. I have wept endless tears of one both blessed to see the good and cursed to know the ever-growing evils of humanity, for I am yet powerless to their sinful whim.

Soon, Damballah will be given to anger. The Great Spirit will move to his mighty wrath for we now behold terrible visions decreeing the setting loose

1

of diverse beasts that will tame his unruly children. That which is contrived of wicked imagination will bring blood from our broken bodies, discarding us as withered husks in a harshly driven wind. Fires will arise from majestic mountaintops.

The ground will rumble from Damballah's fury, and unnamed horrors will tread amongst men. Great and terrible lessons shall he bequeath, causing us to cringe from every sudden sound in every place of silent, brooding shadow. Humankind will suffer terrors untold from the depths of their own souls as the penance of many transgressions. Yet, the lesson will be unlearned, even if only forgotten upon a fleeting heartbeat. In the grasp of madness, warlord demons of genocide will overshadow all, bringing flies that will rule the plains and maggots to pluck our unburied dead to the very bone. From continent to continent, wars will wage for the festering blood of the fallen that boils deep within the soul of this world. All will suffer the price of vanity for seeking powers that are not ours to claim while striving to build earthly kingdoms at any cost. Amongst all that is good in the world, we fall to new depths low beneath an artificial darkness. My children, fouled by the seed of The Satan, are most decrepit when left too long to their own devices.

In all of these things, great and small, the beguiled believe that we are the masters of death and creation. When morose horrors, the very manifestations of the wicked are unleashed, our children shall reap that which is sown by the highest of earthly powers.

Life is the greatest treasure of this borrowed time upon this borrowed land. Life must endure humanity's growing villainy, for it revolves with and without the blessings of the sun. Life, which humanity diminishes with an ill regard for the creator of all things.

This sacred garden will thrive even without humankind's coexistence, so we must reunite with the nature of this once harmonious world or bow to a new species in rule. Because we fail to heed the dark magic of the drums and symbols drawn in blood, an image will be painted for all to see. Because we have failed the conception of Eden, a dark flood soon comes like a sweeping, hollow hunger.

Melissa Parker glances at the clock, closing the book while reflecting and ingesting the haunting words of Kaleem Kinzana's Bible. This is what she has come to consider this most mysterious concoction, though it is impossible to believe. It seems like a Bible that combines many of man's religious beliefs, superstitions, and folklore under one roof.

It contains references to vampires, werewolves...demons of genocide. In a sense, such things are all God's creations, even if the lesser gods that Kinzana mentions at the beginning, created them. There are many unanswered questions for this fifth grade teacher, but she remains taunted by startling religious theories and unanticipated avenues of thought that border—that flaunt—what most Christians would call blasphemy. What she has read so far is nothing compared to what is to come.

This journal is the most bizarre thing Melissa has attempted to read since daring an English translation of Dante's Divine Comedy, but it may have been written by a total madman with impeccable penmanship. Despite Melissa Parker's skepticism and trepidations, the book grows most difficult to put away.

Walking up the steps of their new home, counting as she goes, Melissa approaches her napping husband. It is time to wake Evan for his flight to Indiana.

Somehow, Evan Parker knows that they are his children.

One is a boy and the other a girl. Both have seashell bracelets that click and clatter about their bronze ankles. They are dancing in a circle, smiling and waving to their father while small dust clouds plume around their footfalls. They step in tune with the drums that beat around a circle of several children. These are happy drums, peaceful and harmonious.

While shaking him gently, Melissa whispers, "Evan. Baby, it's time to get up now." He stirs. As he turns to look at his beautiful wife, she sits next to him and says, "You were smiling in your sleep. I always hate to wake you when you look so peaceful."

"Thank you, sweetheart." He yawns as he sits up in the bed. "I'm really sorry that I have to do this, Mel. If I take care of this thing myself, it may alleviate some of the extreme pressure Peter is putting on himself. In times like these, I suppose I must be doing the right thing. You understand, don't you?"

Melissa touches his left cheek and eases his mind by saying, "It's your place as the deputy director. Just make sure you come back in one piece. I'll be fine with Maddy here, so please don't worry about me."

"I love you, baby," he says before kissing her.

"By the way, was I that good?"

Evan asks, "What do you mean?"

"That was me causing you to smile in your dream, right? Was I good or what?"

"Oh…no," he toys with her. "It wasn't you. I cannot tell a lie."

"Okay. So who was she?" Melissa asks, threatening to tickle him. Evan can't stand that kind of torture; a power that Melissa loves having over him.

"Okay, put the fingers of death away. I'll confess."

She arches a brow. "Well, I'm waiting, Mr. Parker."

"Her name was, Alana. His name was, Sonshal," he says while caressing her stomach.

"Sounds kinky. I believe you've been hanging around with your Caucasian co-workers too long," Melissa teases. They giggle.

"I was dreaming about our children, Melissa. Alana is our daughter and Sonshal is our son. Her name means flower and his name means first. I think."

"I see. And just how do you know that they're our children?" she asks. "The first flower twins were they?"

"Well, it was just a feeling I had when they smiled at me and waved their little hands. They had your eyes, Mel."

"I wish I was there to meet them. Can I come next time?"

"I'd like that. I suppose I'd better get my ass in gear if I expect to eat something and get out of here on time."

Evan showers and gets dressed before going downstairs to eat. When he finishes, Maddy insists on driving them to the airport because Melissa is new to the area and traffic can be somewhat hectic. On the drive back to Suitland, the women folk plan to stop at the hospital for a visit with Valerie McAllister. The wife of Evan's boss is having difficulties.

Melissa called the hospital earlier, but they gave her no information. Evan is unable to reach Peter McAllister, which isn't so odd since they expect him to be at the hospital.

Although Melissa has only known Valerie McAllister for a few days, there is a growing connection between them. She feels for Valerie's marital distress, hopeful that their problems will work out.

⇌ ⇋

Jeffersonville, Indiana 9:30 p.m.

As the taxi squeaks to a halt in the driveway of 2119 Paladin Street, Evan pays the driver and asks that she wait for a few minutes. The rather hungry driver agrees because she wants to eat a cold, bagged lunch in peace. The woman makes it clear that she will not wait too long, but the extra fifty bucks buys him some time.

Although the curtains and blinds of the red brick house are drawn, Evan Parker notices that every light seems to be on. For some unidentifiable reason, a creeping ill washes over his skin.

Concealed from sight by neglected rosebushes, something scurries around the eastern corner of the house. The smell of roses in bloom is powerful, but there is an underlying odor of rot and decay. There is no answer, so he rings twice more. Still, no one comes.

Evan knocks on the door, consigned to leaving if it does not pay off, but the red door slips open. Apparently, it hasn't been closed properly.

Contrary to his nature, Evan Parker pokes his head in and calls out. Barrette Holt's assistant, who set this meeting, told Evan beforehand that Mr. Holt is at home recovering from a cold. She also informed that Mr. Holt is in possession of the materials in question and happy to turn them over. Naturally, after knocking and shouting, Evan figures that the man must be on medication and sleeping. He really hates to disturb Mr. Holt, if that is the case.

Something tells Evan to call Holt's assistant back to confirm that she has indeed prepared him for the visit. Because he hasn't traveled all this way for his health, Evan Parker ventures inside only to be astonished by what he sees. Dozens of crosses are scattered about the house, and there are just as many burning candles on every available flat surface. Wax, melting over the sides of furniture, drips onto what must be fire-resistant carpeting.

Bibles are spread about each room. He pauses to look at the one that lies on the end table in Holt's living room. Like most of the others, it is open to Psalms 23. Another lies open upon the highlighted scripture Luke 10:19. Others refer to casting out evil, unclean spirits.

Just before he steps on a sticky puddle of vomit, an odor reminds Evan of Peter McAllister's most recent bout with nausea. He winces in disgust, knowing that he will have to clean it off or carry that scent around until he throws the shoe away. He wipes his foot in the carpeting.

Evan now discerns the pungency of garlic, what he should have noticed when the door first slipped open. Garlands are stapled about every window frame, and draped over hot lampshades that heighten the aroma. The bulbs, traditionally used for seasoning food, trace the handrail of the staircase all the way to the top. Many more wreaths of garlic lay on every other step between the first and second story landings.

Evan peruses his surroundings and mumbles to himself, "This man is sick—in the head. He must be bonkers." Deep down inside, Evan Parker thinks himself mad because an inexplicable something is still forcing his feet onward. He considers walking out, but he is drawn forward by a subtle noise upstairs. Faced with a choice, Evan glances longingly at the front door, then back to the top of the stairs.

In prudence, Evan Parker calls out to Barrette Holt as his magnetized feet slowly carry him up the steps. With each stride, his grip tightens on the briefcase's handle because he is exercising caution that is certainly not caution enough. For a second, he envisions himself arrested as an intruder. After all, he is a strange Black man who met Barrette Holt only in passing a few months ago.

Evan Parker moves on, aching to be outside with every increment of ascent. The aroma of sickness now grows stronger. It thickens with his progress. The unmistakably rancid odor of feces is powerful, as if a dog has been left inside for days. Housebroken or not, it must have answered the call of nature many times.

Imagining himself mauled by a Doberman or worse, Evan stops at the third step from the top to call out. Yet again, there is no answer. Suddenly, he knows how acute claustrophobics must feel when they have to enter cramped, unfamiliar dark spaces.

Up here, even more crosses are nailed to the dry wall like the crooked decorations of a religious fanatic. There is evidence in some places where the cross-hanging maniac has punched holes in the drywall. Barrette, or whoever did this, must have injured a finger because of the stains that look like dried blood.

He has nailed crosses to the floor and surrounded them by wreaths of garlic. Burning candles planted right in the wooden intersection of the crosses lead a clear path down the hall.

The smell of melting wax mingles with all of the other odors up here. As if the stench suddenly lifts some hypnotic veil from his eyes, Evan Parker realizes the sheer lunacy of his actions and decides to go no further.

Parker concludes that Peter McAllister is covering up the fact that Barrette Holt is experiencing a radical mental breakdown. It explains why Peter was so adamant about handling things with Holt himself. He wishes he hadn't come here without Peter's knowledge. In the name of friendship and duty, he's foolishly lit out for parts unknown. Now, it no longer seems like such a keen idea.

As he turns to go back downstairs, there is sudden movement behind him. Barrette Holt appears at the top of the landing with a loaded gun pointed at the back of Evan's head!

Knowing the sound of a slide shuffling a shell into the breach, Evan freezes and slowly raises his hands. He knows the hammer now stands at the ready.

Down in the basement of a nearby home, forced to a dizzying beat, voodoo drums are throbbing in the company of white eyes. Sweat rolls off the drummers' dark bodies like steaming waterfalls. Beneath a black sky that suddenly writhes with angry clouds, the voodoo makers hiss while grasping at invisible talismans of the air.

A crazed grin etches Barrette Holt's grizzled face as his wild eyes penetrate the Black man's vulnerable skull. He begins to laugh. This foolish person is much too tall to sneak up on him, unlike the relentless Pygmy woman that has haunted him. Somehow, Holt knows that he can actually kill this one.

"I got you," Holt rages with his wide eyes blazing. "We'll see who dies now!" he shouts as a wicked little laugh graces his chapped lips. "I got you."

"Wait, hold on. Please don't shoot, Mr. Holt. Your assistant, Amy Lucas, contacted you about my arrival. I know how this must look, but I'm only here to…"

"No talking. You think I don't know what you're trying to do?" Holt shouts. "You are going to pay. Yeah, I got you!" His finger caresses the trigger. The gun pitches with those shaking hands.

"Please, Mr. Holt, don't shoot. I'm the Deputy Director of the Census Bureau. We met once in Suitland some months ago. My name is…"

With spit-slinging irritation, Holt demands, "Shut up, and turn around. I want you to see this bullet coming. Let's just see if you can dodge it from this range!"

Holt is going to shoot this man in the face, intending to empty the clip into him once he's down. Jazzed up on the street cocaine he uses to stay awake, his nerves are bristling cactus thorns; they are hot, frazzled wires. Catching one of the night people, who stalk his wake and dreams, now plies him toward the edge of unchecked jubilation.

Evan Parker slowly turns, fearing that his time has come. Like a vigilant drum, his pulse bangs in his temples. His mouth is as dry as corroded cotton, but sweat flows freely from his open pores.

When the yawning cab driver finally toots the horn, Barrette Holt's breath pauses in his chest for fear that this man's friends are coming to his aid.

He asks no one in particular, "What was that?"

By now, both hearts are pumping pistons. Convinced that he is going to die, Evan Parker decides that he must go for the gun. He holds his breath, but hesitates when faced with the preoccupied gunman's overall appearance. Holt is filthy from his feet to his neckline. It looks and smells as if this man has wallowed in a vat of manure. Blood has dried under Barrette's nostrils, on his shirt, and knuckles.

With adrenaline coursing through his body, Evan Parker is about to make his play. However, when the weapon stops shaking, he knows it is too late.

Barrette's eyes widen as he cries, "Peter? My God, you showed up just as you promised. I'm so sorry. I thought you were one of them coming to get me." Holt drops the gun to hug Evan Parker as if the man is a life preserver on the stormy sea that sunk his tiny craft. Parker is revolted, but he does nothing to agitate this very sick individual. Barrette drags him onto the landing where he hugs Peter McAllister again. And in his bewitched eyes, he is truly embracing the friend that promised to see him soon.

"You'd better come with me, Peter." He whispers, "It's just not safe out here. Well, come on."

When Evan Parker looks at the gun, Barrette Holt follows his eyes to the floor and beats him to the punch. Evan feels foolish for failing to snatch it from the floor the moment it fell from those trembling hands. That had been his second mistake. With a certainty, his initial misstep was coming to this place. Evan complies, wanting no part of the third strike. He follows Barrette, who, for some reason, sees this African American as Peter McAllister.

The door at the far end of the run is riddled with crosses, garlic, and Bibles. This must be his sanctuary, Evan thinks to himself, but nothing imagined compares to the actual sight of it. When Barrette opens the door, he's enveloped by the stench of the central fortress. The room, with a few distinctions, is littered much the same as the rest of the home. In this enclosure, the smell of feces mingles with the candle wax, garlic, urine, and vomit to stifling degrees. It's like breathing the fetid fog of a garbage scow; nearly thick enough to cut with a very dull knife.

The unkempt bed is spotted with urine and fecal matter. Evan surveys the brightly lit room, noting the wounded dry wall. Those are undoubtedly bullet holes. The floor of the walk-in closet is stacked with cases of canned beans, vegetables, and four cases of bottled water. Barrette has also moved the microwave and a wooden dish rack from the kitchen to the bathroom.

The centerpiece of Holt's nightstand is a tiny doll's bed. Strewn about the bedroom floor, lay defaced black dolls. Some resemble ethnic versions of Barbie and Ken. Quite a few are made of plastic, others of cloth. The dolls are mostly female, but each one is mutilated in some unseemly way. Many are decapitated or missing limbs. A few of the more offensive victims are completely dismembered.

Each doll has been impaled with needles, like those used by women to secure hair buns. Some of the dolls are impaled with sharpened crosses that Barrette Holt has fashioned into makeshift stakes. Safety pins and filed crotchet needles protrude from their tiny eyes and crushed skulls. The mouths of the cloth dolls have been sewn, stapled, or taped shut so they cannot whisper their wicked incantations.

Evan Parker fears for his life in the overwhelmingly grim midst of Holt's feverish dementia. He will have to play along by pretending to be Peter McAllister, praying that the pale paint that now colors this man's eyes does not soon wear off.

Once the deadbolts are secured, Barrette whispers, "I did it, Peter. I finally beat those bastards. See this doll?" He removes the effigy from his pocket, showing it to his partner in crime. "I got my own doll. That crazy bitch dropped it, and she'll never get it back!" Now, with creepy deliberation, Barrette Holt places the cloth doll onto the tiny bed and pulls the cover up to its neck. Although Evan Parker remains silent, his body is racked by a frigid shudder. His teeth quietly chatter behind his clenched lips and a wave of nausea threatens.

"Do you understand?" Holt asks. "When I need to sleep, I put me in the bed. They won't get to me anymore, not without a fight. They hate garlic, just like the bloodsuckers that they are."

Holt's eyes dart about as if he expects uninvited visitors at any moment. This pitiful man is the very picture of desperation and unchecked insanity. Since Holt seems so concerned about home security, his behavior prompts Evan Parker to wonder how the front door had been left unlocked. It soon dawns on him that the unlocked front door had been a trap for Barrette's secret fiend.

"Who's after you, Barrette?"

Holt looks at him, strangely. Just for a second, he thinks he sees…a Black man. His mad eyes squint, while scattered brainwaves cause his head to twitch and eyes to blink.

Then he says, "You know. I told you about the Pygmy bitch, with the voodoo stuff. She wants to eat me. She said so many times, but I found a way to stop her from taking me out of the house when I'm sleeping!"

Holt's eyes grow wild, with the crazed grimace of a total lunatic. He is living as a savage, with very savage thoughts because that has been the face and the true nature of his enemies for some time. His brown eyebrows furrow. His clammy forehead wrinkles and small, helpless whimpers escape his nervous lips. Holt is thinking of things Evan Parker could never imagine. His eyes, his very pitiful eyes, suddenly move far away from his wretched body.

"How did you do that, Barry?" Evan asks.

Evan figures that he will end up looking like one of these massacred dolls if he makes the wrong move, so he is locked into this situation. He begins to sweat, profusely, realizing that he should smile. Evan Parker, forced to maintain a pretense of happiness for Barrette's monumental triumphs, caters to his mentally unbalanced needs.

"Can't you see? I just cover myself with nasty stuff. They will not eat me because I'll taste bad. I eat everything with garlic. It will kill them. You and Valerie should start preparing because you're next, Peter." Barrette's eyes grow secretive. His voice becomes a whisper when he stutters, "Shh-she likes to talk about eating your wife's unborn baby." He glances over his left shoulder, listening to shrill laughter and drums that only he can hear.

"What? Who told you that?" Evan asks. "I…I forgot her name."

"Ttt-tu – Tuloni," he stutters. "That midget freak says you're next, Peter. You're next."

Holt's breath, rank with raw garlic, offends Evan Parker's irritated sense of smell. However, he plies Holt further. Unflinchingly, Parker asks, "Next for what, exactly?"

"You're in fucking denial, Peter. Stop playing dumb and wise up. Your nightmares are realer than dreams, aren't they?" His squint grows darker as he zooms in on Peter's blue eyes with a macabre smile to repeat, "Aren't they, Peter? Yes, I thought so. You have to prepare because you can't imagine the awful things those horrible creatures have done to me." He pauses, closing his eyes before asking, "Is God—is our God really dead—like she says?"

"God?" Evan looks at the Bibles, confusion mounting his anxieties like a spooked herd of wild horses.

Holt whimpers, shivering as tears run from his red eyes. "Do you have a gun, Peter?"

Evan says, "No, I don't, Mr. ..." His blood pressure leaps and the temperature begins to rise again. "...Barry. I don't own one, I'm afraid."

Holt approaches, securing the safety before giving the loaded gun to Peter McAllister.

"Well, you'd better take this one. I don't need it as much as you do."

Evan is relieved to have the weapon in his hands, but this dramatization is yet to end. Holding it emboldens the Deputy Director to ask, "Why would you say something like that to me, Barry?"

"Because I'm protected now. When they come for me, I take their dolls and shove pins into them the same way they did me all those times. I like to make them scream in pain, but those godless, black-hearted bastards never give up. They just keep coming and coming!" Holt turns his head to listen. "It's true about God, isn't it, Peter?"

"What's that, Barry?"

"God is really dead, or those things would not be here on earth. He's dead, Peter." Drool runs from Barrette's blistered lips as his eyes dance insane.

Evan Parker pries deeper into Holt's delusions, into its connection with his boss and friend, Peter McAllister. Knowing that he is standing on very dangerous ground, he inquires, "But why do I need this gun more than you?"

Barrette assumes that hurt, confused look again. It quickly transforms into annoyance.

"Oh, no you don't. You are not going to pin it all on me. You know you need it more than I do. I'm not the one who got Cecil Bridges killed. It was you, Peter, not me!"

"Cecil?" Although it feels like a ton of bricks has just fallen on Evan, he contains the emotions to stay the course.

"You made the call, not me. That's it. This is the very last time for me. I am finally leaving here after tomorrow. I'm going somewhere they can't find me, so you can take this stuff off my hands simply because I have finally had it, Peter. Please don't try to stop me this time. Please. I'm begging you to let me go in peace."

Barrette glances at the gun in Peter's hand. For a twitching instant, he spies something amiss.

"Okay, Barry. Calm down." Evan does not want him getting worked up again. Holt seems more excited, knowing that he is about to relieve himself of a most dreadful burden.

Holt goes to his nightstand and opens the safe in the cabinet beneath, where he keeps the delayed census for the year 2000 and others. He snatches the disks and bound reports from the safe, then hands them all to Peter McAllister with a very sincere smile.

"I've given you all of my personal access codes, they're in this notepad. Now you can access this shit remotely, but I wouldn't advise it. Please don't tell Mr. Sterne that I've been keeping this stuff in my house, Peter. He might get angry. That man gives me the creeps. Here, take it. Take it all. I'm finished with it—good riddance. You can tell them to keep their blood money." A twisted little giggle escapes Barrette Holt's dry, cracked lips.

"Thanks, that's just what I came for." Evan wants out more than anything in this world. "Are you going to be okay, Barry?" His briefcase will not hold it all so Barrette Holt quickly tosses him a brief bag.

Barrette hugs Evan, who is glad to have those bulky items in his hands to block a full embrace. It is only now that he realizes just how much weight Holt has lost since their first meeting.

Like a tire going flat, Barrette Holt's voice calms, slowing from the frenzied pace that consumes him from within. He looks up at Peter and asks, "We did the right thing, didn't we? If any of this information had gotten out, we'd all be dead meat, right? You have to know how glad I am to be out of it. I felt so much guilt for what we did, but you kept me going, Pete. For the last eleven years, I thought I was going to lose my friggin' mind, but my good, good friend was always there for me. I'm going to miss you, Peter." Tears streak down his filthy cheeks.

Evan doesn't know what to say. There is too much information coursing through his mind, unimaginable things that must wait like undigested food in his belly.

Holt sighs long and hard. He now yawns, stretching his aching arms wide. "I'm so tired. I just want to sleep forever. You don't mind showing yourself to the door, do you?" Evan doesn't mind at all. "Please be careful, Peter. She's a wicked little woman and nearly unstoppable. She wants to eat your baby because God is dead, and there's no one to stop her."

Holt shivers with a conviction that shakes Evan Parker before he can back away.

"It's okay, Barry. I'll be leaving now. Try to take care of yourself." As Evan turns to walk away, he asks, "Barry, will it be okay if I send a few friends of mine to talk to you? It's alright, they'll help you to find a safe place to rest."

"Can they help me? Yes, of course. Just tell them to hurry."
Barrette Holt begs. "Peter, they... they won't kill me, right? I promise never to speak of it to anyone. You have my solemn oath."

"You will be safe Barry. No one will harm you. I promise."

"Thank you so much, Peter. Thank you so much." With great
relief, Barrette Holt places a hand on his friend's shoulder and
warns, "Please remember to be careful, Peter. They are all around
us now. I can feel them like nagging splinters beneath my skin,
so you'd better run when you get outside." Barrette turns away to
make sure that his effigy is properly tucked in. Oddly, he uses a
piece of string to anchor his doll to the white, plastic bed. He contemplates placing the doll in the vacant safe. However, he considers
suffocation a real threat. In a moment of sudden inspiration, Holt
super-glues the doll's cradle to the surface of the nightstand, concerned that his powerful enemies might cast some spell to spirit
away his entire bed.

This broken soul holds himself for a few quiet seconds before
lying down on a bed of his own filth.

When Evan uses Holt's kitchen phone to call for an ambulance,
he tells the 911 operator that he has a flight to catch and will not
stay. After telling them that Holt is completely insane, and that they
should humor him, he confirms the address. For some instinctive
reason, yet inexplicable even to himself, Evan Parker gives them a
false name. He lets them know that he will leave Barrette's gun in
the mailbox. As with the phone, he puts it there only after wiping
his fingerprints away.

Evan already decided to walk to a convenience store that he saw
on the way to Holt's home, where he plans to call a cab. Although
he was told to stay on the phone, Evan Parker wants to be nowhere
near this place when someone comes to get Holt.

He is pleasantly surprised to find the cab in Barrette's driveway. The snoring driver has fallen asleep behind the wheel with the
engine running. Evan knocks on the window to wake her. Although

the cabby did not intend to stay this long, she receives another substantial tip. Inevitably, there is a comment about the stench.

When the EMT and the police arrive at Barrette's home, they are given a small sense of relief when they find his gun in the mailbox just as the caller said. However, they are shocked at what they find inside this time. The dispatcher's records show that there have been several false alarms at this address, but nothing recently.

Because they are demons of the night to Barrette Holt, the screaming begins upon their entrance into the master bedroom. He thought he was finally safe, but they breached his best defenses.

Barrette Holt's shrieking demons do not heed warnings as he stands in the middle of the bed.

They do not cringe. Nor do they scream in agony when he drives pins into the dolls, which is why he goes for the other gun in the nightstand!

The police officers make terribly novice mistakes as trained observers in this case, but they are very fortunate that Barrette Holt sees things that they cannot.

Barrette points the gun back and forth, but the Pygmy bitch just laughs, knowing that he can never harm her. Holt finally turns the weapon upon himself and blows his brains all over the filthy walls of the bedroom.

Evan's cab stops at a local Wal-Mart, where he purchases some casual wear and a pair of sneakers. He promptly changes clothes in the fitting room, depositing everything he had worn to Indiana in the shopping bag. He ties the bag to contain the smell. Nevertheless, he suffers an odor that seems glued to his nostril hairs by the burning candles in Holt's home. Insanity, he thought. There is no other explanation for Barrette Holt's ravings in references to Peter

McAllister or Cecil Bridges, his old basketball coach and professor. Evan Parker will soon find out just how little he knows about what happened eleven years ago.

Somewhere in the night, the pulsing drums are fading as voodoo worshipers writhe in the grasp of a dark ecstasy. The drums will now cease, but only for a time.

CHAPTER 2
SLIP OF THE TONGUE

Wednesday. August 30, 1990. 3:30 p.m.
Suitland, Maryland

The conference room is crowded with the executives of the Census Bureau. Among them are the supervisors of the Data Preparation Division of Jeffersonville, Indiana, and the Computerized Telephone Interviewing Centers at Hagerstown and Tucson, Arizona. Supervisors of the bureau's twelve regional offices, which are scattered about the United States, are also present.

Cecil Bridges, the first African American Bureau of Census Director, sits at the head of the conference table. A faithful assistant, Deedra Wilson, flanks him. Deputy Director Peter McAllister sits to his right.

Although he still finds the job challenging and rewarding, the past ten of Cecil Bridges' fifteen years at the helm have been rather hectic. His is a presidentially appointed office, having first found favor in the eyes of Gerald Ford, who offered Cecil the position in 1975. At the time, he was asked to replace Director Stuart James, who retired rather suddenly.

Although equally plagued by predictable and unforeseeable problems, Bridges managed to survive Jimmy Carter and two terms of Reaganomics by sticking to long-range objectives. Now Cecil Bridges hopes to outlast the Bush administration.

Standing always in the shadow of imminent cutbacks, the rebounding economy remains the most serious contention. Making sure that his people keep their jobs is a major responsibility, but he sees to it with every means available.

The Bureau of Census was established in 1902. Its major functions authorized and guided by the Constitution, assures that a census of the nation's population will be taken every ten years. Such an enormous undertaking requires vast resources. Under Cecil Bridges, the importance of the Bureau of Census has grown, but so has its budget.

The budget is the main topic of discussion in this meeting of minds. Thankfully, it concludes with Bridges saying, "There you have it, people. We are all on notice now. Despite projections, we have slightly overrun our budget. On top of that, we're also late in painting and framing a picture of national growth for the Congress and the bean-counters in the executive branch."

Quite good at giving equal billing when it comes to staring people down, Cecil inspects the stoic expression of each face in the room. In this case, many of the department heads seem to share an expression that states in its silent effect, "I did my part, so please don't look at me."

Most of the personnel, who fall beneath Cecil's discerning gaze, will look anxiously at the same person with their own reproachful glares. Their eyes are accusing Barrette Holt, head of the Data Preparation Division in Jeffersonville, Indiana.

One by one, they shy away from Cecil's look of disappointment to consider Mr. Holt, who now notices the trend and shrinks into a seat that offers his considerable bulk very little room to hide.

With the temperature suddenly on the rise, the roots of Holt's thinning brown hair prickle in their follicles, threatening to leave him completely bald. In turn, he has a momentary reflex of the betraying eyes, the kind of reflex that causes guilty people to glance at an accomplice in crime when pressured. In this case, Holt's eyes seek Peter McAllister.

Feeling that the silence is both obvious and inappropriate, Peter McAllister clears his throat. He sits up in his chair to address the boss apologetically.

"Well, sir, Mr. Holt is not entirely at fault for the delayed compilation of the data because I have authorized a new program that is designed to facilitate our organization of the hard data transfers from Indiana." McAllister can almost feel his steel blue pupils contract.

"You did what?" The rest of the executives exhale depleted oxygen, relieved by Director Bridges finally finding a specific direction for his ire of disappointment. Barrette Holt is the only other person that does not share this relief.

McAllister clears his throat before straightening his tie to say, "Well, you have a lot on your mind. I thought it best with the budget being in the red and Congress talking about downsizing. I apologize, but I am only trying to come up with a way to alleviate the pressure by looking to the future, should we incur a workforce reduction. I hope I haven't overstepped my authority as your deputy director, Mr. Bridges."

Cecil strokes his graying mustache, a sure sign of irritation.

At this point, Holt adds, "That's correct, Mr. Bridges. The Swifting Program will ease things considerably in the future. I'll admit that there have been delays because the system had to be perfected, but everything is in order now. I promise that every bit of info will have been siphoned through Peter's unit en route to the permanent data banks by lunchtime tomorrow." Holt does that thing with his eyes and nearly bites his tongue, knowing that he is volunteering too much.

Because Cecil notices the look, he becomes suspicious. Of what, he isn't sure, but this collaboration is definitely tainted in its obscure nature. He turns to Peter, whose face barely recovers from the flash of fear and annoyance that bloomed when Holt mentioned the route of information being via his station. What Bridges sees is a pleasant, but detectably phony smile. Peter's skin is still flush. That, he cannot hide.

Realizing that he is not going to get a straight answer, Cecil decides to play along by asking questions for which they will have perfectly reasonable answers. These questions must be asked so that their answers might appear to appease him. Once their guards are down, whatever they're up to will eventually escape them. Obviously, he knows these men quite well.

Cecil leans back in his seat and asks, "Why would you send a decade's worth of data through Peter's station before going to the data bank? I don't understand the reasoning behind that strategy. Quite simply, it sounds to me as if you are trying to kill a charging Rhino with a pebble."

McAllister purses his lips and glances at Holt, whose face begins to display signs of frustration. Tiny beads of sweat are permeating his forehead. Meanwhile, with great interest, the others are watching this cat and mouse drama as it corkscrews, having no idea that, for the time being, almost any answer will be allowed to slide.

McAllister explains, "It's being done this way so that I may double-check some of the more pertinent stats before they're finalized. I'll randomly check for continuity." Dissatisfied with Cecil's expression, Peter adjusts his tie and adds, "You know, I'll be checking for errors in formatting and categorization. That sort of thing. It was my decision to do this, so I should assume the full responsibility of seeing that its maiden voyage comes off without a hitch."

"Ah huh. I see." Cecil Bridges looks at Barrette Holt, who gives an affirming head nod before averting his eyes. After a momentary pause, Bridges says, "Well, if you gentlemen are sure there won't be any more delays I suppose I can live with it. I expect to be updated on this Swifting Program."

"Yes sir." You have my word on that," Peter agrees. He chooses humility on the heels of what some people in the room consider a great save for whatever lies they are telling. Of all the people in the room, Peter knows his professor from the University of South Carolina to be anything but naive. He thinks it best to remain on guard.

Bridges addresses the rest of the troops, who are thinking about fleeing a room in which they're feeling trapped. He takes a deep breath and says, "We've all been under pressure to prove our worth here. I'm frankly amazed that Mr. McAllister and Mr. Holt feel that whatever they've done is so far removed from a budget meeting that they failed to mention it when a bit of good news is in order. Nevertheless, things would be easier around here if we were not burdened with the political aspects or the need for constant justification of our spending methods. However, I suppose I'm here to keep them off your backs so you can do your jobs. Something I cannot do when my subordinates are constructing potentially catastrophic matrixes without my consult. However, you have all done a great job, even if I don't say it often enough. I thank you all for your efforts, but it's imperative that you keep up the good work. I ask that you all remember, no wage increases or unnecessary expenditures for a while. Stay diligent. This meeting is adjourned."

Unlike anxious school kids, these responsible adults restrain the urge to run screaming into the halls after the bell rings. Instead, they gather their files and notes, neatly stacking them in their briefcases. Pens and pencils are placed in their designated slots. They shake hands and make small talk or dinner plans. In an orderly fashion, they walk into a hallway that rings with freedom as they begin an exodus to the elevators of true deliverance.

Much to their chagrin, Bridges asks Peter McAllister and Barrette Holt to stay. Once the room is empty, he looks one to the other and says, "Gentlemen, why do I feel that there could be more to this delay than you're telling me? I want to know everything."

Peter wades in. "Well, Cecil, what do you want to know? I certainly have nothing to hide. I've told you as best I can what has been the problem."

Holt adds, "I don't know what else I can possibly say to reassure you. I had a hand in creating the Swifting Program in conjunction with Algorithmic components of the Defense Department. I'm actually proud to say that this new program is up to speed and everyone will be briefed on its functions soon." Surprisingly, lying is much easier without an audience, which reminds him of all the head turning involved in watching a heated tennis match.

Bridges says, "I seem to recall some obscure memo on the subject. Look, I've been here for fifteen years. Barrette, you've been here for ten or eleven. Peter, when I left the university you were just about to move into your sophomore year. You were one of only two sixteen-year-olds I ever had the pleasure to teach and coach. You were and still are a brilliant young man. However, you've only been here a mere five years or so. My point being, you both know by now that when there are drastic changes to be made, you should seek my authorization first, and foremost. The chain of command, or dare I say, ignoring the chain of command is one of the main reasons that this department, or any other, will incur problems. The chain has its purpose in departmental government, people. There are rules to follow. Do you understand me?" Both men nod. "I'd like more information on this new Swifting Program of yours later. If by some small chance there is a problem with the transfer program, or if you two have somehow managed to screw the data all to hell, I want to know about it before it blows up in my face. Just give me a little time to choose which form of suicide is quickest, and less painful than being fired at my age. I trust that we'll be spared this sort of malfeasance in the future. Got me?"

Both men say, "Got it. No problem, Cecil."

Bridges smiles, sarcastically. "We'll, at least you're well-rehearsed." He excuses them and gathers his things. Because he must deliver a speech at a local college tomorrow morning and needs ample time to unwind, Cecil leaves the office early.

Barrette Holt joins Peter in his office. Once they are behind closed doors, Peter scolds, "Just what the hell is wrong with you? Are you crazy or just a little suicidal yourself? You nearly blew it, Barrette. Cecil is far from stupid."

Holt recedes. His voice is a frantic whisper when he says, "I'm sorry, but he caught me off guard. Having all those assholes staring at me did not help matters much. Jesus." He takes a few deep breaths and tries to stop his hands from shaking before Peter notices.

"He may have bought our story, but not hook, line, and sinker. We've recovered as well as can be expected, but you have to get with it. If you feel you can't handle this assignment, then maybe you should consider another job before you're in too deep because this shit is crucial, friend. We can't afford to let our guards down so get it together, Barry."

Holt stands erect. "I'm over it. When I get back to the DPD tomorrow morning, I'll start up the transfer program. You'd better be here, and remember what you're supposed to do. Just don't drop the ball on me. I can't wait to be rid of this shitty responsibility."

"You'll never be rid of it because it won't just go away," Peter snaps. "And don't worry about me. I can handle my end."

One man goes home to his lover. Meanwhile, the other goes to the airport lounge to have a few drinks before his flight back to Indiana.

CHAPTER 3
MY DUTIES DONE

The unusually chilly weather of the last two weeks now prompts forecasts of an early seasonal change in this region. The singular benefit of which now becomes apparent to Cecil Bridges as terrific bursts of vibrantly colored foliage makes the ride home quite a spectacle to behold. So many colors tracing the roadway's progression gives the sensation of driving through a child's kaleidoscope. It's soothing, most reassuring that all is as it should be even in an ever-changing world where the changing of the seasonal guard, at least, remains somewhat of a constant aspect of life. To him, contrary to the fact that he has held the same job for over a decade, life is about change; anything less is merely existence.

Cecil thinks lovingly of his twenty-five-year-old daughter, who still lives in his hometown of Columbia, South Carolina. She is an only child, so they stay in touch. For them, the Christmas holiday season is a favorite time of year because they spoil his grandson beyond redemption, whenever finances allow. Although the changing of the leaves are a bit early this year, it is a joyful reminder.

Cecil's wife of twenty-six years died in 1985 and he never remarried. Because the loss of true love dwindles more slowly for some, several years passed before he even considered the companionship of another woman. At age fifty-four, however, Cecil Bridges found love again in a woman he has worked with for years.

Upon entering the bedroom, he is greeted by a subtle sweetness lingering in the motionless air like a friendly ghost. Cecil smiles at the scent and goes into the bathroom for a shower before taking a nap. While bathing, he recites parts of tomorrow's speech from memory.

At 7:10 p.m., Bridges awakens to the subtle clanking of pots and the smell of dinner. He puts on an old, comfortable pair of sweats, and creeps downstairs with a wily smile upon his face.

Unnoticed, he eases into the kitchen where she samples something that smells tasty. Listening as she hums, the wily grin of a practical joker stretches Cecil's facial features to retain a boyish giggle. She yelps when he grabs her about the midriff, but quickly turns to kiss her playful man. She is Cecil's forty-nine-year-old assistant, Deedra Wilson.

The lovers with whom they expected to share much more time in this world have widowed both. After working together for more than a decade, they found one another. They were friends long before they became lovers; something in both their opinions that goes lacking, and thereby dooms most of the relationships and marriages of the younger generations.

They kiss for a moment before she rebukes, "Okay, tiger, that's quite enough. We don't want to ruin your appetite with sweets, do we?"

Cecil hugs her tighter and whines, "But, mother, I'm oh so hungry." He flicks his tongue at her and winks.

Deedra Wilson smiles and caresses his cheek. "You're so nasty. Get out. Go on, get! Dinner will be ready soon, so take a walk to cool off."

"I'll go, if you join me," Cecil says. "Otherwise, I'll continue the sexual harassment, while serenading you with my growling stomach."

She laughs and removes the apron. After tossing a sweater about her shoulders, Deedra joins Cecil as he walks out of the kitchen door where the cooling eastern dusk displays its noble splendor. They stroll to the end of his property to stand on a hill overlooking a babbling brook. As they hold hands, the sun slowly fades into the horizon behind them, leaving its mark on rifts of low-lying clouds that float across a lazy sky. Gray, yellow, blue, and a brilliant red hue, paint the darkening atmosphere.

Deedra looks to her man to ask, "Don't you think you were just a little hard on them today?"

He arches an eyebrow and asks, "Who?"

She grunts. "You know, Peter and Barrette."

Cecil chuckles and pats her hand. "Oh, I see. Those two are definitely up to something. I just can't put my finger on it yet, but I'll get to the bottom of it. The nearest I can figure is that they have somehow managed to accidentally erase or misplace some very important data, and they've been stalling while trying to recover it."

"Well, Peter is a nice guy and hard worker. Do you honestly believe he would try to pull the wool over your eyes if it were something major? His explanation seems perfectly plausible. Give him some time and he will fix whatever it is. You'll see."

Cecil sighs in the face of Deedra Wilson's temperate logic. "You're probably right. I just wish he felt he could still come to me, instead of hiding things. It's not as if I'm some evil boss, waiting in the shadows to lop off heads every chance I get." He looks at the quiet sky. "In any event, I have a feeling we'll soon find out. You ready to get back?"

As they turn to walk back, Deedra smiles at him and says, "Speaking of cheeks, maybe their behavior has nothing to do with work or the report." She politely clears her scratchy throat, turning away to cough into a fist.

"What do you mean?"

"Maybe they're both actually gay. You know how those guys like to pinch each other's bottoms and play chase around the office when they think no one is watching." Deedra cackles as he roars, and both continue to be amused by the silly thought until bedtime.

At 6:00 a.m., Cecil Bridges whimpers, "Oh no." He is dreaming that he has gone to school without wearing his pants. Only, in this case, he is the teacher and his students are laughing hysterically.

He wakes, looking about the dim room, somewhat relieved that it had been a dream. To him, however, it represents something missing, something forgotten. Every time Cecil has this particular type of dream, he finds that it foreshadows his lack of preparation for an important event. His speech at the community college comes to mind. As it turns out, Cecil left the revised copy in the desk at the office.

He showers and dresses without disturbing Deedra, whose final act before going to bed was setting out his blue suit and the proper shoes. She is very good about such things.

Because Deedra now sleeps so soundly after a night of fitful coughing, Cecil does not wake her. She doesn't have to be at work until 8:30, so he leaves a note.

He needs to review his speech before doing the dreaded walk to the podium in front of all those young people. The trek to the podium, no matter how near or far, always feels as it must to a death row inmate on the day of reckoning. As he drives, he practices not stuttering, mentally approaching the microphone without stumbling over the cables or his own two feet.

Cecil pulls into the parking space closest to the door and elevators without noticing the new car in Peter McAllister's space. This building is one of the last Federal buildings designed with an underground parking level. It is always cool and quiet here, but a bit too dark for his taste. Cecil never gets out of his car without having his keycard to the secured elevator handy. He stands before the camera and buzzes the security guard, then uses his keycard to open the elevator.

The first thing that comes to his attention when he walks out of the elevator is the stillness and the quiet of the floor. Except for the doors sliding shut, the place is completely devoid of people sounds, an instant affirmation that he should come in early more often. He likes this serenity before the storm, so to speak.

Because the swishing sound of the light trench coat rubbing against his trousers covers the faint hum that comes from Peter's office, Cecil walks by without noticing.

When Cecil realizes that the speech is not in the desk, he is haunted by the dream. Rifling his file cabinets and briefcase fails to produce those sacred papers. It occurs to him that Deedra might have something to do with it, so he calls.

She has always known him to be forgetful, especially after stressful days like yesterday. If Cecil Bridges had bothered to awaken his sleeping lover, the trip to the office would have been unnecessary and the immediate course of his life might have taken a very different path.

Deedra answers the phone with a sleepy cough that grows to the intensity of hacking. She has definitely caught a bad cold or the flu.

When she stops coughing, he says, "Good morning. I'm sorry to wake you."

"Cecil, is that you?" she groans, turning to her left. "Where on earth are you calling from?"

"I'm at the office. I thought I left the revised speech in my desk drawer, but it's not here. Do you have it, by chance?"

Deedra smiles and says, "I'm sorry, sweetheart. Yes, I do. You know I always check behind you, but I forgot to mention it. Senility is no picnic, is it?"

"Thank God. I thought I lost the damned thing, but it's not going to do me much good out there. I really hate to ask you to get up, but can you fax it to me from my study downstairs?"

"See what I mean about senility?" She chuckles. "You know your hub is in the shop for repairs, but there's really no need for that, Cecil. I saved a copy when I typed it for you. Just find the disk entitled, 'Speech'. Let the computer print it for you."

"That was good of you."

"You know, you've practiced that thing a million times. I'd like to think that you have it down pat by now. But don't you worry, I'll still be there to change your diapers, and wipe your chin when you begin to drool." Deedra giggles in his ear.

Cecil's computer does not respond when he tries to turn it on. He soon finds that both it and the printer have been unplugged; probably by someone who cleaned the offices after business hours. He plugs them in and says, "Thank you, Mrs. Wilson. Whatever will I do without you?" He thumbs through the disk caddy.

Deedra replies, "Let's see. You would probably go bald; get old, and very lonely. And you'd probably do all of this just before starving to death." Her giggle turns into a barking cough. "Excuse me. Since you're already sitting there, you may as well reboot to the inter-office system. It's simple. I doubt that it's been offline long enough to degrade any programs. Just turn everything on and hit control and the first function key. Give it a second and you're set."

Cecil does as she suggests and locates the disk. "Got it. Just for that, you get to take time off to deal with that cold. It sounds as if you're coming down with the flu. Get some rest."

"You won't get an argument from me on that one, Mr. Director. Thank you very much."

"You deserve it, Mrs. Wilson. If you need it, you know you've got it because you always take good care of me when I'm whining like an overgrown baby. In fact, I think I'll cook dinner for you when I get home. How does that sound?"

She laughs heartily. "Sounds like death on a plate to me. Lord Jesus, this man is so senile that he done went and forgot that he's the only Southern gentleman in the country that can't cook hot water.

How about takeout? Your choice—anything but Mexican. I still remember those burritos from Marco's."

"If I didn't know better, I'd swear you just compared my cooking to salmonella poisoning."

While laughing with her, Cecil notices a dialog box that offers him the choice of initializing the experimental protocol that links him to the rest of the department. They hang up so he can go about this small bit of business. As he approaches the printer, where an apparent paper jam threatens, the lights flicker. He briefly looks to the ceiling and begins to inspect the equipment. A low rumble, like distant thunder invades the atmosphere preceding a violent tremor. When the lights fluctuate, Cecil detects a vibration through the soles of his feet. Now, all hell cuts loose its moorings. Cecil grabs the hub, but it moves with the floor so he crawls toward the desk. The cup that holds his pens and pencils vibrates across the top of the computer monitor, spilling its contents on the keyboard just seconds before Cecil crawls under the desk. Pens and pencils fall one by one upon the keys, tapping and initiating protocols.

Now, as suddenly as the chaos had taken hold of all the known world...nothing. Two pencils roll to the edge of the desk and fall to the floor as Cecil opens one eye. Still clutching the underside of the desk, he finally remembers to breathe. After thirty seconds of calm, he ventures forth to survey the damage, but there is none. Nothing is out of place, except for the pencil holder.

Cecil goes to the window, looking down on what appears be an orderly world where traffic still moves as usual, and people are walking along the sidewalks as if nothing happened. Two calm pedestrians are pushing baby carriages at their usual pace on their usual route. Apparently, the tremor has dislodged the paper jam. The printer flawlessly deposits page after page in the tray. Then Cecil remembers that his speech is only three pages long.

"What's going on here?" he mutters.

The current screen page is numbered at 1001. It disappears only to be replaced by another page that is numbered the same. Though printing in reverse order, Bridges recognizes the pages to be statistical data from the Data Preparations Division. He would have broken the accidental connection to McAllister's computer had he not noticed something out of place.

Still locked in his office, Peter confirms the successful transfer and hangs up on Barrette Holt. He takes a sip of coffee and continues the tedious job of separating pages. However, in his haste to beat the clock, he neglects to remove the disk from the drive. Because his back is to the monitor, he doesn't notice the upload in progress.

At 8:39 Peter enters the director's office where the blinds are drawn to keep out the morning sun. When he turns the lights on and sees Cecil sitting there, Peter nearly drops the 1990 Census. His voice is a high-pitched screech when he declares, "Jesus Christ! You almost gave me a freaking heart attack. What are you doing here? I thought you had a speaking engagement this morning. What happened, Cecil, got cold feet?" Peter's lips tremble. His face is a vivid blush; this is a surprise that he can certainly do without.

By this time, Cecil is haggard and morose. The old man's silence makes Peter uneasy, but he retains his composure beneath a squinting gaze that seems to plow right through his soul.

After a few silent seconds, Cecil says, "Something came up, Peter. What do you have there?"

Cecil has sat in this dimly lit office, silently plotting how to proceed once he is face to face with Peter McAllister. Despite his shocking discovery, he still wants to be fair.

McAllister gives Cecil the heavy report and corresponding data disk. "This is the final report for your inspection. Signed, sealed, and delivered as promised." He has neatly stamped over 1000 pages with a hole punch, and secured them between brown report covers.

With the turn of every page, Peter's smug expression inflames his boss. Cecil expedites his trip through the counterfeit account, flipping to the final page where never is mentioned the closing of gates. Now Cecil looks up at Peter, who has both hands behind his back. The deputy director is rocking back and forth on the balls of his feet like a kid anxiously awaiting a teacher's approval of a special project.

Cecil's voice is serious and foreboding. "Close the door, Peter. I need to talk to you about a serious matter that has recently come to my attention." After McAllister complies and takes a seat, Cecil stands. "At first glance, although looks can be very deceiving, everything appears to be in order. By the way, did you feel a tremor this morning, sense anything unusual?"

Confused by the inquiry, Peter says, "No. There was nothing unusual. Why do you ask?"

"No matter. Are there any problems with the new data transfer program?"

Peter reads no sign in his boss's demeanor that suggests this to be anything more than a very reasonable line of questioning. Still, he has cause to hope against all hope that this is not the principal topic of their conversation. Undeniably, however, remains that nagging twitch in the pit of his stomach that whispers of impending doom.

He smiles, insincerely, before saying, "None at all. In fact, everything went like clockwork. I'm confident that the new program is going to have a positive impact across the board."

Cecil probes deeper. "Are you absolutely certain that there were no discrepancies or errors that had to be addressed at the last minute? None, whatsoever?"

Peter looks at Cecil's computer. The power cord is no longer visible under the desk. He fears the worst, but says, "Well the only real issue was running out of paper." He chuckles with an insincerity that seems forced even to himself.

"Yes, I seemed to have the very same problem a while ago," Cecil says.

Peter's McAllister's boldfaced lie only prompts Cecil to produce his own copy of the lie. His boss holds it forth with the one Peter has brought to his office as if they are the holy tablets of the Ten Commandments. Like Moses, he casts them upon the desk. Because the unmodified version is unbound, its pages slide to the edge of the blotter, threatening to spill to the floor. Woefully, Peter's reflexes prevent that from happening.

"Well, if there were no problems to speak of, then kindly explain this to me!" Cecil leans on his desk to stare at his underling.

Peter needs only a single glance at the last few sheets, which Cecil has deliberately placed on top, to fully appreciate the distasteful situation. He flinches as if bitten and his hand retreats from the paperwork even faster than it had moved to intercept them. The great nightmare—that seething, black beast—suddenly roars into overwhelming reality. For decades now it has been chained, caged, hidden, and starved. But now, on the morning of its final decimation, it's algorithmic burial, it awakens with a hunger.

Cecil watches Peter's reaction vehemently. Like a summer wind that carries the sweet scent of wild flowers in bloom with the same dedication as it transports that of rotting flesh or the smoke of a blazing forest fire, all doubts are swept away.

Peter rubs his temples and tries to speak. When his eyes leave the time bomb on the edge of the desk, he finds that he can say absolutely nothing. His mouth simply opens and shuts of its own accord. His quivering lips are mute, except for the sound of air being sucked in and expelled.

All of the dreadful prophecies of doom and mayhem flood his mind's eye as he glances at the telephone. For a split second, the phone seems to call to Peter. His watery eyes swear to his rattled brain that it breathes in and out, swelling and shrinking back to its original size. It rings, causing McAllister to flinch as a small, hopeless whimper escapes him. His head throbs and he sees spots from the overwhelming onset of his very first migraine. It would be the first of many.

Cecil snatches the receiver from the cradle to quickly dismiss the caller, promising to be in touch after this meeting. It is, of course, Deedra Wilson, whose curiosity grows into torment.

"I must assume by your response that this is exactly what it seems," Cecil scoffs. "Is that correct, Peter?" It is no great surprise that he does not receive a prompt answer, hardly expecting any at all. Though standing tall, with his blood churning, Cecil's heart sinks deeper as he continues the inquisition.

Peter McAllister is silently perturbed.

"I'd like to know how long this has been going on, and why? Who authorizes it? God damn it, I want an answer!" he shouts, stomping the floor to get Peter's attention. Cecil's gait seems prone to violence when he skirts the desk, waving a few pages of the census before Peter's pale face. "Who put you up to this? I know it goes far beyond you and Barrette Holt. It has to!"

Peter's assistant, Patricia Kidder, is engaged in small talk with a co-worker when Cecil's angry voice resonates from the end of the hallway. She says, "Ah oh. It sounds like yesterday's scat has just hit today's proverbial fan."

The other person discreetly agrees, "I don't know about you, but I think I'll go and find a nice quiet place to practice my disappearing act. This seems like the perfect time for it."

The mailroom seems like a good place to hibernate while the winter storm runs its course in Bridges' office. They will simply torment the newest employees, watching them sweat over a misplaced correspondence that does not exist.

Cecil growls, "Who put you up to this, Peter? Why have you two falsified these stats?"

Although he is tempted to blurt out a hasty lie, and then an ill-advised confession, Peter can only find a weak voice to say, "I…I can't tell you that, Cecil. I'm sorry, but I can't say anything." He raises his hands as if to pray or beg.

Cecil moves behind the desk and kicks his chair hard enough to send it crashing into the printer. "In that case, please leave the premises. Pending a full investigation into this matter, you're hereby suspended until notified of your disposition."

Peter says, "But I had no choice. I had to..." Cecil's eyes tell Peter that he is not interested in excuses; only the truth will do.

As McAllister rises on rubbery legs and turns to leave, Cecil says, "Peter, I've known you since college. You were one of my brightest students. That's why I recommended you for this job, but this is one hell of a repayment. Falsifying federal documents, as you know, is criminal. Son, you've got to realize the seriousness of your actions. Are you so afraid of your co-conspirators that you're willing to risk your entire career or even prison? If you don't come clean right now, and I mean right now, there may be no room for leniency when this shit comes out. I can almost assure you that reprisals will be swift and harshly dealt. Please don't throw it all away, son."

Throughout Cecil's appeal, Peter faces the door to avoid the disappointment in his boss's eyes. Before walking out, he manages to say, "I'm sorry that you found out about this, Cecil. Really, I am."

Cecil says, "Departmental protocol for a case such as this, as you well know, is to have you detained by security until the FBI arrive and takes you into custody to be formally charged, Peter."

While facing the door to leave, Peter McAllister freezes in his tracks with his eyes closed to the threshold of disaster and ruin.

"But I'm going to allow you to go home and think about cooperating willingly before your life is ripped to shreds. I will afford you no more than twenty-four hours to reconsider your mute position, and then all bets are off. Every moment of every hour, henceforth, you will be expecting a knock at the door. There is nowhere to run, Peter."

With that, Peter returns to his office and quickly gathers the few things that will fit into his briefcase. He grabs his file disks and the unbound copy of the true census report, which was never meant to cross Cecil's desk.

Peter McAllister leaves quietly, purposely avoiding curious gazes. He ignores anyone with the nerve to ask what took place in the director's office, choosing to walk his final mile to the elevators in lonesome obscurity. In this moment, he is like a cadet being drummed out of the Citadel for stealing from his brothers in arms.

His disposition, undoubtedly, becomes the hot topic of office gossip and rabid speculation. As he exits the elevator, security personnel take him back inside to confiscate anything pertaining to the Census Bureau. Security thoroughly searches Peter's person, even his shoes. The humiliating experience lets Peter know that Cecil Bridges is extremely serious. His keycard, office keys, and ID are taken from his pockets and wallet.

Despite her illness, Deedra and Cecil share a long kiss. Earlier, she contacted the White House to procure an emergency meeting with George Bush, who is clearing his desk for one of his celebrated fishing trips. Deedra Wilson wants to accompany Cecil, but he won't hear of it. She's feverish and needs to stay indoors. If this mess is as nasty as initial implications, he doesn't want her involved in the scandal.

Likewise, Deedra is very concerned for Cecil's safety, uncertain that he is taking this drama as seriously as it warrants to her sixth sense. She feels danger in the air and his naiveté only enhances her fears. She prays for Cecil Bridges, continuing to do so while waiting by the phone in her own home.

Cecil reaches Washington by car at 2:00 o'clock in the afternoon. He drives to his hotel and checks in. After a meal that he finds less than enjoyable, he goes to the White House.

Meanwhile, Peter McAllister sits at his desk in his home and swallows glass after glass of Scotch whisky, mustering the courage to do what duty requires of him. When a sufficient amount of numbness seizes his brain, he picks up the phone and makes the call.

CHAPTER 4

BLOOD FOR ICING

The African Village. Beaufort, South Carolina. August 31, 1990. 2:22 p.m.

D arkened is the room, though softly illuminated by twelve oil lamps arranged in a large circle. Four-foot wooden poles are firmly planted into the red clay floor to support the lamps.

A small fire burns as the centerpiece. Its smoke steadily escapes the room through a round hole in the domed thatch above. The pungent aroma of burning incense is thick in the undisturbed air. Six bamboo mats lay upon the floor, radiating outward around the fire. Drummers hold stations in each corner of the room, slowly beating the Rada drums before them.

There are twelve people kneeling at the head of the room where a bleating goat protests its bondage upon the stone altar before them. The six men and women are all motionless and bent forward. With their arms extended and their palms splayed outward and upward, their foreheads remain pressed against the clay floor. The faces of the women are white from some form of talcum powder. Meanwhile, the cheeks of the men are painted red, displaying black triangles that intersect at the bridges of their noses. With eyes closed, they meditate in complete nakedness.

When the slow tempo of the drums slightly increases, a shrill scream pierces the relative quiet. The startling cry emanates from the voodoo priestess, a woman named Insanyanga Nozilwane. She begins to sing a song of fertility as she walks through a beaded curtain. She is carrying a heavy clay bowl and a large bush knife as she takes her place behind an altar.

Insanyanga Nozilwane is a beautiful, middle-aged woman of average height, but such detail is not readily noticeable because of the thick coat of red paint that she wears on her face. Even her matted hair has been painted crimson.

The four drummers now join Insanyanga in song. Their voices rise and descend with the tempo of the drums that play in a round. It is both melodic and ominous as each drummer takes a turn, softly plying the drums to become an all-encompassing heartbeat. It seems as if the room itself has come to life, and anticipation is thick in the air.

The tall, dark figure of a man now appears in the dim light beyond the beaded curtain, through which he passes as if it is a liquid screen. His raised hands are painted; one black and the other white. Across each palm, there is a diagonal sliver of brilliant red that is his blood. He is Kaleem Kinzana, the greatest of all voodoo high priests, a man who resided much of his life in Western Africa before coming to America during the coldest day of the year in January of 1950.

When he speaks, the deep bass of his voice floods the chamber. Even the bleating goat falls silent as Kinzana invokes the blessings of Damballah, his God of all gods. While he does so, the air grows dense, and a sudden rumble in the Southern sky warns of an approaching storm. An eerie darkness soon falls upon this ceremony of multiple meaning and great importance.

Kinzana passes before the altar to sprinkle milk upon the heads of the six couples, who remain upon the floor. This milk

41

has been expressed from the heavy breasts of women that recently gave birth.

He says, "The milk of life is your own on this blessed day. Now rise, my sweet children."

The couples rise from the uncomfortable position, but they do not stand. While remaining upon their aching knees, their hands are outstretched so Kinzana can press his bleeding palms against theirs. After touching them all, the priest takes a small dagger from his sash, which he uses to slit the right palm of each male and the left palm of the females they are to wed.

When he joins the bleeding hands of the couples, Insanyanga loosely ties a red, braided string around the left wrist of each bride, draping it over the hand of their mates. This ritual signifies fealty and loyalty unto the end of life.

Lightning flashes and thunder rolls overhead! When the wild wind begins to blow, raising a haunted whistle across that circular hole in the ceiling, their eyes momentarily seek the violent sky. With the rising tempests of the air, the drummers' pulsing beat begins to surge forward.

The couples obey when Kinzana requests that they stand. Then, Insanyanga gives the women earthen pots containing a mixture of five ceremonial wines. The women hold these bowls aloft while their mates gulp mouthfuls. Then, it is their turn to drink of the bowls' strong content. The elixir, laced with exotic herbs, contain properties of extremely powerful aphrodisiacs.

When the drink is taken away, Kinzana and Insanyanga smile as the couples kiss deeply. When they are instructed to enter the circle of light, the drummers begin to beat faster.

Though the violent storm steadily increases in intensity, the newlyweds engage in a ritualistic dance around the fire. In unison, the females lay upon the bamboo mats with their arms crossed and their legs parted while their husbands continue to dance. Moments later, the women take their turn in dance. It is a most sensuous sight, arousing; stirring the blood within them all.

Insanyanga resumes the fertility song while the drumming beat heightens. Now, she reaches into an urn of woven grass. In a moment of pain, her eyes squint and her lips wrinkle to show her brilliant white teeth. She arches her back and slowly pulls her bleeding arms from the basket.

Coiled around each forearm, the rigid bodies of adolescent cobras slowly rise from the darkened well. They hiss, standing poised as if to strike. Flexing, iron scales pave the sloping staircase of their four-foot long bodies. They are Ophiophagus Hannah, vipers of fertility, the layers of a 20 to 40 egg clutch that they will guard with their very lives when necessary. Their massive hoods balloon as Insanyanga slowly spreads her sweating arms and begins to dance something most seductive.

With her dark brown eyes affixed on distant visions, her creaseless forehead sweats rivulets that run to the clinging neckline of her virgin white gown. Mesmerized and obedient to her subtle motions, the snakes sway slightly to join the dance. Their liquid, black tongues taste the air, flicking beyond the forks and curling to retreat again.

Kinzana moves toward the altar and uses his knife to make an incision in the leg of the goat, which resumes its bleating struggle. Its warm blood is collected in the bowl that Insanyanga brought into the room earlier.

At this time, the men are lying on the mats. With the severed foot of a chicken and the blood of the goat, Kinzana scrawls sacred symbols upon their chests and foreheads.

With the completion of each man's markings, his mate ceases to dance, standing over her husband's erect penis on trembling legs. Now, the voodoo man moves about the circle, using the chicken's foot to trace a circle around the swollen nipples of the females. He joins the circles at the center of their sweating, heaving chests, tracing a line of blood down their stomachs to their vaginas.

Each woman kneels beside her mate, crawling about his body baring teeth and nails as if they are possessed. The wine has run its course. The voodoo man spreads his arms before them and says, "The blood of life is yours on this day. Great Damballah commands that ye be fruitful, multiplying like the waves that beat upon the shores in his most violent of storms!"

Lightning whips across the sky as each bride bows her head over her husband's chest and face, caressing his body with beaded braids of hair.

Kinzana returns to his place behind the alter, where a young woman hands him a gleaming machete. When he holds it away from his body, she wets it down with purified water. The blade is regarded with reverence as he raises it to the sky. With blazing eyes cast upon the struggling animal, Kinzana begins to chant a prayer to another of his gods.

The howling wind rushes the side of the hut. Drafts, seeping through cracks and crevasses, cause the oil lamps to flicker and the beaded curtain to sway as if a ghost is playing a muted harp.

The entire room dances in the firelight as the women mount their husbands, each crying out with the pain that accompanies a forceful penetration. The drums' suicide pace is set to escalate still. Each pulsing throb vibrates the clay floor on which the couples lay thrashing and entangled by a burning lust. Their eyelids flutter as they sweat and strain, grasping and scratching at each other's flesh to even draw blood.

Haunting screams of pleasure reverberate throughout the room to mingle with the wind, with thunder, and with the virulent drums. The intense heat causes the smoky air to churn like boiling water in a red-hot cauldron. This ritual is something primal, something... animal.

Each couple reaches a screaming, almost violent climax, which calls the lightning down from the sky just outside the single window of the hut. Thunder shakes the earth and the voodoo priest brings the blade down, decapitating the squirming animal that lay before him! Blood filled with the enzymes of terror jettisons from its pulsing jugular nearly seven-feet to stain a strategically placed map. The animal's life force turns black, smoking as if it has become acid.

Rain falls in turrets, dousing the fire that burns directly below the circular hole in the ceiling. In just mere moments, it seems as though a millennium has passed.

With his prayers completed to Legba, the God of the Gate, Kinzana elevates his blazing eyes to the heavens and says, "The gate is ajar, now comes the waiting. We await the flood!" The crackle of distant lightning offers an eerie affirmation.

The cobras fuss and hiss at each other, threatening to strike. They entwine themselves briefly upon the floor, spreading their hoods in a moment of seemingly angry passion before crawling back into the overturned basket without human coercion.

Insanyanga lies writhing on the floor in some strange ecstasy, as do each bride, whose legs tightly clasp the hips of her new husband. They all bleed between the legs, and they will all give birth to twins, triplets, or more.

Kinzana whispers, "What has taken place here transcends our numbers. Its supernatural affect will proliferate throughout this sleeping America so that that we will someday rise."

The drums suddenly go silent, but Kinzana's bellowing laughter fills the air like a ghost chime, riding the electric wind to somewhere distant.

CHAPTER 5

REMEMBER THY CALLING

The bottle of Scotch crashes to the ceramic tile floor, shattering instantly. Luckily, it was less than a quarter full when his groping hands knocked it from the table by the couch. Peter McAllister wakes up half-crazed, drenched by an acidic sweat. He sits up and runs his fingers through his hair, pinching the bridge of his nose with his eyelids tightly clenched.

He hears the wind chimes singing and assumes that they are what he heard instead of the doorbell, but he is sadly mistaken. When the bell tolls again, dread washes over him like a mudslide, threatening to revive the headache that he tried to drown with liquor.

Vincent Sterne's short, brown hairs bristle at his neckline as his serious eyes pan left to right. He easily assesses Peter McAllister's raging hangover the second he meets that grave expression and those bloodshot eyes.

Without a word, Sterne enters and goes to the den. Peter, who takes a moment to look about his yard, soon joins him. Sterne's driver stays out front with the car, unseen behind a wall of black tint.

Vincent Sterne is standing in the center of the room with his arms crossed. His lower lip covers the upper while he considers the broken bottle at his feet. He takes a deep breath, exhaling with an annoying whistle.

Peter skirts Sterne's position to sit in the armchair. Having always feared this man, he is quiet. Their initial meeting had been clandestine and mysterious, blindfold-mandatory.

Years ago, when Peter McAllister finally dared to accept the intriguing invitation, he found that he'd been summoned to stand before silhouetted faces and serious voices that came from a semi-circular darkness. He actually thought that he was going to be asked to become an American spy or something.

What they wanted of him was exactly that, spying on the American population, never telling what he would soon know. The financial compensation was irresistible. He would never have cause to worry about flying bullets, truth serums, or other stereotypical spy nonsense. It could be lucrative and safe, a real opportunity to serve his country.

Countless hours into the intense interview, something strange had been thrown into the mixture. He was suddenly faced with a music video that had first aired on Black Entertainment Television on April 16, 1985. The Black rap artist's stage moniker was Mystikal. The young man wore short braids that seemed to frame his savagery to perfection. His skin was so dark. Those eyes were angry and intensely driven as he performed the twisted song entitled "Beware!" The song was almost hypnotic, but one of the most disturbingly negative arrangements of imagery that Peter had ever witnessed. The lyrics, which seemed to be consumed by rage, meant little to the others or to him. Yet, little discussion was necessary at the video's conclusion. It was the way the young man crouched in a corner of an abandoned stairwell, lunging toward the camera with his eyes telling the story as well as his lashing tongue. His movements seem primal, and always threatening. His pensive hostility poured from the sound system to threaten every listener, even though the words were never meant exclusively for Whites, if meant for Whites at all. The presentation of this music video was simply a complex tool that served its masters well. Subtly, very subtly, that video changed something deep inside of Peter McAllister.

The BET interview with the rapper that followed the premier of his new hit, however, would have revealed a humbler side of this platinum-selling No Limit Soldier.

In the revealing end, Peter McAllister was completely convinced that this calling possessed great purpose and Herculean justification. Upon emergence from that dark place of silhouettes, Peter walked into the dawn having gained huge responsibilities and the respect of some very powerful people.

Having been seeded by ignorance that did not become him or his background, Peter Quinton McAllister accepted his new role as a keeper of lies. He shunted that ugly aspect of his new life and livelihood into murky corners of his mind and soul where he foolishly believed that it would never rise up to touch him. Here and now, in the context of what futures may lay ahead, his loyalties are called into question.

Vincent Sterne removes his light jacket before sitting down to face Peter. He says, "Tell me what happened." He seems to be very calm, but Peter does not expect that to last much longer.

Peter has grown accustomed to speaking with his hands over the years. They are shaking so badly, he plants them on his knees.

His voice seems panicky when he says, "It wasn't my fault. We were transferring the census data from Indiana when Bridges showed up early and found out. Christ, he wasn't even supposed to be there."

With a careful examination of every twitch in Peter's demeanor, Sterne asks, "Found out what exactly, Mr. McAllister?"

Peter jumps up from his seat, causing a huge throbbing pulse to run from his neck to the top of his head. He shouts, "What the fuck do you think?"

Sterne, however, shows little reaction to the sudden outburst. He isn't surprised that the deputy director finds the game of cat and mouse unpalatable. He knows that there could only be one reason for Peter leaving such an urgent message with his offline service. Still, he asks, "Have we been compromised? Are you saying that the gate has been breached?"

Peter's eyes light up when reminded of the unusual dream, finding it extremely ominous that Sterne has just chosen those particular words.

"Yes. I guess you can say that. Bridges was extremely upset and practically fired me on the spot. Security stopped me on the way out, so he has two copies now. I don't know what he has planned for them. He's given me twenty-four hours to come clean. What the hell are we going to do?"

Sterne doesn't shout, pounce, or sweat, as Peter expects. Instead, he's quite calm as he stares at the horizontal lava lamp that see-saws on top of the television set.

Behind those spectacles are the dark brown eyes of a thinking man, but the room's reflection is lost upon them. His mind calculates and processes the distasteful information before spitting it back into the loop. When the spell finally breaks, Sterne goes into the kitchen to make two calls with his cell phone. Peter hears him mumbling, but the words are lost to him. He is curious, but more certain he does not really want to know what is discussed.

Upon returning to his seat, Sterne emphatically states, "Mr. McAllister, henceforth, you will refrain from drinking. You will keep your wits about you, conducting yourself in a respectable fashion. Is that clear? We still consider you to be the right man for this job. Which is evident in that you made the call as instructed, instead of avoiding the responsibility."

"But the jig is up, I have no job. Cecil has seen to that!" Peter argues.

Sterne points a wicked finger that silences McAllister. "This is the very reason why you don't have one of my underlings as a handler and you report directly to me. No matter how many precautions we took, this was bound to happen sooner or later, Mr. McAllister. By the way, did you discuss this with anyone? Was anyone present to witness the details of your dismissal?"

"No, but I can't be held accountable for what Cecil might have said about me. God, he was pissed."

Sterne's pleased expression is the greatest contradiction to Peter.

"It's highly unlikely that Mr. Bridges discussed this matter with rank-and-file office employees. It will only serve as an embarrassment to him. He may have mentioned your dismissal, but not the substance thereof. Something of this magnitude does not make for good office gossip. His immediate course will be extremely predictable at this point."

Peter flinches when Sterne's cell phone rings. After getting the information he awaited, he hangs up.

"What do you mean, predictable?"

Sterne puts on his jacket. "Bridges is in Washington. He's made an appointment with President Bush. It doesn't take a genius to know what that's all about, does it?"

Peter's head throbs when his heart skips a beat. This is very bad for him and bound to get worse. He's frustrated at Sterne's calm approach, while his future swings in the breezes of a personal hell.

His voice cracks when he says, "He went to the fucking president? That's it, I'm screwed!"

Sterne wheels and places both hands on Peter McAllister's shoulders, staring him right in the eyes. "Mr. McAllister—Peter, get a grip. This situation may not be as bad as it seems, so negative speculation serves no constructive purpose here. Just remember, no matter what happens, to keep your mouth shut. Don't worry about your job. One way or another, you'll be back at the office tomorrow. Trust me. Okay?"

Peter tries to calm down, which is nearly impossible; it's still his ass swinging in the breeze. The thought of being the scapegoat of this debacle is simply overwhelming.

"What can you possibly do to insure that? The man was adamant. You'd have to kill Cecil to get me back into that office tomorrow."

When Vincent Sterne arches an eyebrow, slightly tilting his head, Peter balks as if his shoulders are in the grasp of monstrous tendrils, instead of the Director of the Central Intelligence Agency.

"But you wouldn't harm him over this, would you?" As if he has gotten the answer telepathically, Peter shakes his head in disbelief and backs away. In the face of his panic and fear, Sterne's patient expression changes like the skin of the chameleon. His face becomes brass and his eyes narrow to hardened coals.

"We will only do what has to be done to keep this information under cuff. This is a grownup's game board, Peter, and we're not using play money. Make no mistake, this is for keeps. You must know by now that you're an important man in the grand scheme of things, so remember why you agreed to join us. Remember the projections of things to come if Blacks ever find out that they outnumber us! This isn't about some redneck dirt farmer in Alabama who hates niggers 'cause they been stealin' his melons, son. It's about maintaining the quality of life and the preservation of the system of government in which we've become accustomed. It's about continuity in an ever-changing world!"

"But—"

"No buts, Peter." Sterne scolds.

CIA Director Vincent Sterne now forces his facial expression to soften while he prepares to remind Peter of the things that swayed his decision to become a gatekeeper.

"A great deal of logical thought has gone into the decision to withhold the truth about the White-Black ratio. We've never taken the responsibility or the moralistic implications lightly." Sterne's smile is less wicked to prevent panicking McAllister. "Look. I hate to say it, but African Americans in this country are angry and not just a little violent these days. Just listen to some of the garbage they call music if you don't really believe me. It's all bitch this—bitch that—kill this—kill that. Just watch the news!"

"That's a bit..."

"Stereotypical?" Sterne finishes. "Who knows, Peter?" He turns away and rubs an annoying itch on his neck. "Maybe they have a right to be pissed, but that doesn't mean we should suffer for the people who enslaved Africans early in this country's history. It's time they get over that, but they don't really want to. It has become their swan song for failure. Take a good hard look at how they're out there murdering one another when they should be pulling together. Think about it. If they're killing each other for what they claim that we may or may not have done, just imagine what will happen if they turn all that heightened aggression against us. You must believe me when I say that we are protecting this nation by keeping order in the midst of potential chaos."

Once again, Peter is seduced and consoled by the mesmerizing tone of Vincent Sterne's voice during his impassioned speech. He recalls words like carnage, rioting, mayhem, and change. Would change be so bad, he wonders from the dark recesses of his mind, but quickly realizes that his previous question has not been answered.

Sterne sees that question on Peter's lips, so he answers it by saying, "Peter, no one wants to harm Mr. Bridges. Nevertheless, we must affect damage control to contain the situation."

Peter asks, "What are you going to do?"

"None of your concern, and that is the long and short of it," says Sterne. He walks away, but as he leaves the room, he says, "I need not remind you to control yourself. Lay off of the booze, it's no answer. Just remember your station because if we have to..." He pauses, turning to stare Peter in the eyes with a wry smile. "…well, just don't do anything foolish. Remember your non-disclosure agreement."

Vincent Sterne leaves as he had come and Peter does not lay eyes on him again for the next ten years. They will only speak three times in that period.

CHAPTER 6

THE HOAX

While Cecil Bridges is being guided through the west wing by White House Chief of Staff Lesley Warren, he is a whirlpool of conflicting emotions. He is here to confront the demons that lay at the very foundation of his own house. He's here to destroy specific components thereof because Peter McAllister has left him no choice.

While being ushered to the Oval Office, Cecil recalls his very first visit and that feeling of awe. Decisions made herein affect the lives of every American citizen. Yet the powers that be are not restricted by such simplistic definition. The entire world is affected from here. The policies that are fashioned within that great chamber radiate from its walls to span the country, crossing oceans to leave, virtually, no land untouched.

Nearly sixteen years have passed since Cecil Bridges was first invited to the Oval Office for an interview with President Ford. It has been and continues to be a great honor.

Stuart James's sudden retirement left President Ford in a dilemma on the heels of his recent induction to the Presidency, which came immediately after Richard Nixon resigned to avoid impeachment. The Deputy Director of the Census Bureau, at the time, made it clear that he had his own political agenda to pursue. Therefore, he wouldn't be a good replacement for James, who was dying of colon cancer.

Just how and why Cecil Bridges became a leading candidate for the position was not only a mystery to himself, but to several others in government. Were it not for a senator that he had never met, the opportunity would never have been.

In truth, Cecil Bridges was never expected to discover the hidden facts of the inner workings. If he failed at the Census Bureau, then so be it. The colorful irony is that his failure would assure that no other African American would ever be considered for the position again.

In 1974, Cecil achieved confirmation, pursuing job perfection for fifteen years. His integrity and diligence caught the attention of Jimmy Carter. He apparently won over the Reagan and Bush administrations, since they saw absolutely no need to replace him.

His running of the Census Bureau has been exemplary, even with all of the problems incurred in its growing diversity. Cecil now wonders if it was as simple as successfully clearing the partisan hurdles in the system by working hard and staying sharp. On the other hand, was he set up to play the role of an unwitting a pawn?

President Bush signs a few last minute documents while discussing Vice President Quayle's itinerary during his absence. Bush is casually dressed in khaki pants and a flannel shirt. His fishing vest boasts several pockets and his lucky hat is strewn with an array of his favorite fly fishing lures.

Though he's been announced upon entrance, Cecil clears his throat to get their attention. Bush greets Cecil and apologizes for the delay, then adds the final signature.

Dan Quayle is about to leave the office when Cecil says, "Please wait, Vice President Quayle. I believe you should hear about this recent development."

George Bush jokes, "Why, Cecil, this sounds serious. I hope it's not going to prevent me from catching a trophy trout." His light-hearted wit will go unappreciated.

"Yes, Mr. President," Cecil states. "I'm afraid it will."

"Why so cryptic, Mr. Bridges?" asks Quayle. "What seems to be the problem?"

Cecil gives both copies of the census to the president. Bush glances at them and asks, "The census report? As I understand, it's already slightly overdue, so couldn't it wait until I get back?"

"Frankly, no. It can't wait. If you'll examine them both, you will find that they are essentially the same. However, they are not," Cecil informs. "Not really."

Bush is confused and Cecil sees growing impatience on his face, so he thumbs through the notes he made before arriving in Washington.

Quayle asks, "What do you mean by that?"

When Bush opens the book and asks for an explanation, Cecil answers, "Please turn to page seven-fifty of the book and take a look at the tally numbers concerning Black and White males in the nation's prison population. Please try to keep in mind that these numbers are multiplied by the thousands. Mr. Quayle, please, if you will."

When Dan moves closer, they both examine the numbers. After a few seconds, Bush says, "Okay, Cecil."

Cecil asks that they check the same stats on page 750 of the loose pages. Meanwhile, he checks his notes for other contradicting statistics.

After looking at both versions, Bush says, "I still don't understand. This bound copy states that there are some odd number of African Americans and Caucasian men in prison, while this one states that there are an even greater number of Blacks than there are Whites in prison."

"Yes," Quayle adds. "But the number of Caucasians are identical on both pages."

"That's correct, which indicates that the number is probably accurate. Now, please turn your attention to page eight-thirty. Check the stats on African American males who attended college and successfully graduated between the years 1980 and 1990," Cecil instructs. "And I thank you both for your patience."

Quayle says, "As far as I can tell, the loose pages state that there were fewer in comparison to Caucasians, which obviously stands to reason. After all, we have always been the majority."

Wordlessly, Bush fingers the bound page for Quayle's inspection. He looks at the Census Bureau's director with guarded anticipation.

"Wait a minute," Quayle mumbles.

"That statistic isn't listed there, Vice President Quayle, because the bureau doesn't officially keep such records. Not to my recollection, at least. Are you beginning to see any patterns?"

"Where are you going with this, Mr. Bridges?" Bush asks. "Is it going to get better or worse?"

Cecil offers no verbal response, but he suspects that his eyes have given a sufficient reply. He clears his throat. "I can point out a good number of discrepancies, but the most provocative of them all is located at the top of page ten-sixteen." While they search for the page, he bites on his lower lip in pensive silence.

After comparing both pages at least three times, they look at one another. Cecil watches as Quayle's face sunburns, but Bush suddenly turns pale.

Bush says, "But this states that African Americans outnumber Caucasians the in United States by more than ten-million!"

Cecil clears his throat. "Twelve, sir. There are twelve-million more, Mr. President. With the diversity of our program, you may note that this figure only pertains to those of voting age. And it would seem that an unprecedented amount of the Black population is made up of fraternal twins, triplets, quadruplets and more. Curiously, another statistic that my department doesn't officially tabulate. Nothing, by all accounts, has indicated this trend until now."

Bush is silent, but Quayle assumes, "Well, this book is obviously the correct version. There's no way the other one can be accurate. Right, Mr. Bridges?"

Cecil hears in his voice and sees in both faces a plea for confirmation. However, they're about to be disappointed and uprooted.

"I'm sorry, but I have every reason to believe that it's not. The loose pages have to be those of the true census for the years 1980 through 1990. Of that, I am nearly certain. Even though it seems quite impossible, I'm nearly certain of it."

"This must be a mistake. Just where did you get these convoluted figures anyway?" asks George Bush.

"As you both are aware, we've incurred several problems over this decennial period with the growth of the population and cutbacks. There's also the constant influx of immigrants and illegal aliens to be considered. Because of these things, we had to weed out all of the obsolete methods that have been jamming up the machinery. Therefore, better methods were employed. This morning, all of the information was supposed to be transferred from the Data Prep Division in Indiana with the use of a new program that was supposedly created for just that purpose. But I was never consulted regarding the creation or use of this new program. In fact, I believe that great pains were taken to keep me in the dark about it."

Bush asks, "Who authorized it?"

"And how could something like that be introduced without your knowledge?" Quayle inquires with disbelief.

Cecil takes a deep breath. "Well, to be honest, Deputy Director Peter McAllister and Barrette Holt of Data Prep are my only suspects at this point. I believe, however, that it has to go much deeper than them. They implemented the new program behind my back and I only became aware of it by a slip of the tongue. Apparently, this new program is designed to split certain encoded statistics, adjusting them for Peter McAllister's personal file."

"How did you discover this conspiracy?" Bush asks.

"I had to go into the office earlier than usual. In fact, I wasn't supposed to be there until well after lunchtime. When I realized what was going on, I figured out Peter McAllister's new password with the help of a computer techie. In case of emergency, all employees of the Census Bureau are required to submit their computer passwords to me, with the express agreement that I alone hold the file to insure against misuse. If you will note, page ten-seventeen ends with the words, '*The Gate is closed*' 1990. That page is not included in the bound copy, which was personally delivered to me by Peter McAllister. I can only guess that it's some kind of code from Barrette Holt. By using 'Gatekeeper' as a password, I opened a secret database that includes the 1960 through 1970, and the 1970 to 1980 censuses. I extracted copies of both and what was falsely presented for those decennial periods. The consistency of the numbers, I'm afraid, do not lie."

He takes four disks, secured by a red rubber band, from his briefcase and lays them on the desk.

Bush mumbles, "The gate is closed. 1990. What the hell is that supposed to mean?" He gives the page to Dan Quayle.

"When Mr. McAllister walked into my office and found me there, he was greatly distressed. He was so shocked, that he almost threw that report across the room."

"Then what happened?" asks Quayle with feverish anticipation.

"Well, I asked repeatedly if there had been any problems or glitches with the new program. I asked if there were any last minute changes that had to be made before turning it in to me. He stated, quite emphatically, that there were none. In fact, he seemed extremely pleased with the accomplishment. I want you both to know that I gave Peter many opportunities to indicate that the second report had been the result of a computer glitch without him knowing that I had gotten my hands on the other one. It goes very far to say that this is no accidental misinformation, but that it's the result of a very willful collaboration."

Both executive officials are deeply concerned. Though they are filled with questions, Cecil is allowed to continue.

"When I called Peter on it, he was taken totally by surprise. He handled that unbound copy like a hot potato. I should say that he looked like a person who'd seen something pretty on the ground, but when he went to pick it up, he realized it was a rattlesnake."

Bush asks, "When you presented your findings to Mr. McAllister, did he offer any plausible explanation?" He leans forward on his elbows, close enough for Cecil to notice that a few discrete beads of sweat have formed on his forehead and the bridge of his nose. Quayle thumbs both reports in search of further discrepancies, or possibly, anything that might discredit Cecil's disturbing theory.

Cecil finds it impossible to relax. After an intense moment of practicing his speech without stuttering, he sits back and removes a small device from his briefcase. He places it on the desk and tells them, "I recorded the entire conversation. However, Peter McAllister made no effort to lie or to cover his tracks. He just sat there completely stunned. The only thing he offered in his own defense was that he was sorry that I found out. With the two Census reports staring him in the face, I at least expected him to go back on his previous statement about there having been no mistakes or last-minute changes. I expected him to say that the unbound copy had been the result of an anomalous computer malfunction that he and Holt had to overcome, but he didn't. He couldn't because he was too rattled."

"You mean to tell me that he offered absolutely no defense of his actions? He didn't even try to deny your allegations?" Bush asks.

"He was petrified. This goes farther than Peter and Holt, but he wouldn't divulge anything further. He is afraid. I forbade him from contacting Barrette Holt and I suspended Peter from his duties, pending a full investigation by the Justice Department. I assume that there will be an investigation."

"Yes, of course. There has to be." Bush turns to Dan Quayle and says, "Please see to it that my flight is canceled along with my reservations at the fishery. Also, get McAllister and Holt down here on the double. Have them dragged in by the FBI if that's what it takes." Quayle hops to it.

"Mr. President, I do believe that there are very pressing issues here. For instance, if this turns out to be true, and I feel without a doubt that it is, then the issue of equal representation—or the lack of it—comes directly to the forefront."

As Bush looks up suddenly, Cecil can almost hear the machinery behind his eyes racing out of control before coming to a grinding halt. It sounds just like a racecar flying around the track at 180 miles per hour with an insufficient amount of motor oil to soothe its thrusting pistons.

Bush winces, noticeably.

Cecil knows instinctively that he is about to say, "I suppose you're right, Mr. Bridges. However, this is all just speculation. We have to get hold of Mr. McAllister and Holt to ascertain the viability of these allegations. We have to squeeze them hard until they cough up the truth and their co-conspirators, if there are any." His tone reflects a measure of agitation.

Cecil hastens, "What do you mean, Mr. President? Of course, there are others. Neither man was here to tinker with the statistics in 1960." He sits back, his eyes narrowing. "I see. In other words, you really don't want to think about it."

Though his statement is highly argumentative, Cecil doesn't feel it completely out of line. In truth, he's beginning to wonder if President Bush had no prior knowledge of this cover-up. He is already wondering if anything constructive will come of it. They're White and he's Black, after all. Though it's too soon to tell, Cecil never questioned his course of action until now. He knows that he is doing the right thing, going by the book. But his perfectly reasonable anxieties have caused him to be somewhat clumsy while dancing too near the president's tender toes.

President Bush doesn't like the comment nor the tone in which it's been spoken. He feels slighted by what his sensitivity interprets as an accusation. He looks Cecil in the eyes and says, "Don't antagonize me, Cecil. There's no need for that. I simply mean that, at this juncture, it's important that we have all the facts before we think about anything else."

He is right and sincere, so Cecil takes a strategic retreat by apologizing for being overzealous.

Bush graciously accepts and asks, "Now then, can I put you up for the night or are you already situated?"

Cecil declines the offer and tells him that he is staying at the Milner Hotel in room 404. Almost as an afterthought, but more like an olive branch, Cecil says, "I was very disappointed and extremely upset when I confronted McAllister. He left, but I had security stop him before leaving the building. They confiscated these disks and all other materials related to the bureau. This black disk is a master copy of the latest census, which I believe he planned to turn over to his superiors, whomever they may be."

President Bush acknowledges Cecil's thoroughness. Cecil is assured that he will be hearing from his office the second they get a line on the two men named in the conspiracy.

Deep down inside, George Bush feels that this entire thing has to be a mistake or an elaborate hoax. He even suggests that Cecil's personnel file be examined, hoping that this story could be something cooked up by a very twisted and tortured mind. What he suggests seems a distinct possibility; madness isn't always so easily detected. It can fester in the mind for a lifetime and a day before discovery. Moreover, it is something to hold on to.

Upon leaving the Oval Office, Bridges bumps into a man in a dark blue suit. This fellow is about fifty, wearing lightly tinted spectacles over his dark brown eyes. The gentleman smiles, excusing himself for being clumsy and preoccupied. There is no harm done.

CHAPTER 7

CHARIOT AFIRE

President Bush and Dan Quayle discuss the Cecil Bridges revelations with a growing measure of trepidation. The fact that neither McAllister nor Holt has been located is rather perplexing. Yet, in another way, it is good. They can't be found to actually verify this calamity. The alleged conspirators may have decided to make themselves scarce, or someone else may have decided it for them.

The White House Chief of Staff reports that CIA Director Vincent Sterne requests an immediate audience. Supposedly, it is of the utmost importance.

Bush says to Quayle, "What now? I really don't need any more bad news."

Sheepishly, Dan Quayle asks, "Do you believe this census report is genuine?"

Contemplating the papers on his desk, Bush confesses, "I certainly hope not. Do you realize the hellish upheaval that will result if we find this to be true?" He takes a deep breath and shakes his head. "I can't imagine the damage this inflammatory evidence will cause to race relations in this country, and that's just for starters.

This administration will be submerged in a cloud so thick that no one will remember that you and I had absolutely nothing to do with it."

"Mr. Bridges certainly seems convinced, but it's got to be a hoax."

"Did you get his file checked to be sure that he has no prior mental illnesses?"

"Someone is looking into Cecil's psychological profile," Dan says. "Even if it's true, things might not be as bad as we feel. Race relations between Blacks and Whites, and between Blacks and the American Government have improved immensely since the mid-sixties. This country may be able to absorb the shock with a minimum of damage. That may be especially true if we can prove that only a handful were involved, and not on this administration's executive level. Don't you agree?"

Bush's head whips around, rearing a steely, squinting gaze in Dan Quayle's direction. "Are you nuts? You can't believe that any more than I do!"

Quayle looks away. "Maybe we're overreacting. Maybe..."

"Need I remind you of Dr. Martin Luther King and Rodney King? Some African American people still believe that the government orchestrated the murder of Malcolm X, even though the evidence points directly at their own people. If it's true, this thing will prove to them that this country was built and sustained on their blood and sweat. Furthermore, it will prove just how little credit they get for it. Think, Dan! Suppression, oppression, racism—especially in our court systems and money lending practices. Without a doubt, there will be rioting. These are just a few things that come to my mind. Just what country have you been living in all of your life?"

Lashing out when treated like a total idiot, Quayle snaps, "Then just what the hell do you suggest we do about it, George?"

Neither man knows just how long the door has been open, or when Vincent Sterne was allowed to enter. In their minds, the echo of his announcement resounds in the background noise of their heated debate. He couldn't have just walked in on his own, so somewhere along the line Bush had given permission.

"Damn it, Sterne, you'll just have to wait!"

The papers are clearly in Sterne's sight when he says, "One word sums up my reason for being so insistent, Mr. President. Census." Sterne certainly captures their attention, and it means dreadful trouble if he is involved.

George Bush was appointed the Director of the Central Intelligence Agency, ironically, by Gerald Ford in November of 1975. On the basis of higher political aspirations, he resigned in 1977. In truth, he couldn't stomach most of what took place in the world of the cloaked and of those who hid daggers behind their backs. One final covert operation gone wrong cemented his decision to resign. Those patriots under his direction, those who died as a result of his indecision during the secret op in Germany will forever remain the hidden collateral damage beneath the headstone of his tenure as CIA Director.

The Central Intelligence Agency was established on July 11, 1947, to conduct subversive operations abroad. In any case, the agency was not to conduct law enforcement in the United States. In other words, they were involved in spying strictly for the gathering of intelligence to protect this country and its citizens from those who would do harm. The CIA works closely with the National Security Council. Neither agency is very successful at separating covert activities from the personal lives of the citizens they are sworn to protect.

Operatives of the CIA often take occasion to investigate fellow Americans, and not just because they are suspected as spies. The abuses of this organization are far more extensive than that, and at times, things get downright personal. Innocent American citizens have even died at the hands of the CIA, which was George Bush's true reason for resigning the post.

Vincent Sterne was once Richard Milhous Nixon's choice to head the Central Intelligence Agency. In the wake of the snowballing Watergate scandal, President Ford was strongly advised to abandon most of Nixon's choices of officials and their alternates. There was still a matter of Senate confirmation to consider. Moreover, the Senate's opinion of Nixon was at an all-time low.

President Ford was encouraged to make his own selections. Otherwise, his administration would most certainly have been overshadowed by the indiscretions of his predecessor. He chose George Bush, who felt it an honor at first, but gave up the helm after only two years. His resignation left the door open for Vincent Sterne, who had faded from the limelight just long enough to lose the stench of Richard Nixon's presidential imprudence.

It is a little known fact that Vincent Sterne immediately created the Department of African American and Latin American Analysis, although the CIA was not supposed to be overly concerned with U.S. citizens.

George Bush is very familiar with the dark heart of the CIA, which he discerns as a regrettably necessary facet of American defense. He regards the department as a cure that often contributes to its own diseases. He's happy to be rid of its terrible delegations and often ugly responsibilities, which once lay at the leading edges of the Cold War with Russia and growing anti-American sentiments in the destabilizing Middle Eastern region.

Sterne approaches President Bush's desk. Though adept at reading upside down and backward, he uses an index finger to turn some of the papers. Vincent Sterne doesn't adjust the slanted angle of his head to look at Bush and Quayle, he only raises his eyes from the papers.

Silence from the nation's leader seems indicative of fear and indecision. Sterne prefers it. Having caught the tone of their private conversation, Sterne figures the angles favorable to his agenda. Unsettling fear in the nation's leader is the sweetest sentiment of all.

Sterne unbuttons his jacket and sits on the couch. He sighs before saying, "Mr. President, Dan, this silence is very awkward. Please sit and let us talk."

Neither feels like sitting. Bush asks, "You know about this already?"

"I do, Mr. President," is Sterne's simple reply.

"Then you're undoubtedly here to tell me that Cecil Bridges is a crackpot and that his allegation of falsified census reports is totally unfounded. Right?" Bush asks with a bit of urgency.

"I'm afraid it's an actual fact, Mr. President," Sterne says rather nonchalantly. Effectively, his unemotional inflection is designed to get under George Bush's skin. If a much needed calm can be established in the wake of the anticipated storm, it will best be achieved in these outsiders by its resolute personification.

Vice President Quayle demands, "Damn it, Sterne, cut the cat and mouse crap and just tell us what you know about this mess!"

When Bush finds his voice again, it nearly cracks. "Are you trying to tell me that there really are twelve million more Blacks in the U.S.? Are you telling me that McAllister and Holt are not acting independently but under your supervision?"

"Yes, on all counts, Mr. President. And if you will sit and calm down, maybe we can deal with this illumination together."

"Don't presume to tell me what to do. I am not amused, nor in the mood for your mind games!" Bush warns. "It will serve you best to remember who you're talking to."

"My apologies, Mr. President. Please stand if you like, but it won't change anything," Sterne says with sincerity. He isn't one to be flustered by the threatening display on their faces.

By all accounts, attitude and fear are his best tools. He knows once this secret is learned by any sane, White American, there are very few avenues of choice. Sterne's job here is simply to help them to realize that fact.

Sterne, a very elaborate thinker, possesses the ability to ponder many questions ahead of his opponents. Thusly, in most situations, he directs his opponents to a logical conclusion that will eventually reflect his own.

He was once the Director of Research in the U.S. Department of State, as well as President of the National Intelligence Study Center in Washington. Sterne graduated Harvard Law School as well as the Defense Intelligence College at the top of his class. Psychology is his favorite tool of manipulation. His credentials are limitless, for it takes a very special type of man to hold his position.

When it comes to this gatekeeper's secret, he feels that no Caucasian man or woman will resist his logic. He is about to put that theory to the test yet again, not that many officials discover the truth on their own.

President Bush finally sits down. Vincent Sterne watches him with great intent, noting the rigid posture. It is time for the breakdown.

While assuming a very thoughtful facial expression, Sterne admits, "Mr. President, now that I've verified this unsettling truth, I realize that this looks bad from all angles. And you could be right about that. I only ask that you hear me out before making any rash decisions." He sighs. "As you now know to be fact, the African American population has increased exponentially. We have conducted extensive research into this phenomenon since the trend was first isolated in the early 1950s. There are many distressing factors that we haven't been able to nail down. It's simply epidemic. So, for the most part, this is really old news to us."

"Are you saying that your people have been operating all of this time?" Bush probes. "Just who the hell are we? That's what I'd like to know, Sterne. Who are we?"

"I assume that Mr. Bridges has brought the words, the gate is closed, to your attention. Well, Mr. President, we are the keepers of that gate—this immensely volatile secret. For the time being, however, I must refrain from naming names."

Bush relents. "I suppose I'll have to accept that for the time being. Now, tell me what the hell has been going on here for the past forty years."

Dan Quayle remains quiet but studious.

With his sights reset, Vincent Sterne begins by saying, "Believe it or not, you're one of us, Mr. President. Both of you are, and soon you'll know that to be true because we're all patriots." He gauges their posture before going on. "You must first realize that our actions should not be considered racially motivated in any way, shape, or form. This whole thing is about keeping the peace, maintaining life as we know it. If I may be so bold, I believe we all know the adages about this country being stolen from the Native American Indian. It was then built on the blood and the backbones of African slaves and Oriental and Hispanic immigrants. It doesn't sound very pretty, but it's nonetheless true. The South tried to secede from the Union, refusing to give up certain practices, pushing for the expansion of slavery into new territories in fact. They lived lives of leisure at the expense of the Black man, whose leaders have been destroyed, ruined, discredited, imprisoned, and assassinated throughout American history. I believe that you mentioned Martin Luther King and such, which leads me to believe that you already suspect the very dangerous ramifications of this information."

In the face of Bush's silence, Quayle asks, "But who gave you the right?"

Sterne almost ignores him, but thinks better of it. "With all due respect, Vice President Quayle, you wouldn't have to ask such an asinine question if you were to put it to an all-White vote."

Dan, despite the insult, allows Sterne to continue.

Sterne sits back down and says, "As I've already stated, Blacks have been experiencing a population explosion since or before the early fifties."

"Get to the point," Quayle says.

"The increase in their population was heightened by things like the Civil Rights Act. Blacks began to get better jobs. Not all of them, mind you, but they enjoyed a certain amount of prosperity. The evidence seems to support that this went far toward allowing them to have and support larger families. Not to mention those who live in the cast society—welfare mothers who simply have bastard kids to increase their monthly checks, for an unpleasant example. Then you have to take into account all of the advances of modern medicine, which have given us all longer life spans. African Americans have also benefited greatly from health education, which translates into less hypertension and heart disease."

Sterne pauses, knowing that he's agitating the nation's leader. His sweeping diatribe is a mirror filled with broken images that are purposely brought together to form an ugly picture in its entirety.

"Like it or not, you must take into account that African Americans are dying at older ages and have been reproducing five children in comparison to the average White couple's one or two since the early fifties. Without having seen the latest figures, I'd say that approximation has probably increased to six or seven to one. At these rates, for the past fifty or sixty years, they have not only managed to catch up, they have surpassed us in numbers. And, unfortunately, these numbers are expected to escalate. It's almost as if Mother Nature herself has some hand in this anomaly because the epicenter of growth is most evident in the lower-middleclass. This trend is not as rampant in the most affluent or the poor families, where it would be more noticeable, but right where it can hide in plain sight. This is a staggering revelation."

Sterne is pleased by Bush's expression, but their emotions have to be further drawn into the ambush attack.

"Now, I know that this will sound ridiculous, but think about it for a second. Who's been pushing for the practice of birth control and social reform? Who has been pushing for cutbacks in welfare and health care?" He waits a moment before answering his own question. "You have, Mr. President. You and every money-making White man in this country that contributed to your campaign."

"This is preposterous and you know it. How dare you make such a leaping implication? This is outrageous!" says Bush.

Sterne shifts into overdrive, getting serious. He says, "Please be realistic, Mr. President. On a subconscious level, at the very least, I believe that most White men and women in America have mulled over the unsavory thought of Blacks gaining numerical advantage after everything that's happened to them. Every man of power has entertained thoughts of having an African American boss telling him when to break for lunch or when to take a crap. And every White man has had that nightmare where he's looking down into a valley filled with small dark figures crawling about like ants. The ants begin to crawl upward, climbing toward you. As they get closer, they get larger. Suddenly, they aren't ants any longer. They're angry Black people. They're coming like a black tidal wave that's going to drown you and trample you like a raging herd of stampeding cattle, but your feet just won't move you out of harm's way. Both of you know that dream, or something like it. Only this time—this time—you can't wake up because it's real. It is very real."

Neither man utters a word while horrible images fill their minds. Their silence pleases Sterne even more than before. President Bush is no longer so rigid, slumping deeper into his seat. That self-righteous attitude slowly dissipates. He is being seduced by a professional hooker, a political hooker. Sterne, however, is not done. Before it's over, Eve's snake in the garden will pale by comparison. They're both being swayed.

Sterne asks, "What do you suppose will happen to your own way of life and those of your children's children? Do you really believe that this kind of damning revelation can be absorbed without very distinct—very deleterious repercussions? I think not."

Bush says, "Maybe it will all work itself out." There is very little conviction in his voice as he reiterates the words of his running mate before Sterne's appearance. His words sound more like the mutterings of a man who's having a bad dream.

"Mr. President, Vice President Quayle, are either of you really willing to take that chance? I suggest that you both think long and hard about this. At least as long and hard as we have. We weren't present when the slave trade was alive and well in this country. Nor are we responsible for all the atrocities they have endured at the hands of institutions of hate, like the KKK. None of us pulled the trigger that killed Martin Luther King. We have no responsibility in any of these things. Or have we? It matters not when the mere implication is simply more than damning enough."

Again, he pauses during their silence.

"Truthfully, we will all pay a terrible price. Yet, that's only if you make this public knowledge, which can only prove to them that we are the monsters they perceive us to be. I can guarantee that they will riot and they will kill. Yes, kill. They can be an angry, warlike people by their very nature. I'm sorry to say, in many cases, they seem to have every provocation. You both know it as well as I do. If you tell them about this, you'll not only hand them the smoking gun, but you'll be aiming it and pulling the trigger for them. In that very grave moment, that profoundly grave moment, life as we all know it will cease to exist, undergoing an upheaval like nothing in the history of the entire world. There will be anarchy, total revolution, and for the worst I'd wager." Sterne sees Bush's mind grinding away behind those placated eyes. He is wordless, finally yielding. With the fight drained from his posture, his mirror image is Dan Quayle.

Still, Sterne is not finished.

"And what of the world, Mr. President? What of the world? Not to mention the many issues of equal representation, the eventual capture of the presidency and a majority rule in both houses of Congress. Do you think they can run this country better than you can?"

Bush glares at Sterne, but holds his tongue. Dan Quayle does likewise, although he expects Bush to rail down on his insubordinate CIA Director.

"What exactly will the world feel toward this government's credibility when the possibility of damage control will not even exist for you? How much will the rest of the world allot a nation that is ultimately based on something that will suddenly become as flimsy and meaningless as democracy?" He waits for an answer that won't be forthcoming. "I must put to you this question. Who among them will remember that our efforts to free Nelson Mandela was finally rewarded with a rare and happy outcome just this past February? Who will remember? They will brand us all hypocrites. I also ask, who will remember that we've effected the near complete dismantling of the Communist Russian threat?"

Bush and Quayle are speechless. Vincent Sterne's monologue has been a chariot afire, racing down a mountainside, completely unimpeded or thoroughly challenged. His chariot sets ablaze all obstacles of the imagination, which would feign to stand in its way. It is designed to conjure issues and images of insurmountable chaos, which now reigns undeniably in the mind of both men.

Sterne now feels it time to deliver the coupe de gras, his most telling blow. He leaves his seat to say, "Wall Street, among other things, will come crashing down. Ultimately, war will be the direct result of divulging this information. We've ruled this country because we've had the upper hand, which only comes with superior numbers. But we will no longer enjoy the luxury of that advantage. When this news goes public, you will have a civil war on your hands that, short of killing enough Blacks to tip the scales, you can't possibly hope to win in the end. It is a lose-lose situation that will haunt you both to the grave."

Sterne watches them, wondering if they even notice that he's shifting the weight of blame and responsibility onto their shoulders.

"I suspect that you already know what will happen while we're engaged in the difficulties of civil disobedience. The world will turn on us while the nation is at its weakest! When the United States is being ripped apart from within, the Castros and the Saddam Husseins of the world will be picking it apart from without. Even the descendants of Hiroshima and Nagasaki will have to consider the opportunity for revenge. Every friend this nation has will turn its back. So you see, in the end, this nation dies, and absolutely no one will love you for being men whose morals are above reproach. Moreover, anyone in this room who stands against all of these reasons is certainly not in full control of his mental faculties. He is unfit to run this great nation because he couldn't be a true patriot for a lack of love for it. Hell to pay, gentlemen. There will be hell to pay. Do you really want that responsibility?"

It's done, and Sterne knows it without a shadow of doubt. Love for the country is a compelling fixture in the basic reasoning behind most decisions to enter the political arena. With it comes the hope of making this country a better place to live.

Sterne thinks to himself, "Do it, Mr. President. Do it for mom and for apple pie. Do it for the red-blooded/White American way, and for all the other crocks of shit most politicians pretend to believe in until you are elected to office."

Since childhood, Vincent Sterne has raised dogs as pets. He is especially fond of the Rottweiler breed. They are such powerful, intelligent creatures. His experience with such large dogs has taught him that they are usually loyal and obedient to their master, but subject to lose respect when the master finds himself on their eye level. When a man is on all fours, he becomes one of two things; a subject or a playmate. In either case, he is vulnerable to its temperament and power. On this level, Sterne is master and in total control. However, he will soon return to President Bush his dignity and power, which is ultimately the power to do absolutely nothing.

World-class debates rage in their minds where logic is pitted against morality, each stammered with powerful emotions. In the end, however, there is only one conclusion; a moralistically logical conclusion. They are trapped in a vicious loop that has been sealed by the credo: To Protect and Serve. Vincent Sterne waits until all the rats have run the maze. He will leave soon.

CHAPTER 8

AN OFFER NOT REFUSED

Cecil Bridges sits before the television, resisting the slumber that now threatens to spirit him away. He has paced holes in the carpet while wrestling with weariness and the anticipation of President Bush's call. Having had no chance to rest since the discovery of Peter's treachery, he's become a churning ball of emotions. Knowing that the mercy of sleep could be his only relief for the upset stomach he still fights, he's slumping in an armchair that seems much too comfortable.

NBC is airing a special report, on which, a prominent political figure is being grilled by investigative journalist Allen Peterson. Cecil readily concludes that there will be a big stink in light of the damning evidence Peterson has just exposed on national television. Peterson's data links the Louisiana senator to unethical practices involving private sector lobbyists from New York, Chicago, Florida, Nevada, and Texas. Of course, this senator was not appreciative of what he called 'ambush journalism'.

There is a knock at the door.

Once Cecil is assured of the man's credentials, a second person enters the room with a heavy suitcase. Cecil soon recognizes

Vincent Sterne as the same man that bumped into him at the White House. Upon relief of his burden, the second man returns to the hallway to make sure that they are not disturbed.

"What's all this, Mr. Sterne?" Cecil asks concerning the case. He wonders if it's polygraph equipment, which is an insulting scenario. "And why the CIA?"

Seeing no need to mince words, Sterne simply says, "With plausible deniability always being a backdrop for everything that we do, Mr. Bridges, you can be made to disappear in the blink of an eye. Just like that!" He snaps his fingers as Cecil's eyes narrow. "But we're both civilized men here, you and I, so I chose to deal with you personally on this matter. This case contains an offering of ten million dollars, Mr. Bridges. You see, I'm one of the keepers of the gate that has been your utter misfortune to discover. Quite frankly, we feel that this sensitive information is much too volatile to expose to the American people all at once."

Cecil's heart races, highly distrustful of this visitor since the snap of his finger. His hypersensitive ears are tweaking, and his eyes pivot back and forth with Sterne centered.

"I thought you said that you were sent by President Bush."

"I was. We had a very long talk after you left the White House and he agrees completely. There's really no need to call. I believe he went on a fishing trip."

"We'll see about that, won't we?" Cecil says defiantly. He is soon shocked to find that Sterne is telling the truth. At least, that is what he's told before slamming the phone down in disgust. A wry smile leaves Sterne's lips by the time Cecil turns to face him.

"Mr. Bridges, what do you hope to accomplish by making this information public knowledge?"

"I hope to right a lot of wrongs, mister."

"How—by igniting a fire that you can't possibly contain? By making African Americans angry enough to engage the system, you stand to lose much, except for the amount of blood that will be on your hands. Do you want that on your conscience?"

"Contrary to what you may believe, all of my people aren't gun-carrying murderers," Cecil growls.

"But don't you see, Cecil? Clearly, that's exactly why you can't win."

"What are you so afraid of? Would change be so bad that you'd incite civil war rather than give the African American race its due?" Cecil asks, fuming.

"Correction, Mr. Bridges, it will be you who incites civil unrest and needless bloodshed. I strongly suggest that you take the money, sir. I know that you've lost a great deal on unsound investments over the years, so you can use the windfall. Your grandson needs braces and your daughter is trying to raise him alone. Rearing a son on a kindergarten teacher's salary is very tough these days. Is it not? Give it some thought. You'll be set for life and your family will want for nothing."

Cecil clearly reads a threat to his family between the lines of Sterne's appeal. While standing beneath the discerning gaze of a man that shows no fear in this boldly obtrusive approach, Cecil's mind races. He deduces that it must be very dangerous to cross such a person.

He paces the floor before approaching the table where the suitcase lay for the taking. He touches the smooth outer texture and glances over his shoulder to catch the slight smile on Sterne's face. Cecil is used to being the one with x-ray vision, but the tables have turned to make him the subject of visual dissection.

When he opens the suitcase, he whispers, "My God. So much money."

"Believe me, you'll be doing the right thing by accepting this gift. You can retire and watch little Nathan grow up with the best that life and the world have to offer. He'll never have to sell drugs or join street gangs because his mother is always away and struggling to make ends meet. In that way, eventually, lies prison or death. You can prevent such ugly things from becoming a part of his life equation. What do you say?"

Cecil stares down at the pile of green happiness, rubbing the stubble of his chin and neck. The case is filled with currency of large denominations. Ending a moment of very deep thought, he whispers, "Okay."

"What?"

"I said okay, damn it!" Cecil spits.

Sterne is somewhat relieved but suspicious. "You've made the right decision, Mr. Bridges. You have my personal guarantee that nothing will ever happen to you or your family, just as long as you keep your mouth shut. If you should suddenly decide to retire, no one will raise a fuss. But if you choose to stay on at the bureau, I must insist that Peter McAllister retains his post. Agreed?"

"Do you really think I'm going back to work? Fuck that noise. Now get out, I have some packing to do."

"As you wish, but aren't you forgetting something?" says Sterne, still locked on to his objective.

Cecil turns and says, "What? Oh, sure." He goes into his bedroom and brings back five disks and another copy of the census. He feels dirty after placing them in Vincent Sterne's anxious hands.

Sterne looks him in the eyes and asks, "That's it, right? Can you assure me that there are no other copies and you didn't discuss this with anyone?"

"No. Those are the only copies. I didn't discuss it with anyone other than President Bush," he lies. He tries not to give Sterne any reason to doubt his words, but stutters slightly.

Vincent Sterne reaches out to shake Cecil's hand, expecting him to hesitate or refuse. To his surprise, Cecil takes his hand without any discernable delay. He even manages a smile.

Sterne seems satisfied, so he turns to leave. He's already activated a team to hack and wipe all of Cecil's computers.

"Wait. I have two questions."

"Sure. What is it, Mr. Bridges?"

"Is the money real? I won't be arrested for counterfeiting if I buy a car or a new house, will I?"

Sterne smiles. "Yes. Of course, it's real. In fact, you can deposit the entire amount in the bank. As an added bonus for your cooperation, the I.R.S. will not bother you with the details and this windfall will never be taxed. Enjoy. Just remember, no one is to ever know about any of this." Sterne reaches into his blazer for a letter. "Oh yes. Can't believe I almost forgot this one small detail. This is an ironclad non-disclosure agreement that you will sign under penalty of death. Are we clear on this, Mr. Bridges? Death."

Cecil nods and scribbles his signature on the contract. When Sterne leaves, he hears Cecil whooping it up as if he's a lotto winner. He whispers something to his operative as they enter the elevator. The door slides shut and Cecil Bridges never lays eyes on Vincent Sterne again.

CHAPTER 9

DOUBLE-CROSS

August 31, 1990 10:30 p.m. NBC Studio, Washington, D.C.

With his feet crossed atop the desk, Executive Producer Turner Ross sits languidly in the big chair. He secretly relishes the conversation with a friendly competitor, Martha Richards, an executive of CBS News in Washington, D.C.

Although the NBC exec is gloating on the inside, he graciously accepts praises from his former colleague for the masterful exhibition of Senator Anderson's guts and the more private parts of his anatomy on NBC's exclusive broadcast.

Displaying a playful smile, Ross coyly proclaims, "Really, Martha, I can't take any credit on this one. It was Peterson's baby all the way. Despite the spineless reservation of others, he dug it up. Then he spit-shined and polished it before impaling that crooked bastard for all the world to see. Did you notice that suddenly feverish look on Senator Anderson's face? I thought he was going to give birth to a king-sized hernia!" Hearty laughter roars from Ross's lips.

She says something that catches his attention.

"What? No way, forget it. Peterson is my pit bull and he's extremely happy here at NBC. In fact, a new contract is being drawn up as we speak. He and I are just like family. Peterson's one of the few who can go over heads without getting crushed at my door. He has an uncanny instinct for choosing such battles. Hell, all bullshit aside, Martha, I'm actually thinking about introducing him to my daughter. Journalistic genes like his should be harvested."

After knocking, Allen Peterson pokes his head in. Upon seeing his crusader, Ross excuses himself, but not without a promise to buy Martha Richards a conciliatory dinner.

"Come in, Allen. You're just the man I want to see. Great job, as usual."

As they shake hands, Peterson bows and says, "Thank you, Ladies and Gentlemen."

"Go ahead, take another bow. Take three."

Having just snorted two huge lines in his personal lavatory, Allen Peterson feels quite pleased with himself. His smile is absolutely radiant.

"Did I get him, Turner, or did I really get him?"

They laugh merrily because both have been duplicitous in the most recent journalistic exploit. Having gambled and won on the wordplay that trapped a thief and liar, they make jokes about how Peterson exposed the underhanded dealings of Louisiana Senator Clifton Anderson.

Ross makes it known that he especially enjoyed the part of the broadcast when the good senator could offer no coherent explanation in regard to the hooker. The blonde call girl often did him special favors, for which she was always handsomely paid by the lobbyist pulling the strings. His mistake was in striking her on a previous rendezvous for flirting. She lost two teeth and suffered a split lip, but he hastily paid for dental surgery and trips to a plastic surgeon. Vengefully, the woman captured the next four meetings on both audio and videotape.

Anderson is a pig. With big money behind his negative ad campaign, he took the seat by a massive margin. He lied through his teeth to win the election and completely abandoned his constituents once in office. When one of Peterson's contacts hinted that Senator Anderson was involved with his sister, the prostitute with a grudge, the journalist dug deeper. Natasha Trident was paid five-thousand dollars for each videotape she'd made of Anderson's reckless pillow talk. But Allen Peterson convinced Turner Ross that the same amount of money was the prostitute's asking price to meet with Anderson again. This time, she offered to pick the Senator with a set of carefully orchestrated questions about his attitude toward the minorities that voted for him.

Allen Peterson convinced his boss to commit to the creation of a false media forum of praise and appreciation from those minority voters, who wanted to thank him on television because Senator Anderson was regaled as a moral Christian that procured an unprecedented minority voter turnout. The Senator had no idea that the ad campaign for this interview was all just an elaborate rouse to get him in front of the cameras. Anderson fell for it, but his own mouth became the shovel that would bury him. Instead of clamming up when the trap was sprung, he babbled like an idiot on national television. In this political graveyard, the soil will be rich for years to come despite his threat to sue.

Peterson baited Anderson by asking him to come on the air to answer the fictitious admirers who would have the great man run for the White House. Even his lobbyist friends were taken in by this aspect. He had agreed to the live interview, feeling smug and safe. The Senator felt honored in fact, but he was taken totally by surprise when the former prostitute appeared from the shadows to sit in the vacant seat before the lights and cameras. He undoubtedly deserved what he got. Thanks to Peterson and the Senator's hooker friend, a full investigation will be launched into Senator Anderson's dealings with 'Big Oil' and pharmaceutical companies.

There will be stiff penalties to pay, starting with an immediate call for his suspension from office and the hooker's spiteful lawsuit. The "Pillow Talk Videotapes" are pure journalistic gold. Needless to say, Anderson's wife is none too happy. The politarrazzi would sell their collective souls just to be a fly on the wall when he gets home.

Turner Ross informs Peterson that he is practically a shoe in for the Peabody Award and the fifth annual Chritton Award for Excellence in Journalism.

They are celebrating with a toast to things to come when Turner's assistant buzzes the office to inform the reporter that he has an urgent call. Peterson takes the call, gives the caller his email address and runs out of the office a few moments later. His hasty explanation of the five-minute phone conversation to Ross is only that it could be bigger than Watergate and Louisiana Senator Anderson combined. Peterson proclaims it to be too juicy to ignore because the caller sounded serious. With an enigmatic gleam in his eyes, floating just above the floor, this reporter is again a confident man on a mission. His accomplished investigative experience certainly gives him the ability to discern the crackpots from the genuine articles. All that need be said to Ross is that the mysterious caller claimed to be a government official with proof of something monstrous; proof beyond all recrimination.

As Allen Peterson waits for the elevator to reach the underground parking structure, he checks the batteries in his mini-recorder. He walks out into the garage, listening to the city noise that makes its way down into the concrete vault. It gives him comfort, anything to break the silence.

In the interim, he wonders if he hasn't gotten excited over nothing. The phone call could be some cruel prank or a setup by Senator Anderson's goons. Because Allen Peterson has reported the news from New York to Washington, D.C., he's confident in an ability to discard the loons that crave media attention, but that talented instinct is constantly tested.

Allen Peterson is the secret finder, the man quietly deemed by peers and fans as the Crooked Politician's Nightmare. With little more than time to lose, he has a feeling that the man claiming to be the Director of the Census Bureau is about to give him the big one.

A blue sedan passes Peterson, who holds his breath in anticipation. He recognizes the young lady from the secretarial pool when she waves with a smile that could only mean that she wants him. He often feels that way about women when he's high.

Cecil Bridges enters the parking structure, stopping in the middle of an empty row of parking spaces, well away from the elevator where Peterson paces.

His hands shake as he opens his briefcase to remove the disks he'd kept from Vincent Sterne.

The suitcase containing the ten million dollars lies upon the back seat of the car.

Cecil was forced to soil himself with the bribe money so Sterne would back off. Being aware of the price of this potentially deadly double-cross causes glaciers of sweat to fall from his brow. His crawling flesh is a living oil slick with a thousand legs.

After accepting the risk to himself, Cecil called Deedra Wilson from the same pay phone he had used to contact Allen Peterson. He sent the information via email with his laptop just as he asked Deedra to warn his daughter of any strangers that might suddenly show up. Finally, Cecil made his lover promise to keep quiet about the census lie, no matter what happens. He made her repeat the promise she's already made before he left Suitland.

Now Allen Peterson moves toward the grey Cadillac, waving. The driver is an older man, who looks genuinely harmless. Peterson's voice echoes with his hurried footfalls when he says, "Mr. Bridges, Cecil Bridges?"

As Peterson draws within five parking spaces of Cecil's car, a black SUV screeches to a stop at the entrance, never actually leaving the street.

As though he is some kind of savior, Cecil Bridges looks desperately at the reporter. As he tries frantically to get out of the car, Peterson hears him say, "Oh shit!"

Before their bulging eyes, time stalls. All else in the universe ceases to exist, but for two heartbeats. These two souls are locked in a frantic stare, enveloped by a moment of urgent, ominous silence. Then a searing shriek erupts from within the Cadillac as living fire engulfs the cabin and driver! The glass of the windows seem to melt within their frames from the intense heat of an incendiary device, bubbling outward faster than Peterson's eyes and mind can process. There comes a monstrous explosion, tossing the car into the air where it slams into the low-lying ceiling of level one!

Peterson is an ice sculpture of a paralyzed shriek as the fire spreads toward him. The laughing flame, slow of motion, begs him to let it give chase. Running, however, will do Allen Peterson little good at this point.

The laughing flame flicks its red-hot tongue out across the ages to kiss Allen Peterson upon his screaming lips! He starts to back away, but the overpowering heat reaches him just before the evil redhead engulfs him in her suffocating embrace. It sears his mouth, throat, and lungs as a hasty breath draws the heat inside of his body.

A second explosion ensues when the fuel tank goes, slamming Peterson to the concrete floor several yards away. Cecil Bridges is burnt to a cinder seconds before being ripped to pieces. The evidence and money now burns with him.

Having the inside track allows NBC to scoop the tragic story. With tears in their eyes, newscasters offer the nation a firsthand view of the underground parking structure. One such reporter is telling the world of her brilliant co-worker, Allen Peterson, who was present at the time of the blast. He's been transported to the nearby hospital, having received second and third degree burns over most of his body. According to early speculation, Allen Peterson is not expected to live through the night.

Were it not for a quick-thinking security guard, who used a fire extinguisher to put him out, Peterson would have perished on the spot. Peterson and the guard are the only witnesses. FBI forensic investigators are attempting to ascertain the identity of the body in the car. Bomb experts are already searching the debris, looking for anything that might shed light on the type of explosives used.

When someone gives the reporter a sheet of paper, she says, "This just in—the FBI has tracked down the man they believe responsible for the bombing here at NBC Studios in Washington. He is believed to be a member of an Al-Qaida terrorist faction, who may have entered the country with falsified documents. In the FBI's attempt to apprehend the suspect at an abandoned warehouse where the terrorists have apparently set up shop, there has been a heavy exchange of weapons fire. Sources say that during the fray there has been another explosion, which is believed to have killed the Iraqi terrorist known as Aziz Basra and several others of the terror cell. It was a very brief but bloody battle. Several members of the arresting task force have been injured by the heavily armed terrorists." She clears her throat. "It would seem that the gunfire accidentally detonated some form of explosive device, which officials believe Aziz Basra and his group were planning to use to terrorize American citizens right here in the nation's capital."

She tilts her head and touches her earphone, listening for a moment. "Moments from now, we will have a live, exclusive interview with a government representative who will try to shed some light on just how something like this has happened on U.S. soil. Apparently, the CIA and the FBI were involved in joint surveillance of the terrorists. They were watching the suspect when he came here to detonate the bomb, but they had no prior knowledge of its placement. Please stay tuned as we try to get a clear picture of the tragic events that have just taken place here at NBC Studios Washington. Right now, we're joining Jeffrey Thomas at the scene of the burning terrorist hideout. Jeffrey?"

The television screen seems to blur. An open pack of Rolaids rolls to a stop on the desk. President Bush watches the newscast on television as the prelude to a pounding headache bears down on his pulsing temples. He no longer feels like going fishing.

The cell phone in his pocket startles him from his dreary malaise. The man on the other end says, "It's done. Now the gate is truly closed."

The phone goes dead, and with it, George Bush's innocence. Like it or not, he is now a gatekeeper. Later, within the depths of night, he awakens to the pulse of drums and a faint, ghostly laughter that rides the electric wind. It is a darkly ominous, forebodingly malicious laughter.

CHAPTER 10

DARK PROPHECY

President William Jefferson Clinton survived impeachment on May 13, 1999. Though Clinton finished the second term, both his marriage and brilliant presidential career were marred by his internal tryst. Amid the resulting media storm, it was suspected that Hillary Clinton filed for divorce, but such supposition remained the domain of political hearsay until she pursued her own political agenda and remained married to Bill.

White House intern Monica Lewinsky, once voted Most Likely to Become Famous in her high school retrospect, is a woman whose infamy had become bait for worldwide exploitation. To the great shame of her family, she tried to sell the publishing rights of her tawdry memoirs to the highest bidder, but lost sight of the fine print of the France based contract. She reserved little control in the upcoming motion picture of her scandalous affair, which was aptly entitled "My American President". The motion picture's poorly written, slightly pornographic format gained it no honors and very little recognition. The movie's European debut garnered more laughter than serious scrutiny; more scorn than accolades.

Al Gore was expected to easily assume the helm, but it is strongly believed by many that the distractions of the Lewinsky scandal muddied the political waters so greatly that the Republican Party's dirty work was long set in place before the 2000 election. Al Gore nearly lost to George W. Bush, even though he won the popular vote. The voter polls in the state of Florida, run by Governor Jeb Bush, turned into a disastrous nightmare. Many ballots were misplaced in the key swing state. Thousands of Al Gore's supporters found out that they had actually voted for the wrong candidate. Absentee voters, many of whom were disabled or military personnel stationed abroad, had been all but erased from the electoral process. The election was an ugly, tarnished affair that caused many voters to lose faith in the integrity of the system.

⇒+⇐

April 1, 2001. Saturday.
North Charleston, South Carolina.

At 1900 Blair Street, the home of Jarvis Parker is bustling with activity. Most of the family is gathered in the backyard. Jarvis is a tall, dark-skinned man with kind eyes that sparkle as he watches his grandchildren hard at play. The short grey hairs of his beard prickle as he smiles to himself. Most of his family has come together, except for his daughter Talia. His wife of forty years, Alvina Parker, passed away in 1994.

Talia Parker's children have enjoyed the week of spring break with their grandfather. The ten-year-old little girl's name is Reesha. Her twin brother's name is Shaquile. At the far end of the backyard, the children are engaged in a rather strenuous game of tag with their cousins. It is no accident that they stay well away from the meaningless gabble of the grownups, who are going about the rituals of the spring barbeque.

Blue jays and mockingbirds are squawking their jurisdictional disputes in the trees and shrubbery that encompass the backyard of the Parker family home. Thankfully, the mosquitoes are yet to reach a swarming population. No one misses their bothersome presence in the low country.

Jarvis Parker retired from the railroad where he worked for nearly forty-two years. Although he started out as a lowly porter, he'd worked his way up to conductor. By being studious and dedicated, against all odds, he became an engineer. His upward mobility in the company was no small accomplishment during that period. It had taken a lot of hard work and a relentless drive, both tempered with a reasonable degree of humility. Jarvis Parker instilled these qualities in his children.

The job once required that he travel extensively, but he never allowed it to interfere with the raising of his only daughter or his older twin sons, Evan and Kyle. Jarvis Parker was proud of his children, who graduated from different colleges to embark on equally fulfilling careers. Alvina Parker, who had been taken from them in a tragic automobile accident, also played a big part in their success.

Jarvis's daughter is in her early thirties. Talia Parker is in the process of completing her residency at University Hospital in Augusta, Georgia, where she has lived for several years. Her college career was interrupted by an unanticipated pregnancy, but she managed to handle going back to med-school with only a few hang-ups. Her parents volunteered to keep the children for a few years when they were old enough to be separated from their mother. It was the time of the grandparents' lives.

Kyle Parker is an unmarried Captain in the Air Force Nuclear Weapons Division. Evan Parker, the elder twin by a few minutes, is an economic statistician. He was recently hired as the new Deputy Director of the Census Bureau. Because of tragic personal conflicts, he'd left his career as a professor at his collegiate alma mater in Columbia, South Carolina.

Evan and Kyle attended separate colleges on academic scholarships, having reaped the benefits of accelerated learning programs in high school. These tall, strong men are very easy on the eyes. However, there are distinct differences in them, other than physical appearance. Evan is married to the very beautiful Melissa Parker, who is five months pregnant with their first child. Children have always been Evan's desire, but his brother has no cause to be so serious about such things. Until recently, marriage and children were next to having teeth pulled on Kyle Parker's list of fun things to do.

Jarvis' sister, Thelma Jacobs, works furiously to add the finishing touches on the family barbeque. It would not be complete without generous helpings of her famous potato and shrimp salads, or the sweet potato pies that are cooling on a rack beneath an open window.

Although people are coming and going, Aunt Thelma is being helped in the kitchen by Melissa Parker. They have enlisted the help of Alicia Markham, Kyle's girlfriend and co-worker at the super-secretive missile installation high in the Allegheny Mountains. Their base is one of the few missile sites in the Mid-Atlantic region of the country. It is the only one of its kind in the world, for the time being.

The three women have engaged a probing conversation while Evan and Kyle play a competitive game of horseshoes in the backyard. After Jarvis finishes smoking his pipe, he decides to wrestle with the children, who enjoy the advantages of youth. They wrap themselves around his legs and pile on until they conquer the mighty, snarling beast. Once the old man is felled, they rain kisses and hugs on him. The infamous Magugoo plays dead for a moment, and suddenly resurrects to attack the young warriors.

Thelma laughs, pointing at the scene through the kitchen window. "That old fool is going to throw his back out or break a hip," she says.

"He's too tough for that," Melissa Parker says. "Aunt Thelma, I don't think Jarvis even knows the meaning of getting old."

As they giggle, Thelma sees the perfect opportunity to ask, "You know, speaking of getting old, when are you going to make my handsome nephew an honest man, Alicia? Am I going to have to break out that rusty, old shotgun?"

Alicia gasps at the unexpected change of subject, but her surprise affords no mercy because this is not an entirely new subject.

With Thelma's unanswered question looming still, Alicia looks at them coyly and answers like a soldier. "Markham! Lieutenant. Serial number Sierra 1234..."

Melissa pops her with a drying towel and warns, "Sister, you better give up the info, or we'll tickle you until you have to change your clothes. If that doesn't work, I'll just whip out one of Kinzana's infamous voodoo dolls and make you talk. So what's it gonna be?"

Aunt Thelma moves in, humming her allegiance to the plan if they aren't given immediate satisfaction.

Alicia confesses, "Okay. He asked me yesterday and I said—yes. We're getting married!" She removes the engagement ring from her pocket, placing it on her finger to properly show it off. She is smothered with congratulatory kisses and a few tears of joy are shed.

"I have two stipulations, okay? You have to act surprised when we make the announcement, and you have to keep it a secret. We haven't told our commanding officers yet. God, I felt like I was going to burst. Thankfully, you guys just dragged it right out of me."

"I can understand you wanting us to act surprised, but I just don't get the rest of it," Aunt Thelma says. Melissa Parker waits patiently for the answer to a question that was about to roll from her very own lips.

Alicia says, "Well, you see, until around the late 1980s, coed missileer teams were considered taboo. Theoretically, conflicts between team members and their spouses would result. One would be on the outside looking in, wondering what might be going on underground. You know, simple jealousy and suspicion. It took a lot to change those perceptions, but our commanding officer is still liable to split us up as a team. Doing us a big favor, to hear them tell it. Another theory is that a married team will experience problems brought on by overkill. In other words, they'll get sick of seeing one another all the time. Presently, there are no husband and wife teams in our line of work."

"Oh, that's ridiculous," Melissa replies

"I tend to agree," Alicia says, "But I really enjoy working with Kyle. We make a great team. We're complete and whole, you know? Heaven forbid, but if there is a nuclear war and we are ordered to launch our birds, I really don't think that I could do my job without him. I don't know, I probably would execute my orders. I'm a professional. Being with Kyle will just make the ordeal a little more bearable. Do you understand?" Her eyes plead with them to comply with her request for secrecy because they don't know that missileer are often followed when they go on furlough.

"Well, I suppose it wouldn't hurt us to keep the secret a little longer. Come here and give your Aunt Thelma a big hug."

"So you do understand, right?" Alicia asks in the midst of a group hug. "It's just until we get the feel of things from our commanding officer."

"Certainly. We understand," Melissa assures.

Aunt Thelma adds, "But we can't vouch for Evan's and Kyle's cousin, Mary the Mockingbird. You know, the really hungry one in the spandex. She never stops talking unless she's stuffing her mouth, and sometimes that doesn't make a difference. Maybe you should wait until we're all out of food to make that announcement. I can guarantee she'll be long gone by then."

Alicia Markham points out the window and asks, "You mean her? But she's so skinny. She can't even fill out the spandex."

Aunt Thelma says with a grin, "That's 'cause she has such a high metabolism. It takes a lot of energy to talk that much."

They cackle hysterically and guiltlessly when Mary starts talking with her mouth full of potato chips, crumbs sticking to her heavily applied lip-gloss.

When the hysteria finally subsides, Lieutenant Markham admits, "I really love that man. I love him so much that I don't think there's anything I wouldn't do for him. I've never felt this way about anyone. I want to go wherever he goes, come what may." She is smiling, and her eyes have taken on an enchantment all their own.

"Aunt Thelma, I think she's got it really bad," Melissa teases. "Alicia, are you having an out of body experience right now?"

They share another girlish giggle as Thelma shuffles off to the bathroom.

"I never thought it possible. It would seem that I've become so much closer to this family in the past two years that almost all traces of my own dysfunctional family have nearly faded away. Just letting my own father know that I'm getting married is something to think about. Even if I did, I doubt that he'd be able to crawl out of the bottle long enough to give me away."

"You've got all the family you will ever need right here," Melissa says, noting a hint of sadness in Alicia's eyes. Melissa, who was once very shy, recalls the shyness Alicia showed when they first met. It is something that Melissa can appreciate in this person, who must have felt as if the women of the Parker family circle were once interrogating her.

"Thank you so much for saying that, Mel," Alicia says with a new measure of sadness in her eyes. "My mom is gone. My dad is a dedicated drunk. Two brothers doing ten to fifteen for a crime that only one committed. My younger sister is on drugs, in the streets somewhere selling herself. God, what the hell happened to us?"

They are hugging when Thelma returns.

"Alright now, let's get this food outside to those hungry people before we start crying again or laughing." Right on cue, Mary walks in. They cackle and go about the business of serving up healthy portions of good southern cooking.

Before they sit to eat, Kyle and Alicia announce their engagement. With many members of their family gathered at the home of Jarvis Parker, this is truly a joyous occasion.

After the feast of meats and sweets, as the sun fades, the children rebel against the siren of sleep by challenging a final game of hide and seek. Yet one by one, they'll succumb to the siren's call. On this day, everyone has enjoyed the best of times. With unforeseen changes coming, this is icing on the cake for grownups and children alike.

The young twins are to return to Augusta tomorrow evening. Melissa Parker's day of departure is also at hand. For the first time since Evan's career change, she is finally going to join her husband in Maryland.

Jarvis will not be alone with Thelma to fuss over him, and his children will visit whenever possible. His roots are spreading out in the world, and he's very proud to be their father. The benefits of knowing that he and his late wife have raised them well are infinite in the advancing years of life. All is good. It is well.

While the women wash and dry the dishes, the men chat and clean up outside. Satisfied and full, most of the others return to their own dwellings with their favorite assortments of leftovers. As the last visitor leaves, Jarvis retires to the front porch; his favorite place to sit as the dying sun casts its longest shadows. Moments later, a sleek Mercedes glides to a stop in the driveway.

Evan and Kyle are now talking by the stone fence at the very end of the shaded backyard. They're leaning on a cool stone ramp, reflectively picking their teeth. Kyle looks at his fraternal twin to say, "I wish momma was here to see me get married."

Evan looks to the ground and then to the sky. His voice is thoughtful and serene when he says, "I miss her, too. Sometimes, I can still hear her voice and see her smile. We were lucky to have her as our mother."

All of the bitterness that normally accompanies the wrongful death of a loved one has faded from their hearts with the passage of time. The memory of Alvina Parker no longer causes them to grit their teeth, so only the good things rise from thoughts of her life and untimely death.

"Yeah, you're right about that. I feel as if she's still with me. There are times when I'd swear I can smell her favorite perfume. What was that fragrance she used to wear?"

They both say, "Channel Number Five."

Evan grins, looking at an old tree that now only bears plums every other season. "I can see her tanning your ass for eating that whole jar of preserved pears. She was going to use them to make cobblers for the church's bake sale when we were eleven. That was one of the times when I was glad that we were not identical twins."

Kyle says, "You can't eat just one and walk away. Well, you did, but I couldn't stop. I'd probably do it all again, if she could be here to cut my ass. Do you remember how she cussed out the old man for an entire week when he began building that 'damned infernal' bomb shelter in the backyard? Jesus. She was cussing and asking God's forgiveness with every other word."

Evan attempts to mimic his father's voice and demeanor when that conversation was held many years ago. He waves his hands about just as Jarvis did when he said, "'Damn it all to Judas hell, woman. You got the Charleston Naval Base right over there. You got the Naval Weapons Station right down the street. The damn Air Force Base and airport are out that way. Shit if we ain't a prime target to get nuked by the Russians!'" It was one of the few disagreements Jarvis had actually won outright.

"Wait, wait. I've got one," Kyle says, barely able to contain himself. "How about the time she waded knee-deep into the old man's shit for letting the voodoo man tell us those scary stories about the evil zombies of Makuunda on that stormy Halloween night?" Evan grunts, but says nothing else because he knows where this is heading. "Kinzana's story must have kept us awake for about a week. That old oak tree outside our bedroom window kept creaking and changing shapes. You pissed in the bed because you were too scared to go to the bathroom alone!"

That memory really cracks them up. It was one of the few times Evan had ever lost his composure. The zombie story was truly terrifying, and it was told to them as only one man could.

When the raging laughter finally passes, Kyle asks, "How is the old witch doctor anyway?"

"Well I haven't seen him in nearly two years. I meant to take a ride down to the African Village for a visit. There just never seems to be enough time, especially with all that's been going on. But the last time I saw them, he and Insanyanga still looked as fit and strong as they did when we were kids. I swear they haven't aged a day. It's uncanny," Evan observes.

"I really miss them. We had lots of fun down in Beaufort. Every visit was a new adventure, especially when those crazy people were playing with their snakes. That shit used to make my skin crawl, but those were the days. Remember when we were playing and that really big one got loose? God, that thing stood as tall as we were, staring us in the eyes with its head ballooning. I thought we were both dead. I looked it up only to find that it was actually a King Cobra."

Evan Parker admits, "So did I, after peeing my pants. We couldn't even scream for help. It hissed, looking back and forth, trying to decide which one of us to bite first. If either of us had moved, it would have. Then Kinzana came around the corner and tapped it on the head. I forgot the words he said, but it just went back to its home like a pet dog obeying its master."

In perfect harmony, both will sigh and smile at the fading sun. After a moment of silence, Kyle says, "Well, I'd better go and steal a kiss from my lady."

"It may have taken forever, but I see you've got it pretty bad. If your nose were opened any wider, I could probably see your brain." Evan squints when he grins at Kyle.

"Careful. This brain is highly classified and you just don't have the security clearance. You may be twenty minutes older, but I out-rank you there," he says. As they walk, he drapes an arm over Evan's shoulder. "So how about you and Melissa? Are things really okay now?"

"Fine. Melissa's a great woman and she'll make an even better mother. She's been feeling a little guilty about leaving the old man here alone."

"I know what you mean, but he'll be alright."

"Man, to just think. We both went to college at age sixteen. It's taken us this long to conceive our firstborn. And at age forty-two, you finally want to settle down."

"Yep. It's a good year for us both, big brother. So how's the new job working out, Mr. Deputy Director?"

Evan says, "Good. I'm all settled in at work, hitting my stride. It's different from teaching, but I like what I'm doing. We have a big ole house. Did you see the pictures?"

"Mel showed them to me. I get the feeling that she's a little disappointed about that part of it all," Kyle Parker says.

"She's going to love it when she actually sees it for the first time. Those were the pictures that I took before the renovations. Naturally, my wife wanted to be a part of it all, but I didn't think it wise because of the problems with the pregnancy. However, I had fun doing it all by myself. It allowed me to influence the ambience of the house. Of course, I left the nursery and bathrooms alone. She'd just change them anyway."

Kyle says, "Sounds like perfection. I'm happy for you, Evan. I think it was wise of you to deal with the bulk of things. It did take you guys forever and a day to get pregnant. 'There is never the need to rock a leaking boat', as the old man would say."

As they approach the kitchen door, Evan says, "Oh! I forgot to tell you, my boss is none other than Peter McAllister."

"Get out of town. Your crazy college roommate is the Director of the Census Bureau. How the hell did he manage that trick?"

"Yep. Bush gave Peter the appointment when Cecil died back in 1990. He's been in charge ever since. Two Presidents later and he's still there. I guess that's saying something."

"I don't believe it. That guy must have turned over a whole new tree. The South Carolina Gamecocks have invaded Maryland, once again. The Terrapins must be shaking in their boots. Tell the Critter-getter I said hello."

"Sure thing," Evan says as he laughs. "Critter-getter...I forgot about that nickname."

Kyle stops on the top step and asks, "But didn't I hear something about a security breach at the Census Bureau? What happened?"

"Well, about eleven years ago, the bureau integrated all systems and departments throughout the country. It was like one big umbilical cord that stretched from the headquarters to all the regional offices. More like a crude Internet type system. Anyway, some egghead with a sick sense of humor hacked his way into the mainframe and introduced some kind of super-virus that wrecked the system. They called it a Reticular Sleeper Virus. Apparently, the virus remained dormant until it had spread to every department within the Census Bureau. Once that was achieved, it activated itself and all hell broke loose. They believe it was introduced into the system years before, sleeping until it had been encoded throughout. It destroyed all the electronically stored data for the last decade and then some. The stats had to be retrieved, reconstructed and transcribed from files to software. That's why we're still working on the last decennial census in the year 2001, and we've already begun working on the 2010 census report."

Pausing their steps in sync, Kyle winces and whistles. "Man, I know there are some mad mothers out there. Nobody wants to do the same work twice."

"Ten years' worth—squared," Evan adds.

"Did they ever catch the guy who did it?"

"Not to my knowledge. According to Peter, the FBI believes that there had to be more than one person involved in pulling it off, maybe even employees that introduced the Retic Sleeper at different points. Each segment of the virus was like four sections of a snake. Each part heading in one semicircular direction with specific objectives, seeking out its own encrypted signature. Essentially, it was just like the Reticular Python, circling until joining as one. Once the circle was complete, it activated and strangled the department by destroying a lot of data. I'm just glad that I'm coming in on the ass end of it all. When I get back to Maryland, we should be just about finished with the retrieval process."

Kyle asks, "Wow. But what's to stop them from doing it again?"

Dubiously, Evan says, "Anything's possible, but I don't think so. The entire system underwent a massive overhaul and the security protocols are constantly upgraded to prevent that from happening."

"Let's hope so."

They enter the living room where the women are sipping tea or coffee. All abeam, they fall silent when Evan and Kyle come in. The brothers know instinctively that one or both of them had been the subject of the suddenly abandoned conversation. The brothers look at one another, each with a comically raised eyebrow. Finding their expression amusing, the women soon burst into wild laughter.

A familiar voice, thick with an East African accent, flows over Evan's and Kyle's shoulders to their ears like warm butter running downhill. The woman says, "Children, am I so old and thin of a ghost that I've faded from the sight of my most cherished godsons? Have you finally outgrown your love for Insanyanga?"

The brothers turn to see their godmother, approaching quickly to rain kisses upon her cheeks. Insanyanga is indeed a welcome sight. They exchange pleasantries before the brothers go to in search of her husband.

To their astonishment, Kinzana and Jarvis are sitting on the screened porch smoking a rather healthy joint. The pungent aroma of marijuana assaults the brothers as they walk onto the porch. They're quite shocked to find their father drawing on a left-handed cigarette with its fiery tip flaring in the twilight.

The tall figure of a man arises and is hugged. They exchange greetings before the brothers turn to inspect their father, who is coughing up a lung.

Evan scolds, "Pop, I know better than this. You're actually smoking reefer, man."

Jarvis tries to shush him, but only manages to raise his hand to protest the volume of Evan's voice. The pitiful display causes the other three men to chuckle as his chest heaves to hold the smoke.

Kinzana says, "My two godsons, tall and handsome like the mighty oak tree. How good it is to see you when so long it has been."

Evan says, "Yes. It's been much too long. How are you?"

Kinzana reaches out to turn on the porch light. In its soft illumination, he spreads his wings like a runway model and slowly turns. He bids, "Take a good look and envy, for I am the very picture of health."

"What's your secret, Kinzana? I mean, you haven't aged a day in forty-two years. Let's bottle it and get rich, what do you say?" asks Kyle.

They all laugh, including Jarvis, who's regains the ability to speak without the use of his hands. Without falling victim to another bout of spit-slinging coughing, Jarvis passes the joint back to Kinzana as they sit.

In disbelief, Kyle asks his sixty-two-year-old father, "When did you start smoking grass?"

Jarvis has begun to feel the effects of Kinzana's personal touch. He wears a grin from ear to ear while floating just above his rocker. He can barely feel the smooth wood beneath his bottom.

His eyes water when he says, "Mind your place, boy. I'm retired, so why shouldn't I be allowed to try new things? Look at my friend here. I've known this man for over forty years, but you don't see him getting old and withering away, now do you? Hell, I want to live forever, too. In fact, I feel pretty strong for my age. I still have most of my teeth. God bless the righteous dead, but if your mother was still here, I'd chase her upstairs for some nostalgia right about now!" Jarvis puckers his lips and wraps his arms around an imaginary lover, which brings a roar of laughter. Jarvis coughs, as well as Kinzana, who has taken an ill-timed toke. Jarvis says to Kyle, "Turn that fan on, son." Then he uses a can of spray to dampen the aroma.

The stuff must be pretty good. It certainly smells that way, so Evan chances a toke himself. He takes a draw on the joint, which would eventually render him just as senseless with its rapid-fire high. One toke is enough for this lightweight. Kyle declines because he's subject to undergo a urinalysis upon his return from leave.

With a rather serious look on his face, Jarvis scolds his eldest son. "Boy, what the hell do you think you're doing? I thought I raised you better than that. Or to hide it from grown folks, at the very least."

They burst into tear-jerking laughter as Jarvis struggles to maintain the insincere reprimand of a son he taught to avoid drugs.

Evan admits, "Well, I hate to disappoint you, but we've sneaked a puff or two while growing up. Because you did raise us well, it was only a phase." Kyle looks at his brother, who just divulged one of their biggest secrets.

Kinzana smiles, thinking this well. He gazes at the red firefly in the darkness and muses, "Too much of a good thing can be very bad for anyone, but this is not the poison it is often made out to be. In my native land, it grows in our gardens next to stalks of corn. It still flourishes wild in jungles and forests where the water and sunlight are plentiful."

Nodding his head as if he's urging on a preacher during Sunday morning service, Jarvis says, "Go ahead. You tell it now."

"Damballah sprinkled the seeds of this plant upon the earth to serve as a bridge for man to heaven, and even for man to himself. It is good to have when wicked voices intrude upon our peace and goodwill toward others. It can be most helpful when those voices clutter that of the inner being, which seeks rejuvenation and expansion in a world of mass sorrow and infinite pain. Also, it does not come with a laundry list of side effects that can turn out to be much worse than the disease one tries to cure. Tell me now, how can such a thing be bad?"

Jarvis blurts out, "I'd buy that for a dollar, Doc. I bet you can take that speech to Congress and they'd probably re-elect Bill Clinton for a third term, seeing that he wasn't such a bad guy. Damn it, I'm telling you that the man had insight!"

Jarvis is on a tear and they cheer his statement because he has known too few reasons to laugh so loudly since Alvina Parker died not long enough ago. It is good to see him spinning the yarn again.

"So, Kinzana, how are things at the village?" Evan asks. "Everything okay?"

"Yes, my son. We are enjoying prosperity. There are now thirty such villages across this country, each in different states. In the future, there will be more. Of this, I am certain."

"That many? Wow," Evan muses.

"Whenever people hear the mention of African villages, they always think of poverty," Kyle states. "They think of women running around with their breasts hanging out, and a baby at each nipple."

Evan adds, "And don't forget the naked children that don't have enough to eat, but you seem to be doing quite well for yourself."

"Ah, you mean the Mercedes. Well, I do perform certain services for people in their times of need, and the village benefits in turn. By patronage and Damballah's blessings, my people will someday take their places among rulers of the world," Kinzana graciously proclaims.

Kinzana offers the joint to Jarvis, who declines. He's reached a plane of consciousness that he so enjoys.

Unwisely, Kyle says, "You'll have to tell a lot of fortunes for that, Juju man."

His statement is made in poor taste and Jarvis takes instant offense. "Mind your manners, Kyle. I never taught you to mock another man's beliefs. In many cases, his beliefs are mine, too."

Kyle retreats, but Kinzana says, "There is no need to apologize, but to honor your father, for I am what I am. However, Kyle, you do not know all that I am. I walk the boundaries between this world and the next plane of existence, as you and Evan shall. It is no mere coincidence that I am here on the eve of your departures because we are all connected you see." Even in the dim lighting it is plain to see that a cloud of seriousness has passed over Kinzana's countenance.

Kinzana's voice is deep and thought-provoking when he says, "I fear that time is nigh upon us to embark on a journey that leads us all on separate paths. In the end, however, our destinies shall have been as one."

At a loss for meaning, Jarvis grows rigid. "What do you mean, Kinzana? Are you saying that something is going to happen to my sons?" He seems almost panicked. Evan notes his reaction especially.

Jarvis has only doubted his friend once since they met long ago. Since that time, nothing Kinzana predicted ever failed to manifest itself in some form or another. He fears for his sons. Kinzana's cryptic words resurrect terrible memories of his wife.

"Relax, my friend. What I have to tell is all that I am allowed to tell, lest the circle will be broken by doubting our true instincts. Yet, to everyone here, it may mean very little until the wheels have begun to turn on their irreversible course. Then the interconnection of our personal destinies will reach the pinnacle of significance, for it is of great importance that we have always been bound together."

Kyle grins at Evan. He is never one for hocus-pocus because he's a professional soldier who works closely with machines that bite and think for themselves once unleashed. He is a man of discipline, logic, and science, dwelling in a mechanical world where there exists little room for superstition.

Evan Parker, on the other hand, holds to a peripheral judgment of Kinzana's strange powers of prediction. He remembers, as a child, overhearing Kinzana telling his father that their mother would die after raising her sons to adulthood. To Evan's dying day, he will remember that this beloved man told his father that their mother would be taken from them when a man of power loses sight of the road on which they both travel. He recalls Kinzana saying that she would only suffer for an instant, which was little comfort. It filled his heart with childish fear, but the thought of the terrible prediction had faded from his mind until the day of his mother's fatal accident. He secretly blamed Kinzana for her death, even hated him for a while, but Jarvis Parker was an attentive father. He noticed the change in Evan's attitude toward Kinzana and Insanyanga, keeping after him until his burning tears spoke of his secret knowledge of their previous conversation concerning his mother's fate. Even in his most painful moment, Jarvis assured his grown son that his anger was misplaced.

Indeed, Alvina Parker died at the hands of a drunken city council member, who was engaged in a game of pull my other finger with his secretary. He was doing sixty-five miles an hour in a thirty mile an hour zone during a light afternoon drizzle. The council member and his secretary survived the accident, but their marriages and his political career had not. There were too many witnesses and his political competitors would not allow them to be silenced or easily dismissed. Especially after he was found unconscious with his penis sticking out of his zipper with her lipstick all over it.

The four men on the porch are seemingly unaware of the three women standing quietly in the doorway. Thelma is upstairs making sure that those sleepy children had taken their baths before going to bed for the night. She cleans out the tub and collects their soiled clothing, which will be cleaned and folded by the time they depart tomorrow.

Kinzana stands and beckons, "Come. We should make a fire beneath this striking blanket of stars." Evan and Jarvis do not hesitate to join him. Kyle, however, remains less enthusiastic. A mere second passes, in which he finally admits to himself for the first time that such things always cause him some small, unjustifiable fear. Kyle has never admitted to Evan that he pissed the bed on the same night long ago. He's never admitted the substances of his dreams, the visitations. The second memory passes with a shiver.

Without looking back, Kinzana says, "You lovely ladies should join us, for this journey is not ours to walk alone. Whether it will be side-by-side, in spirit, or in flesh, this trek will also be your own to endeavor. I am here, this night, to deliver a message."

Neither Melissa or Alicia knows what Kinzana wants of them. In fact, they find his ominous words a bit disturbing. Though Melissa Parker is more familiar with this man, she is just as anxious.

Insanyanga walks quietly behind them. As they make their way to the backyard, Alicia whispers, "What is he talking about, journeys and spirits? I'm not marrying into some kind of weird cult, am I?"

Masking her own anxieties because her husband has told her certain things over the years, Melissa only shrugs her shoulders playfully and smiles.

Insanyanga notices apprehension in Alicia's voice, and sees it written in the nature of Melissa's uneasy smile. Her liquid voice is furtive, but firmly rooted in conviction when she says, "Be still, children. Fear not, for Kinzana is a great man of powers untold and his invocations should not be so readily mocked. Know that his words will come to pass, but he is not the enemy. Be still, I beg of thee to fear it not."

Kyle takes the folding chairs used during the cookout to the mound in the backyard. Evan takes splinters of wood from the pile to set before the row of chairs. Kinzana instructs the women to place those chairs in a semicircle on top of the raised area of the yard that represents the ceiling of Jarvis's underground bomb shelter.

Kyle douses the pile of wood with lighter fluid he's retrieved from the picnic table. Standing at the open end of the semi-circle, Kinzana's gaze falls on the match that Evan uses to ignite the fire. It blazes up as if the wood is soaked with raw gasoline. The hairs of Evan's forearm are slightly singed just before he snatches his hand away.

Playfully, Kyle says, "Dad always warned you about playing with fire. Some things never seem to change." His statement brings little more than an uneasy chuckle from most of those who are gathered here.

Kyle sits next to Alicia, taking her hand. He sees questions in her eyes and feels uneasiness in her touch. He has no answers, but whispers his love and seals it with a simple kiss. Melissa strokes the back of Evan's head and squeezes his hand. Briefly, he caresses her swelling stomach with loving care. Kinzana witnesses these things and sees that they are good.

When everyone settles in, Insanyanga begins to hum a sadly melodic lament that eventually touches each of them. Although she utters no words, the song resonating from her angelic throat holds some meaning for them all. The meaning is different for each individual, yet it is the same. This is a song she learned as a citizen of Africa that mourns the ravages of war. Many mothers have hummed it while slowly rocking back and forth with dead or dying loved ones until the suffering from the wounds of war finally ended. That seems so very long ago.

The stars twinkle in their heavenly stasis. Their radiance, as well as the light of the rounded moon, cast a sublime aura upon these people. Around this circle of love, the warmth of the fire keeps at bay the wandering tendrils of mist that crawl along the cooling earth.

Though quiet, they're all electrified with anticipation. However, this apprehension is contradicted by the calm brought to them by Insanyanga's sad lament.

Kinzana says a prayer as he stands alone in the firelight. Jarvis and his wife observed the Presbyterian faith in practice, so had their children. Melissa was raised to observe the Baptist faith and Alicia Markham was Catholic when she went to church. Irrespectively, there is only one God in this circle and no one is offended. This is to be a moment of prophecy.

In the deep bass monologue of Kinzana's voice, they will span time and space to a place where the imagination can be guided to some alternative path of the future. Looking to the stars, Kinzana says, "There is a black tide rising, my children, and we are summoned to ride its foremost waves to the very heights of Damballah's glory. It is prerecorded in my journals. All, or most of it is there. Be advised. The past often represents the future. Nevertheless, to manipulate the present day is to command what comes, for it is the greatest power to know it." He smiles, sadly.

Melissa shivers in Evan's arms, snuggling closer to him for warmth.

Kinzana continues, "I would like to see myself as an accomplished writer someday, one with an ability to describe the worst of things in the benign, able to express what is the worst of a good thing so that all sides may be equally examined. There are times when it is necessary to peer into the insidious darkness until we can see the good and the light of day."

His audience sits wordlessly, listing slightly as his words, mixed with Insanyanga's melody, washes over their minds.

"I would like to paint a picture of the world as it was and will be in its new diversities. But this picture has great cost, for I fear it must be painted with a measure blood."

Alicia Markham recognizes Kinzana as a man given to speaking in riddles, and crazy riddles at that. She remains still, however.

Kinzana spreads his arms. "I am riding the furious wind of great and terrible things to their final destinations! It is to be the new beginnings of reunification and glorious change when He Whom Is Greatest sees fit to reset the hourglass on the running sands of man's reprieve. And so, we've been summoned, for this gathering may be the doorway to our final forgiveness."

No one utters a word while Kinzana speaks. No brow is raised in ridicule or skepticism. No sighs of boredom escape their lips.

"I am called to stand upon the precipice of evolution, which may be an end of life as you now know it. As a price, I may even perish in witness of it all. However, children, that will be acceptable when the gates have been torn down and the scales lifted from the eyes of our brothers and sisters. Then life upon this world will be changed forever unto the end of man." Tears stream down Kinzana's face as he continues. "The drums are vibrant in our souls. For some of us, they will be replaced by glorious trumpets and horns. The shadow of death will claim the souls of many where the scarred earth shall serve as a reminder. In that place, there will be nothing to reclaim by anyone, if it is not claimed by all. Damballah, the God of all Gods, will have quenched his anger with blood and fire. But it will be only after the angel of war, shielded amongst the clouds above, has ruled the skies to drive his mighty sword of destruction into the earth. And its sparks will be brighter than stars. There will be a quaking of the earth. The land will crack open and the ocean shall reclaim even the new Sodom. The rumblings of our hearts will be felt around the world. Where one peninsula must fall into the unforgiving sea, setting apart man's cradle, another shall be the birth of the Island of Angels. The ocean shall rise upon the desert sands, bringing life as well as destruction. There will be wailings of war. For three days and nights, snow shall fall on the African equator. And then...we shall all know the true meaning of darkness."

Shards of burning wood begin to pop as splinters settle with the loss of material. Kinzana shivers as cold sweat runs down his spine. "Three of the seven seals of cataclysm will rise from their sleeping places and they shall not rest until they are joined again, serving as our final warning! But that is another story to be written by new authors some terrible day. After the cock crows on these lowly people, time will stand still for the full turning of the clock. Most brilliant will be the light that sparks a new beginning. And in it, a wound will be opened, bringing a final surge of blood to the lips of Almighty God. Its fire must burn the wounded earth to cleanse its flow. These scars will be reminders that the time of healing must begin and that it is never to be hindered in our hearts and deeds. These things have been decreed for a dark future, but it is always—always—darkest before the dawning of the brightest days."

A subtle breeze caresses their skin. At first, it is warm and gentle, but it rises and soon falls cold.

The stars are no longer a blessing, for clouds have come from nowhere. A subtle rumble moves the earth.

Kinzana pays no heed to the atmospheric changes as he says, "Most of us shall bear witness to three days of utter darkness, where the blessings of the sun will abandon mankind. Many will perish. It, for me, is almost comforting to know wherein death most likely dwells, and that nothing will have been in vain. Those of us, who survive will be blessed with the task of affecting the process of change as living pillars of remembrance. Though it will be as a curse upon thee, fear not, for your efforts will set in motion the commandments of a future way that is not to be abandoned because of personal strife and the agony of loss. Your own children shall carry the words and text in diary and song, and the meaning of all that will come to pass will be embraced by their hearts in their time."

Lightning strokes the sky as if invisible angels are crashing to the ground.

"Mankind must learn and remember which god is God, for his name is Damballah. He is the Great I Am, the Allah, The Great Creator, and the Great Destroyer. Our Master is much more than what you've been taught. It is most important that you remember this, for his wrath comes with a quickness and a surety that none shall deny. We are the chosen instruments of his bidding and his will is most superior. Please remember these things, for in the darkness yet to come these words may be your only comfort. Remember!"

Rain pelts the embers, making a sound reminiscent of bed sheets flapping in the wild wind, but no one feels the tapping rain until they're all nearly drenched by it.

A voice in Melissa's mind, his voice, whispers, "In this world, whosoever weeps in the utter depths of despair will not do so in vain. By reason that we as a people have striven, then withered in the grasp of countless sorrows, how can we not wonder of an alternative future that is to be conceived within the endless possibilities of what will soon become the alternative past? There are very dark days creeping over the horizon, child. So very dark are the days to come, Melissa Parker. Please forgive this intrusion. It is not maliciously contrived."

CHAPTER 11

HOMECOMING

Easter Sunday. April 2, 2001

The Federal Bureau of Investigations finally arrests a suspect in the New Year's Eve Millennium bombing of Time Square. The alleged bomber, Alexander Smolenski, shows no remorse and offers no pretense of innocence. Federal investigators have discovered two simultaneously recorded videos from different perspectives of Smolenski while sitting before the television set on December 31, 1999 at 11:55 p.m.

This Vietnam veteran, a disgruntled city worker with mental problems, has no known terrorist affiliations. The demolitions expert simply believed planting the six deadly devices in Time Square to be the work of God, signifying the apocalypse.

Authorities claim that two of his shaped charges exploded simultaneously, each sending thirty pounds of steel washers and ball bearings into the carousing crowd with deadly accuracy. When the opposing street lamps ignited, they killed approximately 263 people instantly. Hundreds more were injured by the blasts.

As Alexander Smolenski watched the televised drama unfold, he urinated on himself while praising God in the home where he'd already murdered his wife and two stepchildren. They were dead for at least four days and walled up in the basement, where Mrs. Smolenski accidentally discovered his insane plans.

As the bloody mayhem ensued in Time Square, with terrified people trampling the fallen, Smolenski wept tears of joy. Then, approximately thirty seconds later, a second set of deadly devices went off below the streets as well. He showed amusement at the futility of the multiple victims' panicked flight as four hydrocyanic clouds rose from the manhole covers and storm drains to engulf them. As it choked the life from the innocent victims' bodies, the acid ate at their eyes and nostrils while virtually dissolving their lungs.

Evan and Melissa Parker have missed the parades and all the confections of the day by traveling north right after the early Sunday morning service, but Easter comes every year for the blessed.

Melissa Parker turns the radio off with a disgusted shiver and says, "Jesus. All those poor souls, nearly six hundred people are all dead or were severely wounded because of that maniac. Just to think that we were all ready to go to war over this makes me cringe. What's worse is that some slick lawyer, looking to make a name for himself will probably find a way to have him declared incompetent to stand trial."

Evan hums his agreement as they exit the freeway, which is a relief for them both with Melissa's anticipation peaking and her bladder filling.

On the day after Kinzana's dark prophecy, they'll arrive at their new home around 6:58 in the evening. During the trip, both had occasion to think about last night's slightly bizarre events. Everyone questioned the meaning of Kinzana's frightful words, but he only told them that all would be revealed in the near future.

Later, after the sudden downpour subsided, Kinzana had drawn Melissa aside to give her an old, handwritten journal that he claimed to contain many aspects of his travels. The heavy journal was bound in timeworn leather whose shallow, crimson fissures congregated like the tributaries of a vast river system. It was sealed with a simple lock at the edge of a sewn on appendage. When Melissa accepted his gift, the initial touch caused her skin to prickle.

She still has no idea that the only dated entries are those of August 31, 1990 and April 1, 2001, the very day he presented it to her. The inscription on the last written page simply states: April __ of the year 2001. To be recorded, henceforth, by Melissa Parker.

After Kinzana gave Melissa the journal, Insanyanga whispered to her, "It is locked, I know, but you already have the key."

She found that key in the briefcase that she used as a teacher. Last night, Melissa browsed its yellowing pages, but she wasn't sure of what she was reading, so she shut it and moved closer to her sleeping husband. Something buried deep inside of her had no desire to know the contents of that book. It was a baseless fear, but it was real, nonetheless.

Their brick home is a masterpiece and Mrs. Parker loves it beyond words. Evan has stolen the white picket fence, which encompasses a carpet of lush green grass, directly from her childlike fantasy. A tiny garden, once tended by an elderly couple, still struggles to bring new life at the very end of their backyard.

Inside and out, well-trimmed hedges run along the red brick privacy fence that borders the entire backyard. A greenhouse also stands in the backyard, which boasts a glass-enclosed walkway that connects directly with the house. Melissa has enjoyed gardening since her childhood. It was one of the few things that she and her mother seemed to have in common. And like her mother, she discovered early on that she possessed quite a green thumb.

Though she enjoyed it so, gardening was destined to become her second love. Her strongest passion had grown for teaching. Of course, her mother doused her fire some, citing gardening to be only a hobby and hardly worth structuring a life thereupon. However, Melissa likens teaching to gardening in that she could plant the seeds of the future and watch the minds of her students grow. The analogy is a profoundly personal viewpoint that she shares with very few.

Evan was sold on the property the moment he saw the greenhouse, knowing that his wife will resume her relaxing dirt hobbies while he is busy at the office.

The home is a testament to sound architecture. Its spacious rooms are constructed with large windows that let in plenty of light. The odors of new paint and new furniture still hang in the air, but that is fine with her.

Hardwood floors announce Melissa's hurried footsteps from room to room as she peruses the ample closet spaces for their closet things. Evan has taken the liberty of purchasing new area rugs to compliment the decor of the den. Paintings and African artwork are carefully arranged on the walls and along the mantle of the fireplace.

There is an island in the kitchen, which comes complete with a dishwasher and a self-cleaning range. Melissa is at home in the kitchen and she knows right away what their first meal will be.

Four spacious bedrooms constitute most of the upstairs. One room, the nursery, has been left empty. The housekeeper, who is to stay with the Parkers for two to three days of each week, will use one of the other rooms. She has also agreed to move in during the final month of Melissa's pregnancy. Melissa protested the need for a housekeeper, but Evan convinced her that it will give him peace of mind. He was quite insistent on that point.

The centerpiece of the master bedroom is a queen-sized rice bed made of fine mahogany. Nearby is the antique bassinet, which rocks back and forth with the slightest touch. Embedded in the wall that faces the bed is a complete entertainment center, the twin of the one downstairs. A daybed soaks up the light of a large picture window. A comfortable rocking chair sits nearby, so Melissa can rock their child to sleep after a feeding or a moment of bonding.

This is perfection and Melissa Parker is certain that she will never doubt her husband again. When he suggested that they sell nearly everything from their previous home and start anew, she was very skeptical, but nevermore.

With the help of Madeline Perkins, their housekeeper and former nurse, Evan located a reputable OB/GYN and Pediatrician. Melissa's medical records have been transferred, so an appointment is scheduled for Monday.

Madeline Perkins, an African American woman in her late forties has undergone many tragic events in the last few years. In Evan Parker's opinion, the smile that she always manages seems so sad.

Melissa Parker stayed behind with Jarvis Parker for the three months it took Evan to get situated in his new job and close the deal on the house. In the latter two months, Evan and Madeline gained each other's trust and admiration. Theirs is a symbiotic relationship; each fulfills needs of the other.

Madeline Perkins' teenage sons of fifteen and seventeen had inadvertently found themselves caught in the middle of a shootout between the Philadelphia police and two rival gangs. On that wintry day in 1996, she had sent them to the neighborhood store to pick up a few things needed for dinner. That was the very last time she saw them alive.

The sight of their bodies in the bloody snow crushed the woman. Naturally, she blamed herself for their deaths, but so did her husband, Carl Jamison. To her great torment, he constantly reminded her that their children died doing her errands. She was too busy talking with her sister in Florida, whom she hadn't seen in three years.

Carl Jamison chose to batter his wife with harsh words, rather than grieve the loss of their sons. Tormenting their mother seemed to be his only way to deal with the pain. Beneath the grief and heartache, succumbing to the mounting depression, Madeline often contemplated suicide. Because she was a devout Christian, however, Madeline Perkins never attempted to take her own life.

Nevertheless, seeking professional help became her only recourse. After three long years of intensive therapy, Madeline finally walked out of that cold, dark tunnel. Because the increasingly abusive marriage hindered the progress of therapy, she divorced her husband. It was best that way. She then found the strength to leave Philadelphia, moving to Suitland, Maryland, where she built a new life.

Madeline enjoys working for families with small children. Since she is unable to have more of her own, they are welcomed substitutes. Her therapist tells her that it is natural and healthy, as long as she does not become fixated. Her medical background is a plus in any event. Why Madeline Perkins, a woman who obviously loves children, never considered adopting remains a mystery to her therapist. She seems to have lots of love to give a child in need of a stable environment, but her therapist understands that, for some patient's, it would seem wrong to replace a child with that of a stranger. She respects her patient's idealisms in that regard, knowing that it often changes over time for many who have lost children to tragedy.

Evan has told his wife all these things over the course of their temporary separation, but a reiteration seems appropriate over dinner. They always talk over their meals. It is a time of informal connection between husbands and wives.

As expected, Evan finds his lovely wife a veritable fountain of ideas and suggestions for decorating the three bathrooms. She has very special plans for the nursery.

After a moment of silverware and China noises, Melissa looks up from her salad to ask, "Steak okay, honey?"

Evan prods, "Oh, it's a little tough. Do you think we can use real meat next time, instead of the rubber substitute?" They look at one another and laugh. Then he says, "It's perfect, as usual. You know I love your cooking, but you just wanted to hear me say it. Nobody cooks like a southern girl."

She blushes. "Thank you, sweetheart. You know me so well. By the way, if I haven't said it quite enough for one day, I love what you've done with this house. Are you sure you didn't use an interior decorator? The way things are arranged and everything, I really have to wonder."

"Thank you, and no. Little old Evan Parker done it all by his lonesome as a labor of love."

Melissa smiles. "So you really have gotten in touch with your feminine side. I see." She brushes a lock of hair from her lips and flips it with a deft head toss. The act itself is a playful insinuation.

"Funny. Really funny. I'll admit that I did take a few pointers from Maddy," Evan says.

"So it's Maddy now. You sure are taken with this woman, aren't you? Should I be worried?"

"Maybe," he teases. "You're going to love her, you'll see. As for your second question, I love you so much that you probably won't have to worry until you're about fifty-five or so. Then, when all of the delicate parts have gone south, so will I...by my damn self."

When Evan grins, Melissa shrieks and throws her napkin across the table, which would have been a cardinal sin in the eyes of her prim and proper mother. Such rude behavior would never have been tolerated during her younger years when her mother would scold her endlessly.

Although Melissa has never uttered a word of it, there had been a tremendous weight lifted from her shoulders when her mother was laid to rest. After the very first operation, the cancer eviscerated her body and shredded her mind to turn her into a godless, unholy thing. She died so miserably. Her father died many years ago and being the only child of an only child, left her few to lean on during her mother's struggle. If her mother had survived, she wonders if their relationship might have improved.

Thankfully, Evan asks, "So, what are you going to tackle first?"

"Well, after my appointment tomorrow morning, I'll go shopping for a crib and the other things I'll need around the house. I'm so excited."

"Okay, as long as you promise not to overdo it. You must agree that Maddy will be with you at all times."

"I promise. Besides, it'll give us a chance to get to know each other," she complies. "Since you seem to like her so much, I'm sure we'll get along just fabulously, dahling." Melissa is doing her pitiful Marilyn Monroe impersonation, blinking her brown doe eyes. She puckers her lips while twisting a lock of jet-black hair.

"Sounds good, Marilyn," Evan says. "But, all jokes aside, I hope you two become friends. She just seems so quiet at times."

"It's got to be hard to recover from what she's been through, losing both sons at the same time. I'm glad she asked you to tell me all of that. It may help matters, and I promise not to bring it up unless she wants to discuss it."

Later, during the course of their meal, Melissa says, "I'd like to invite your boss and his wife over for dinner tomorrow night."

"I'm not sure that's such a great idea, Mel? Don't you think you may be taking on a bit much for one day?"

Melissa's reassuring smile is a gripping bribe when she states, "Not at all. The baby and I are fine now. You'll see, Evan. I've been cooped up for three months and I really need to breathe while this excitement is upon me. Besides, I promised to let Ms. Perkins help with every aspect of the day. If I get tired, I'll just shut down the mommy machine and rest. Okay?"

"Alright, if you're sure. I'll ask Pete in the morning."

"So, I will finally get to meet the legendary Peter McAllister, the man who got my husband into all kinds of trouble in young adulthood. I can't wait to get the filthy little details. What about his wife?"

"Valerie? Tall, blonde, blue eyes, and very pretty. She still has a hint of a British accent. Peter always had a thing for blondes. They make a very good couple, but she's been worried about him lately. I promised to convince him to see a doctor about those migraines this week."

"Really? That sounds serious. Migraines can mean that he has a real problem. It could be a lesion or something," she says.

"Yes, Doctor Parker."

"I'm serious. My father experienced terrible migraines before his first stroke. Some people on his side of the family claim that mother was the underlying cause, however." She grins, guiltily. "So, unless you're after your friend's job, I suggest you get him to see that doctor. It certainly couldn't hurt."

"I will. But please leave my loving mother-in-law alone because we don't want her to wake up and move in. God bless the dead." Evan knocks on wood and rolls his eyes as if he hears something move in the corner. Although they laugh at the idea, Melissa experiences another twinge of guilt.

After the dishes are done, they bathe together, but they don't make love before going to sleep. Evan Parker is extremely needy, but he is still very tentative about her condition.

Melissa failed to tell him that she had a dream about their child during the trip to Maryland. It started out as a scene of the fetus inside of her womb. At first, there was a heartbeat that faded into the soft background beat of drums. For Melissa Parker, this dream was both disturbing and surprisingly soothing. She has the same dream during the first night's sleep in their new home.

CHAPTER 12

DAMBALLAH'S WILL

The long day following the Parker family barbeque is also an eventful one for Kinzana and Insanyanga. This day of feasting is of great importance as they greet a multitude of visitors, but this gathering could never have anything to do with Easter. At the end of it all, Kinzana's woman needs desperately to be heard. Insanyanga fears what may become of the man with whom she has spent a lifetime. Although she is strong, she is still a woman of fathomless emotions.

In the solitude of their bedroom she approaches and whispers, "Husband, we have come far together. Must it end this way, with our happiness traded for so much uncertainty? Must this be the price for you and me?"

After much contemplation of its placement, Kinzana adds a single stroke to the canvas. A swath of crimson pierces the face of the pale moon. Lunar glory shimmers down on the seascape, where a thriving wave rushes to meet the shore of some lonesome beachhead. The wave's white crest contrasts the serene waters beyond the break with its foam pausing, standing still before something out of place. The turmoil is frothy and alive, but forever frozen before a flaring splash of red upon the sand. Kinzana and his wife are actually standing in the center of six easels. Each canvas is now completed. If placed together, they would form a single, haunting portrait.

Her husband places the brush into a cup of solvent, watching the crimson stain as it swirls upon the surface. As Kinzana backs away from the last canvas, turning slowly to see the entire picture, he draws a deep breath and says, "Mother, it is a destiny long foretold unto you. And yet, there still lies hope for you and I."

"Yes. But I want to be with you, even on a deathwatch that is our own. I would die with you, my beloved Kinzana." She leans on his chest, holding him tight as she buries her face in his black robe.

"Mother, it is not your destiny should I perish because of the evils of men. You, however, have already paid such great duties to this cause, but the journey is not yet complete. Although you have suffered in silence since the beginning of our time together, you are still required to play a role in what Damballah has made to be the sum of our countless days upon the earth. It would seem that this wondrous garden is for you after all, Insanyanga."

"But I am so afraid of what is to come. I have danced with venom on the cusp of death. I've consulted the bones and the whispering wind, but Damballah has chosen to blind my vision into the future. This treacherous path no longer offers me light, Kinzana. Who or what am I if I can no longer see?"

"In many ways, you are the path you seek, dear heart. My price to see this thing through is bloodstained and, perhaps—perhaps—one more death to endure. Meanwhile, you have suffered a thousand deaths at my side. Always blessing the children, always helping to bring them from their mothers' wombs. Yet, you were never allowed to have children, never to know the exquisite pain of bringing forth life from your own body. That was your price, dear heart, and your reward is to be godmother to all the children of this world when the healing comes. Then, your children will bring unto you the many exquisite pains you've missed. Such a task shall be greater still. Please believe in this, my beloved Insanyanga. I only hope that our friends will forgive my trespasses, and that they will still have love in their eyes if we should meet where the sun shines eternally. On that glorious day, I shall miss thee with all that is in me to love."

Kinzana kisses her gently and dries her tears even though they are both weeping together in the silent dignity of candlelight.

According to Kinzana's beliefs, Insanyanga is to become a future figurehead. She has been told in prophecy that she would someday escort special children to the top of a new America.

Insanyanga already has thousands of godchildren, but she is to become so for billions. Yet those special ones are never to be far from her influences. She is to stay close to them until they have been taught everything necessary to reach the status of rulers in whatever is to become of the future.

Insanyanga is to possess the influence of a queen from the shores of America to Africa, eclipsing the rein of Cleopatra and all other pretenders to the earthly throne. Woman—the undeniable ruler of mother earth. Such aspirations could be perceived as the ravings of a madman. These two, at the very least, are true believers.

Africans, Haitians, Jamaicans, and the last great chief of the South American Szinjala tribe have come to America in subtle drifts. Dressed in everything from traditional tribal apparel to Italian suits, nearly three hundred priests and priestesses have come.

The most notorious of these are Abongoma Nosinyanga of the Sect Rouge vodou cult of Haiti. There is Nimjara Kinzara from South Africa, who is Zulu Red Sect. And there is the West African voodoo priest Abatu Abuutu. The Szinjala chieftain, Szinja Szin, stands tall among them with his iron gray hair framing his gaunt features. These men, however formidable, are no nastier than the red witch from the African Congo. She is Princess Tuloni, the Pygmy priestess.

These five are among the most powerful of all voodoo masters. They are the strongest of those who pay homage to the dark gods in the strangest, most mysterious practice of religions in the world.

In the practice of voodooism, many priests prefer to deal with the benevolent gods, but it is almost impossible to completely separate from the injurious entities.

As Damballah was alone before creating The Satan and other lesser gods, they too, created gods of their own lesser powers. Such is the cornerstone of all their beliefs. Kinzana's rule as the high priest is all-encompassing, but completely devoid of any traits and symbols of Catholicism that have seeped into the culture over the centuries. His dominion and those of the other priests, are things of a staunch purity.

Kaleem Kinzana walks between both courts, light and dark, but he feels more comfortable when invoking the powers and favors of the benevolent deities. He knows, however, that it will be imprudent to fall short in invoking the powers of the Red Sect gods, which would probably mean failure in his appointed task, again. Because he made that very mistake eleven years ago, Kinzana is certain that it will be a dangerous insult to ignore their part in this great and terrible thing. Therefore, he relegates such matters to the others, even though his favor with the lesser gods still outweighs that of those priests in combination.

Blood is required of Kinzana, who will commit himself to the infinite darkness when necessary. There is no way to totally exonerate himself of the ensuing turmoil. Unlike the fabled Lady Macbeth, he will not attempt to wash his hands. Not again.

Kaleem Kinzana's entire existence is committed to the will of his God of Gods. No one knows of his real age, only that he doesn't seem to age as normal men.

He is in charge of some mystical black tide, commanding its waves to the very steps of a nation's capital that is to be changed forever. Kinzana is to witness his work firsthand, which is to be considered a privilege, but the question of his own survival and that of countless others is not all together his to decide. It is ultimately not even God's to decide, for the choices of men and women will have far reaching effects.

From the African Congo, via Haiti and Jamaica, he had come, sowing seeds of mysticism that would finally come to a head in this country. Kinzana cannot dissuade the supreme power from this calamity of blood, but he will facilitate its inception per his duty.

Since his arrival on American soil in 1950, Kinzana has visited his native land only once. His most powerful subjects in South Africa then joined him in 1989, where they conspired with the gods until the day Nelson Mandela was freed from prison by F.W. de Klerk in 1990.

Terror had caused the release of Mandela from his immoral imprisonment. It was fear of insanity and twisted deaths that forced the hands of Whites to finally unclench the throats of the true South Africans. There was much to be done from whence he had come, so Kinzana did not tarry any longer on African soil than was necessary.

Again, it is commanded that terror be used to finally bring the Negro nation and lesser people their due. His work is aimed at transforming this country into the truly United States of America, an example to be followed by all men. He strictly believes the utter annihilation of humankind to be the unsavory alternative.

Damballah intends to use Kinzana and his followers to heave against the established system and bring down its walls. Then, in nakedness, humankind can begin the hand in hand process of rebuilding this place with neither hand clasped in chains of iron, nor metaphorically speaking. Such things make up the prophetic scenario Kinzana paints for the leaders over whom he is leader.

Sacrifices are made at the village where magic, drinking, praying and feasting consume most of the day. The Rada drums of eleven years ago are now joined by the Conga drums to vibrate relentlessly into the darkness where no woodland animal will find rest within reach of their terrible harmony.

Until Damballah's thirst is quenched and the drums are summoned to pound a message of peace, rage, hatred, and anger are unavoidable tools.

He tells his followers that Legba, the God of the Gate, has chosen which side he will champion. He tells them that this deity is on the side of the tides. After the wars and the fires, the gate will no longer exist.

They gaze up into eyes of ivory glass as Kinzana says, "Scorched will be the earth where mountains of useless paper will burn, for that place shall become a museum of our unnatural history. It will be viewed only from wings on high because the ground shall be uninhabitable!"

They bow and scrape, trembling in fear.

On the morning of April 3, most of the visiting priests disperse throughout the country, traveling to distant places where they will anew the Vigil of the Drum. This is a time of strange magic, for dark powers are to be unleashed.

CHAPTER 13

SHANGA'S TOUCH

Monday. April 3, 2001

When morning comes, the housekeeper lets herself in. She starts breakfast and goes upstairs to make sure that Evan Parker has gotten up for work on time. While his wife sleeps, Evan showers in their private bathroom.

Understandably, Madeline is nervous about meeting the mistress of the home for the first time. However, she remains hopeful. Evan has done an equally good job of selling his wife to her.

When Evan comes down, he is greeted by the smell of brewing coffee and the sizzle of bacon that serenades his growling stomach.

Madeline hums quietly, noticing Evan when he walks into the kitchen. "Good morning, Mr. Parker. Did you and your wife get settled okay?"

"Good morning, Maddy. We made it just fine. How are you?"

"Fine, sir. Hungry?"

Evan says, "We had steaks for dinner, but I'm starving now. Is that red-eye gravy I smell?" He sniffs at the air like a hungry jackal, tasting the airborne nuance of a long awaited meal.

Maddy is pleased. "Why, yes it is. I told you that my mother was raised in Georgia. She taught me all of her recipes, so you will never go hungry with me around. Now have a seat."

Evan is sopping up the last of his breakfast when he hears the sleepy yawn of his wife.

Melissa whines, "Oh, honey, I wanted to fix breakfast for you on my first morning. I'm sorry that I overslept, Evan."

Evan turns to her. "Good morning, Snoring Beauty. I didn't have the balls to wake you. Besides, you need all the rest you can get before your busy day." He rises to kiss her sleepy cheek and says, "Baby, this is Madeline Perkins. Maddy, this is my wife, Melissa. Please remember that she only growls in the morning. Just feed her well, rub her tummy afterward, and she'll purr like a kitten for the rest of the day. Now, I have to go, so you two have fun. And don't let her overdo it."

Smiling politely, Madeline and Melissa shake hands and commence the getting to know process.

⇒✠⇐

At the John B. Hawkins Federal Building of Suitland, Maryland, this conference is reminiscent of Cecil Bridges' final meeting eleven years prior, but with four distinctions. Peter McAllister now dictates the terms of such meetings. Evan Parker, the newly appointed deputy director has taken the place of Norman Todd, who drank himself out of a job. The Director of the Data Preparations Division, Barrette Holt, is absent due of sudden illness and unavailable for video conferencing. Finally, Deedra Wilson, who is still remembered by some, has resigned her post.

Peter wraps up things by giving everyone a pat on the back for completing their tasks despite the many problems. Because of their efforts, he can take a much-needed vacation. When the meeting ends at 10:45, the various department heads disband without the door-watching anticipation they used to experience when Cecil Bridges manned the helm. Only Peter and Evan remain.

"Well, old boy, how did the final move go? You and Melissa get back without incident? I know holiday traffic can be a bitch." Peter places an arm around Evan's left shoulder.

"Everything went according to plan. My wife loves the house, thank you very much," Evan says. He's feeling quite pleased with himself.

Peter McAllister grins at his friend. "Does she?"

"Oh yeah. It's a grand slam home run. She feels right at home, but her head's already filled with decorating ideas of her own."

"That sounds great, Evan. Just don't give her the credit cards like I did when we moved into our new home. Man, Valerie went nuts."

"Trust me, the woman has her own credit cards. My only real concern is that Melissa doesn't put too much of a strain on herself, but she insists that she's feeling fine. How is Valerie's pregnancy coming along?"

Peter says, "Perfectly. My wife loves the idea of giving birth to our first child." His grin grows wider. "Actually, I don't know why I waited this long to have kids, but my wife is just horny as hell all the time."

"Yeah, I think I know what you mean. It's as if they're trying to load up on sex before the big bang," Evan embellishes.

"That could be it, or maybe they're just making sure that their husbands are sexually satisfied before hitting the streets among all those beautiful, non-pregnant, home-wreckers."

They share a chuckle upon Peter's totally logical assumption. Evan has lied, innocently, in a way. The fact that he and Melissa haven't made love since her troubles with the pregnancy is an extremely personal subject.

"By the way, you're both invited to join the Parkers for dinner tonight. That's if you guys don't have plans already."

"Sounds good to me, roomie. I'll check with Val, but I'm pretty sure we can make it."

"Good. Let's say around seven…seven-thirty."

Peter says, "Sure thing. Well, Evan, it looks like we've come full-circle. Who would've thought that all those damn stats in Professor Darwin's class would land us both here?"

"We do make one hell of a team. By the way, my brother says 'go Gamecocks!' He also mentioned your former nickname, Critter-getter." They both howl for a moment.

"Speaking of which, in my own perverted sort of way, but with absolutely no sexual connotation intended, I can't wait to meet the woman who tamed the mighty Tarzan. She must be some piece of work."

Evan warns, "Whoa, now hold on there, Kemo Sabe!" He shakes his head from side to side in protest. "Let's keep the legends of Tarzan our little secret because I don't think Melissa would appreciate knowing how many vines I swung from back in college." There is a hint of seriousness in his voice and he knows Peter is going to rag him for it.

"Oh, I see," Peter says, thoughtfully. He rubs his chin. "It suddenly makes sense. Jane meet Tarzan. Jane tames Tarzan. Now Tarzan, he no cheetah?" Peter chuckles.

"Yeah, well I can also tell a few tales about my ex-playboy roommate, but I'm sure that the story about the Delaney twins is enough to land us both in the doghouse for several years. You for the despicable acts performed with those two, and me for just knowing you."

"Okay. Okay, I give. I'll keep your secrets, if you'll promise to keep mine."

"Agreed, although, I should warn you that Melissa may rake you over the coals for the sordid details. I'm afraid that I may have mentioned a few things about our checkered past over the years, but like all things, we'll face it together."

Suddenly, Peter's head throbs and he pinches his nose in noticeable discomfort. He mutters, "Oh man. Not again."

"You need to see a doctor about those headaches, Peter. Intelligent people are kicking the bucket every day, leaving their loving families behind because they're too stubborn to seek help when they can still be helped. If you let this thing go much longer, you may regret it."

Peter's voice is barely more than a whisper when he says, "I'll be okay. I just need to get some rest. You just got here, but this has really been quite a long haul. That's all it is."

When Evan asks, "Are you still having those nightmares?" Peter's glance reveals both surprise and a hint of annoyance. "I know about those, too. Your wife is concerned about you, so she asked me to convince you to get some medical attention. We're all concerned, for that matter. It is pretty obvious that things have finally taken a toll on you. You should ask yourself if a pregnant woman needs to worry about her unborn child and her husband, too. Think about it."

"All right. Just stop yelling, mother. I'll see a doctor, I promise."

"Good boy." Satisfied, Evan pats him gently on the shoulder and leaves the conference room.

"See you around seven-thirty, but if it gets too bad, let me know." He returns to his office to dictate a letter.

Back in his office, Peter McAllister sits at his desk for five minutes with his head in his hands, and then decides to take some aspirin and a drink from the bottle of Jim Beam.

When he unlocks the drawer and blindly reaches for the bottle of pills, his fingers discover something foreign. Something scaly moves at his touch!

When Peter yanks his hand from the drawer, his knee bangs against the underside of his desk. Out of simple reflex, he looks into the drawer and nearly screams when he sees snakes crawling around his liquor and aspirin. They writhe within the confines of the drawer, hissing at him maliciously. His eyes bulge when he shoves a palm across his lips to quiet the scream.

Making a hasty retreat, Peter stumbles over his chair. His hand is clasped over his lips to prevent himself from crying out. As he rises, he sees the flexing hood with the third and fourth eyes of a massive Indian Cobra before it turns its attention to him. It hisses and twitches as he moves.

Peter's head throbs; the pain is brutal. He feels sick to his stomach as he kicks the drawer closed. The bottle of whiskey bangs against the interior. Yet, his ears insist the sound of it to be proof that nothing else is in there with the two bottles.

Peter replays the sound of the loud clanking noise and the rattle of the pills in his mind. He eventually convinces himself to reopen the drawer to be sure that this was just another wicked hallucination.

He looks about for something long enough to open the drawer without getting too close. The pointer he uses on board diagrams will suffice, so he snatches it up. As added insurance, he lays claim to the statuette of Shanga, the African God of War that Evan gave him upon arriving in Suitland to signify their unified attack on the agency's problems.

Peter eases within a yard of the desk, raising the statuette. His sweaty hands tremble as he works the tip of the pointer into the handle of the drawer. He yanks hard, snapping the pointer just as the drawer slips open with another loud bang.

Peter pumps the statuette in midair, ready to strike at anything that might hurl itself out of the shallows but nothing comes.

Although it causes his head to throb, he holds his breath, standing on his toes to be sure that there are no squirming reptiles. Sweat falls from his brow as he stares unbelievingly into the small space that only contains a few folders, the aspirin, and a pint of Jim Beam that has been cracked. The rank elixir has begun to seep from its cap.

The single bead of ice-cold sweat that falls past his stare to land on his cheek causes him to shudder. The sensation reminds him to breathe, but when he inhales, the angry pain in his head makes him lurch. He's forced to lean upon the desk for support. The agony reminds him of why he opened the drawer in the first place.

Peter whispers, "God. What's happening to me? Am I going insane? It seemed so real; I felt them move."

Moments later, he reaches tentatively into the drawer for both bottles and puts the God of War back on the desktop. Peter pops some pills into his mouth, following them with a gulp of whiskey that would cause any novice drinker to gag.

He's about to take another swig when he notices blood on his trembling hand. He wonders if he has somehow injured himself on the chipped lip of the bottle, but he had been careful not to cut himself on the jagged glass. His hands are fine, so he licks his lips. There is no retaliatory sting. After noticing a bloodstain on his shirt, he rubs his face to discover another nosebleed.

Peter snatches open the middle drawer and uses the small mirror to look at his face and shirt. He backs away from his magnified image and drops the mirror, which cracks upon impact with the desk. He is shaken because the bloodstain on his shirt looks strangely familiar.

Peter realizes that the stains are nearly identical to the symbols he always sees in nightmares. Suddenly, it dawns on him as to why he feels such an aversion to Evan Parker's gift of a god. Similar symbols are embossed on the base of the statuette. Despite his efforts to avoid looking at it, his eyes wonder to its base. And for a split second, the statue breathes in mockery of him.

Peter nearly jumps out of his skin when his assistant, Patricia Kidder, walks in unannounced. She's saying something about needing his signature, shocked into silence at the sight of his bloody shirt and terror-stricken eyes.

"My God!" She approaches, taking hold of his clammy hands. "Peter, what happened? Are you all right? Did you fall or something?"

Patricia surveys the spilled pill bottle and the bottle of liquor precariously perched on the edge of the desktop. She uses her right hand to push it further onto the surface.

"You're trembling and your nose. Let me get a wet towel for that." She goes into his private restroom and brings back some paper towels. Patricia helps her boss to clean himself up, but the shirt is a lost cause. She asks, "Should I call a doctor or your wife?"

His reaction is swift. "No, don't do that. I'm fine now. I think I'll go home and get some rest. Please don't say anything to anyone about this, Pat. Promise?"

She promises to keep quiet, something that is always difficult for her to do. After asking her to replace the files that have been soaked with alcohol, he changes shirts and leaves with the Jim Beam.

Nearly at the bottom of the elevator shaft, Peter takes an ill-advised swig of the liquor, nicking his bottom lip on the jagged mouth of the bottle when it stops. He discards it when the elevator opens.

<hr />

The Rada drums are beating their dark rhythmic pulses at the end of Kwani Drive, near the outskirts of Suitland. They are plying the forces of life, plying the forces of magic, coercing spirits to rise from a fetid slumber.

The parking spaces of the single level structure beneath the John B. Hawkins Federal Building are designated to executives and visiting VIPs only. The other employees have to park outside, where subject to the elements of nature. At this moment, Peter McAllister sincerely considers that to be a luxury. He wishes that he, too, is forced to park outside in the open air, in sunshine, or even in rain, and snow.

For the past eleven years, he has experienced an irrational fear of going to his car in the gloomy underground parking structure. Peter's claustrophobia has much to do with the fact that his was once Cecil Bridges' parking space. He hates the short walk, but he hates the designated parking space more. It serves as a daily reminder of how he'd gotten his job. It reminds him of his part in the death of his mentor, his former coach and Business Calculus professor. It's all too personal. Such is the essence of the deeply embedded guilt consuming Peter slowly from within. It is beginning to affect his mental stability.

For years, he's been forced to put on the happy face for his wife and co-workers. Then Evan Parker's name was added to his list of woes. Peter wonders what he could have been thinking when he selected Evan's name from the list of qualified replacements for Norman Todd's vacated position. He was convinced at the time that he couldn't ignore Evan's qualifications. Having his old college roommate working by his side was a great temptation. It now appears that he has only been fooling himself.

Every time Evan Parker mentions something of a personal nature or brings up a memory of their old coach, Peter's headaches rage. His heart races, or his stomach rolls within a wave of vertigo whenever the past is raised to issue. The truth of what he's done is killing him inside.

On some subconscious level, he may have felt that by replacing Cecil Bridges with Evan Parker, he could somehow exonerate himself of guilt. It could go far in making up for something he can never truly live down. It no longer seems like such a keen idea. Having Evan around only adds to his mounting distress. His nightmares have returned tenfold. Now he is beginning to see things again.

"Why?" he often asks himself. "Why did I do it?"

As McAllister approaches his automobile in the gloom, his footfalls resound like military taps, interrupting the stillness of the concrete crypt. Its disquiet seeps into his soul. The combination of stale gas fumes and his irrational fear is thick and suffocating. So that he may see whatever monsters there may be lurking in the shadows, his wary eyes let in the stinging sweat that now saturates his forehead.

Without warning, a cold wind gusts. A scraping sound suddenly penetrates the stillness and Peter nearly falls to his knees when his feet get confused.

When he shouts, "Who's there?" his voice echoes, bouncing from the low-lying ceiling and the emotionless concrete walls.

There is no answer, other than a whisper in his mind declaring, "Cecil died in a place just like this. Just like this."

Peter slowly expels a deep breath. Despite the pain in his head, a little smile creases his lips when he decides that he's being ridiculously paranoid. And yet, he resumes his short walk at a slightly quicker pace.

He takes one last look around the deserted garage before deactivating the car alarm. He gets into the Lexis and starts up. As the quiet engine purrs, he sits back with the air on its highest setting. While kneading his aching temples, he relishes the cool air on his clammy skin.

Peter closes his red eyes and says, "I've got to get my shit together. Things will be okay, if I can just learn to relax."

He shrieks when he reaches for the gear, feeling something furry and alive! A huge Tarantula perches on the head of the gearshift, staring back at Peter with its forelegs raised as if it's a boxer poised for battle.

Terrified of spiders his entire life, Peter finds himself temporarily paralyzed. But when his motor senses return, his left hand is stricken with clumsiness in a futile attempt to find the door's handle. He's unable to take his eyes from the bluish black thing on the gearshift. However, if he could, he would see that his windows are now covered with them.

Finding the courage, he grabs the coffee cup from the console with his right hand. As he slowly raises the cup, the spider pivots as if in anticipation of his next move. When it issues a wicked squeak and bounces on its hinged legs, Peter panics, thinking that it's about to pounce. With a disgustingly girlish squeal escaping his lips, he brings his ceramic weapon down! Spider gut splatters the dash, his clothes, and face as he slams the cup into the gearshift repeatedly. The cup, which was a gift from his wife, finally shatters during the assault. The only thing left intact is the part connected to the handle. The rest of it is scattered on the floorboards and the front seat of the car.

When Peter stops beating at the spider, he glares at the stick with disgust. Part of the spider's head and two of its forelegs ooze off the side and hangs in midair. It swings lazily from the slimy part that sticks to the gear shifter. Now it falls slowly to the console and sluggishly oozes to the floor mat next to his right foot.

McAllister struggles to catch his breath, loosening his fresh tie with one hand while he tries to wipe the slime from his face with the other. A terrible odor fills the cabin of the car. It combines with that slimy feeling on his crawling skin to make him sick to his stomach. He opens the door to vomit only to find that large arachnids now surround his car.

Peter quickly shuts the door and raises his eyes to survey the darkened windows where glints of light intrude. When Peter McAllister looks to the rearview mirror to survey the back windshield, he's stricken dumb with terror and his heart skips more than a beat. His mind is seized by the sudden appearance of Cecil Bridges' charred face in his rearview mirror!

Cecil's face resembles meat that's been left in the oven too long. His nose and lips look as if they've melted together. Only one of his nostrils is left partially open. The crusty flesh of his cheek exudes a lime green puss, holding a strong resemblance to the spider guts or phlegm from a serious case of the flu. But those dead eyes are what causes Peter's mind to scream. One of Cecil's eyes is perfectly intact, much too perfect for the face in which it's affixed. The other eye is just a hollow socket, however. The only thing that moves there is a black dung beetle that appears to be enjoying the tastiest of meals at Chez Cecil's.

Peter clutches his hand to his thrumming chest where his heart races unchecked. He is unable to squeal, speak, or scream. He is helpless to avert his eyes from the long dead thing in the mirror. Then it speaks to him in a raspy voice that sounds like gravel being swished around in water somewhere far away. He closes his eyes, waiting for the hallucination to disappear.

Now, it groans, "You killed me, P-e-t-e-r!"

"No! Who the...who the fuck are you?" asks McAllister.

The corpse in the mirror snaps, "Ask not silly questions. You know damn well who I am. You're going to die, Peter, but there will be so much death before you join me." Cecil's voice is slow, flowing from his blackened lips as cold molasses flows across a cracked plate. A horrifying rattle follows every ending syllable.

McAllister is in tears. His hands try to block the sound of Cecil's voice as he shouts, "Why are you doing this to me? What do you want?"

"The truth will out, Peter. You will die a painful death at the hands of those you have sworn to protect, but death is so sweet. Death is so complete, Peter. Oh, sweet, sweet...d-e-a-t-h!" Cecil lunges without warning.

When McAllister stops fighting, he's alone. There is no evidence of a smashed spider. There is no scorched living corpse in his car, but that stench lingers. The shattered coffee cup that used to say Daddy, remains. His windows again allow light to penetrate the glass.

To his disgrace, Peter has pissed on himself, forced to drive home in a pool of urine. He drives with one eye on the road and the other on the mirror, where no face suddenly appears to haunt him.

Upon entering his home, Peter slams the door shut and leans against it until his knees stop shaking. A car's horn blares as it passes by and his mind nearly splits the roof of his pulsing skull.

Finally satisfied that he is alone, Peter fixes himself a stiff drink, but not before breaking several glasses. Then he runs upstairs to the medicine cabinet to retrieve a bottle of Valium. Peter swallows three of the tranquilizers before taking a much-needed shower to clean the filth from his body. The tranquilizers do not get a chance to work because he vomits in the shower. He pukes until the dry heaves take over. Then he slumps to the tiles in the stream of hot water until his legs could support his weight. Afterward, he takes more of the pills, able to keep them down this time.

The last of his worrisome thoughts dictates that the car has to be cleaned before the pills really kick in. Hours later, Valerie McAllister comes home from her shopping spree to find her smiling husband calm and well rested.

CHAPTER 14

GOOD OLD BOYS

Winston County, Mississippi.

Farm country during spring is flourishing. New green life is abounding in this part of the country while bitter humans still nurture old wounds.

As the evening sun administers the last of its life-giving rays, the cloud of dust over the dirt road slowly settles. A man named Barney Jasper parks in front of Terry Black's farmhouse in his twenty-year-old Chevy pickup. While beating at the grime accumulated on his clothes during a hard day in the soybean fields, he sneezes. With an index finger, he deftly flicks away a relentless yarn of snot that hangs from his mustache. Then he rubs his face on a sleeve.

Barney's throat is dry from his strenuous toils so he brings a chilled twelve pack. They mix the beer with Terry's special brew to wash the thirst away, a combination that always makes for a good high; makes for a good drunk.

As the evening progresses on its preordained course, they sit on the front porch to reminisce on the good old days when the Ku Klux Klan was strong and buried within American Government.

Terry Black is a cousin of former United States Senator Peter Black, who was once a heavy hitter in Ezra T. Krantze's new and improved Ku Klux Klan. Senator Black was an integral component of the Klan's attempted takeover of the U.S. Government from the inside, but everything they'd striven to achieve was destroyed in 1995 when they had a run in with an African American attorney from Atlanta named Keith Williams.

The Governor of Mississippi, Jud Martin, and several others were killed as a result of a dramatic hunt for Williams that ended in the Rocky Mountains of Montana.

Senator Peter Black had been named as the intended vice presidential running mate of Mississippi's governor. Other affiliations were discovered in deeply probing investigations. However, it was Peter Black's attempt to hinder the FBI investigation that ultimately shed light upon himself. He was then sought out and ejected from office.

Like many in office at the time, Peter Black was arrested and convicted of treason, and conspiracy to overthrow the American Government. Hundreds were accused as accessories to murder and a variety of crimes, which left a lot of people very bitter.

These relics of the violent past are two of those bitter souls.

While pouring a third can into a mug of moonshine, Barney Jasper groans his discontent. "Terry, it just done gone straight to hell."

Terry grunts his agreement and says, "I'll drink to that. Now the damn government is thinking about telling people how many kids they can have. Where the hell do they get off? This ain't Japan."

"May as well be," Barney Jasper said. "The gooks are buying up everything in sight. Wetbacks are everywhere you look and those damn towel heads keep blowin' shit up."

"Before that nigger lawyer and his traitor bitch brought down the house of cards, we were on top. We could see the dream coming true."

"Yup. You sure are right about that. Can you believe that whore helped a spook to kill her own father? Jud Martin was the best damn governor Mississippi ever had, and he was going to be the best president this godforsaken country could ever hope for."

Either these two are misinformed or they simply choose to ignore the fact that their salt-of-the-earth governor participated in the brutal gang rape of his own daughter after being told that her father was really an African American. His sole purpose for being in those mountains in 1995 was to hunt down and kill her because she had taken an African American lover, a secret that could not be exposed to his followers. The truth of bitter matters often falls short upon chapped lips and within the poisoned hearts of men such as these.

"I'll tell you this," Terry mutters. "With Jud Martin and Peter in the White House, things were finally going to change in this here country."

"No more nigwaums spreadin' AIDS. No more of them nasty, lazy welfare bitches cloggin' up the system. No damn greedy Jews trying to take things over, and no more of those dirty wetbacks stealin' good paying jobs from American citizens. That's what it was all about," says Barney.

"And it all went belly-up because of a spook mouthpiece. I swear, if I had a dollar for every time I thought about killing that fucker, I'd be as rich as a coon's age," Terry spews.

"Amen to that, brother," Barney says. "Now, I hear that lawyer is running for office in Georgia."

Terry growls, "You don't say. The nerve of that coon. Somebody will do a right proper job on him if he does. Him, his white trash wife and them zebra kids of theirs will get it sooner or later because long is the memory of a righteous man."

"I tell ya, it just ain't natural. If God had intended for us to mix breeds, then he wouldn't have made but one breed. It ain't right, her marrying that boy after he killed her old man. Cats and dogs were never meant to mix."

"My friend, no truer words have ever been spoken. No truer words," adds Terry Black.

Mr. Black casts his bloodshot eyes over the beer can graveyard that is his front yard. He crushes an empty before tossing it to the porch floor. The can bounces to the ground, clanking among the other relics of swill.

"All us god-fearing, White folks ought to just round 'em up in a corral and shoot down the lot of 'em like the mangy dogs that they are," Black growls.

His motley wife mutters a curse word over the kitchen sink, knowing that they're already good and drunk.

"Damn right. Send 'em back to Africa. Give those bastards a paddle, but keep the boat. Shark bait and tackle, my friend. They'll be shark bait and tackle," says Barney Jasper.

"A-fucking-men!" agrees Terry Black.

Less than thirty minutes later, the last can is drained of life and so is the quart of corn squeezing. These bitter souls are slouching in their creaky chairs with their blurring eyes closing. Out of simple reflex, their sleepy hands swat at the flies that attempt to mate on their grimy faces. They snore in unison, and in their dreams, many trees topple. The forest of Negroes is burning. The trunk of every tree is covered in black soot. They scream before hitting the unyielding ground, never again to stand where they can block the White man's glorious sun.

A benign pebble flies through the air to tap the wooden siding of the run down farmhouse. Moments later, Marla Black slips quietly from her bedroom window. She holds her breath for a second and dares a peek around the corner before sneaking into the woods.

The drums are playing a dangerous melody here. In this sleepy county, they woo a frenzied cauldron that stands on the brink of a very bloody boiling point.

CHAPTER 15

TWIN DISPARITY

The night sky is clear and full of stars that glimmer down on all who could appreciate their beauty and quiet serenity. When the doorbell rings, the Parkers welcome Peter and Valerie McAllister to their home.

Peter cradles a bottle of wine. Meanwhile, knowing that Evan Parker's wife is also expecting, Valerie carries their gift of a baby's rattle.

The couples move into the living room where proper introductions are made. Although they have never actually met, Valerie says to Melissa, "Hey, wait a second. Don't I know you from somewhere?"

Melissa devotes all of a split second to search her passive memory files before saying, "I don't think so. Oh, wait. Marston's. Maybe that's where it was. You do look sort of familiar."

"Oh my God, that's it. You know, I think that was a really nice thing you did earlier today," Valerie says, reaching for Melissa's hand.

Without a clue, Peter and Evan glance at one another, and then they look at their respective wives. In accord, their raised eyebrows signify that they are totally in the dark.

Being humble in the presence of those who offer her praises, just as she was raised to be, Melissa blushes before saying, "Thanks, but I really didn't do very much."

"Are you kidding? The way those cops hassled you really stunk," Valerie continues.

"Cops?" Evan asks out of serious concern. "Just what happened today?"

Melissa says coyly, "It was nothing, Evan. Several things happened today that I've told you nothing about, but all in due time."

Madeline smiles, then takes the bottle of wine and places the guest's light jackets in the hall closet. She tries not to, but a small giggle escapes her.

Valerie says, "Oh, this is for your baby. I picked it up at Marston's Baby Supplies. Peter told me that you are expecting, and it looked so adorable when I was picking out a crib. I just couldn't resist it, so I bought two. I have this sneaking suspicion that our kids are going to spend a lot of time together. Wow. What a small world, huh?"

Melissa opens it with Valerie's insistence. "Look at that, it's beautiful. Thank you." She shakes it gently, listening to the soothing chimes within. Though they are essentially strangers at this point, Melissa and Valerie hug briefly.

"This day has been one heck of a coincidence. I feel like I know you already," Valerie says.

Coming out of the lull, Peter turns to Evan and comments, "I've got to hand it to you, Evan. You've really turned this old mausoleum around since the last time I saw it. I can't believe you made so many changes in so little time and never came into work late. From what I can see, you've got yourself a terrific wife, too." He smiles at Melissa.

"Why thank you, boss. Next time, when you're complimenting me, please put the wife first," says Evan with a smile. "Shall we have a seat?" They sit facing each other, wives with their husbands.

Peter says, "So you're Melissa Parker—the Melissa Parker. I almost feel as if I know you, also. He talks so much. You know, Evan has always been a shameless braggart." Peter's warm smile remains, and his eyes twinkle with a happiness that only comes from the true peace of really great drugs.

"And you are the notorious Peter McAllister, the man who turned my sweet, lovable husband into a collegiate ruffian. Shame on you."

"Well, from what I've heard, he can't take all of the credit," Valerie rebuffs.

Melissa smiles at Val and says, "Sounds to me like we've got to sit down and compare notes, girlfriend."

"Okay, that's enough on that. I'd like to hear about the police incident, if you don't mind," Evan plies as he places his arm around his wife's shoulder.

Valerie and Melissa will take turns telling their husbands about the incident at the baby store. Apparently, there was a four-year-old child wondering around on the sidewalk in front of the bakery. Melissa and Madeline had stopped to get some fresh pastries before going down the block to Marston's.

While Madeline waited at the door of the crowded bakery, Melissa noticed the child because she was alone and in tears. She had her own childhood memories of being lost and frightened, and that four-year-old child was the very mirror of those images.

Several people passed by without paying very much attention. That's why Melissa approached and gave her comfort, keeping after her about the parent's possible whereabouts. The child had apparently followed a messenger with balloons and gotten confused.

It seemed hopeless for a while, but Melissa finally figured out that the child's parent might be at Marston's when she said that her mother promised her a baby brother to play with. Maddy was at the register when Melissa told her where she was headed. She and the child walked to the opposite end of the block, stopping to check other shops along the way.

The young mother was frantic when she discovered her daughter's absence. Deep down inside, however, she was even more concerned about her husband's reaction. Something similar happened less than a year ago. Terrible images of the precious little girl swept through her mind. The mother envisioned the very words her husband had shouted at her. They were such ugly things, even to one so irresponsible. She had checked the sidewalk only twice before making the call and waiting for the police in the middle of the store.

The police finally arrived, rushing into Marston's right behind Melissa and Lisa McCoy. The child saw her mother in the distance and ran screaming into her embrace. They were both in tears. It should have been a happy reunion, drawing a better ending that often plays out with less fortunate outcomes throughout the world.

The child's mother reacted to Melissa with undue hostility and her example was followed by the police officers. They treated Melissa Parker like a common criminal, instead of a pregnant woman who went out of her way for a child in need. The investigating officers threatened to take her in for questioning, but Madeline Perkins arrived to confirm Melissa's story.

The little girl became upset because she was essentially ignored. She was very confused by her mother's hostility toward the nice chocolate lady. By the time Maddy came in, Melissa was irate at being treated so shabbily. Maddy was overwhelmed by blushing surprise when Mrs. Parker proceeded to flail them all with very choice words of profanity. While fuming in a moment of anger, it did not matter that the child's tough-acting mother chose to relent. Melissa used words that she hadn't in years; words she ordinarily would never utter in the presence of children. But she hadn't forgotten how to combine them to paint a detailed picture of what she thought of them all.

Overall, the story is quite intriguing to their husbands.

"They had no right to treat you that way. God!" Valerie proclaims. "That bitch should have been keeping an eye on her daughter. She should have been grateful to you for taking the time to help. I'm sorry. I was right there, near the door when you came in holding the child's hand. We were looking directly into each other's eyes when the police burst in and ran right past you. I saw it all, but they even had me convinced that you'd done something wrong. Please excuse my cussing, but that shit really sucked!"

Melissa says, "Look, Valerie, I'm certain that you know by what you witnessed today, the word bitch doesn't offend me. I'm sure that I used it in and out of its context and gender on several occasions."

Maddy, thinking aloud, said from another room, "Lord knows she did. You could have been an artist with your use of such colorful language." She giggles again.

They all laugh. Evan is satisfied by the explanation, so he shows Peter his office, while Valerie receives the grand tour.

As the guys go to the ground floor study, Peter says, "Well, it's official. They're hitting it off. I'd say it's an instant match."

"Yeah. I think they're best friends already, but women are like that when they feel no threat to their territories. They meet. They sniff. They rub bellies, and boom, sisters for life," Evan adds.

Peter grunts. "There would probably be a lot more gay men in this world if we used similar techniques for initiating male bonding. Know what I mean? They meet. They sniff. They get stuck and then God pukes on a cloud!"

The two will laugh until they enter the office. When Evan turns the lights on so Peter could see his final arrangement of the study, the smile wipes away. The many books on the shelves and the personal computer and fax machine are normal enough.

Above all, Peter is struck by the various forms of African artwork, which are arranged throughout the room on stands and on the walls. Original paintings are neatly staggered along the walls with tapestries that look authentic. There are masks and statuettes about the room also. One statuette in particular catches Peter's attention. He must have bought two of those damned things.

On one wall, there was an oil painting depicting a tall, thin man. His skin was dark in the paling light of day with rolling hills in the backdrop. He looked to be a proud warrior with a long spear in his hands, staring across some distant horizon. He wears a flowing white tunic with a smudge of drying blood or mud upon his majestic left cheek. It seemed so oddly familiar and unnerving for absolutely no reason. Unbeknown to Peter McAllister, Evan had purchased this particular painting because it reminded him of a man named Kinzana.

Embedded in the center of the floor is a black and white tile setting of Yin and Yang, the Chinese symbols of male and female; the symbols of good and evil. But the overall theme of the sizeable room somehow meshes without the blaring clash of cultures that one might expect. Peter manages to smile, concealing the rush of anxiety that courses through him when Evan asks his opinion.

McAllister says, "This is very nice with...with...the combination of artwork and everything."

To his haunt, the snakes flash before his eyes with Cecil's emaciated face following. Peter's skin grows hot and it becomes hard to swallow. He is glad when Evan suggests that they look at another room. He can feel the sweat building up enough steam to erupt from his pores. For some ungodly reason, Peter feels suffocated in a room he cannot exit too quickly.

When the tours are over, the couples go into the dining room where Madeline serves the dinner she and Melissa had collaborated to create. The delicious meal consisted of the usual salad and homemade garlic bread. The shrimp Creole, with spices toned down a bit, is spread over a bed of fluffy white rice. The flounder stuffed with real crab meat rounds out the meal. It was quite nicely done, a complete culinary success.

Melissa graciously asked Madeline to sit and have dinner with them. She was delightfully surprised by an invitation she could hardly decline.

They make good conversation over dinner, continuing to do so when they return to the living room. Evan and Peter test the wine, while their wives sip cups of decaffeinated tea they secretly spiked with a touch of brandy. Just a touch.

Amid the engaging conversations, Melissa kisses her husband, affectionately. She says, "Honey, I have another surprise for you. As I said before, this has been a very eventful day."

Valerie blushes, having learned Melissa's exciting secret during her tour.

Peter notices his wife's expression and warns, "Ah oh. Something's up, Evan. Better hold on to your hat, cause here comes the big one. Earthquake!"

Valerie nudges Peter in the rib with a benign elbow.

Melissa is also blushing when she says, "Well, you know that beautiful rattle that Valerie was kind enough to buy for us?"

With his eyebrow raised, Evan slowly says, "Yes." He knows he's being tortured deliberately.

"My new obstetrician gave me an ultrasound today. According to him, we're going to need one more rattle and two of everything else. We're having twins, honey." She does that happy little squeal that women do.

"Twins? We're having twins? But how?" Evan asks as he leaps to his feet in pleasant surprise. His eyes light up as he kneels to hug his wife, raining kisses on her lips and cheeks.

Valerie McAllister is delighted for them. She looks over her shoulder at Peter, expecting to see surprise and happiness on his face, too, but he has suddenly gone pale. He is speechless when he glances at Melissa's stomach and then at that of his own wife.

It's happening right in Peter's face. He could hear the voice of Vincent Sterne saying that Blacks in this country are having babies at a ratio of four to one in comparison to Whites. He sees the data streams that grew year after year with ratios, real-time stats, and future projections. All of which are disproportionately unbalanced. Here it is in living color, slapping him in the face within brutal proximity. Reality is a bitch that is never too shy to make her undeniable presence known. Certainly not here, and not now.

Snapping to, Peter feigns a smile when his enthusiastic friend shouts, "Did you hear, Pete? I'm going to be a papa squared!"

"That's great, buddy," is all the joy Peter can summon. He gets up to give Evan Parker a handshake, which becomes an enthusiastic hug. When forced to return the gesture, Peter fakes it well enough.

Evan turns to his wife, taking her hand as he sits. He's smiling from ear to infinity when he says, "But you had regular appointments with Dr. Prior in Charleston, how could this happen? Don't get me wrong, I love the idea. I just don't understand how it could have gone undiscovered at this point in your pregnancy."

Melissa isn't clear on that either, since she has listened to the single heartbeat of her growing fetus on several occasions. She tries to explain the numerous things that Dr. Ward claimed to be possible reasons for the anomaly. But, be it due to faulty equipment or whatever she means by delayed embryonic separation, it is a welcomed surprise. It's something that might be better viewed as a modern miracle, since getting pregnant seemed so difficult.

The proud father-to-be finally throws his hands in the air to proclaim, "To hell with it. If it weren't such good news, old Doc Prior would be getting his dentures sued out of his mouth right about now!" They all laugh together.

The McAllisters soon part under the pretense of leaving the happy couple alone to celebrate.

Having seen Peter's truer expression confuses Valerie to no end. There will be questions later, none of which Peter will answer satisfactorily. Nothing he tells her remotely resembles the truth.

Seeking to dodge the issue, Peter blames his expression on a sudden wave of nausea. While that part of his explanation is true, it has nothing to do with bad seafood. Valerie does not buy it, knowing instinctively that there has to be more to it than a forty-minute illness.

Without an acceptable answer, she is left to her own womanly devices. Therefore, Valerie is convinced that Peter must be disappointed that she is only having one child. Naive of the truth behind Peter's expression, she does that thing that females often do, which leaves her feeling slightly inadequate. Valerie is right about things in one sense, however, very wrong in all others.

CHAPTER 16

KINZANA'S JOURNAL

April 4, 2001

As Evan watches a local news program, Melissa kisses his cheek and curls up next to him with Kinzana's gift to her. Because Melissa had only glanced through those ancient pages while in South Carolina, and had not started at the beginning, little understanding was gained.

Melissa realizes that she has been more concerned with Kinzana's reasoning; why she was chosen to read something so personal. She decided to give it an honest read from the unnumbered beginning because it seemed to mean a great deal to both Kinzana and Insanyanga.

During her busy day, Melissa purchased a stand for Kinzana's journal. She intends to honor the book by displaying it on that pedestal in the corner of the living room like a piece of artwork or something from an archeological dig. It, however, refuses to stay planted there where it nags at her constantly and seriously. She tested its pages during the road trip to Maryland, finding her thoughts immersed within its tales ever since.

Sitting with her back to the pillows and her head nestled in the bow of Evan's left arm, she ventures deeper into its pages. While seeing the world from a new perspective, her eyes are intense as she readily turns from page to page.

She stops reading and glances at the small key that lay between her legs. She reaches for its leather strap and looks at her husband with a question.

"Evan, do you remember what I said to you during our honeymoon?"

Evan thinks for a moment. He looks at the key, relieved to have a clue to her rather ambiguous inquiry.

"I believe you told me that Insanyanga gave you a key as a wedding gift, but it didn't seem to open anything. You said that they have a way of giving very curious gifts. We concluded that it probably held some philosophical or symbolic meaning regarding the key to a long, prosperous future together."

She smiles at his thoughtfulness. "And now, here we are. Years later, we find that this key is for this book. What do you think it means, Evan?"

He returns the smile. "Ah. I do believe that the lady is intrigued."

"Guilty as charged, sire. Kinzana told me that this was just an abridged edition and I'm supposed to get the others at some future date. Can I ask you something?"

Although Evan is interested in the news segment, he chooses to listen to her. "Sure, ask me anything," he says while gently caressing her shoulder.

Melissa hesitates for a moment before asking, "Well, just how old is your godfather, really?"

"Kinzana?" Evan's brow furrows. "Why on earth would you be interested?"

"I'm just wondering. Do you have any idea?"

"To tell you the truth, I don't really know. I'm not even certain that my father can answer that. I mean, that has got to be the last thing I expected your burning question to be. Why do you ask, Mel?"

Melissa looks at her husband for a moment but retreats. "Nothing important, I guess." She pouts, staring off into to space as her hands absently caress the book in her lap.

With genuine interest he says, "Tell me what's on your mind, Mel."

Melissa takes a deep breath. "It's just that this book is more like a kind of Bible, like an ancient diary that parallels the Bible and opposes it at the same time. At one point, it seems like some brilliant work of fiction, from what I think I understand of it. At other times, it seems like a step-by-step progression of the history of mankind. Maybe I should say the earth's history and maybe even beyond."

"Okay. What's that got to do with Kinzana's age?" Evan asks, searching for meaning in her intense line of thought.

Melissa sits up. "Kinzana's words are very lofty, to say the least. The way this thing is written, it can be difficult to understand, and even harder to accept what you do."

"You mean it's confusing as hell."

"No. Not exactly. His meaning seems clear enough, I think. However, there are some things in here that…" Melissa pauses while shifting her weight a bit. "Don't get me wrong. I'm sure that I'm less than an authority of theology, but this stuff is so spooky. I really started to read it on the way up here, and I…"

"I remember. You hardly looked up, even with that annoying crick in your neck," he interjects.

"…I had to start all over again. I felt compelled to start again."

"What do you mean?" he asks, pressing for conclusions. "Is it that entertaining or that badly written?"

"This thing, if there is any truth to it, whatsoever, would rival many of mankind's preconceptions about God, about how men and women came to be on the earth, and even the devil himself. Everything. In a way, this book refutes both the theories of evolution and the King James version of the Holy Bible with avid deliberation.

It's closely aligned with the Bible, but it's also very different. And yet, it seems almost...almost genuine in its accounts."

"Get out of here. Maybe the old man was smoking some of that special homegrown weed when he wrote this book." They laugh, but her laughter fades quickly.

"You're probably right, but still." Melissa slips into that private place again.

"What, Mel? Something has obviously made an impression, so why don't you tell me what's gotten you so hooked?"

The intensity of her thoughts is apparent; her face is a muse of conflict. As her puckered lips go in one direction, her eyebrows go in another. For a moment, the expression is quite comical.

She turns to him. "The way Kinzana has written this journal, in this high-handed fashion of his, makes you wonder if he wasn't really there. No, I really mean it. And I know it sounds like I'm headed straight for the madhouse, but it's like reading a history book about a history that never was. I say this because there seems to be more to Kinzana's strange religious beliefs than what we were all taught in Sunday school about creation. It's comprised of more than just anecdotal folklore and subjective superstitions. This journal is incredibly deep. It supplies both the meat and the teeth, as my father once said when I was young. I never understood that saying, nor have I ever had occasion to utter the words myself. Until now."

"Hmm. You know you just said a mouthful, right?"

"And then some," she says with a sigh. "Kinzana has written this in first person. Do you realize that? He even entitles one of the first entries Genesis. In the beginning, he talks about the creation of the earth, what he refers to as the garden. Most of it mirrors the Holy Bible. However, before that, he speaks of Lucifer as an entity created, not as a servant or an angel, but as a companion for Kinzana's God of gods. Twin entities were also created and they were all given the powers of gods, powers that Lucifer, The Satan, eventually used for evil. I'm telling you this stuff is really wild."

"Sounds like the kind of shit that might revive the witch hunts of old," Evan comments.

"Humph," she grunts. "I know a few Southern Baptists of today who'd certainly consider burning Kinzana at the stake, and they'd probably do it in a very public place." She does not stray long from the subject. "And then there's the story of Adam and Eve, which is also closely related to that of the King James version. However, sweetheart, your godfather claims that Eve was not created by Damballah, by God, but by one of the twin gods. I believe he calls her Dossa. Because Dossa was made to doubt the viability and worth of her own creation, The Satan was able to tarnish the Garden of Eden, introducing evil disobedience into the very fabric of mankind. Later, he speaks of Cain and Able in the first murder. They may have been in some sort of competition for their younger sister's hand in marriage. Incidentally, he makes the point that Cain was fair of skin while Abel was of a darker complexion." Melissa looks at her husband with a grin when she says, "And now I suppose we know where we got the term White devils!"

Evan arches his brow and grunts, wondering if his wife is pulling his leg.

"To be perfectly honest with you, it sounds almost as if he is talking about himself as the first man. He tries not to, but from time to time, it slips through. This book is also full of very strange, very dark, and frighteningly ominous prophecies."

Melissa pauses because she's beginning to listen to her own words, feeling a bit silly.

"You're serious, aren't you? You can't possibly believe that Kinzana has walked the face of the earth for more than a millennium." When Melissa says nothing, Evan realizes that she feels self-conscious. "Okay. I'll tell you what, read some of it to me and maybe I'll see what you're talking about."

Feeling that her husband is merely patronizing her, Melissa says, "That's okay. I'm just being foolish, you don't have to do that. It's just that I've known you for nine years, and we've been married for seven. The thing is, I've never seen Kinzana or Insanyanga age a hair. Not one gray hair, and he has to be at least sixty. You've said it yourself. Okay, now I know I sound obsessed. Just forget it, honey. Let's attribute this one to the dreaded pregnancy hormones." Her voice trails off, lacking the proper inflection to deliver one of their inside jokes.

The night around Kinzana's fire is heavily impressed upon Melissa's mind. The sudden birth of that storm was so well choreographed that it no longer seems so coincidental. Nor is the stirring in her womb, which caused fleeting fright and an inexplicable exhilaration when she initially touched this journal.

At that moment, her womanly intuitions were vibrant hairs standing on end in a cloud of disorienting static. There's been a quiet worry growing inside of Melissa Parker for days, so she believed it to be the anxious energy of anticipating the move to Maryland. However, something deeper down than is her soul now searches for something more to attribute her anxieties. That something seems to have greatly, if not everything, to do with this interesting collection of pages.

Much of what Melissa read greatly offends her Christian orientation, but that key forces her to remain open-minded. Because Kinzana's view swings her like a pendulum between utter disbelief, disgust, and awesome wonder, she manages a degree of objectivity. Like a nagging itch, there has to be more.

When Evan and Melissa met years ago, she was a very shy person. Her very quiet disposition intrigued him because still waters often run deep. Her interest in him was mutual, but breaking through her shell was still quite a task. Over the years, Evan has learned to recognize her lack of confidence. At times, he still has to urge Melissa to freely speak her mind, something that's not always so natural a thing for some. He really wants to know what has gotten her so involved with this book and its author.

Evan's voice is that of a whining child when he begs, "Please, Momma. Please read to me." She punches him for it, but it also brings her cherished smile.

"Okay. I'll do it, but only if you promise to keep an open mind. Just remember, you asked for this." He anxiously agrees, so Melissa makes herself more comfortable. She finds a page, but thinks in silence for a moment.

"What's the matter, Mel?"

"One more thing before I begin, Mr. Parker. I would like you to try to hear these words in Kinzana's voice, with his inflections. I think it's more effective, somehow." She offers one last playful glance and warns, "Just remember that you actually begged for this. What I'm about to read is very strange. You should be forewarned to expect it to mess with your head a little. Lord knows it certainly messed with mine. This comes from the section Kinzana has named the New Testament, of all things."

Thunder rolls in the distance to herald a spring storm. With it, comes a great wind that bends the tips of trees as it howls around the eaves of their new home. As the rain begins to beat upon the windows, she reads, "I—the renaissance of Adam—was summoned unto the desert sand where Damballah decreed that I travel far by night as the star of Bethlehem lighted my path across the dunes to bear witness. Once more consumed of his insatiable malice and envy, The Satan has called unto Damballah to challenge his children again to the test. Then did he whisper unto the Lord God, 'Not by guile or by my own powers, shall I offer thee proof of their unworthiness. Into the fold, I will go unto them. Not as I am, but as a mere man-child, and subject to the laws of nature and mankind. Let the brightest star among them herald my long foretold coming. I will suckle at the teat of your most blessed servant. I shall eat at my earthly father's table and learn, as a child becomes a man. I shall bless the children, bringing unto them thy wisdom and holy commandments as thine own son and heir. I will show them wondrous miracles as thy emissary. Not by guile shall I offer up my very life as thy oracle and sanctified vessel to the very gates of heaven, and yet they will surely destroy my body as a testament of their disloyalty unto He whom has created them. More wondrous still, I will rise up days thrice to prove thy powers, for they will surely fail thee to utter misery. I wager that ye shall render this world asunder with thy mighty wrath, damning their petulant souls unto my charge. Shall a man have faith in his God of all gods even when his God finally has none in him? What say ye, Lord of Hosts?'"

Melissa Parker glances at her husband, suspecting that his eyes and attention have wondered back to the television. She's pleased by the contrary, realizing that Evan has turned off the television set during the thunderstorm.

She falls silent, looking away in a thoughtful, though troubled daze.

Evan asks, "Honey, are you all right?"

"For God so loved the world, he gave his only begotten son," she utters. "What does it sound like to you, Evan?"

He reflects on those words for a moment, sighing long and hard before saying, "Well, as crazy as it sounds, it seems that Kinzana believes that, dear God forgive me, Jesus Christ was really Satan in disguise." Evan rubs his right temple and shakes his head in disbelief of what he's just heard from his own lips.

"Yeah. I thought that would grab you. It threw me for a loop, too."

"You know, you were right about it rivaling many of our pre-conceptions, but maybe this is just a basic component of Kinzana's beliefs," Evan theorizes.

"I think..." she says. "...well, I don't know what I think to be truthful."

"It makes you wonder if Kinzana hasn't gone completely mad. What's even more incredible is that his followers actually believe this stuff. Man it goes deep."

Evan brushes a lock of hair from her face, one that she doesn't seem to notice. Melissa has become silent again, looking at the journal.

She says, "That's as far as I've gotten. I'm not sure that I want to go any further. Its premise is so disturbing."

"But?" he prods.

"What if this isn't just religious belief and conjecture? What if it really holds even the smallest measure of truth? Don't get me wrong, I'm not suggesting that Kinzana really is the resurrection of Adam, but the rest of it. I mean, think about it. If Christians are really worshipping and praying to The Satan, it could actually explain why there is so much evil taking hold in this world. God forgive me."

Evan smiles at his wife, who quickly drifts into other deep thoughts. "What are you thinking, Mel?"

Melissa looks at the Bible on the nightstand. She picks it up and searches the index to find a certain passage. Once she finds it, Melissa Parker inhales deeply before saying, "I realize that this may be taking things a bit out of context, but just listen to these words spoken by Christ. 'Think not that I am come to send peace on earth. I came not to send peace, but the sword. For I am come to set a man at variance against his father, and a daughter against her mother, and the daughter-in-law against her mother-in-law. And a man's foes shall be they of his own household.' St. Matthew 10:34 through 10: 36 of the King James Version." She looks at the picture of Jesus Christ upon the bedroom wall.

Evan arches his brow and says, "Wow. That was...wow. Mel, what's the matter?"

She relents at this point. "Nothing. This is madness. The storm has passed."

"So it has," he yawns.

"It's getting late and you have to go to work tomorrow, Mr. Deputy Director." Melissa places the book on the nightstand, using the red leather strap of the key as a bookmark.

They kiss before turning the lights out.

She is feeling silly, having experienced such unbridled excitement over something that's just too far out in left field to hold any credence. But what if?

For quite some time, Melissa Parker has trouble going to sleep. Then, while listening to Evan's peaceful breath, its gentle rhythm finally lulls her into the arms of slumber.

Somewhere in the dark of night, the drums have stopped throbbing. Somewhere in the dark of night, Kinzana smiles to himself.

CHAPTER 17
THE PACKAGE

Leiber Maximum Security Prison. Ridgeville, South Carolina.
12:00 midnight.

Although Warden Maxwell Carson has always been a particularly cruel person, his prison seems the picture of impeccable order to visiting authorities. Within its concertina-wired fences and barred windows, however, Carson is party to horrible crimes against the Black and Hispanic inmates. Every now and then, he will have some poor White trash put out of his misery, but all of the really unlucky ones are tortured into oblivion first.

Warden Carson's most compelling reason for killing usually involves money. When an inmate or an outside influence has a vendetta, they can have that prisoner discretely executed for the right amount of cash or drugs. Impeccable references are a must.

The local coroner and the prison's doctor are deeply lodged in Carson's pockets, so it's relatively easy to cover up a sudden death or successful suicide. If the target happens to be an extremely newsworthy inmate, then there must be other considerations.

Maxwell Carson is a devout family man and a church-going racist, whose prison population is over seventy-percent Black, providing more than a small herd of cattle to slaughter at his whim. He has controlled Leiber for nearly twenty-two years, and in that expanse, prisoners have been sold to the Ku Klux Klan for their barbaric manhunts. Others are subjected to chemical testing by unscrupulous cosmetic and pharmaceutical companies. Those who are the misfortunate amongst test subjects often die in unimaginable agony like so many lab rats or stray cats and dogs. It is all neatly done for the beautification of the world, and so modern medicine can find its much-needed cures. Most of these prisoners are only animals after all, siphoning segments of their humanity for small stipends to struggling family members on the outside or the promise of special consideration by the parole board, if they should survive testing.

Carson reigns over his prisoners like God and they are scarcely allowed to forget his lofty status.

Standard procedures dictate that no inmate is allowed to receive or send mail without the contents being thoroughly searched. Every letter is read and every package inspected. It means certain death to expose Carson's cruelties, though many have died trying.

There is one other contributing factor in the warden's indiscretions being so well concealed within the walls of the Leiber facility, possibly the most important of them all. He systematically weeded out all but one of the African American or Hispanic prison guards. The rest transferred at their own requests, mostly. Nelson Ammatha, the one that stays, is a naturalized citizen from Nigeria.

Nelson Ammatha is hated by many and branded a sellout. It is widely believed that he's a willing participant of Carson's tyranny. Meanwhile, the White inmates live in privileged luxury, as far as prison life goes. They're allowed to sell drugs within the population with the warden being a primary beneficiary.

On many nights, while reliving the horrible accounts of the day, Nelson Ammatha privately weeps. He endures multiple death threats, knowing that at any moment one of the inmates can make an attempt on his life. However, his true feelings have to remain hidden and few inmates know of his allegiance to them. It is never easy to work in a place where the masses wish to see his head on a pike, but he remains for their sakes and much more.

The reason that Nelson hasn't been attacked or terrorized right out of Leiber is solely due to a lifer named Alunga Abuutu, the brother of one of the priests that just visited Kinzana's village.

Alunga Abuutu was sentenced to life without parole for the manslaughter of two White men in 1991. This voodoo priest survived a brutal attack by three men with clubs and chains just to end up in prison. The ages of his assailants ranged from 18 to 20. After getting stoned on pot, crank, and Wild Turkey, they set out to find some action. In that state of mind, action always translated into trouble.

On that fateful night, Alunga still wore ceremonial symbols that had been painted on his face and forehead because he had just performed a wedding in Goose Creek, South Carolina. It was unfortunate that a tire had gone flat on the way back to his quiet Summerville neighborhood.

The young men spotted Alunga while fixing the flat along the roadside. They turned around and tricked him by offering their assistance. The first blow was with a tire iron and he was beaten quite severely. In the end, he prevailed against the assailants who, surely would have taken his life. Alunga Abuutu was an excellent fighter, having been trained in hand-to-hand combat in his native land of Zaire, now known as the Democratic Republic of the Congo. Upon reverting to his military training, his instincts deemed it necessary to exert deadly force.

The one survivor is forced to live out his life in a wheelchair. When this nephew of the Summerville Chief of Police ended up beneath Alunga's car, the jack dislodged during the fight. The weight of the old Lincoln crushed two of his cervical vertebrae, severing his spinal cord. It was a miracle that he survived at all.

The two that died as a result of their unwarranted attack on Alunga Abuutu were full-blown members of the Ku Klux Klan. One of them perished on the way to the hospital, but the other was dead at the scene. He was impaled by the same jack handle he used to attack the Black man.

Severely battered and bruised, Alunga barely escaped a lynching before local police took him into custody. By the time he reached the hospital, he was in much worse shape.

Somehow, Alunga Abuutu was found guilty of two counts of manslaughter by a so-called jury of his peers; an all-White jury of peers.

During the trial, however, the defense presented an elderly White couple, who came forward to testify on Alunga's behalf even under threat. They witnessed the bloody incident from their front porch, but the determined prosecutor discredited the couple's testimony. He basically ignored the truth, citing the thickness of their glasses and poor vision at night. The fact that they both used hearing aids did not help matters, when maybe, it should have. Of course, the bitter, paralyzed survivor lied about Abuutu's vicious, unprovoked attack on him and his poor dead friends.

With the urging of members of his community, the NAACP, and the Black media rallied behind Abuutu. Because they made so much noise, he was only doomed to serve consecutive life sentences for his crimes. Alunga's many appeals had fallen wasted on deaf ears.

It is often whispered that the gods are protecting Alunga Abuutu from Warden Carson's angry friends on the outside, but he was never forgotten. It is only a matter of time before he will be spirited away in the dead of night to be hunted, burned alive, crucified or much worse. They are waiting in the shadows for the tenth anniversary of the slaying.

On the night of April 4, after Alunga Abuutu withstands another brutal beating, Nelson Ammatha will bring him a secret package.

The prisoner is completely naked. No mattress has been allocated for his stainless-steel bunk. Partially, to wash the blood from his battered body, the inmate had been recently hosed down. Moreover, it is a form of torturous physical abuse.

This time, he is being punished for merely preaching to his following, which absorbs Muslims and Christians alike. He is reaching men of nearly every faith, and even a few of those with none. Alunga is considered a dangerous influence because of the control he's gaining over these inmates. Decreasing incidents of violence has become noticeable. Though it's impossible to dissuade all of his brethren from drug use and violent reprisals, the warden's profit margin is beginning to suffer.

Nelson Ammatha opens the heavy door to look down upon a naked, beaten man. The air is dank and stale, smelling of Alunga's feces and urine. The stained filth, now pooling in the middle of the floor, proves that the drain has been deliberately plugged. The water that supplies the toilet has been turned off.

As the dim lighting of the corridor assaults his puffy eyes, Alunga slides along the floor until he backs himself into a defensible position in the corner. The blood from his broken nose dries between his nostrils and upper lip. His gnarled, wet hair glistens like the shackles that bind his hands and feet.

Alunga bares his teeth, snarling like a caged beast. His wild eyes blaze an undying defiance as he wills his trembling, arthritic hands to curl into fists.

When he suddenly shivers, a hacking cough burns his lungs and throat. Greenish phlegm escapes his broken teeth and lips. He suffers from bilateral pneumonia, and the antibiotics that Nelson steals from the infirmary fail to halt its progression.

"It is only I, Baba," Nelson whispers. He places the box and a tray of food upon the bare steel bed and hurries to Alunga's side.

"Why have those dogs beaten you again? What does Carson hope to gain by such savagery?"

"They want to break my will before they take me to his friends, but I will not be broken!"

Ammatha covers the shivering prisoner with a thin blanket and holds him for a moment. The intense heat that pours from Alunga's body indicates that the fever has worsened, but Nelson's empathy is quickly spurned when Alunga forces his arms away.

There is a look of insanity about him, like that of a rabid animal when he says, "It makes no matter, Nelson, because I am free. I am already free!"

Because Alunga Abuutu hasn't been fed in two days, he eats accordingly. Meanwhile, Nelson Ammatha removes several items from the box for his inspection. It contains two wooden flutes and a bongo drum, which is a poor substitute for Conga or Rada drums, but it will do. There is also a container of dead, Africanized bees and wasps hidden inside. The untranslatable symbols indicate where the secret compartments have been hidden in the wood, and how to open them.

The letter is from his brother, Abatu Abuutu and Kaleem Kinzana, giving him instructions for the near future. Hollow spaces in the wood of the drum also conceal small bags of powder and darts that are to be used in blowguns, those harmless looking flutes.

At night, Abuutu will beat his tiny drum to conjure foul spirits. His solitary confinement for what is called an incitement of riotous behavior turns out to be a blessing. The savage beatings he has taken over the three week stretch will soon be forgotten.

Within the confines of Alunga's small cell, his eyes gleam in the darkness when he reads the letter before swallowing it.

After Nelson Ammatha leaves, Alunga Abuutu whispers to himself, "I am the lion, and I am already free. For all the unjust insurrections, there shall be blood!" Before long, these very words become the deadly whispers of Black and Latin-American prisoners. The very same is repeated in several prisons around the country, where potent drums begin a rhythmic throb after lights out.

Boom da-da doom! Doom da-da boom! Drums, beating in the night, their deadly pulses decreeing, "We are free and there shall be...blood!"

Boom da-da doom! Doom da-da boom! Boom da-da doom, da-da doom, da-da doom!

CHAPTER 18

THE VOODOO DOLL

*O*ne *hour beyond the moment of the black witch. Doom da-da boom!
The drums are pounding in his ears. Tortured screams are inescap-
able as he runs past torn, partially eaten bodies. Corpses are strewn about
the ground as if a cemetery has just disgorged.*

*The insane eyes of some unspeakable thing leers at the passerby, hissing
its malcontent for the disturbance of its rotting, human meal.*

*Torches burn all around, planted in the spongy black earth that falls
beneath his panicking feet. Half-decayed, living corpses are dragging themselves along the ground, moaning the chorus of the undead. Their prayers
for forgiveness of some unredeemable trespass and freedom from purgatory
raise the hackles of his neck. His ears will not go suddenly deaf, as he wishes.*

*He is running at top speed, fearing that his rubbery legs or burning
lungs will succumb to the exhaustion that follows sustained bursts of adrenaline. The painful stitch in his side worsens as he works his way through
vines that hang like black spaghetti from the darkened treetops. Such pangs,
minor by comparison to what will happen if he's caught, have to be ignored.*

*Like a wild animal, he is hunted through the jungle by unseen maraud-
ers that crave his tender flesh. He knows within his mind and heart that his*

eyes will be plucked from the sockets—sucked until they pop on their tongues like plump, juicy grapes. This terrified runner knows these malicious cannibals, and he knows them well.

The canopy above is so thick that the face of the full moon is revealed only in glimpses. Stopping to rest, gasping for air, he holds onto a thick vine that transforms into a snake that wriggles in his grasp. When it lunges at his face, he screams for an uncontrollable moment, before shoving a fist into his mouth. As his wild eyes search the malicious darkness, he bites down hard to quiet himself. There's danger everywhere as he whimpers helplessly.

This brutal, unforgiving night world has been thrust upon him time and again. Thus far, the instincts of self-preservation have sustained this man against the escalating terror, but his resolve is severely battered. The walls of his will are crumbling like the porous blocks of a home that has been built within a thriving swamp.

Barrette Holt is petrified, sensing that they are coming for him. He can hear their rushing footsteps between the pulses of the Rada and Conga drums. The relentless drums are telling them just where he can be found. They are coming fast.

The Director of Data Preparations continues to run, stumbling blindly in the darkness until tripped by a root protruding from a bed of moss. He rolls down a small hill, landing face down in soupy mud that reeks of animal excrements. Human skeletons are littered about. Their tattered bones are unmistakable when the clouds retreat from the face of the full moon. He looks at the bones, knowing that they died horribly.

He looks up and sees a highway with modern day cars blaring as they pass beyond the ditch or whatever he's fallen into. It is safety, he's almost home free.

His insane smile quickly fades because some large something is slithering forward in the mud to the right. The crocodile growls a low, guttural sound that nearly paralyzes him as its iron-scaled belly plows through the mire.

Barrette Holt screams and scurries for footing, falling repeatedly with the slithering beast bearing down on him. It is gaining ground as Holt flounders about, so he's forced to crawl on hands and knees until he hauls himself out of the slime. When he reaches the top, wiping the mud from his face, the crocodile lunges at him! Those sharp teeth shred the air, but its jaws snap shut just short of Holt's face. Its mouth waters at the thought of devouring such a large meal.

Holt will never forget the crunching click that its vile, yellow teeth make when those jaws close merely inches from his chin. Nor will he soon forget the foul odor that exudes from deep within its gullet, just before its weight causes it to slide back from whence come.

Barrette Holt scoots backward, dragging his ass and the palms of his bleeding hands across the soggy earth. The road to freedom is right behind him. He can hear and feel the rush of tires as the cars zoom by.

He smiles, having outrun the footsteps. The drums have finally fallen silent behind him. But to Barrette Holt's woe, he can no longer hear the footsteps because the pursuers already surround him!

Their sudden appearance burns a white-hot flash across Barrette's brutalized mind. He collapses upon weakened knees, looking into angry eyes that are wholly consumed by malicious intent.

They are the voodoo-makers, things of dark magic with blazing eyes. Their skin has been painted with white dots and symbols that eerily reflect the light of the moon above. Adorned with beads and bamboo that rattle and click with movement, they stare down upon him. Their hands clench sharp spears and bush knives, which they beat against animal skin shields while stomping their bare feet into the ground.

Holt hears no car horns, feels no rushing wind from the highway of imagination. His road to safety has vanished.

Encircling their prey, they make horrible shrieks that force Barrette's hands to his ears, but he cannot block those sounds. Nor can he ignore the drums that resume in his head, for this is madness.

"What do you want from me?" he screams. "Please, God. Somebody, help me!"

Suddenly, a fire blazes up from the ground. There's no kindling, no wood, just fire from nothing at all. The circle parts and a short woman struts into the mysterious firelight, ranting something incoherent. She is a dwarf or a pygmy, something definitely out of place.

Her long, matted locks boast bone and teeth accessories that clatter with her small steps. Smelling of sackcloth and sweat, this detestable little woman grins when she produces a cloth doll. She thrusts it into Barrette Holt's face, grinning—always grinning.

She glares at him and says, "You call on God, but you know not whom He is, White man!" Her wicked eyes squint to puncture his heart.

Holt begs, "Who are you people? Why are you always doing this to me? I'll give you anything if you'll just leave me alone."

"Anything?" she asks. "You would give me anything I ask?"

Feeling a sense of hope, Holt sheds tears and says, "Yes, anything. Just name it."

Priestess Tuloni smiles at Barrette and caresses his scruffy cheek. She looks about the circle of warriors with those black, loveless eyes and asks, "Are you certain?"

Barrette Holt whimpers, "Anything." He crawls toward Tuloni, bowing at her dusty, sandaled feet without shame.

"Then, I want you to die!" shrieks the nasty little woman, who drives a long pin into the doll's head.

Barrette grabs his temples, screaming from the exquisite pain that rips through his brain. As he twitches and convulses, his ears and nose begin to bleed before Priestess Tuloni finally withdraws the pin from the doll's cranium. When the pin is fully withdrawn, Barrette gasps for air.

"Please," he begs. "Please, no more."

She screams something to the others in her native tongue, pointing at the helpless victim. Now, she reverts to English to say, "You are one of the gate conspirators, a man who would kill to keep such dreadful secrets. Now, Legba and Shanga demand that you die!"

She places the point of the needle into the flames and stabs the doll in the genital area, bringing about a reciprocal reaction in Barrette. He lies on the ground, writhing in pain as he clutches his fiery groin.

Tuloni yanks the needle out, but before he recovers, she stabs it into the doll's chest. The woman works it around and around, pulling it out and shoving it home repeatedly. Invisible agony tears at Holt's body and he prays for death.

The drums are pulsing in Indiana.

Tuloni leans toward Barrette and pierces his effigy in the groin once more. Then she draws another pin from her hair and stabs into its back. As Barrette arches and grabs at the pain, she watches him scream from very close in.

He stares into her smiling grimace, which smells of rotting flesh. She points her stubby index finger at him and proclaims, "Pasty man, you will soon know a thousand deaths. Simply because you are in my charge, I will kill you night after night. Each demise will be a more painful death than your puny little manhood can imagine. You will cease to be or I will come for you until you are driven mad. Either way, you will die twisted like the trunk of a mighty devil tree!"

Without warning and no more effort than pulling a fig from a tree, she reaches her tiny hand into Holt's gaping mouth to pluck out the molar with a gold filling. She pulls the pins from the doll's groin and back, laughing aloud as she gazes at the bloody tooth that glistens in the firelight.

Just when Barrette thinks that his torment is finally over, the hunters close on him with their spears and machetes raised to do him harm. His screams resume as he's stabbed and hacked limb from limb.

The drums are beating at the end of Karma Drive, pounding on the outskirts of Jeffersonville, Indiana.

Sweat-laden, Barrette Holt's racing pulse thuds in his temples. His chest heaves from the strain of severely taxed breathing as his hands search the nightstand for his nearly empty inhaler.

Holt realizes that it had been just a dream, even though it was the nastiest thus far. Those very powerful images seemed so real. He experienced such pain. He could almost taste his own fear and the rancid mud.

He takes a puff and tries to relax as the constriction loosens in his chest, flinching when he looks down to see that his clothes and one remaining shoe are filthy and covered with slime. His right foot is bare of shoe and sock. Mud is drying between his aching toes. His bed sheets are ruined and he also notices blood.

Barrette leaps from his bed. His entire body aches as his legs protest his weight, threatening to buckle at the knees. Struggling to maintain his feet, Barrette limps into the bathroom where the mirror of the medicine cabinet stands open. It was left that way after his last search for the tranquilizers that he's already used on his relentless anxiety and insomnia.

When he swings the mirror closed, his breath seizes. His eyes grow exceedingly wide from the sight of his own reflection. Fine trickles of blood run from his ears and nostrils. Dark rings encircle his sunken eyes. His lips are cracked and blistered. He opens his mouth, and as expected, his bloody gum is missing a molar.

It is the sight of his own skin, however, which causes Barrette the most concern. It's gray, like that of a man who's been long dead; flaccid and toneless. Barrette Holt looks dead to Barrette Holt.

His gut contracts without warning, allowing a wave of vomit to erupt from his lips. His rushing purge traces a wide band from the bottom of the mirror, down the wall and onto the vanity. Now, through watery eyes, he sees something squirm. When the maggot wriggles, Barrette vomits again. He is sick from something awful. When his dry heaving finally runs its course, he turns on the tap to rinse his mouth, splashing cold water on his hot skin.

Barrette's stomach rolls again when he sees a maggot squirm on the bottom of the mirror. This has to be an illusion, yet he cups his hands beneath the tap to dash the mirage away. When he looks again, the voodoo priestess is sitting on the shoulder of one of her minions, glaring at him with that accursed doll in her teeth! As his eyes bulge, the mirror cracks down its center.

Forgotten, the water seeps between his trembling fingers. Holt squeals as a virgin does when an insensitive lover rams the very first penis home.

Her haunting laughter fills his world, slowly cascading into an echo. Then, she is gone. His heart jackhammers and he knows that he's gone completely mad because overwhelming guilt can do this to an emotionally broken man.

Moments later, Barrette tentatively peers out of the bathroom to survey his empty bedroom. When he's certain that nothing will spring from the shadows, he moves toward the bed and the telephone.

Along the way, he kicks something on the floor. At first he thinks it's his missing shoe, but it is soft. Nor is it the displaced sock. He looks down to find his effigy, a voodoo doll that bleeds real blood from several puncture wounds.

Holt jams a fist into his mouth to quell the swelling eruption in his throat as a new scream forces its way to his tongue. His eyes are saucers, racing from one corner to the next, scanning every existing shadow for movement.

Afraid to look over his shoulder, Barrette snatches it up and runs to the phone. He calls Peter McAllister at 2:30 in the morning, cradling a weapon from the drawer that is never in hand when he needs it most.

Valerie McAllister's grumpy voice comes across the line. "This had better be really good."

As Peter's wife yawns, she yanks the phone from her ear when Barrette shouts, "Let me speak to Peter. Please!"

"Do you know what time it is?" she scolds. "Who is this?" Peter rolls over. His own sleep has been fitful. If not for near exhaustion, his eyes would have opened on the first ring.

"It's Barrette Holt. I need to speak to your husband right away!"

"It's Barrette," Valerie growls. "And he sounds wasted." She drops the receiver on Peter's chest and rolls over.

"Barry, is that really you? Why are you calling so late?" Peter asks.

As his muddy eyes search the room for his secret enemies, Holt shouts, "You know damn well why I'm calling. It's happening again, for Christ's sake. But this time, it's much worse."

Peter says, "Wait, just slow down." He looks at his wife and decides to move out of earshot.

Holt is hysterical and skittish. Peter's certain that he's crying when he says, "I just...I just can't take it anymore. Someone knows and they're out to get me." His voice pivots between the axis of frantic whispers and unchecked ranting.

"Barrette, you've got to get a hold of yourself. Nobody knows a thing. Do you hear me?" Peter reassures.

Quite by accident, Valerie overhears that part of the conversation when she gets out of bed to use the toilet, but her husband is in the bathroom with the door slightly ajar. The urgency in his voice tempts her to listen as Peter whispers warnings.

"Don't do anything rash. No one knows. You just go and..." His eyes jerk about. "What?"

"You heard me. It's not just a bad dream anymore. It's fucking real!"

"What the hell are you talking about? They're just nightmares, Barrette. I can't explain why we are having similar dreams, but that's all they are. That's all."

"You don't understand, Peter. They were in my fucking house tonight. They chased me through some crazy graveyard in a swamp. Hell, I have no idea where I've been, but this time I saw her. I saw her as plain as day, Peter. She was right here while I was wide-awake, damn it!" Barrette Holt snivels, crying outwardly.

"What are you talking about? Who was in your house?"

"That bitch, that midget woman with the doll. She left it here and I've got it in my fucking hand right now, so don't you tell me it was just a dream!" Holt's eyes snatch from one well-lighted corner to the next. He thinks he hears a noise. Then, a whisper in the rising wind carries deadly threats to his tortured mind.

Peter advises, "If someone was in your house, you should call the police right now."

"No way. Please don't hang up on me, Peter. I tried the police three times before. They think I'm nuts or on something." He pauses when a thought occurs to him concerning the dangers of sleep. His head twitches once, then twice. "The cops threatened to arrest me the next time I call in a false alarm. Don't you see? No one can help me."

"What do you mean, Barry?"

Peter seems worried to Valerie, who pushes the door open a little more.

"I'm a dead man. I can see it in the mirror. I think they did something to me when she stole my tooth. I'm so sick, Peter."

"Okay, Barry. I want you to go back to the doctor and I promise to see you in a few days. I swear it. I swear I will," Peter says, hoping that the man can hold on that long. This is certainly the worst of Barrette's episodes over the years.

"It's over, man. I'm through dealing. She told me that she'll see me dead." Barrette's voice is beginning to sound distant and Peter is very concerned about that last statement.

"Calm down and listen to me." Peter licks his dry lips. He takes a deep breath and says, "Okay, here we go. No one knows what happened eleven years ago. It didn't come out then and it won't happen now. It's just nerves because the new census is due, and we're getting close to the end of it all. You'll be okay. I know that because I've been going through the same anxieties. I've been having the same problems, Barry."

"Oh yeah? Well I'm bleeding, man. My tooth is missing. I look like a fucking ghost, and I'm covered with alligator shit! And you think you've gone through the same thing. Have you, Peter? I can't take it anymore. I'm losing my freaking mind here. I'm just losing my freaking mind."

"You're talking crazy." Peter bites his tongue and recants. "I'm sorry, Barrette. Just see a doctor.

We'll begin the transfer program day after tomorrow and the stress will subside. It will be over. You have to trust me on this."

Valerie recognizes desperation in her husband's voice. He seems very disturbed as she does the pee dance from one foot to the other.

"They're coming for you next, Peter," Barrette says in a tone of voice that suggests that he wants it to happen, just as long as they leave him alone.

"No one's coming for me, Barrette. Stop talking like that."

"You'll see. You'll see, Peter. This shit has been eating me alive. I have to talk to someone." Barrette seems so defeated, but he is calmer. He is suddenly too calm.

Peter cups his free hand over his mouth and warns, "Don't do anything stupid. You know what happens if you disclose this information just to clear your fucking conscience. You'll just end up like he did, so keep your yap shut if you want to stay alive. Got it?"

When Peter sees his wife in the mirror, he's sure that she heard nearly every word. The burden of new lies begins to clutter his mind immediately.

"This isn't living, Peter," Barrette sobs. "By every holy definition of the word, this isn't living."

The line goes dead.

CHAPTER 19
THE THEMES OF DESTRUCTION

Geddon Air Base is no typical military installation. It is considerably small in its complement of buildings. Most of these soldiers are security personnel or military scientist. Because the base has only two full-length landing strips, it poses insignificant; the very effect its founders hoped for.

This place of secrets is a den of deadly new toys that are filled with nasty surprises. It's a world where weapons of the future berth, brooding in their traces. The Allegheny Mountain range parallels the Appalachian Mountains. Together, they provided the seclusion that Geddon required when construction was finally completed in 1990.

The base's entire perimeter is protected by several rows of electrified razor wire fencing. These fifteen-foot barriers are formidable, but the more technological defense systems are constantly upgraded.

Geddon is so secretive that the Russians and the Chinese scarcely know of its existence. Its personnel are among the best soldiers and scientists in the world.

Missileer are very important human components of this base, and they always work in pairs on twenty-four to forty-eight hour shifts. To begin their shift, a team descends to the underground command capsule where they monitor the nuclear missiles buried deep in the heart of Angel Mountain.

Missileer hopefuls are required to undergo extensive interviews and batteries of psychological testing before and after they're accepted into the Inter-service Nuclear Weapons School. The students of this institution are some of the most intelligent minds in America. They have to supersede the rigorous standards of aptitude testing needed to be selected for jobs of such sacrosanct importance.

These men and women take an oath to launch their missiles if given the secret enable codes, which allows the missiles to leave their berths. These code combinations are rotated hourly. Each person entrusted with this power is forced to watch endless film footage of the act and aftermath of the bombings of Hiroshima and Nagasaki. It's a requirement that one dares not shy away from. It is imperative that each candidate knows exactly what it means to launch their nuclear ordinance. They see fried and mangled bodies in the midst of massive destruction. They know that, potentially, this job may require that they do it again with unimaginably more human and collateral devastation.

Many are traumatized by the themes of infinite death. Like a rock climber's spike, it's driven home that this is the job for which they train. There can be no doubt. Countless have asked for reassignment following the films. Others drop out after the dead rise in their nightmares. They suddenly discover that they simply aren't as tough as they once thought.

Some will dream about scores of diseased people, dying from radiation sickness. From the dark halls of the hopefuls' imagination, the sick reach out with their ragged hands to beg for food and water, or medicine. The ravaged most often ask, "Why...why have you done this to us and our innocent children?"

Countless soldiers scream themselves from the depths of slumber, searching the darkness for moaning people with sunken eyes and patches of scorched hair that cling to their melted flesh. This job is no symphony, before or after the diploma.

Over twenty-seven thousand officers report to the Chairman of the Joint Chiefs of Staff General Bradford Smith. Smith reports to Secretary of Defense Marquis Slater, who bows in turn to the President of the United States, their Commander in Chief.

Together, Smith and Slater have siphoned the resources of the North American Air Defense and Combat Operations Center, better known as NORAD and appropriated congressional funding to conceal the super secretive testing of the missiles on Angel Mountain.

The weapons system was perfected at White Sands, New Mexico in a completely separate department from the main weapons testing center. The existence of these weapons are undisclosed in every disarmament treaty ever formed in conjunction with counter-superpowers.

The Angel Mountain installation is about destruction, making sure that in the event of nuclear attack, there will be little of an enemy's land left habitable by man or beast.

What was once known as Viking Mountain has been poetically renamed Angel Mountain on all of NORAD's maps. This innovative military exercise is littered with themes. Geddon is actually short for Armageddon Air Base. Buried deep within the mountain are twenty-two missiles with nuclear warheads, and forty-four without, making up the deadliest arsenal on the face of the planet.

The missiles with nuclear warheads are called Gabriel 1 through Gabriel 22. The others are called Michael 1 through Michael 44, but they're just as essential to nuclear defense. With these weapons named after the Avenging Angel and the Angel of War, archangelic are these themes of war.

The Gabriel missiles contain enough plutonium to produce a blast ten thousand times more powerful than both bombs dropped on Hiroshima and Nagasaki combined. The Soviet Union and China are large countries, but with the spread distribution of these missiles, most of either could be reduced to useless wastelands. However, the blast potential of the weaponry is the very least of what makes it unique, for these are very intelligent machines.

The engineers of the Armageddon weaponry successfully integrated three new concepts into the basic technology of nuclear devices to make them incomparable. First, stealth technology is incorporated into the Gabriel missile. It's essentially the same technology that played such a giant's role in the defeat of Saddam Hussein's forces during the Gulf War of 1990. On board the Gabriel missile is the Cross-7000 Supercomputer, which is capable of simultaneously processing one-hundred trillion bytes of information. It avoids detection by absorbing the known signals of satellites, aircrafts, and all ground-based detection devices. It will duplicate—exactly—the signal frequencies of each individual detection device, sending it back to its origin showing whatever should be reflected. It was thought to be impossible, but they also displace infrared tracking as well as sonar and most microwave detection, welcome surprises for the engineers.

If an orbiting enemy satellite sweeps an area, the Cross-7000 would absorb and compute the signal's angle to instantly calculate the direction of the sweep while making its own sweep of the terrain below. The satellite would see what it's supposed to see, land masses or the ocean; essentially, nothing at all. An aircraft's radar or ground-based radar detection is also impossible.

During the testing stage, unarmed and then armed Gabriel prototypes were launched over the deserts of White Sands and pitted against the most sophisticated spy and fighter aircrafts known to man. Pilots were instructed to get close enough to the missile to make visual contact, but their radar screens were completely blinded. Visual identification or manual interception of a Gabriel 1 is the only plausible way of shooting it down, but even these aspects are countermanded by its genius.

The second protective measure of the Gabriel missile requires that it be maneuverable in both high and low atmospheric flight. If the sky happens to be overcast when the missile explodes from its silo, it will instantly adjust its altitude and trajectory so that it can hide in the cumulonimbus. However, it will never go too far out of its way to do so, simply using them when available. These missiles are different in that they do not automatically go into the upper atmosphere like the Titan Four, Titan Five or an ICBM. The shortest distance between two points will forever remain a straight line, but if there is sufficient cloud cover, Gabriel uses it extremely well.

No matter what, this missile is designed to deliver its highly classified megatonnage on any dime it aims at because the Avenging Angel will be at its side. A single megaton equals one million tons of TNT. The mathematically incomparable threat of Gabriel is simply staggering!

The slightly smaller Michaels are the Gabriel's deadly escorts. Its range is just as extensive so where Gabriel goes, Michael is sure to follow. Each warhead-equipped missile is shadowed to its blast site by two of the smaller missiles. Their sole purpose is to annihilate any hostile aircraft or antiballistic type weaponry sent to bring down the Angel of War.

Each Michael is equipped with sixteen smaller, very deadly Sidewinder type missiles, only bigger. These rockets, designated as Sabers, are affixed to the fuselage and hidden beneath retracting panels fore, aft, and midway. If something like a Patriot missile is launched at the trio from ground level zero, one or more of the Saber missiles will arm. The retracting panel would do just that, slipping into the missiles hull. The Saber would be ejected from the fuselage of the missile. Its ignition system would then activate away from the Michael's body to avoid changing the parent missile's trajectory, and then its booster will kick in. Instantaneously, the panel reseals the vacated launch site to annul air drag, staying true to its flawless aerodynamic design.

Before the point of ignition, the Saber would already have acquired the target. A second Saber will launch to destroy the hostile weapon's point of origin on the ground. And since the Gabriel always monitors the terrain below, it will have acquired the launch site of the hostile weaponry upon launch. This is important because the U.S. designed Patriot missile and most comparable surface-to-air weaponry employs both automated and visual laser tracking capabilities that conceivably threatens the Gabriel entourage.

In all of their extensive testing, however, nothing ever comes close to harming the advanced killing machines. The same goes for any approaching enemy aircraft.

If nuclear war is to break out, the President himself will have to give the missileer the correct launch enable codes. Using keys that hang around both their necks, the missileer will open a cabinet in the command capsule. The enable codes are encased in red plastic covers. For each warhead, there are fourteen of these cards in the cabinet of the Angel Mountain facility, but only three of these cards will contain the correct codes at any given hour. They have to be used in the proper sequence. Using the wrong code or the wrong sequence of the correct code will cause the auto-shutdown of all command functions. Therefore, it is virtually impossible for missileer to launch the nuclear weapons without authorization.

Smith and Slater have near complete trust in the mental stability of their personnel to hold true to their appointed duties and nothing more. Surprise drills and simulations are constantly thrown at the missileer throughout the nuclear program, but more so for those of the Geddon facility. None of the appointed few has folded, thus far.

Captain Kyle Parker and 1st Lieutenant Alicia Markham are sitting next to each other in the briefing room. Surrounded by the twelve members of the other six missileer teams, they face yet another drill announcement.

Kyle Parker is tempted to caress his fiancée's thigh, but he decides not to tempt the wrath of Colonel Terrell or Base Commander General Austin. They're being briefed on the upcoming assignment, which requires that each team participate in another stress test. This one means that they will be sequestered underground for twelve days and nights, or possibly longer.

The test is designed to determine their capability and efficiency ratings under stressful situations beyond the scope of what they have already proven safe. This exercise is also in conjunction with the stipulations of the U.S. Congress and President Al Gore, who want to be sure that the human factor should remain in the deadly equation.

While engaged in the matters of work, the missileer monitor the hatchlings for malfunctions. Computers persistently run checks on the missiles' launch mechanisms. They monitor the deterrent, guidance, and propulsion systems, as well as assuring the full containment of deadly radiation.

Down there is another world, connecting the command capsule with the missile silos by a system of secured tunnels. After the initial launch, the eleven silos are designed to automatically reload a secondary set of missiles. This is truly an awesome wonder of modern-day killing technology.

With the command capsule centrally located, the missile silos are spread out in a staggered circle. They cannot be accessed unless the team releases the security protocols so technicians can get inside. Silos are chiseled out of earth and solid rock, lined with two-feet of tempered steel throughout each chamber.

The conventional silos of old were usually perfectly vertical and had to be built on mountains because digging that deep would bring water from underground river systems. Nevertheless, with the power and maneuverability of these weapons, vertical placement is not necessary. The forty-five-degree angle facilitates the reloading system because the missiles are arranged on revolving turrets that position them into the empty space left by previous launches.

Once the team enters the facility, they will activate the perimeter security systems of the above ground elevator entrance. A ten-foot thick titanium door, which can only be opened from within, slams shut. The elevator stays at the bottom of the shaft. Six seven-inch steel pylons that are simultaneously forced into place by the missileer secure the car itself. Three horizontal doors, which are two-feet thick, slide into place at thirty yard intervals to seal the shaft from top to bottom. This installation is constructed to keep these men and women untouchable from any hostile threat. These deadly weapons never need to be fueled before launch because they are propelled by atomic reactors that also go critical when the target is reached.

Upon completion of the briefing, the orders of shifts are posted and the first twelve-day stretch is scheduled to commence sooner than liked. Captain Kyle Parker and 1st Lieutenant Alicia Markham are to be the leading team down.

CHAPTER 20
POWER SURGE

At 11:45, Evan Parker walks into Peter McAllister's office with the new budget projections he's been working on since joining the Bureau of Census. This pet project is something he'd actually volunteered to take on. His findings are very promising for the government entity, which has been running in the red since the Sleeper Virus awoke to wreak havoc on the network. Evan Parker's data model suggests that they could operate below the budget spending of the pre-viral years if innovative strategies are implemented.

Parker expects Peter to be sitting at his desk with his nose buried in one official notice or other, but he is not. The slightly disappointed deputy director places a copy of the in-depth report on the desk, and is about to leave when he hears Peter retching in the tiny restroom. Peter's drawl sounds much the way it will when a person prays to the porcelain god after drinking too much rotgut. The sound causes Evan to cringe, sympathetically.

"Pete, are you okay?"

"Oh G-o-d!" Peter prays as he heaves.

There is a splash as Evan Parker reaches the doorway. While Peter kneels at the altar, his back arches, heaving up and down. Evan Parker does not know that the bowl is full of maggots, but that awful retching sound reminds him of the old sump pumps at the African Village when he was just a kid. The pumps almost always needed to be primed with water before drawing water from the underground stream.

The memory of the first time Peter McAllister had gotten him drunk in college also surfaces. He recalls the awful moment as if it was yesterday and a wry smile forces his lips when he thinks of how Peter and other veteran drinkers ragged him the entire time. Being the man that he is, Evan Parker feels a twinge of guilt for gloating and that glorious moment of possible retribution is gone.

Peter's hair is matted, as if he's just taken a morning run. Evan figures that he's suffering from symptoms of the flu. His necktie is loose, tossed across his left shoulder, and his skin is flush. When Peter's collar moves from his sweating skin, Evan notices an oozing red pimple on his neck that looks infected.

"I won't bother asking if you're alright. It's pretty obvious that you're not." Even with a prevalent stench of stomach acid and partially digested food, Evan Parker ventures inside and places a hand on his friend's shoulder.

Finally, Peter hawks up some spit and catches his breath. His vision blurs, hazing out of focus for a second and the maggots are gone. When he tries to stand, he slips on a dabble of slime that splashed over the rim. Evan Parker catches him.

"Jesus! Thanks, Evan. I'm alright," Peter says with an attitude. He jerks away from Evan's grasp and flushes the toilet.

Just then, Evan experiences that overwhelming urge people often have when their eyes are drawn to the disgusting; things they don't necessarily wish to see. At such times, the eyes do seem to have a mind of their own. Evan does a double take as the chunks of grapefruit and bits of bacon swirl down the red funnel of water. This causes him genuine concern.

Evan Parker's friend and boss splashes water on his face. Peter is rinsing with mouthwash when Evan says, "Tell me that's not blood you just threw up."

As if annoyed, Peter looks at both their reflections in the mirror. He starts to straighten his tie, but decides to leave it be. He sighs before saying, "Not at all. I had some red wine that just didn't agree with me."

Peter uses his fingertips to examine the dark rings that have formed around his eyes, flexing his lids when the focus hazes over for a second.

"Yeah right. Remember who you're talking to. Since when do you drink red wine this early in the morning? You haven't even gone to lunch yet, Pete."

With unexpected hostility, Peter McAllister scowls at the image in the mirror. "Look, mother, I'm fine all right." For a split second, something blazes in Peter's eyes. Then he jokes, "It's just morning sickness, man. Valerie decided to share her pain." His smile isn't returned as hoped, which annoys him even more. It means that there will be more questions.

"Looks like you have developed a bleeding ulcer. They do tend to kill hard heads like yourself, so I'm not buying into that very weak wine story, my brother."

Peter snaps, "I'm not your goddamn brother, or your responsibility, for that matter. So fuck-off, Evan!"

Evan Parker's cold stare in the mirror could have shattered souls. He walks out, but Peter runs him down just as he's about to enter the hallway.

"Hey, Evan, I'm really sorry. I had no right speaking to you that way. Please forgive me. I'm just not my lovable self these days."

After a fleet moment of looking at Peter's outstretched hand, Evan shakes it and says, "You're losing it, Peter, and you look like shit."

Peter McAllister returns to his desk. "I know. I feel like shit," he confesses, while running fingers through his damp hair. He takes several deep breaths and flexes his eyelids.

Evan takes a seat and asks, "What's that on your neck, one of Valerie's hickeys gone bad? Rabies, perhaps?"

Peter doesn't laugh as expected. Self-consciously, he touches the irritation on his neck. As a defense mechanism kicks in, his accent suddenly changes as if possessed by his late Irish, Uncle Clement McAllister, during one of his drunken blathers. "Valerie and I had a silly little dust up in the wee hours of the morn, don't ya know? She just wouldn't stop pestering me, so I ventured outside for a bit of a cool down before my riches turned to rags. And just my accursed luck, a fauckin' bee sent straight from the pit of hell stung me. At five o'clock in the morning, a faucking bee assailed my saintly personage, and for the second time in two months, I might add. I'm asking ya, Jimmy Tom, what the hell's gonna happen next?" He tosses his hands into the air in frustration.

Evan hisses and crosses his index fingers as if warding off bad spirits. "You know, in my vast experience with unforeseen calamities, I've learned to never ever ask that particular question when I'm already having a bad day. Never ask because you'll soon find that every demon in hell has a different answer, my friend. Every demon in hell."

"You're probably right, but it's too late. What's done is done, so I guess we'll find out if your theory holds any basis."

Evan asks, "Does it hurt? Certainly looks that way."

"Not really. It's a little numb to tell the truth. I'd almost forgotten about it."

"Looks infected. Did you treat it, at least?"

Peter says, "Yeah. Val took one look at it and she wasn't upset with me anymore. It actually turned out to be a godsend, but the old man upstairs could have sent a smaller bee to patch things up. That damn stinger was huge. It must have been a bumble bee or something similar. When my wife yanked it out, it hurt much worse than when it went in. I searched for the bee, but I couldn't find it. All I wanted in this world was to smash that bastard into ant food."

Evan hesitates for a second before saying, "I know we've covered this ground before, but you really need to see a doctor. You look as if you haven't slept in weeks. I only say this because I care about you, Peter. As far as I'm concerned, we're like brothers, no matter how much time has passed in absence. At least, that's how I feel. You, however, have been acting crazy almost since the moment I arrived. I mean, is it me? Do you regret the fact that you selected me for this position? What is it?"

"No, of course not," Peter lies. "No way, Evan. I'm just tired. I'll tell you what, I'll let my wife make an appointment for me." By tossing him a bone, Peter slightly offends Evan Parker, who sees the bone coming. Evan decides to drop it and returns to his office, leaving Peter to discover the budget projections on his own.

Doom da-da boom! On Kwani Drive, the drums have long resumed vigil. They are pounding hard, forcing the supernatural breach to answer Peter's question with something unimaginable.

⚔ ⚔

While sitting at a traffic light, Marsha Lawrence checks her lipstick in the rearview mirror of her red BMW. She's only a block away from destination and destiny. Her very red dress is very short. She is wearing no stockings in her red pumps. When the light changes, she peels away in the springtime warmth with no fear of the black and white patrol car. As it cruises by, she pays the officer a wink, a smile, and an enthusiastic wave.

When she pulls into the visitor's parking space at the Federal Building, she raises the top on the convertible and locks it down. Mrs. Lawrence covers her blonde hair with a rather modest silk scarf and gets out of her husband's latest peace offering. Her blue eyes are anonymous behind her two-hundred dollar sunglasses. No purse weighs her down, just a simple shopping bag.

This is the wife of Suitland's Mayor Jack Lawrence, a rather reserved fifty-year-old politician approaching total baldness. Marsha Lawrence is having an affair with bad Boyd Wagner, the Harley riding chief of security at the federal building. He's brutish and manly. And in her well educated opinion, Boyd is ten times better in and out of the sack than her husband, who's mostly prone to missionary style sex.

The two have not seen one another in a week. Boyd left town to attend a conference in Atlanta to discuss new security protocols that might prevent disasters like the 1995 bombing in Oklahoma that claimed well over 100 innocent lives.

As Marsha walks into the lobby, her radar locks onto her sex partner. Boyd is heading for the elevators when she goes through the metal detector. She runs shouting for someone to hold it for her. He does, but someone else enters by the time she gets there. The lovers will stand next to one another in pensive silence, until the other passenger exits on three. They are all over each other when finally alone.

They exchange affections as they descend into the basement. Without any annoying little stops, she playfully wraps a leg about his hip. Boyd knows that his buddy is watching the elevator's security monitor.

He has a hand up her dress, which doesn't travel far to reach her feverish wetness. There are no panties to impede the penetration of his probing fingers and she moans with the pleasure of his hands feeling her, needing her.

When the elevator door finally opens, he carries her down the dimly lit corridor to the room where the mainframes are housed. He locks the door behind them so they will not be disturbed unless they are extremely unlucky.

Having dispensed with the usual foreplay, they reach their first climax only after five minutes of rather strenuous huffing and puffing. Marsha Lawrence is pleased by his quick release, which means that he might not have strayed while away. Even if he has deviated for a one-night stand, the experience obviously hasn't satisfied him.

Parched, Boyd opens the champagne she's brought in the shopping bag. Because sex is such thirsty work, they both drink deeply, despite the bubbles.

They giggle and tease for a while before things begin to get serious again. "Well, Mr. Boyd, I think it's about time for round two," she cooed. "Would you like your most favorite thing?" She purrs like a contented kitten sitting in its master's lap.

Boyd's eyes light up and a sly, blushing smile visits his face. With her dirty little connotation, Marsha sparks the beginning of another raging erection.

They take another swig from the bottle before Marsha gets down on her knees to give him the best of blowjobs, looking into his eyes all the while. She never closes her eyes unless he does. She loves to watch her bad boy squirm. And squirm he does while leaning against one of those large, humming boxes to fully enjoy the unbelievable pleasure she gives.

Boyd's heart pounds like a drum in his chest and ears as Marsha increases her supple strokes. His knees weaken so he reaches back, grasping for purchase on the mainframe's top. His arm knocks over the half-full bottle of champagne, but he makes no attempt to rectify it.

Marsha also moans because the act is just as much of a turn-on for her, maybe even more so. The foreplay feeds that bone-deep pressure, straining the sexual valves to erupt into the sky while the drums are beating in their heaving chests.

Suddenly, as if life depends upon it, Boyd begs, "No, baby, please stop. I want you now. Please, please stop."

He pulls the mayor's wife from the floor by the hair, something she seems to like. After all, her personal philosophy would often question the value of sex without some measure of pain.

Boyd is close to another climax. She could feel his throbbing penis threatening to explode in her mouth, so she obeys. Though she would equally enjoy swallowing his children, the mayor's wife heeds his lust and mounts him where he stands. He's certainly strong enough to hold her up while she grinds against the hardness inside of her shivering body. With their synonymous rhythm growing harder and faster, deeper and deeper they stride, while outside, lightning walks the cloudless sky.

One of the things they enjoy most about making love is their simultaneous orgasms. There's simply no better sex than that. It's hot, forbidden, secretive, and nasty. They pant and moan in ecstasy as Marsha stands on the precipice of a screaming eruption, which she muffles by biting his shoulder hard enough to draw blood.

Together, they shake and vibrate with a heightened sexual energy, joining in a rapture that is truly electric when the champagne makes its lethal connection with the power supply and the metal casing of the mainframe of love. They convulse with the current racing through them before the overload finally trips the fuse box.

The computer's server is destroyed and so are they. Both mouths are agape, but no screams escape them; only smoke. They will be found that way when someone from maintenance comes looking to track down the problem.

At this very moment, the drums cease throbbing, falling silent in the midst of white eyes that seek the blinding sun.

When the lights upstairs fluctuate, Peter looks up from his monitor to face Shanga. "What in the ..."

Sparks fly from his keyboard! The flat screen flashes lime-green, then gray, and goes black. Peter stands much too quickly, causing the blood to rush downward in the tow of gravity, but he refuses to yield.

"Fuck! Jesus H. Christ, what now?" Moments later, Peter McAllister snatches his door open and heads down the hall. He's joined by Evan Parker, whose face is riddled with the same questions.

Confused computer zombies begin to poke their heads out of their cubbyholes with blank stares and their shoulders raised to question. Without warning, they have been torn away from the Pentium God and it's simply traumatic for some. A quarter of them were surfing the Internet anyway, toying with e-mails that had nothing to do with work.

The entire system has shut down on their floor, bringing those who were working to an abrupt halt. Many of them will eventually ask themselves, "Why am I upset, isn't this is a good thing?"

When the fire alarm starts to ring, the police and fire departments are alerted automatically. The building is evacuated by stairwell. Mere moments later, media personnel are practically running one another down to get a story.

Because they are reminded of Oklahoma City 1995, bedlam breaks out in constricted stairwells. A viral panic grows rampant among these normally peaceful and well-organized people. These frightened U.S. Government employees exit the building only to stare back at it from a safe distance, waiting for the building to collapse after a loud noise.

A senseless act of terrorism is everyone's first thought. They soon downgrade speculations to a surprise drill. It becomes some practical joker's idea of fun, until the coroner shows up and two people are brought out in body bags. For the media, this turns out to be a juicy story after all. It is an absolute scandal.

Standing beneath the noonday sun, the government employees raise their hands to shield their eyes from its brightness, while exchanging bits of gossip or guesses as to who has been murdered inside the basement.

Peter McAllister feels a stab of pain in his temples and chest. He doubles over from a new wave of nausea while sweat pours from him. Someone has just told him that the only system to sustain any real damage in the tragic affair is that of the Census Bureau.

Disaster looms in Peter's mind. With the data transfer scheduled for the very next day, his plans are seared, not to mention the possible loss of decades of information. That is not really an immediate concern. There are now backups and archival records of almost everything at alternate locations.

He faces red tape to no foreseeable end. Rerouting the transfer program to the Silver Springs facility will be too great a risk with the hacker problems they have experienced over there. This mess could not have come at a worse time, but he accepts that it's not impossible to deal with.

Peter will simply have to kill two birds with one stone by retrieving the hard data and checking on Barrette's condition in one trip to Indiana. It would be a far better thing to deal with both problems away from Suitland. He'll be able to get Holt some help, if necessary.

If his counterpart has truly gone over the deep end, however, Peter will have no choice but to call Vincent Sterne. Of course, he knows all too well what Sterne is capable of doing while protecting their almighty secret.

McAllister's concern over Holt's mental deterioration is growing, so he worries about the man's safety. Holt will conveniently disappear if he is really cracked beyond repair, and Peter will have to be the one to make the fatal call. When he asked what could happen next, he had no idea that the answer would be this severe. "Every demon in hell," he mutters in disgust.

Evan Parker tries to convince Peter to go home when they are finally allowed to enter the building, but he refuses. Parker should have expected as much.

The building's superintendent, Carl Little, enters Peter's office while Parker is present. While sucking on the unlighted stump of a cigar, Carl gruff voice sounds the horns of doom when he says, "Mr. McAllister, I'm sorry to report that the overload has nearly fried your entire system. It's a wonder nothing else caught fire besides a few keyboards or Mr. and Mrs. Slap and Tickle's hair. Can you believe that crap?"

Evan asks, "Is it true that she's Mayor Lawrence's wife?"

Carl nods to affirm the suspicion. "Oh yeah. It was her alright."

Peter slouches, grasping his aching head. He says, "That's what the police seem to think. Her car was found in the parking lot. Was her hair really smoking, Carl?"

With a grunt, devoid of human remorse, Carl says, "You bet. I was the first person to go down there. I guess they really got off on getting it on in strange places, if you know what I mean. When I opened the door, the first thing I saw and smelled was her hair smoking. They had to peel Boyd's body off your server and she was still wrapped around him. To die like that, with a stiff cock up that pretty little ass. What a way to go." The giggling grunt that escapes the tactless New Yorker is curtailed by the disapproving glares of both Mr. McAllister and the new guy.

Rather impatiently, Peter growls, "Thanks, Carl. Is that all of the bad news, or is there more?"

Carl Little seems to enjoy being the bearer of bad tidings; evident in the sly little smile that cracks his lips. "No. That's basically it, except for the fact that you're niche in the Department of Commerce is officially out of business.

At least here, anyways. Now, I'm no computer genius, but me and my crew went sniffing at all of the units on this floor, and I'd say that more than half were tied-in when the two lovebirds got themselves hard-boiled. Yours and most of the others are cooked well done. If I were you, I'd requisition immediate replacements. Some of them may be salvageable, but they'll have to be sent back to the factory to be sure. And we all know how the government feels about fixing things."

"Oh my God!" Peter shrieks. "Shit me straight to hell!"

"Of course, you must know that there's going to be a big stink about this. And not only because she was the mayor's darling little wife," Carl adds.

"What do you mean?" asks Evan.

"Well, for the life of me, I can't figure out why the circuit breaker didn't trip the instant the juice was shot to the box. Nor do I know why your desktop units didn't just shut themselves down, as I understand they're supposed to do during a power surge. Every safeguard failed I tell ya, every single one. There must have been at least three that didn't perform, and it cost two people their lives. Because of it, there's a possibility that this entire building may be decommissioned."

Carl falls into silent reflection, which holds no particular remorse for the victims just mentioned. He's only thinking about circuitry, wiring, and shady electrical contractors who take shortcuts.

"Why?" asked Peter. "How could something like this happen?"

"Well, I haven't got the slightest idea. I mean, you don't call them safeguards unless they are safety tested. Right? It's simply beyond me. Well, I guess you two may as well close up shop and take your pretty little wives to some tropical island paradise. Let someone who's qualified come in and do his thing. It may take the electrical engineers at least a week or two to fully investigate the extent of the damage and submit a safety assessment for this facility, so there is very little you can do about it. Dispersing your department's personnel to other facilities like Silver Springs is your best bet. It's been a real pleasure, gentlemen."

Carl feels pretty important when he leaves. He experienced quite a rush while dictating doom and gloom to the bigwigs.

With a sigh, Evan Parker observes, "A real pleasure? He's a piece of work, that one."

Peter adds, "That man is a pig. How can he chew on that filthy looking thing all day long?"

"He is a pig at that, but he does have a point. While we're down and out, this may be a good time for you to take that break. Just let go."

"I can't right now. Maybe after I come back from Indiana. Maybe."

"Why Indiana?"

Peter is annoyed. "I'll have to go out there to retrieve all the data from Barry myself so we can make our new deadlines. We're scheduled to transfer the 2000 finals tomorrow morning, remember? Now this mess. Fuck!" As if to question some higher power, he tosses his hands up in frustration.

Parker suggests, "You don't have to do that. We can just have things rerouted to Silver Springs. Or, if you don't trust that, use a courier. Hell, I can take care of the arrangements myself. I can even go to Indiana for you. I really wouldn't mind."

Peter barks, "No. I have to do it myself. I'm the director here, it's my job!"

In retaliation, this time Evan snaps, "All right. You do what the fuck you want as far as your job goes, Mr. McAllister. Just know this one thing, I'm officially through taking your goddamn verbal abuse. You can stow that shit until little Peter is born, since you insist on talking to me like a motherfucking child. You got me, my brotha?" Fire burns in Evan Parker's eyes, which he refuses to avert.

"Evan, I'm sorry I yelled," Peter says in retreat.

Standing to leave, looking Peter directly in the eyes, Evan smirks. He says, "Mother-fuck-you, Peter! That just doesn't cut it anymore, Jack. You've been highly irrational and increasingly irritable lately. You need some serious help with whatever the fuck is your problem. I'm out of here. There are a number of fertilizer companies that will gladly take the shit you apparently love to shovel, but not me. Not anymore because there's only so much fucking shit one fly can eat!"

He walks out, slamming the door.

Looking directly at Shanga, Peter McAllister asks, "What the hell are you looking at?" As he rises to leave, he slams his secret liquor drawer. When it bangs shut, the God of War statuette topples to the floor where it cracks down the middle of its skull. Peter just stares as its blood seeps from the wound and runs toward his feet. He blinks and the blood is gone. McAllister shivers. He refuses to pick it up because that will require physical contact. He simply cannot abide that. After another sudden wave of nausea runs its course, Peter decides to leave. The room seems so cold.

The drums will beat heavily throughout the night, for within their dark harmony the lines have already been drawn. Peter McAllister and Evan Parker are at odds. Doom da-da boom!

CHAPTER 21

CONFESSIONS OF SHAME

"How did it happen, Melissa? I mean, were there any warning signs at all?"

Melissa Parker glances at Valerie McAllister, deciding that she can be trusted with something so personal. "Hmm," she says with a moment's hesitation. "Let's see. Where exactly should I begin this terrible tale?"

"I'm sorry. You really don't have to go there if it is too painful. I must apologize because I realize that I'm displaying my rather macabre sense of curiosity. I suppose it does tend to get the better of me at times," Valerie says with genuine regret. It is only now that Melissa Parker truly hears her unfettered British accent. It somehow makes her seem more attractive; more trustworthy in some small way. Curious.

"It's okay. The ordeal is behind us now and, as you can see, there are happy endings."

Trying not to seem so intense, Valerie takes another bite and a sip of tea. "This chewy is really delicious. It's going to be my new pregnancy food, so you must share the recipe."

"Why thank you. However, it's actually Madeline's recipe and she's been holding out on me. We may just have to crack that tough nut together."

"Just name the time and the angle of attack, and I'll have your back, Melissa. Count on it." They hold hands and chuckle.

Melissa places her cup and saucer on the coffee table, sitting back with a long and thoughtful sigh. She gazes at the stand she purchased for Kinzana's journal and says, "It all started several months ago. I was still teaching elementary students and my husband was secure at the University of South Carolina. One ordinary night over dinner, he told me about a sophomore that seemed to have developed a king-sized crush on him. I know what you're thinking, but I took it in stride. These things tend to happen in the teaching profession. God knows I was stricken with my share of crushes when I was a student." She pauses before saying, "But neither of us had any idea just how far it would go, or how much our lives would be impacted by what was never really a crush at all."

"Apparently things got a lot worse before getting better," Valerie interjects.

"Much worse, believe me. The student was a spoiled little rich girl, used to getting her way. She probably went to U.S.C. thinking that college would be a breeze and spent her time partying instead of studying. Her grade point average reflected it. Anyway, she tried to sway my husband by offering sexual favors. Evan put her in her place, of course, but she was facing academic probation and daddy dearest was breathing down her neck."

Valerie's eyes become mere slits when she says, "I knew girls like that in college and high school. Some of them succeeded by working their way through half of the male faculty by the end of their senior year. Shit like that used to burn me up."

"I know what you mean." Melissa's brief smile is more like a grimace. "This girl, however, turned out to be a fatal attraction. I mean the genuine article. She started spreading nasty rumors about my husband. Of course, I never really believed any of that stuff, but it did begin to put a strain on things." Melissa pauses, but with a deep sigh that Valerie feels. She touches Melissa's hand to see that she is all right. "And here is where the hammer drives the nail into the wood. I was discussing the importance of social awareness with my fifth-graders, citing television news programs and newspapers as the most popular means of keeping up with current events, even though the internet was bound to surpass both in the future. Imagine my surprise when I turned on the midday report and saw that little bimbo with torn clothes and running mascara, crying rape no less. My husband was being forced into a police car in handcuffs for all the world to see. To make things worse, my kids recognized Evan. He was once kind enough to speak to my classes during career week and obviously made an impression."

"Christ. I would have died right there and then. You must have been absolutely mortified."

"It wasn't pretty, that's for sure. I just froze, couldn't even turn the television off. The student was hospitalized and given a rape examination, the whole nine yards. They were positive that she was telling the truth and the media was playing it for all it was worth. I never actually told Evan this, but I had begun to doubt him. I believe he suspected as much, but it would kill him to know for sure. To this day, he won't talk about that aspect of it all."

"Please don't leave me hanging. It was all just a lie, correct?"

"A monstrous lie. One which dragged on when the lab claimed to have lost the semen sample and Evan's DNA, so he was subjected to that humiliation all over again. To make things worse, the university refused to back my husband publicly because they had already begun termination proceedings behind his back. After all those years, they just abandoned Evan, which gave that little bitch even more credibility. Two women in the college's administration had been raped or molested themselves, so they just kept that pot stirring. When I discovered that I was pregnant, the situation turned a moment of joy into pure vinegar. This foul, loathsome, cruel little voice in the back of my mind kept saying that I was possibly pregnant for a rapist. I hated myself for feeling that way, and I'm afraid that it had begun to show despite my best efforts. I should have known better. Anyway, as you can imagine, Evan was furious and growing more so by the day. By the hour. By the minute."

"Who wouldn't be upset?" Valerie asks.

"Yes, but I...I just wasn't there for him the way I should have been. Not really. It was most evident in the way I bristled or seemed to shrink away whenever he tried to touch me as an expression of his need for intimacy. I basically shunned any physical contact. I'll never forgive myself for that and I don't think he would either. I believe that's why he doesn't really want to know for sure. I've tried several times to bring it up to bare my soul and ask his forgiveness, but he won't allow conversation to go there."

"I understand, but you must forgive yourself for being human, Melissa. Much greater sins have been committed between men and women to rend families apart in this world," Valerie McAllister offers. "Any woman in your position would have doubts in the midst of such horrific turmoil. We are none of us, impervious to a media bombardment of innuendo and supposition."

"Up until that time, I'd never had problems with things like blood pressure or hypertension. The whole scene was taking a toll on my health as well as my marriage. One stormy night, Evan and I had an awful argument. Who knows what it was really about now. I suppose he walked out on me because that was about as close as we'd come to the unspoken truth of whether or not I believed in his innocence. Evan left in that nasty weather without a raincoat or umbrella, and it was raining cats and litter boxes. We lived near campus, so I had an idea that was where he'd gone to clear his head. It was the one place he was forbidden to go. All of a sudden, a very concerned co-worker called to ask if I was watching the news.

I usually watched, but not then. When she told me not to turn on the television set, I simply could not resist."

"Dear Lord. What happened?" Valerie asks on pins and needles, hanging on every syllable emanating from Melissa's lips.

"God only knows how much I truly wish I had listened to Beverly's warning. But there she was, hanging from the rooftop of the Russell House. The building is at the heart of the South Carolina campus, and she was deader than two Abraham Lincolns." Valerie clutches her chest. "Someone claimed to have seen a dark figure running away from the scene. When Evan was recognized in the crowd, he was arrested as a trespasser and then charged under suspicion of murder."

Valerie winces. Her British accent fully resurrects when she asks, "Oh my sweet Lord, whatever did you do?"

"That's when I almost miscarried. I got sick and dizzy. I felt as if the floor just...it just disappeared from beneath me. My blood pressure was over the top, so I fainted. Luckily, my co-worker was still on the phone, so she heard it and myself hitting the floor."

Valerie touches her hand, again. "Oh my God."

"Beverly called 911. When the firefighters and ambulance finally arrived, they could see me through the window, lying on the floor. All of the doors were locked, so they had to break in. I was bleeding like a stuck pig, as they say. When I finally came around, I was in agony. All I could think about was my baby, my poor husband, and..."

"What? Don't stop now."

"...the lightning," Melissa continues. "It was so intense that every stroke seemed to hurt my eyes. Even with my eyelids closed, it seemed to pierce my entire body."

Melissa Parker thinks briefly of the strange woman that she must have imagined. The stranger stood over her before the ambulance arrived with something that looked like the branch of a shrub. Melissa recalls having a very bitter taste in her mouth. She recalls the stranger's deeply accented voice, oddly familiar at the time, but the words were beyond comprehension. Melissa felt...

She shivers as a single tear spills from her eyes. "I was so afraid, and I have never felt so alone in my entire life," Melissa whimpers on the verge, but she soon regains her composure to trudge on. "As it turned out, there was someone else at the scene when the young woman died, but it was not Evan."

"Who was it, Melissa?" Valerie asks while resisting the urge to drive a freshly polished fingernail between her teeth.

Melissa manages a smile, signifying a happier turn of events. She wipes the tears from her eyes and says, "It was the girl's boyfriend. The very same boyfriend who unknowingly donated the bruises during rough sex, and the semen sample that the incompetent lab claimed to have lost. He claimed to have no idea what she was up to when she accused Evan of rape. The angry young man even attacked my husband while he was cuffed. He truly believed her. When the truth finally came out between them, she convinced him to keep quiet. The young man had suddenly found himself caught up in this ugly little melodrama. Also, he had publically and physically attacked my husband while in police custody, for which he should have been arrested on the spot. When it finally started sinking in that the result of the DNA testing was bound to prove that she had lied, he wanted no part of it. Especially, after her rich father had taken up such a publically vocal crusade against my husband. Realizing that she'd backed herself into a corner and time was running out, she chose to commit suicide. Instead of facing the truth, she got sloshed on liquor and pills that night, went to the roof of the Russell House and tied a chain around her neck. Her boyfriend found her suicide note and went looking for her. The kid nearly grabbed her before she jumped, but he was a second too late. The young man freaked and ran away when someone looked up and screamed. He eventually gave the suicide note to the police. The letter exonerated my husband and we left Columbia,

South Carolina for good when I got out of the hospital. Before then, however, Evan shoved the university administration's apologies up their asses with reckless abandon. I've never seen him so cold... so vengeful. His lawyer sued everyone involved in his smear campaign, including two television news networks for neglecting to use the words 'alleged rapist'. Evan never really has to work again, if that is what he chooses. He sued everyone, and won each defamation case without long fought battles. He made them all pay, everyone. All except for, Dustin, the young man who had beaten him while he was helpless in those handcuffs. Although his father warned him to stay away from us, his mother helped him secretly. She brought the young man to seek Evan out, both apologizing with tears in their eyes. My husband placed his arms around the distraught kid and forgave him every trespass. I think that single act of contrition reminded him of who he really was. That brief, but very powerful moment of compassion healed him, and probably saved our marriage as well. And well, Valerie McAllister, here we are."

"Wow. That's some story, Melissa. Thank God the young lady still had that ounce of decency left inside before she died. I must give you the utmost credit. I probably would have ended up in the boobyhatch before all was said and done."

Melissa Parker giggles before asking, "What about you guys? It took so long for me to get pregnant, I really wondered if I was barren, but what's you reason for waiting to have a child?"

Valerie thumbs through her own list of regrets in regard to the question.

"Hmm. Our thriving careers, respectively, I suppose. I had several engaging business interests that required just as much of me as Peter's career at the bureau demanded of him. In many regards, it just didn't seem so important to us until recently. We were talking one night over supper and we both asked where has the time gone. All of a sudden we both concluded that something was missing from our lives, something long overdue." She caresses her tummy and smiles. "As you said only a moment ago, 'and here we are.'"

"I'm happy for you."

"Thanks. And I you. I can't believe it really took this long to realize why I was working so tirelessly at the law firm. I partnered with some very astute attorneys, established my dominant place at the top of the hierarchy, and took an extended leave of absence. I wonder, do you suppose my lack of paternal desire will make me a bad mother?"

"Oh. Of course not, Valerie. Some people tend to get so wrapped up in their careers and desire to succeed that they lose sight of other important issues. And I suppose when you are in the thick of it, the hustle and bustle of the daily grind, things tend to become a distant echo of a basic instinct. Meanwhile, others, like myself, hear it resoundingly because it seems so elusive."

"Wow. Now that was an absolutely poetic reminder that I had completely forgotten that I was a woman, and capable of bringing life into the world."

They giggle, girlishly.

A car pulls into the garage.

It isn't until Evan throws his briefcase to the floor that he realizes Valerie McAllister is there. He wishes that he'd found some sudden inspiration to stay in the garage.

After taking delivery of a new car this morning, Valerie had invited Melissa to lunch. When she arrived, they just started talking and never actually left.

Immediately after an exchange of tense greetings, Melissa asks, "Evan, what's wrong? And please don't say, 'nothing, Mel.'"

"Nothing, Melissa. I'm fine." His eyes do that trick, seeking Valerie for an uncontrolled instant.

Valerie stands and says, "It's Peter, isn't it? Please don't deny it. I saw that look, Evan. Level with me. Please." Her eyes admonish him as well.

"I'd rather not talk about it right now," he says, looking away.

"What's the matter, baby?" Melissa asks as she reaches up to loosen Evan's tie because he looks like he's about to pop.

Valerie is worried. She approaches and says, "For the love of God, please tell me what happened today."

"We had a nasty altercation, I guess you'd say. Not a fistfight, but I wanted to bust his ass so bad I could almost taste it. Some very harsh words were exchanged. That's all."

"But why, Evan? You two have been getting along famously, what's changed?" Valerie McAllister probes.

"Peter's sick and refuses to seek help. I spoke to him as you asked, but he's being extremely unreasonable. I can't figure out what's eating him. Maybe it was a mistake for us to come here. I get the feeling that he regrets hiring me. I'm beginning to wonder."

Valerie retreats toward the window where she gazes at the front lawn and weeps quietly. When Melissa moves to her side, Valerie McAllister admits, "I don't know what's happening to him. Peter's always had bouts with insomnia and bad dreams. Lately, they seem so much worse. His nightmares must be extremely violent. He screams and thrashes about as if he's being strangled or something. Now, when he can sleep, it's become a nightly occurrence. You should know that this all started long before you came here, Evan. Please don't blame yourself."

Holding his ground in the living room's entrance, Evan asks, "Does he ever tell you what those dreams are about, Valerie?"

"Never. I've tried to pry it out of him, but it only makes him angry. It seems as though Peter is holding the weight of the world on his shoulders, and refuses to share his problems. It's almost as if he's hiding some deep, dark secret from me. Maybe something from his past. I don't know."

"That must be hard on you. Why won't he seek professional help?" Melissa asks while gently stroking Valerie's shoulder.

"I begged him to do just that. You know, I used to think that Peter was having an affair so whenever his thrashing about woke me up, I'd listen for her name. Sometimes, I'd even ask him questions in his sleep. I know that sounds pathetic," Valerie says, feeling great shame for having made such a personal and degrading confession.

"Not at all," Evan says as he draws closer. He empathizes, having gained an understanding of what she must be going through.

Valerie snips, "Please. It's pathetic and we all know it. There's really no need to patronize me, Evan, but I appreciate the effort to make me feel better about myself."

Melissa says, "You shouldn't take it that way. He's just a man, after all." No one smiles, as hoped.

"I'm sorry," Valerie says. "I can never make any sense of what he's mumbling in his sleep. I do know that he sometimes dreams about his former boss at the Census Bureau. In fact, Peter calls his name quite frequently."

"You mean Cecil?" Evan asks. "But why would Peter have nightmares about Cecil Bridges?"

"I don't know. I used to believe that Peter really cared about the man and misses his guidance. I'm now convinced that my husband has developed a full-blown guilt complex over assuming Cecil's position, and that it has been festering inside him for years. It seems possible, I suppose. You probably know that Peter was quite ill at the time of Cecil's funeral, which prevented him from attending. I suppose he never really got the chance to say goodbye because the family had the body buried in South Carolina."

"Maybe. I don't know. I can't offer you any constructive answers without Peter's cooperation," Evan admits. "I wish I could help, but we seem to be at an impasse."

"I met him a long time ago, when Peter and I first started dating. Mr. Bridges seemed like a very nice man. Peter used to be full of life back then. He was so funny with his voices and those silly impersonations of people in his family, you know. But now, he's very moody and distant, and he's always nauseous." She pauses and inhales deeply. "My husband looks," Valerie sobs, "...he looks so...so haunted." She seeks the shoulder of her newfound friend and ally, weeping guiltlessly. However, this display is not without its graces.

When Melissa searches Evan's eyes, he could almost feel Valerie's sadness, as if it's passing through his wife by their visual link. However, Melissa sees in him no solutions, no answers.

Under the pressure of her gaze, Evan hastens to suggest, "Well, maybe, we can all go on vacation together. The four of us can just fly away."

Although money is no issue, Evan couldn't possibly take a vacation after only three months of employment, but it is the positive thought that matters. Not knowing that the vacation horse has already been run into the ground and beaten to death, Melissa thinks it a start.

"That sounds like a terrific idea, Val. Why don't you run it by your husband tonight? If he doesn't agree, we'll just make the reservations anyway. I'm sure that he wouldn't let you leave him behind. You aren't that big yet, a bikini will still look good on you. He'll change his mind, you'll see."

Melissa's words are medicine to her, the tonic of hope. Somewhat encouraged, Valerie says, "You may be right. I'll give it another try." Her eyes have assumed an unmistakable measure of shy humility. "Thanks, both you guys. I really hate dumping all of this crap at your doorstep. Please forgive me."

Evan moves closer and they hug, briefly. After purging what she's never confessed to another soul, Valerie McAllister leaves their home feeling better. She chooses to remain hopeful because she and her husband desperately need to get away. Evan's ghastly news about the fried computers is almost welcomed. If Peter still refuses to get away from it all, she'll take a trip without him. For a mere instant, she thinks about making it permanent, but she shakes her head to banish the thought. This has been a day of tears for her and for her new friend. The heartfelt sharing of which often bridges ironclad bonds that are rarely broken.

Later, after Peter explains the horrors of his day, Valerie seizes the opportunity to make the vacation pitch. After plying Peter with Kidd gloves, he finally agrees to take time off. He promises to take a vacation right after his return from Indiana. They toss vacation spots into the air, but the final decision is Valerie's. As if heavy clouds have suddenly parted after days of chilling rain, hope springs from the drenched earth like seedlings to sunshine. All seems well at the McAllister household.

In case there is some act of God that might prevent his return according to schedule, Valerie helps Peter to pack an overnight bag. They enjoy a light supper and retire for the evening.

CHAPTER 22
NIGHTMARE

Somewhere in the heart of this black night, Kaleem Kinzana converses with spirits that tell him much. Somewhere in the depth of darkness, Nimjara Kinzara works his magic to the beat of the Rada and the Conga drums. His woman visited the McAllister home on the previous night, lurking in the shadows until the White man came outside in a moment of anger. That was when she sent the tainted thorn of a Mobeku Tree flying at him. Once again, Peter was touched by the magic dust, as had Barrette Holt so many times before. With the final dosage administered, Nimjara seeks to rule Peter's soul by shrouding his life in a velveteen cloak of gloom. The fact that Peter's innocent wife will have to suffer with him makes no difference. It is the will of Damballah.

Dark, angry clouds begin to fill this night sky. Boom da-da doom, boom da-da doom, boom da-da doom! The Rada and the Conga drums pound as lightning flashes across a sunless sky.

Peter McAllister and his wife lay spread eagle. Their eyes open to the rhythmic pulse of drums that will now mingle with their startled heartbeats.

Peter hears a child crying as he looks at Valerie, who lays next to him com-pletely naked. Her ripened stomach, full of new life, moves up and down with her panicked breath. To his dismay, Tarantulas now stand poised on each of their extended limbs. The arachnids hold positions on each of their ankles and wrists. They are motionless with their half-inch fangs glistening in intermittent bursts of light. They seem to be tied down by invisible tethers. Valerie's struggle to be free is useless.

With some of them crawling about on the satin sheets, one of Peter's secret fiends paws at his naked rib cage. Feeling every hair of its jointed body, he can only watch as it climbs to his chest. Once there, the creature stands poised between Peter's heaving lungs with its furry gloves raised to challenge him. The terrified man is powerless.

When Peter's paralysis breaks, he cries, "What's happening? Oh Jesus, what the hell is going on here?"

At first, the thunder drowns out Valerie's voice. Her mouth seems to move silently before him. When he can finally hear, she is pleading for help that he cannot give.

Again, from somewhere deep within the vibrant darkness that tor-tured baby begins to scream. This is the sound of ghetto children, whose crack-addled parents have left them in filthy diapers. It is the sound of naked kids that haven't eaten in days, with no end to hunger in sight—the sound of fever and helpless, infantile terror.

"Please help me, Peter. Help our baby. They want to eat my son!" Valerie's eyes begin to flutter and she shrieks, "It hurts. Oh God, it hurts!"

While Valerie writhes in pain, Peter looks at her stomach, which moves inconsistently with her breathing. It seems as if the child inside is pushing against the inner walls of her womb, trying to claw its way out.

Another Tarantula scales the dampened locks of Peter's head. He fran-tically tries to dislodge its grip by thrashing back and forth, but it clings relentlessly.

"What the fuck is this?" Peter repeats to no one in particular. He feels the arachnid's forelegs scraping at his sweaty forehead as the one on his chest begins to bounce and threaten. Within the harried confines of his mind, its

sound shreds what little resolve Peter still has, for nothing so small should ever make so loud a sound.

Lightning flashes. Immediately, thereafter, thunder shakes the McAllister home to its very foundation. The tree outside their bedroom window falls, crashing to the yard in flames. The drums—beating—beating faster.

Valerie's fruitless struggle continues, but there is no help for her. When the lightning flashes again, her eyes widen. She peers beyond her husband, screaming from the sudden appearance of her newest terror.

Peter slowly follows her frightened gaze to the left. When the lightning comes again, he discerns the painted face of a tall, muscular African man. Across his broad shoulders and groin, he wears the skin of dead predators. From his neck, there gleams a necklace of fangs, claws, and what looks like tiny, shriveled fingers! It hangs loosely, clattering as it swings freely across his sweating, hairless chest.

He is Nimjara Kinzara, and from his right hand protrudes the grayish green head of a snake that has coiled the entire length of its body around his wrist and forearm. Dendroaspis polylepsis, tightly wrapped and hissing. Its metallic eyes are as black as an oceanic cavern.

Both that child and its mother scream. When the lightning drenches the bedroom again, the couple can see the whites of Nimjara's insane eyes. In their centers, stones of coal scowl back at them with a frigid, unyielding glare.

This face has to be something born within the horrid wastelands of humanity, from some motherless hole in the molten earth. He smiles a terrible smile, for his teeth are razors in the flashes of light. Fresh blood now drips from his lips.

Though fearing for their lives, Peter demands, "Who are you? What is the meaning of this?" He receives no immediate answers from the grinning intruder to his home and sanctuary.

Nimjara now sniffs the air with his wide nostrils flaring. His gate seems effortless in the sight of gravity when he moves toward Valerie's side of the bed.

The drums! Boom da-da doom! The drums wail for them.

When the lightning strikes again, the room is awash with brilliant blue. In this light, the helpless couple on the bed realizes that the voodoo man is not alone. They now see strange men beating the drums in each corner of their bedroom. Their faces are ashen gray, and their eyes seem to have no pupils.

Now even harsher cries pierce the turbulent air. The unborn child is screaming more fiercely, as if seeing through its mother's terrified eyes. Its shrill demand for protection shreds Valerie's heart because she cannot comply.

"Stay away!" she bellows. "Get away from me!"

When the dark man uses the hand with the snake to caress Valerie's stomach, it hisses, puffing its head. The inside of its mouth is an immaculate black, seeming to possess the ability to absorb all light. Its lower jaw flexes once before striking her stomach with its venomous fangs! Valerie and Peter can do nothing as the Black Mamba sinks those deadly syringes into her indefensible gut.

Between the towers of lightning, a woman materializes from the shadows as if she's walked through a blackened doorway from another world. Her hands are cupped at the base of an earthen bowl. From it, the voodoo man takes the severed foot of a chicken that drips coagulating blood. As he draws it from the bowl, Nimjara stares directly into Peter's terror-stricken eyes, feeling nothing for his pleading anxieties.

Valerie has fallen silent, convulsing violently, foaming at the mouth as if possessed by savage demons. Her breathing is severely labored as the Black Mamba's lethal venom attacks her respiratory and nervous systems.

Nimjara goes on to paint mysterious symbols upon Valerie's swollen belly. His wild eyes dance as he snarls, "Blood for blood spilled. Blood for blood that is yet to be spilled upon the earth. For your actions in this terrible thing, angry spirits shall drink the life that flows through this child's veins. And I, Peter McAllister..." He takes a large knife from a little boy that emerges from the shadows. "...will eat your child without salt!"

Nimjara's laughter rakes across Peter's mind like an ice floe. It's a sound that would haunt the mind of even the most analytical person, one who would never believe in such things. His laughter mingles with the thunder, the lightning, and the rhythm of drums that can be beaten no faster.

Without warning, Nimjara raises the knife and brings it down in a vicious arch! Peter and the child scream, but Valerie's head turns toward him in a silenced lull. Her glazed eyes see nothing as a steady stream of bloody froth flows from her purple lips onto their bed sheets.

In the back of his mind, Peter just knows that this is the part of the bad dream where he is supposed to scream himself awake. Even though his wife lies next to him with a dead stare, suffocating from the poison and bleeding to death from a huge gash, he has not awakened.

Peter's cries continue as the voodoo man slowly licks the long blade and turns the knife over. He sees its razor sharpness glistening as if it has a living desire for more blood. The blade is still upturned when Nimjara slides the large knife between Valerie's separated legs, thrusting it mercilessly into her womb!

Lightning flashes and the crashing thunder rolls. The noise of which could not drown out that sickening, wet, slicing sound as the voodoo man saws back and forth, forcing the blade upward through Valerie's stomach. She offers no protest as the blade splits her navel in two.

There is so much blood. Like a living shadow, its spreads across the sheets beneath the hairy feet of the Tarantulas. Meanwhile, the baby's cries diminish and die away completely. Peter weeps, wanting badly to awaken.

The voodoo man places the knife beside Valerie before reaching into her with his free hand. The foul odors of bowel and urine grow as thick as gasoline in the room. Over the storm, Peter can hear a revolting splatter as several feet of his wife's intestines slither onto the bed. Now, that man yanks his unborn child from its mother's womb by the foot!

Nimjara holds Peter's bloody child aloft, laughing as he places the hand with the snake closer to the dead infant, whose eyes and mouth are agape. The reptile flicks its forked tongue as if to taste the skin slicked with blood and amniotic fluids.

"Oh God, no. No!" Peter's voice is defeated when huge worms wriggle out of the baby's mouth and nostrils. They hang in midair for an instant, before falling into the open wound in his wife's lifeless body. Peter continues to whimper as the voodoo man turns the child to ascertain its sex.

The lightning, the thunder, and the drums are relentlessly driven by something that science would fail to explain to anyone.

The voodoo man grins when he says, "It's a boy, papa!" Then he opens his mouth wide to rip the child's penis and scrotum away with his razor teeth, proceeding to eat the child's genitalia as if most sumptuous.

"Oh God," Peter whimpers in horror only a fraction of a second before spraying puke onto his silk underwear.

That quiet woman now produces a large map of America. Nimjara turns and spits, spraying it with a red stain that quickly runs to its lower edge. When he turns to face Peter McAllister, his eyes are as white as polished ivory.

Nimjara says, "Call on God if you will, but you have sinned against your brothers, White man. Yet, your deeds will not go unpunished long beyond this crimson night. You and yours will be repeatedly dashed against the rocky shores, and it shall make you so tender, for we will eat you all with no need for salt!"

"God, help me. Why is this happening to us?" Peter howls. He unclenches his straining fists where the five-hundred pound spiders refuse to relinquish their unearthly grasp.

"Remember that man who would span the turbulent waters betwixt ebony souls and their true destinies? In fire, he was consumed. However, he was but one. Now, Peter McAllister, we are many!"

"What are you talking about?" Peter cries. Recognizing the wordplay, Peter already knows that Bridges once tried to span very turbulent waters and he was murdered for it.

"Even now, in this place—on this plane of existence—you would deny truth, but you will soon yield to our awesome power and all that is within it to do the greatest evils unto you. Even if you do not yield, you will be crushed beneath the angered waves of this black tide!"

Nimjara tosses the infant's ravaged corpse onto Peter's stomach, laughing a haunted mockery that augments Peter's horror. The spiders begin to squeal. They stab into his flesh. Blood runs from his forehead into his eyes.

Blood springs from his neck where the spider's fangs sink into his pulsing blood vessels.

When the drums at the end of Kwani Drive cease to throb, the voodoo man fades with the very next stroke of lightning.

By 7:00 in the morning, the rain has stopped. The air is clean and fresh. Birds are singing while Valerie McAllister shouts, "Peter, it's okay. You're just having a bad dream. It's just a dream. Calm down."

Her husband is hyperventilating. His wild eyes are darting about in their sockets while he thrashes and slaps at things that are no longer there. It seems that he cannot see the face of his loving wife merely inches from his own. She holds his feverish cheeks firmly in her hands. His side of the bed is soaking wet.

As Peter says, "Huh? What?" spittle slobbers over his lips to run down his sweaty chin.

When he finally focuses, he is ever so glad to see Valerie unharmed. He looks at her face and then his eyes race to her stomach, which he touches as if he's found his long lost puppy.

"Thank heaven you're okay. It was just a dream, just a fucking dream." He looks away and nearly smiles, but his rebellious lips fight the gesture.

"It was about me? What happened to me in your dream, Peter?" she asks.

He runs his trembling fingers through his wet hair and whispers, "It was nothing, sweetheart. It's not important, really." Valerie knows better than to push, so she kisses him gently and climbs out of bed. "Where are you going?" he asks. "You never get up this early."

"Well, it's seven o'clock. I'm going to take a quick shower. I feel so sticky. I'm going to make breakfast while you shower and shave, unless you'd rather join me in a noble effort to conserve the planet's water supply," she says with a halfhearted smile.

Peter doesn't want to take a shower with his wife, but he chooses not to hurt her feelings. "Sure, but you don't have to go through all the trouble of breakfast."

"It's no trouble, and I'm going to the airport to see you off."

"Oh, Valerie, you really don't have to do that," he protests, but not too strongly. At least she isn't suggesting that she make the trip to Indiana with him.

"I know. I want to do this, and I plan to be there when you return." Valerie turns on the shower and brushes her teeth before slipping out of the white granny that she likes to sleep in. Though it isn't very sexy, it's extremely comfortable. Their bathroom always steams up quickly, so she turns on the exhaust fan to clear the mirror by the time she showers.

She teases, "Honey, are you coming, or don't you think you can stomach seeing your pregnant wife in an unabashed state of nakedness so early in the morning? Is there a problem, mister?" When the steam finally begins to clear, Valerie can see her grin in the mirror.

"I'm on my way," he groans, forcing reluctant muscles to propel him out of bed.

Her hair is up when she sticks her head out to say, "I didn't hear a word you said."

"I'm coming, mom." Peter's eyes suddenly grow wide and his breath retreats into his chest with a hiss.

Mistaking his abrasion, she says, "Gee whiz. Am I that fat?"

Peter says nothing. His Adams apple works up and down. His mouth falls agape. When Valerie McAllister looks down at herself, she screams, uncontrollably. Her blood pressure shoots through the roof and she faints dead away, hitting the floor.

Moments later, unsure how long, Peter's eyes move to the floor where his wife lays unconscious. When the shock of it brings him back, he hurries to Valerie's side. He tries desperately to revive her, saying all the while, "Please let her be all right. This is all my fault."

She is out cold and Peter must force himself to leave her side to call 911. He runs downstairs to unlock the door, leaving it ajar for the paramedics. An ambulance arrives ten minutes later to rush her to St. Francis Xavier Hospital, where Valerie's obstetrician meets them on the ramp.

Two hours later, the very competent doctor tells Peter that his wife is going to be fine, but she has to be hospitalized for a few days. Though Valerie has sustained a minor concussion, the child is okay. The mother has to be watched for at least forty-eight hours, possibly longer.

"Spotting? What do you mean?"

Dr. Harrelson says, "Bleeding, Mr. McAllister. The blood on Valerie's stomach. As I mentioned, the child is fine, displaying no discernable signs of fetal distress. So I'm confused as to the..."

"That's not her blood, doctor. Valerie was fine until she saw it, but I'm sure that she wasn't bleeding. There was no blood on her underwear or on the sheets. She went to bed wearing white and there was nothing on her nightgown," Peter says. He stares off into space, thinking.

"If it wasn't Valerie's blood, where else could it have come from?" the doctor asks.

"I'm telling you, it's not her blood. Check it!"

"Try to calm down, sir. You've had a terrible ordeal and it's understandably distressing for you. When's the last time you had a checkup, Mr. McAllister?"

Harrelson reaches for Peter's sagging red eyes, but McAllister prevents it. "I'm fine, and I'm not crazy. That isn't my wife's blood!" A blank stare crosses Peter's eyes again. His voice becomes a mere whisper. "Those bastards were really in my house."

Dr. Harrelson says, "Did I hear you correctly? Mr. McAllister, if you feel that a crime has been committed, you should talk to the police."

Peter snatches the doctor by the collar and snaps, "I know what this sounds like, but I'm not crazy. Check it out, damn it!" He quickly lets go when he realizes that he's being watched.

An hour later, following Melissa and Evan Parker's visit, the doctor returns. Doctor Harrelson removes his glasses and regards Peter McAllister in silence for a long moment. The worried man is out on his feet, oblivious of the doctor's presence until he says, "Mr. McAllister, I'm sorry--"

"What? What's happened to my wife and baby?" Peter shrieks in a frenzy. He is struck with panic, about to tear off down the hall past the water fountain where he's just taken the longest drink of his life.

The doctor grabs him and says, "Wait, they are both fine. I apologize, Mr. McAllister. It was insensitive of me to begin what I have to say that way. It was a very poor choice of words, forgive me. Please allow me to start over." Peter listens. "What I meant to say is that you were right about the blood not belonging to your wife or her baby."

"Christ, you scared the hell out of me," Peter says.

"Now, this is in no way a judgment of you, but do either of you happen to practice in the occult, Mr. McAllister?" His voice was hushed and serious.

"What is this? Are you nuts or just some kind of very expensive quack?"

"I'm sorry. However, I had to ask because according to the lab, that was clearly the blood of a chicken."

"What the hell are you talking about?" Peter shouts. His eyes seem to glaze over, but only for an instant.

"It was unmistakably the blood of a chicken. Does Valerie have a tendency to sleepwalk, maybe to the point where she may have gotten into the refrigerator?"

"No way. If you're done with this bullshit line of questioning, I need to see my wife now," Peter growls.

When a security guard eases closer, the doctor waves him off and says, "By all means. Valerie is very frightened so I administered a mild sedative. Right now, she needs to rest. No matter what you do, please don't upset her any more than she is already. I've assured her that she'll be okay and you must try to do the same. I feel that her pregnancy is safe, but fetal distress may lie just around the corner."

When Valerie's doctor returns to the nurse's station, a nurse gives him the Polaroid photo she had taken of Valerie's stomach. She suspected that those had been markings of some kind before they were washed away. This is certainly one of the strangest things that either of them have seen. Dr. Harrelson decides to hold on to the picture, wary of Peter McAllister's state of mind. The security guard is asked to remain in the area, just in case.

Timidly, Peter enters Valerie's unit. Her doctor is making arrangements for the maternity ward where she will be more comfortable.

Peter sits next to his sleeping wife, taking her hand. She moans and turns her head toward him, but her eyes remain closed for the time being. When he kisses her hand, his mind flashes back to the dream that wasn't. He sees the severed foot that the intruder used as a crude paintbrush. He sees it being stroked across Valerie's chest and stomach, writing with crimson ink that bubbled and sizzled as if it was acid. Peter shuts his eyes against the images and begins to cry, but he can still see it all. He can't help thinking about the nightmare that was not real, in part at least. Its meaning seems unfathomable. Barrette Holt had warned of their coming.

Vile intruders, from which there seems no protection, have entered their home. His mind reels as he recalls the lightning storm, which had to have been an actual event. The ground was wet when he followed the paramedics to the ambulance. But what about the dead men who were beating the drums? There were spiders, but neither of them had been bitten until after the snake…

A violent shudder racks Peter's aching mind and body. He still hears that sound of the evil man slitting Valerie open as if merely gutting a fish. He recalls the sound over the drums when that man reached into her to end her pregnancy by ripping his child from her womb. It should not have been possible to hear over that storm and the drums. Yet it is imprinted into his memory. The child then screamed in agony no longer.

He sees that wicked person tearing his son's genitals away. The tender skin runs down the child's stomach until it reaches the umbilical cord and snaps away from his body like a rubber band. The cruel intruder sucked it up as if it was spaghetti and nothing more. "It's a boy, papa!" Peter mumbles and flinches.

"Excuse me. Did you say something, Mr. McAllister?" asks Dr. Harrelson as he checks Valerie's chart.

Peter is startled, unaware that he's spoken aloud. His head snaps about and he asks, "Dr. Harrelson, do you know if our child is a girl or boy?"

"Yes. We've done extensive ultrasounds. However, your wife specified that she didn't want to know just yet."

"Just spit it out."

"It's a boy, Mr. McAllister, and he's just fine."

"A boy? We're having a son," Peter whispers with a smile. That blank stare comes again.

Harrelson is uncomfortable in regard to the oddities surrounding his patient's hospitalization. Peter's strange behavior prompts him to consider added precautions. Not sure if he should leave the couple alone, the doctor walks out.

When Valerie comes around, she's disoriented, but knows by his touch that Peter is there at her bedside. He's fallen asleep with his head in the cradle of an arm. She smiles as she strokes his hair, causing him to jerk fully awake.

"Hi. You look worse than I feel."

"Shhhh. Don't talk. Get some rest, sweetheart."

"I'm afraid, Peter."

He forces a smile, trying to sound reassuring when he says, "I know. Hush now. The doctor told me that everything is going to be okay."

"But I almost lost the baby, Peter."

She knows how Melissa Parker must have felt. The story was unimaginable when she listened to her accounts of a near tragedy on the day before. She recalls her friend's words about those looming uncertainties, even with her physician's reassurances.

"But you didn't lose our baby, sweetheart. They want to keep you because you have a slight concussion and you're just a little anemic. The doctor assures me that our child will be healthy and happy. Please try to relax. Rest now."

Peter is relieved that she isn't asking about what landed her in the hospital. His hopes, however, are soon dashed against the rocks when her eyes suddenly reflect the recollection of something terrible.

"What happened to me last night? I was all bloody, like someone painted those awful symbols on me while we slept." Tears are streaming down her cheeks.

"Try not to get upset. Just don't think about it, okay?"

Valerie's respiration begins to elevate. She squints at Peter and says, "What do you mean, try not to think about it? How can I? I wasn't bleeding. It would have been all over my nightgown!"

"We can talk about it later," Peter says. He starts to worry. She's getting excited, reeling in a flood of emotions that cannot be good for the baby.

"Don't patronize me, Peter. I can see in your face that there's more to this thing. Isn't there? You grabbed my stomach when you woke up, damn it!"

Pain stabs at Valerie's groin and she squeals. Peter completely forgets about the call button clipped to her bed.

"Oh Jesus, it hurts!" she shrieks while clutching at her bed sheets.

Peter runs out of the room, shouting for the doctor. Then he collapses in the hallway, sliding to a stop near the water fountain. Now there is only darkness, utter and complete. The drums. Doom da-da boom! Doom da-da boom! The mighty drums are calling!

CHAPTER 23

THE INVESTIGATION BEGINS

April 6, 2001. 7:18 a.m.

T he housekeeper quietly rummages around the kitchen, unable to find the flour sifter that she used moments before. Melissa Parker appears in a nightgown and slippers, "Good morning, Maddy. Did Evan make it back from Indiana last night? Did he call?"

"Oh, good morning. Your husband is in his office."

"The return flight from Indiana was scheduled for one o'clock last night. Was it late?" Melissa asks.

"I heard him come in at about two o'clock, Mrs. Parker."

Melissa places her hands upon her hips and says, "Maddy, please, we've been over this. Call me Melissa or Mel. Agreed?"

"Agreed. I took him some coffee a little while ago, but I think there's something bothering him," Maddy says.

"I wonder why he didn't come to bed when he got back."

"Mr. Parker asked if I had other jobs like this one because he may want to hire me exclusively. He asked if I'm willing to travel in case you have to leave suddenly."

"What on earth?"

"He's in a very strange mood, Melissa. I believe he's been up all night." Maddy shakes her head when she realizes that the flour sifter is on the counter looking right at her.

"I just got here. Where in the world would I be going?"

"There seems to be something awful bothering Mr. Parker. I've never seen him this way, so sullen and sad."

"Go on," Melissa says with growing concern.

"I think he's been drinking. He keeps muttering something about lies and deception. Maybe you should go check on him, but whatever you do, please don't get yourself upset. Remember those precious babies of yours."

"Drinking? Thanks, Maddy. Can you bring me some decaffeinated tea in a little while?" Melissa Parker begins to walk away, but turns to asks, "He's been drinking, are you sure?"

Madeline Perkins opens the dishwasher and removes the glass that smells of liquor, allowing the mistress of the house to sniff it. She points out an empty bottle in the recycle bin, which was half full with Vodka yesterday.

Melissa is wordless when Maddy informs, "Thus, the two cups of coffee. I believe he's just a bit hung-over. Maybe all he needs is to see his beautiful wife to snap out of it." She offers a hopeful smile, praying that this sort of thing isn't the beginning of an awful trend for this nice couple.

Because it seems to be the proper thing to do, Melissa knocks on the door of Evan's office. When her husband fails to answer, she enters.

Evan sits in the deep leather chair, facing the window in a dour malaise. To her, he seems to have fallen asleep with books in his lap, but Evan is staring through the pane as the morning develops before his eyes. Sitting there, in his mind, he scoffs at that age-old adage that so erroneously claims: What one does not know will never hurt one.

"What a lousy cliché," he mumbles.

"Evan, are you asleep? Baby?"

His voice is listless and dazed when he says, "I'm awake, Mel. Come on in."

Melissa approaches, placing a hand on his shoulders as she draws near. The only times she's seen her husband cry was when he discussed the death of his mother, and when she nearly miscarried. She looks at the material in his lap, knowing that his mood must have greatly to do with those tear-stained pages. She kneels before him, touching his face gently.

"Evan, what happened?"

His voice is distant and hushed when he says, "It's all a lie, Mel. Just one big lie."

"What are you talking about, baby? What's the lie?" she probes, searching his eyes for the meaning of such sadness.

He taps the census data in his lap. "This is the biggest lie of them all."

She grows frustrated when he isn't forthcoming, and yet a large part of her doesn't want to know.

"I don't understand, Evan. How can the census be a lie?"

"Not only is it a fabrication, but Cecil Bridges must have discovered the truth. This is probably the real reason that he was murdered." Evan has gone over it repeatedly, testing every angle. In the end, his is a very reasonable conclusion.

"Honey, you know that Cecil was killed in a terrorist attack. How could it have anything to do with this census report? You told me that his death was just a senseless act of violence."

Evan shakes his head to the contrary. "You're right about the senseless part, but I really doubt that he was killed at the hands of terrorists if these reports are what they seem. His murder was not at the hands of foreign radicals as we've all been led to believe. It was a government cover-up." He turns the book around so she could see, pointing out a couple of columns. "It's all right here in black and white, Melissa. No pun intended, but it certainly applies." He grunts in disgust.

A moment later, his wife says, "I'm no expert, but this seems to state that..." Her eyes bulge. "Oh...oh my God."

"It states that, right now, there are approximately nineteen million more African Americans than there are Whites in the United States. The other census report is from the previous decade, which coincides with the time of Cecil's murder."

With growing desperation in her voice, she asks, "This is unbelievable. Are you sure that it's reliable and not just a misprint of some kind?"

Evan looks into Melissa's eyes, needing her to understand and accept the distasteful possibilities of this development. "It makes sense to me, however, I can't be sure. I got it from a very disturbed person."

"You mean, Mr. Holt, the guy you went to see in Indiana?" Melissa asks, clutching her chest in a moment of consternation.

"Yes. The man has practically barricaded himself inside of his own bedroom. It's horrible, the way he lives in such filth. Crosses, bibles, garlic, and candles are scattered everywhere." His nose wrinkles as a reflex to an unpleasant memory. "Barrette Holt is convinced that someone is out to get him. If this census turns out to be accurate, compared to the one they want us to make public, he's been sitting on a powder keg that has driven him insane. The man's so crazy that he actually thought I was Peter McAllister. You wouldn't believe the things I've seen and heard. You can't even begin to imagine."

A selfless thought crosses Melissa Parker's mind. "I know that this is a terrible burden to bear alone, but I don't think you should tell Peter about it right away. He collapsed in the hospital yesterday. Valerie told me that Peter may be released later today or tomorrow. They've been running tests."

"That fucking bastard ought to be hospitalized!" Evan says with bitterness.

"Evan, I realize that you two may have your differences right now, but he's your best friend."

"He knows, Mel. Peter knows everything."

"What? But how can he?" she asks.

"According to Mr. Holt, Peter is a part of it. Apparently, he played a major role in Cecil's death. Fucking bastard slid right into the driver's seat afterward without a care in the world."

"How can you be sure about any of this, Evan? He's your friend, and he couldn't do such a thing. Could he?"

"I guess I don't know him as well as I thought. If you'll allow yourself to think about it, this shit makes perfect sense. Perfect sense. Valerie told us that Peter calls Cecil's name when he's having those violent nightmares. The guilt of what they did has been tormenting Peter and Barrette Holt all along, eating them up from the inside out. It's coming to a head because of the delays in updating the lie. The introduction of the computer virus that destroyed all that data years ago has thrown them off schedule. The mounting stress of keeping this secret is killing them both."

"If it's true, what can you do about it now?" she asks.

"I don't know, Melissa," Evan says with a sigh. "I have to be certain beyond a shadow of a doubt before I do or say anything. This revelation is extremely volatile."

Very unsettling thoughts now race through Melissa Parker's mind. Her worried voice is high-pitched when she says, "This thing is too dangerous. You'll just end up like Cecil if you pursue it. Just throw it in the trash and never take it out, Evan. Please, I'm begging you!" She takes the books from his lap, moving swiftly to the paper shredder near his desk before he stops her.

"I can't do that, Melissa." He gently coerces the books from her hands and places them on the edge of the desk. Evan tries to put his hands around Melissa, attempting to soothe her sweeping anxieties.

"Why not? Why can't we just forget this ever happened? Just give it to the police, let them handle it." Melissa begins to sob, not wanting to be touched or quieted.

"Because the coach was a friend of mine and that of my family. That's why. You know he meant a great deal to us all. His name should be cleared, Melissa. I would want the same for myself, wouldn't you?"

"But you're not him. Why does it have to be you, Evan? You're just going to get yourself killed. You're going to leave me and our children alone in this world, Evan. Please."

"I have to, don't you see? This goes way beyond us now. The last fifty or sixty years might have been very different, had it not been for the suppression of this information. There's been a lot of suffering because we haven't received the representation that our numbers demand. There are issues here that we can't even begin to imagine—billions of dollars diverted from the places that need it most—businesses that don't even know that we exist—programs and opportunities lost. If I don't get involved, it will be buried. If that happens, the same may become our fate. Doing nothing means I'd see a coward every time I saw my reflection in my children's eyes because I will have let them down, too. Don't you understand that, Melissa? There is no running away from this, win or lose. There's no going back for us. Sooner or later, the people Peter and Barrette work for will find out that I know everything. What do you suppose will happen then? Can you be strong for us, Mel? I need you to trust me, knowing that time is of the essence. You do understand, don't you, sweetheart?"

Evan's head is pounding, and the smell of liquor exudes from him. Reluctantly, she nods her head in affirmation. Though bitter still, Melissa Parker allows her husband to embrace her heaving shoulders.

Madeline knocks and brings in a cup of tea. Seeing Melissa in tears prompts Maddy to excuse herself, but Evan asks her to come in and have a seat. He tells Madeline everything, apologizing for not giving it to her straight from the start. He acknowledges that she could be caught in the middle of something twisted. After Maddy chews on his story, she accepts the apology without malice, agreeing to do as he asks. This is also her fight.

Evan wants the women to leave Maryland and visit his father in South Carolina. Melissa refuses, of course, but she's eventually convinced with Maddy's help. He writes Madeline Perkins two checks totaling five-thousand dollars, which she will deposit into her own accounts. They are to make flight reservations from the housekeeper's bank accounts only, taking the next available flight. But he insists that absolutely no one is to know, except for his father, who will remain alert in case of unforeseen events.

Melissa realizes that her husband has given this a great deal of thought. She vows to trust him to know what is best for them all in the long run.

Evan explains that he may find some kind of evidence at the office, thinking of a conversation that he had about a month ago with Peter McAllister's mouthy assistant, Patricia Kidder. She casually mentioned that Cecil Bridges was having a love affair with his assistant, a woman named Deedra Wilson. Supposedly, Cecil had left something in his will for Mrs. Wilson. Evan figured that she could be the one person the coach would have told about his discovery, if the rumor is factual. When asked about the interaction of bureau employees back then, Patricia reported that everyone used to get along just fine. Things were great, stressful at times but good. Apparently, Deedra Wilson was a dear woman and liked by everyone.

After Cecil's death, however, she changed. For no apparent reason, the woman had just gone sour on Peter McAllister. Patricia assumed that it had something to do with the fact that Peter was taking Cecil's place. Mrs. Wilson retired soon after Cecil's death, remaining in Maryland where she currently owns a bakery.

Before leaving, Evan decides it's best not to call and ask his father for permission to send him two guests. Melissa will have to explain the details in person.

Though Melissa hates her husband's determination, she does her part by packing a bag and copying the disks as he asked. Meanwhile, Madeline Perkins will visit two banks to deposit the substantial checks written by Evan Parker. Ultimately, credit cards can tell tales, but only if someone is looking closely. Evan promises to be back in time to see them off.

The ride into town is filled with dreary thoughts. Evan begins to rethink his theories, feeling guilty about his eagerness to believe Peter McAllister's involvement. Barrette Holt may not be the most reliable source on which to base such damning assumptions. He's second-guessing himself, looking for excuses to refute the evidence with any means of rationalization available to him. Deep down inside, he knows the truth, and it fills him with more sadness than fear. It fills him, for the time being, with more sadness than the anger that is still growing within to sustain him on this quest. Whether he wants to see it or not, there is a trail forming before his eyes where seemingly unimportant conversations and coincidental sequences of events have come together to place his feet upon this path. It seems a path that he's predestined to follow.

⇥⇤

Discretely turning Peter's office inside out avails nothing of use. He thinks it prudent, however, to leave no evidence of his snooping.

With the floor nearly deserted, Evan asks Patricia Kidder to locate something that she will easily find. He quickly maneuvers Peter's assistant toward his goals, but not without the minimum of small talk.

"Thank you, Patricia," Evan says. "By the way, you mentioned a bakery a while back. I believe it's owned by Cecil's old assistant."

She thinks back for a moment. "Oh yes. What about it?"

"Well, how's the food? I'm thinking about trying it out."

Patricia smiles, warmly. "It's also a delicatessen. The food is excellent, so are the baked goods. I think Deedra and her daughter are running the business together. They make the greatest strawberry tarts. Mm! I was addicted to them, but I had to give them up because they go straight to the waistline. Know what I mean?"

"Sounds good to me. I wish I knew how to get around a little better. I've been here for three months and really haven't been anywhere. Between starting this new job and getting the new house ready, I hardly know anyone in this town."

"I can give you directions if you like," she offers.

"I'll tell you what. If you don't already have plans for lunch, why don't you join me? I'm buying. I'll even sweeten the pot by making it an early lunch. How's that sound to you?"

"Sure, why not? Don't look now, Evan, but you are the boss," Patricia says, smiling innocently. She is never one to turn down a free brunch, and it is beginning to show in some places.

"Good. I'll see you at ten-thirty," he says on the way back to his office.

Evan Parker has done all he can to discredit his suspicions, but they continue to drum in his mind. He feels he owes Patricia a free meal. Her gossip has provided the direction in which to begin his investigation of an eleven-year-old drama where the scent is long cold.

At the end of Kwani Drive, the Rada and the Conga drums are beating once again. The priest, Abongoma Nosinyanga, holds a serpent aloft. His eyes are whites, and his black nostrils flare as he sniffs the troubled, smoky air.

She parks and they walk into the Happy Oven Bakery and Delicatessen, which is already crowded. Evidently, the place is doing much better than when it was just a bakery.

Patricia makes a takeout order for a mixed dozen of blueberry and strawberry tarts. She intends to pay for them herself, but Evan wouldn't hear of it. Then she orders the tuna melt and salad, which she'll eat at the restaurant. Evan orders the fried shrimp plate and salad, eating sparingly. He is nervous and disappointed that Patricia doesn't see Deedra anywhere in the deli. If Mrs. Wilson isn't there, he will simply return and ask for her without Patricia's knowledge. He makes it a point not to seem too anxious about meeting the woman because Patricia is such a busybody.

Evan looks at the passing traffic, not really listening to Patricia Kidder's gabble. Every now and then, he offers a reassuring, "Ah huh," or "Is that right?"

"Mr. Parker, can I ask you a personal question? Evan?"

"Oh certainly, what is it you'd like to know, Patricia?"

She shakes her head, changing her mind.

"No. Really, what is it? I have nothing to hide, and since we are going to be working together, ask what you will."

Patricia Kidder says, "I looked you up, you know, during your background check and qualifications for this position. I really wasn't prying, I swear to God. Just doing my job."

Evan Parker smiles at her bashfulness, never thinking a woman so talkative could be that way in earnest. He feels he has been judging her a bit harshly, acknowledging that she isn't to blame.

He says, "Go on."

"Well, you're filthy rich. What the hell are you doing here sniffing ink and flipping digits?"

He chuckles before saying, "So you know just about everything there is to know about how I became financially solvent."

"Oh no. I mean yes, but that's not...that's not...well obviously you proved your innocence and you did nothing wrong. But that wasn't what I was getting at. I promise. I think I should just shut up now. I'm sorry for being so nosey."

"It's okay, Patricia. I get why you are curious because, in truth, I could be sailing around the world right now instead or working a nine to five."

"Really, Mr. Parker. It was none of my business and I apologize."

It is an extremely personal question, but also a welcomed distraction so he answers. "I suppose there are a few reasons for me being here, doing what I'm doing when I don't have to. It would seem that God wants me here. Idle hands are the devil's workshop. I love number crunching, seeing patterns that most people will never see or correctly interpret. The census really is important in the grand scheme of our economic growth. The proper distribution of tax revenue, for example. There is always the need for updating changes where growth is lacking, or reconstructing programs that can be deleted or recreated to assure that there is balance for the wellbeing of our entire nation are all extremely important tasks. The accuracy of the American Census plays a huge role in all of these things. That's why I'm here. Besides, I'm not one for sailing anyway. I get seasick."

She looks at him and says, "Wow. When you say it that way, it almost sounds sensual."

"Why, Patricia Kidder, if I didn't know better, I'd swear you just made a pass at me."

"Well I was getting a bit tingly for a moment," she says with a smile. They laugh for a few moments, and then the quiet resumes as she wonders if she was actually being a little flirtatious.

Approximately ten minutes after their orders arrive, a woman's voice comes to them. This is the moment. "Patricia Kidder? Don't you have time to stop and say hello anymore? Is the food that bad, child?" Although Deedra Wilson's hair has grayed, her disarming smile and kindly eyes are the same.

"Deedra, hi!" She rises to hug her old friend. "It's been so long."

"Yes it has. Don't you love me anymore?" Deedra asks, putting her arms about Patricia's shoulders. Evan's heart races when he stands to meet her.

"And who is this tall, handsome gentleman? Once you go Black, Patricia, they say you never go back," Deedra says with a chuckle.

"You're so bad. Deedra Wilson, this is Evan Parker, the new Deputy Director. Evan, meet Deedra Wilson."

Evan offers his hand. "Pleased to meet you, Mrs. Wilson. I've heard a lot of good things about you."

"Thank you, Mr. Parker. Patricia, don't you think he's a little young for you? Now I can take him off of your hands if you can't quite handle the heat, but I may have to hide him from my daughter."

Patricia blushes. "You are so bad. I don't believe you."

Deedra joins them at the table. While they talk, she has someone bring them a few samples of her newest dishes. Evan politely compliments her on the cuisine. He even comments on the decor of the deli.

"You know, Deedra, Mr. Parker and Peter McAllister went to college together. In fact, Mr. Bridges was both their coach and professor," Patricia offers freely.

Patricia is talkative, indeed. Parker decided long ago that he will never trust her with anything of importance. Yet, in this capacity, her willingness to talk is perfectly suited to his purpose. She volunteers information just as Evan hoped, and silently thanks her for every public service announcement.

"Is that right?" Deedra says.

With mention of Cecil Bridges and Peter McAllister in the same breath, Evan notices a subtle change in Deedra. He sees—almost feels—the measure of sadness that touches her eyes.

"Yes, ma'am. Coach Bridges was one of my favorite professors at South Carolina. He was different from the others in that his classes were never so large that he didn't take time to answer my questions or offer me pointers. There were quite a few times when I really needed his input. But he never left me hanging, whether in class, on the court, or life in general. He was a good person."

Deedra tows the line of conversation by saying, "Yes, Cecil was a very dear man. He may have even mentioned you to me once."

"Well, I wouldn't be surprised. He kept me out of trouble on many occasions. I owe him more than I can say because I may not have graduated on time, were it not for him. Maybe not at all," he embellishes.

"Really? Tell me something, Mr. Parker. Were you the student that fell from the balcony and smashed in the roof of his new car?" asks Deedra Wilson.

Evan's eyes light up and he blushes. This is the first time that Patricia realizes that even African American people can blush. She recognizes that blushing is more than a sudden rush of color to the cheeks, but that it is also a feeling and an attitude; a mystique unveiling.

"Yes, ma'am. I'm embarrassed to admit it, but that was me alright. We were celebrating our victory over Clemson University. I'm afraid I was a little drunk and extremely lucky that I didn't break my neck."

Patricia is shocked. "You fell from a balcony and smashed up his car? Boy that must have gone over really well with your parents."

Deedra says, "Cecil wouldn't have told them, unless it was a serious injury and absolutely necessary."

"That's true. He never said a word to my parents, and allowed his insurance to take care of the damage. In fact, I sprained my ankle in the fall. Coach took me to his home where he and his wife got me healed up in time for another really big game. We became very close and he visited my family during spring breaks and summers. He and my father became very good friends. His wife and my mother were as thick as thieves. Unfortunately, both passed away within a year of each other. It was good that my father and Coach

Bridges were close, so they consoled one another," Evan confesses. He isn't lying about these things, nor is he acting when he speaks affectionately of Cecil and his wife.

Patricia looks at her watch with a grimace. "Well, sir, it's time to scoot. I have a few more things to move to my temporary station on the fourth floor. Deedra, I promise to come in more often."

"If you do, I'll let you have a few tarts on the house. Just don't wait another five years to do so." They hug.

Not intending to leave, Evan asks, "Mrs. Wilson, are you very busy?"

"Not really. I've hired enough help so my tired old bones don't have to endure as much strain as they used to. Why do you ask?"

"I'd really like to talk to you a little more about Coach Bridges. This visit brings back some really fond memories that I'd love to share with you. I promise not to take up too much of your time."

It's evident that Deedra silently protests the idea. His eyes plead, fearing that she's had quite enough nostalgia as far as the memory of Cecil Bridges is concerned.

"Okay. We can talk in my office, but I'm afraid that this can't take very long," she relents with a long sigh trailing her words.

Evan tells Patricia that he's going to hang out for a while longer. Such is one of the benefits of being the director/pro tempore. He will take a cab back to the office, and she's not to discuss his slightly unprofessional behavior.

Evan follows Deedra through the kitchen and the storage areas to her office, where recipe books are stacked neatly about the room. Her office is pleasant, but private most of all. Deedra invites him to sit before doing the same.

"Okay, Mr. Parker, what's on your mind," she asks rather impatiently. The change in her demeanor is sharp. She isn't as bubbly as before, and it's obvious that she wants to cut to the chase. She must suspect his true motive.

"Mrs. Wilson, I realize that this is highly unusual and I appreciate you taking the time to talk to me. However, I have reason to hope and believe that you and Coach Bridges were more than just fellow employees."

She balks at the statement. "That's very presumptuous of you, Mr. Parker, and just what business is it of yours?" She squints, almost spitefully. "That woman has been running her big mouth again. While at the Census Bureau, it will serve you best to consider your sources, Mr. Parker."

The drums are beating harder and faster. One by one, the eyes of the drummers roll up in their heads to quiver in the dark ceilings of each socket.

"Please don't be upset with me, ma'am. This is very important. I believe you could be the one person who may know."

"Know what?" Deedra asks harshly. "Just what the hell are you getting at?"

"The census report is a total lie, Mrs. Wilson, and I believe you know it," he whispers, looking directly into her reactive eyes. Brisk tension fills the air, mounting quickly between them.

She rises from her seat to say, "Get out. You get the hell out of my office. I don't know what you're talking about." Deedra turns to the small window, staring out at a barren riverbed littered with bad memories. The woman's hands are trembling, and she holds herself as if her blood has suddenly gone cold.

"I know this is hard for you. I believe that you cared for him. I can see that, Mrs. Wilson. I believe that Cecil wanted to protect you and that is why you've been silent all these years. We both know that Cecil was never involved with terrorists. You know that someone in the U.S. Government must have had him murdered because of what he knew. It's no coincidence that he died at a television station."

"I don't know anything, Mr. Parker. Now, please go," Deedra begs. Absent of mind, she reaches out to caress a picture of her grandchildren on the wall. The acidic tears of mourning are destined to return as she briefly relives happier times cut short with the tragic death of her lover. That feeling of being watched, even years later, lurking like a low-lying cloud with a bellyful of pain, comes to mind. It was a suffocating fear that encompassed her hopes for every member of her family.

Evan Parker circumvents the desk. Though his heart goes out to her, he presses on. There is such rigidity in Deedra's shoulders when he reaches out to her.

"Please, Mrs. Wilson. I loved him, too. Cecil was like a second father to me and I feel I owe him his memory and good name. I can't imagine what you've dealt with all these years, but I can't live with myself knowing that Cecil is turning in his grave because he has been branded a traitor to his country." It's a very low blow, a ruthless tactic that's sure to hold consequence.

Deedra cries in Evan's arms. "Why have you brought me this pain, again, Mr. Parker? Why? Why?"

He holds her, fighting back his own tears as her sorrow washes over him. She had truly loved Cecil.

Evan whispers, "I found evidence of two completely different Census reports, and it scares the hell out of me to think that my suspicions are true. But if I'm right, this can't be kept a secret any longer. Cecil's name should be cleared. If you help me, I promise to keep your name out of it. The responsible party has to be brought to justice. They are the real traitors here. They have to be punished for his death and so much more. It may not be easy, but with or without your help, I will find a way to prove it. Cecil Bridges meant that much to me. Please help me, Mrs. Wilson."

The drumbeat intensifies. The priests and drummers hum dark songs as an animal struggles beneath the knife!

"I can't. I just can't, don't you see? I promised him that I would tell no one. It was the very last thing I said to him and I cannot break my promise," she sobs. "Don't you understand?"

Evan releases Deedra. Deeply searching her eyes, he says, "Please help me. It's only a matter of time before they find out that I know." He takes a photo from his wallet and shows it to her. "This is my wife, whom I love very much, and she's carrying twins. There's just no going back for me now. A breadcrumb on the path is all I ask—a name—a place. Anything at all."

Deedra withdraws. It seems hopeless. Seeing what he's done to her, Evan apologizes for pushing the way he had. When her wordless gaze returns to the window, Evan walks to the door in frustration. He's tried and failed here.

As Evan Parker lays claim to the doorknob, her sobbing voice comes to him, broken and shaken. "Go. Go to Macedonia Sanatorium in Seat Pleasant. There was a patient there named Allen Peterson, but he could be dead by now. He was the reporter Cecil contacted. Now, please leave. Never return here, and for god sake, do not mention my name."

Evan thanks her. When he walks out of the office, he pauses, leaning with his back to the office door. He is feeling quite guilty for having twisted the knife in that sweet old woman's heart. Inside the office, Deedra is saying that she hasn't broken the promise. She speaks to Cecil Bridges in the afterlife with her eyes raised to heaven, while asking his understanding. She wants forgiveness. Not for breaking her oath, but for sending that young man to his probable death.

The pulsing drums cease. Something convulses to its end on the altar with its protest forever silenced.

CHAPTER 24
GHOST OF MACEDONIA

B efore walking to the boarding gate, Evan kisses Melissa and
holds her close. He promises to be careful, and asks that she
not worry so. Madeline pledges to take care of her, but there's an
inevitable shedding of stifled tears.

As flight 407 takes to the sky, Evan watches from the terminal's
window. As it disappears into the graying ocean of air, he promises
that he'll see Melissa again. Though on separate paths, they are
tied together by invisible bonds, sharing both the longing and the
dread.

After leaving Deedra Wilson's deli earlier, Evan made a
quick stop at the local newspaper to dig up and copy micro-
fiche records from eleven years ago. Now, while sitting at traffic
stops, he reads the accounts of Cecil's alleged treachery and
very violent death.

At a four way stop, Evan Parker comes across Allen Peterson's
name twice in a 1990 newspaper article. Peterson, who sustained
massive burns, was not expected to live. Apparently, he survived for
some time, since Deedra Wilson pointed Evan in his direction.

Evan Parker discovers that Allen Peterson's story is even more tragic because he had no surviving family members to see him through the suffering. The fact is a rather maudlin thing to cheer, but it presents an opportunity. The first article suggests that the television journalist may have been close to exposing the terrorist cell when the blast occurred. It's an interesting twist, but Evan sees it for what it really is; suffocating smoke and cracked mirrors.

As Evan Parker enters the highway, his cell phone drags him from deep thoughts. Veronica Sellars, his assistant, is calling to tell him that the Jeffersonville Police are trying to get in touch with him.

Evan's heart thuds, but she puts his mind at ease. The detective in Jeffersonville was trying to contact Peter McAllister, but because he is indisposed, Evan Parker is next in line. Barrette Holt is dead by suicide, with Peter McAllister's name on his lips and scrawled on his filthy walls. Telephone records show Peter McAllister to be the last person that Barrette called. Although the news of Barrette's death comes as a surprise, Evan Parker is on a mission.

"I can't speak to them right now, Veronica. They'll just have to wait. Oh yeah, I'll have to go to Washington some time tomorrow." He hates the congested drive.

"Really? You know, there's a seminar I'd like to attend in Washington tomorrow afternoon. And since there's very little that I can do here with the system down, why don't I join you? Would that be okay?"

"Sure. Why not?" He hangs up, continuing his two-hour drive.

After giving a false name at the gate, and stating his business as visitation, Evan parks the car. When he gets out to take a good long look at the hard face of Macedonia Sanatorium, Evan shivers and decides to never grow old. The bleakness of its main building, where dark water stains mar the stone-gray walls, is strikingly macabre.

Behind barred windows, patients stare out over the parking lot at the woods across the fence. He wonders what those poor souls must be thinking. With every passing second, the place resembles a morbid prison. It seems so gloomy, so utterly desolate.

He approaches the front desk, noting several elderly people sitting unattended in the halls. There is an underlying odor mingling with the Betadine and a few other disinfectants meant to cancel it out. This is the miserable smell of lingering death after it has been hosed down with perfume and alcohol. It strikes a nerve.

"May I help you, sir?" asks Nurse Greta Sparks, who is spelling a co-worker due back from lunch at any moment. She's a pleasant looking woman of about fifty or so, with just a touch of gray in her short, brown hair.

Evan snaps out of his funeral home viewing day regrets and says, "Yes, I wonder if you might. I recently hired a private investigator to locate my uncle. You see, he's my last known living relative and I have gone to considerable expense to find him. I've lived abroad for the past fifteen years, so I've been out of touch, to say the least. The person that I hired, Mr. Winslow, informs me that my uncle has been committed to this institution." The only thing missing from Evan Parker's performance is a phony British accent, which might be pushing it a bit.

Nurse Sparks displays genuine sympathy, hoping that this is going to have a happy ending for someone under her care. She says, "May I have your name and the name of the patient so I can check our records?"

"Yes, of course. Do you require identification?" Evan asks while patting his pockets.

"No, sir. That won't be necessary," she says with a polite smile. Because of her answer, it isn't necessary to tell the woman that he left his wallet in the car or at his hotel.

"My name is, Tom. Thomas Peterson. My uncle's name is Allen Peterson. As I understand it, he was badly injured about ten or eleven years ago," he says, looking a bit saddened by the prospect. The nurse is obviously shocked by Evan's request. His stomach tightens into a knot, and dread seeps into his resolve.

"Mr. Allen Peterson?"

"You know him? Is he here?"

"Not to worry. Yes, your uncle is here. In fact, I work with Mr. Peterson on a daily basis. I must confess, however, that he's been one of our more difficult cases in the past ten years. Then, who wouldn't be? That poor soul of a man." She briefly looks away while giving herself that internal speech about maintaining professional distance.

"Would it be possible to see him? I mean, I know I didn't make an appointment."

Greta Sparks smiles at his enthusiasm. "I think that can be arranged, Mr. Peterson, seeing as how I'm the head nurse. We were always under the impression that he had no family."

"Really? I was orphaned when I was very young. The folks were victims of a drunk driver."

"Oh. How awful. Both parents?"

"I'm afraid so. Fortunately for me, I was taken in by family members on my father's side so I grew up on the West Coast. I came home for a family reunion and someone made mention while discussing the family tree. To my shame, I barely remembered my uncle after all of these years."

She looks at her watch. "Let's see. Your uncle should be enjoying his favorite place in the shade right about now. An orderly took him out to a quiet place that our residents refer to as Tree Island. I'd be happy to take you to him myself in one moment."

Evan forces the tense muscles of his cramped abdomen to relax. He breathes a sincere sigh of relief as the walk down a long, gloomy corridor commences. Herein, the truth of dread is awakened in him. When they reach the activities yard, Evan is glad to be outdoors and away from the desolate stares of old people, who look as if they would ask perfect strangers to take them away from this dreary place. In a moment of sudden sunlight, Evan Parker thinks of leaving forever this place. However, he is driven forth.

As Evan first entered the gates of Macedonia, where he assumed an alias, there seemed to be heavy clouds looming over the main building. Yet the contrasting sunlight over the activities yard does not escape him. This is like another world. When his eyes adjust, he sees cheerful nurses in immaculate uniforms and orderlies that look more like wrestlers than caregivers. The patients here seem so much happier than those inside. They're more alive, somehow. Evan Parker considers the sky and figures that there must be a God for those who wish to live in the light rather than the depression of gloom.

As if he's a mariner, launching an unproven vessel into the mysterious sea, he looks over his left shoulder and approaches the truth of his mission in life. It's dark back there, signifying that he should continue toward the light of truth.

"If you don't mind my asking, where did you live while you were away, sir?"

"Well, I lived in South America for much of my adult life. I'm a botanist. My pharmaceutical company is involved in cancer research, experimenting with various compounds from rare plant life and things of that nature."

"How interesting. You know, I could swear that I've seen you somewhere before," she says to stop Evan's heart. He recalls that nasty business at the University of South Carolina and the many times his face has been on the tube.

"For the oddest of reasons, I seem to be getting that quite a lot."

"In any event, I pray that you haven't come all this way to be disappointed. I'm afraid it may not be easy to get through to your uncle. It has been years since he's received any visitors. It's very sad to be forgotten by the world that used to love you so much.

Your uncle has had many problems to contend with, and it's a miracle that he has survived all these years. Mr. Allen was once a famous television journalist, but then you should know that. Please forgive me."

"Not at all. Please go on, Mrs. Sparks. The private investigator dug up what he could, but there are quite a few blind spots."

"His producer and another lady used to visit, but no longer. The woman only came a few times and she always left in tears. I suppose she found it extremely difficult to see Mr. Allen that way. As I said earlier, he can be quite a handful at times. I seem to have better luck in dealing with Mr. Allen, so chin up. You may have success. I certainly hope so."

"Can he speak? Is there any realistic chance that he might remember me?" Evan probes. The question is double-edged; however, she need not know his real reason for asking beyond the scope of a long lost nephew's concern.

"Yes. He has a lisp, but he can speak. He may choose not to, however. Then again, he may go off into a fit of profanity. One simply never knows on a day-to-day. Let's just try to stay positive. That's always very important in cases of the elderly or the tragically deformed."

"I suppose you're right about that."

She stops to face Evan. "In truth, Mr. Peterson, most people come here to die. I hate to say this, but this can seem like one big cemetery waiting to happen at times. I know it sounds awfully abrupt, but that's the truth. It is my duty to make certain that you come to terms before the reality of your uncle's existence slaps you down," she warns. "Now, Mr. Allen is a miraculous exception to all of the rules. Most patients, who have sustained such extensive damage, die from a variety of complications that range from infections to pneumonia within days or weeks of their injury."

Evan remains quiet as they resume the walk across the lawn.

"I'm sorry about the things I just said, but it gets to be so depressing at times. It's difficult getting close to the elderly or terminally ill just to watch them fade away. All too often, they do so in lonesome obscurity. Children who would rather not be bothered have abandoned many of these gentle people. I sincerely hope that this visit turns out well for you both. God knows this is no place for family reunions."

As they continue toward the circle of trees, Evan says, "Your candor is appreciated, Mrs. Sparks. I was out of the country for so long, I never realized. After being reminded of things and people from my childhood, I felt it my duty to seek him out. Please tell me, just how bad is it?"

Greta Sparks clasps her hands behind her back, tapping the clipboard. She contemplates blades of grass that fall beneath their slow steps and sighs. "It's bad, Mr. Peterson. It's really bad. As I'm sure you must know, Mr. Allen sustained second and third degree burns over fifty-percent of his body. The doctors did what they could for your uncle, but there just wasn't enough good skin to make successful graphs or transplants."

"I'm sure that he appreciates all that you've done," Evan offers.

"Every effort was made to save your uncle and to give him a semblance of a normal life, but the regenerative powers of the human body can only be asked to do so much. Since his tragic accident, the technology of synthetic skin grafting has made giant leaps and bounds, but the treatments are extremely expensive. This facility is only partially funded by the state, and you must imagine that Mr. Allen's care has long since consumed his insurance. However, the spirit of charitable institutions still exist in our nation, and someone sends us money every year to help with his care. I was told that these are the reasons he hasn't been sent to a facility that's run completely by the state. He probably would have died long ago, had that been the case."

"My God. Do you know who that person may be?" he asks, suspecting that it may have been Deedra Wilson. He wants to keep her out of this, realizing that it may be quite impossible to do so.

"I'm told that the personal funds always came anonymously. I believe that the sender may be that woman I mentioned earlier. I can check if you think it's important. The list of visitations may be active in his files, even that far back. I'm not sure, but it could be the same person."

"There's really no need to trouble yourself. If she sends the money anonymously, then I suppose we should respect her wishes. No need to pry."

The nurse stops once more to look Evan in the eyes. "Your uncle experiences excruciating pain, so he has to be medicated constantly. Nearly all of the upper body hair follicles have been fused. He's almost completely bald, except for a few random patches on his head." She takes a deep breath before continuing. "You must understand that your uncle isn't a very pretty sight. I'm telling you this because the initial reaction to disfigured patients can have very adverse effects on their self-esteem when a visitor shows shock or revulsion. I really hate to say these things, but I simply must." They resume the slow pace.

"I understand. Thank you for warning me, Mrs. Sparks. I'll try to be strong for both our sakes. He's still family, and I wouldn't want to do anything that will make him feel uncomfortable so thank you for telling me this."

"I would be remiss, sir, if I fail to caution you that he also experiences periods of extreme paranoia. Your uncle has developed a strange fixation in which he actually believes that someone is going to harm him even after all these years. There are moments when he's highly irrational. Even under sedation, Mr. Allen can be very irritable. Nonetheless, there are times when he's one of the sweetest people in my care. Ah, there he is. Please remember everything we've discussed."

While Greta Sparks speaks, Evan is already certain that the man in the shade, with the plaid blanket over his legs, is Allen Peterson. As they get closer, Evan acclimates himself to the sight of the pink and black skin that frames this man's face like an eerie jigsaw puzzle. What's visible of Peterson's body, like his hands and neck area, are clearly scorched beyond repair.

Mr. Allen Peterson simply stares at the ground ahead. His fingers are gnarled, the nails are barely existent. A dull expression is entranced upon his face. He almost looks comatose, completely oblivious to all outside stimuli. The sight of Allen Peterson prompts Evan Parker's childhood mind to recall the evil zombies of Makuunda in Kinzana's scary story.

Peterson's nearly useless hands tremble slightly as they hang limply over the arm bars. A fearless squirrel scampers about in what has to be directly in this man's line of sight. As he draws closer to Peterson, Evan discerns that those eyes fail to register any awareness of the animal. There is absolutely no reaction to the acorn-foraging creature, which displays a constant twitch of its nervous tail.

Peterson has regained the use of his eyes, which suffered heavy trauma due to flash burns, but his black eyes still look dead. They seem never to witness the scampering squirrel, which suddenly retreats when living humans approach.

He stands nearby as Greta Sparks kneels beside the wheelchair. She's careful not to allow her stockings to touch the ground while gently rubbing Peterson's right hand.

In a soft, patronizing voice, she reaches for the mind of a man who is exactly the same age as his visitor. "Mr. Allen, can you hear me? This is a special day. You have a visitor that wants to talk to you very much. Would you like that, Mr. Allen?"

Evan's gut twists, even though Peterson fails to speak. The burn victim does lift his eyes when she says, "It's your nephew, Mr. Allen. It's Tom Peterson. Look, he's all grown up now. Isn't it wonderful?"

Peterson slowly swims to the surface of his depressive stupor. His eyes twitch as he looks up with a kind of hope that encourages both the nurse and his visitor. At first, Peterson remembers his fabled kin. Then he remembers that he has no nephew, or anyone else for that matter.

To Peterson, this must be the person sent to kill him, finally. His eyes search Evan's face for deception or malice, but the eyes of a man who looks to do him no harm dishearten him. Peterson's slow logic deduces that the government might have found a man who'd dispense with him for a price without question. The tall visitor could be wearing an expression of concern just to fool the nurse, and his wordless sympathy is just an act until they are alone. He's glad in a way.

Nurse Sparks says, "Now you be good, Mr. Allen. Talk to your nephew because he has missed you terribly. Please be nice." She stands, gracing Evan Parker with a difficult smile. "I'll leave you two alone. If there are any problems, please don't hesitate to ask for help."

Evan Parker's mouth is dry. His voice threatens to squeak when he says, "I will. Thanks again."

She is about to walk away, but thinks it prudent to give the visitor another warning. The nurse calls Evan Parker out of earshot to whisper, "There's one more thing. I'm afraid he can't do without the morphine drip. Normally, it's secured, but the lock was just removed. Unfortunately, the key was accidently broken off in it earlier. Another unit should be available within the hour, but your uncle has no idea that it's only taped shut right now. If he talks to you, he may ask or even beg you to increase his medication. As you should know, the PCS pump is a very sensitive piece of equipment and can kill him if it's adjusted by anyone not strictly trained to do so. Your uncle can't reach it because of where it's situated. Please don't give in. Promise me that."

"You have my word, Mrs. Sparks."

Nurse Sparks walks away, writing down the name of Peterson's visitor. Now that she's far enough away, Evan gets down on one knee and forces himself to look Peterson squarely in the eyes. The man nods when asked if he can hear.

After an awkward moment of silence, the severely burned man speaks in the absence of his visitor's tongue. His voice is badly slurred and distorted. He speaks with great difficulty because the skin of his face is so taut. Amazingly, there is still a man inside of this broken vessel.

Peterson asks with a very distinct lisp, "You come to kill me?" His eyes jerk about until they see those of his visitor clearly.

In the most reassuring voice that he can muster, Evan Parker says, "I'm not here to harm you, Mr. Peterson. Please forgive me for lying about being your nephew, but you have nothing to fear from me."

"Why noth? Sh-shomebody goth to k-kill me. Pleath, please seth me free."

Moments later, Evan will confirm the reason for Cecil Bridges going to the NBC studio in 1990. Peterson tells him of the brief, hurried conversation he had with Cecil before going downstairs to meet him in the parking garage. For the better part of a decade, this wretched man has lived a drug-hazed existence while waiting for his deliverer to come in the night to snuff out what is left of his miserable life. Because that did not happen, living in more pain than fear of death, he finally broke silence. However, when he tried to explain the circumstance before his tragic burning, no one listened. He was just a severely traumatized burn victim, who suffered a psychotic break and no real threat to the men who did this terrible thing to him.

The Crooked Politician's Nightmare, the one-time super reporter who feared no man or issue, now slumps in his wheelchair to tell his tale. He is the picture of pity as he weeps with nearly dry eyes. The tears are both born of the deepest sorrow and the height of joy because he's finally found an audience. Little water comes from his puffy eyes, for there are so few tear ducts to secrete them, but Evan Parker sees and feels them coming from this man's soul. Peterson has finally gained an ear, someone who knows the terrible secret that White men cannot bear to have revealed.

Throughout his residence, Allen Peterson was certain that his enemies would come to spirit him away and end it. Upon that sweet moment, he would attain more freedom than could be known by an entire nation. By a divinity not to be questioned, Evan Parker represents the fact that his black angel of death has finally come. It will not be long now.

At the end of his tale, Peterson reaches for Evan Parker's lapel. His lisp worsens as he stutters, "My God, I've waited for you for ten long years—for ten year-th. I'm not crazy, mister. I been sss-sthuffering alone, but I'm noth crazy."

Evan Parker is moved to tears while this terribly burnt man holds onto his grey blazer as if holding onto life itself. Only, in this case, Peterson clings to death. He yearns for it like a suckling child yearns its mother's touch. Evan is silent, drying his tears and forcing the emotions back.

As Evan Parker replays the recording and deciphers Peterson's slurred narration of the events of 1990, he no longer doubts the elemental dangers involved. Parker finally says, "Are you're saying that Mr. Bridges went to Washington, D.C. to see President Bush, but he was given ten million dollars to keep it hush-hush? Bridges decided to double-cross them, so he was bringing you the money and some kind of proof. However, he was killed before he could give it to you. Is that the way it happened, Mr. Peterson?"

Peterson only nods and whispers, "Yeth," to confirm. His pitiful weeping resumes. He releases Evan's lapel because of the cramping pain in his feeble, trembling fingers.

"You have suffered in silence, living in fear. When you decided to say something, no one listened. They think you delusional because you are always heavily medicated. You're probably still alive today because no one takes you seriously. Also, the newspaper articles suggested that you were probably about to expose the fictitious terror cell. They interviewed the last person you spoke to before the explosion, your boss, who claimed that you were on the hot trail of something big. As it turns out, he didn't know anything about the census or Cecil Bridges. The government's lie about terror cells and the Turner Ross interview made you somewhat of a hero. They expected you to die from your injuries, but you didn't."

Peterson says, "Yes, and now I wanth to die. N-no more bad dreams abouth the red flame. No more shadows. Pleath tell the world what they did. Pleath." His jerky eyes make contact with those of Evan Parker again. "Tell them what they did, pleath!"

There's a click from the machine on the back of Allen Peterson's chair. The morphine is on its way.

"I will, Mr. Peterson. I'll see President Gore and…"

"No!" Fearful fire flashes in Peterson's eyes. "Don't mmm-make the sh-shame misthake!" A miserable cough erupts from his lips in this moment of panic.

Careful not to squeeze, Evan takes Peterson's hand. "President Gore is a good man. He'll do the right thing."

Allen Peterson's fear isn't based on himself. The concern is that Evan Parker's naiveté will get him killed before he exposes the truth. Cecil Bridges made the mistake of following the sainted chain of command, which was essentially White in its creation and longstanding foundation.

Allen Peterson has had eleven eternally tortured years to mull over these issues, drugs or none. After eleven years in a living hell, he knows beyond all shadows that no White man, politician or otherwise, would willingly open that vial of poison to public recriminations.

Allen Peterson, without the details of discovery, clearly sees what Evan Parker's emotional trek leaves his racing mind lacking. It's something so obvious and blaring that even a blind man should see the missing links of Evan's faulty thinking.

"You can't trust him to turn on his own race, but they will expect it of you. Deep down inside, they think they are better," Peterson pleads. "Are you crazy?"

Evan Parker says, "I'll be alright and so will you. I have to ask, sir. If you're protected, will you be willing to testify so those responsible for what happened to you and Cecil can be found and brought to justice? Would you be willing to testify, Mr. Peterson?"

Peterson nods. "No cameras. No cameras…pleath."

Evan manages a smile. "No cameras. I promise."

"I used to be handsome. My girlfriend abandoned mmm-me. Sho ugly now."

Evan rises, unwilling to look upon the man's face as dry tears threaten to flow once more. He cannot imagine how this man has survived in this condition. If he were in Peterson's shoes, Evan Parker wonders just how long it would have taken to find some way to end his own life.

With the taped interview tucked in his pocket, Evan Parker leaves the island of trees. He does not notice the squinting eyes of the orderly that watches with great interest from afar. When Evan disappears into the building, he moves toward Allen Peterson with a scowl of retribution etched upon his face.

At the African villages in South Carolina, Seat Pleasant, and across the nation, the Rada and Conga drums are pounding where white eyes have rolled back into their private theaters. Sacrifices are made beneath the steely gazes of snakes that flick their forked tongues from within their deadly coils. They taste danger in the air, the space between the doors of chaos are widening.

Amazed and bewildered, Evan Parker starts his trek back to Suitland. He's stricken with an unseemly shame for having considered Peter McAllister, who'd been party to such cruelties, to be a friend.

CHAPTER 25

NO FRIEND OF MINE

5:15 p.m.

U pon his return to Suitland, Evan goes to the office to make hard copies of the bound 1990 and 2000 Census Reports, making certain that every page wears the official watermark of The bureau so there can be no doubt of their authenticity. Without the watermark, Melissa could have performed the task easily at home, but he'd neglected to buy paper and ink. Still, it's better this way. Evan doesn't expect anyone to be here, but Veronica Sellars catches him before leaving with the heavy burden.

"Hey, boss. I made reservations at the Monarch Hotel. I tried to explain the situation here to the White House Exec, but he still couldn't promise anything before five."

"I really appreciate it. If I haven't said it before, you're a godsend. Thanks."

She looks at his load and asks, "What's that?"

"Just garbage that I should have taken care of by now," Evan lies with his eyes averted. The old bag is sagging, so he adds another wrap around his fist, hoping the bottom doesn't fall out. "I'm just going to toss it in the shredder on my way out."

Evan's mood has been altered from what she's come to know as normal. His clothes are a bit disheveled, and he's slumping in the saddle. His demeanor prompts Veronica to ask, "Evan, is there something bothering you?" When she touches his arm, she detects a slight flinch.

"I can't tell you right now, but you'll find out soon enough," he says.

"They say you and Peter had a falling out. I hope it's not something you guys can't fix."

"There are problems all about us, Veronica. Some of them can be fixed while others can only get worse. Only time tells all."

"Well, in that case, I should tell you that the bureau is picking up the tab for our suite at the Monarch. I hope I haven't overstepped."

"It's business enough, Veronica. Don't worry, I won't hang you for misappropriation of funds," he says with a forced smile.

"Are you sure? If it's a problem, I can pay my half of the expense. I don't want to cause any more problems. God knows we have enough of those around here." She glances at the abandoned desks and cubicles about the floor.

"It's okay. Besides, our light-skinned cousins do it all the time," he says in a near whisper. "So, what kind of seminar is it anyway?"

With glimmering enthusiasm, Veronica says, "Well, it's not so much as a seminar as it is a formal merger. You see, this could possibly turn out to be the biggest thing to happen in Black History in a very long time."

Evan's certain that he can go one better. "Really, how so?"

"Where have you been, in a cave? Louis Farrakhan and Jesse Jackson are finally coming together. Think of it. What they have proposed surpasses the Million Man March of 1995. You do remember the march. Just think about it for a second. The leader of the Nation of Islam and that of the United Christian Rainbow Coalition have somehow worked out all of their petty differences in order to win back today's wayward youth and the family unit. It's really going to happen, and I'll be there as a witness."

"Is that right? I seem to recall hearing something about the Muslims and the Christians coming together for the greater benefit of African Americans. I hope it works out because I'm certain that it's something to be feared by many. God knows the timing couldn't be better, unless you'd say that the shit should have happened long ago."

"It's going to be phenomenal. No more petty bickering and dissension. Picture it, Evan. Let's just hope that Farrakhan doesn't start talking about his crazy number theories or pulls out the tarot cards." She giggles, expecting him to do the same.

He glances at his watch. "It sounds great, but you'll have to fill me in later. I'll see you, Veronica. Don't bother coming in tomorrow morning, there's really no need. A team of building inspectors are scheduled to arrive to begin fully assessing the damage." Before walking away, Evan is besieged by a new thought, which he quickly dismisses.

His beautiful, twenty-seven-year-old assistant watches as he walks away. She continues to do so with a wave and a smile until the doors slide shut. Her smile, however, refuses to fade with the interior lights of the elevator. During the three months of their working together, Ms. Sellars has developed quite a crush on Evan Parker. She wants him for herself, or parts of him at least.

Veronica Sellars is quick of mind, but her desires are just a little unscrupulous when it comes this particular married man. With a pregnant wife, who may be fragile to the touch, combined with the sexy teddy she has in mind, Veronica figures Evan Parker could be vulnerable. The opportunity to seduce her boss looks promising. The short trip to Washington holds both merit and hidden agendas.

Because of Evan Parker's conscious efforts to hide his attraction for her, Veronica is still unsure of herself. Her unchaste energy only seems to add to her sensual allure, most evident in his avoidance of eye contact. He maintains his fidelity only because he truly loves his wife and holds to the sworn oath to be faithful. However, Veronica Sellars has caught Evan looking a few times, even wetting his lips. Extremely determined women can purge a faithful man's heart of guilt, for a time, when they really put their minds to it. And if Veronica has her way, there will be lots of guilt to purge. Perhaps the time is right.

Back at home, Evan Parker places the disks in Ziploc bags. He arranges them and the original hard copies into sturdy plastic bags, which he takes to the greenhouse. Buried in large trays of soil beneath a few flowering plants ripped from their potting cradles. Then he goes back inside and places the copies in the open briefcase on the desk of his study. As he places the disks on top of the papers, he detects a slight tremor in his hands. He finishes the cup of coffee and goes upstairs.

Evan is packing his garment bag when the doorbell rings. His heart pounds as he descends the stairs. He retraces his steps from the onset of this misadventure, which began with Indiana, up to this very moment. Certain that he's covered his tracks with false names, he's apprehensive about the identity of the person at his door.

For the first time, he notices the discrete little squeak of the hinges when he slowly opens the front door to look into the face of stark terror. Peter McAllister is the ghost of Barrette Holt. Like ebony vipers, bruises have coiled around his eyes. As if all of the blood has been drained from his body, Peter's face is pallid, sallow.

The Census Bureau Director now searches his surroundings as if he expects someone or thing to pounce from the hedgerows garnishing the Parker home.

Because all of the anger Evan has endured comes rushing back like the blast of a cannon, he walks away from the door without saying a word to Peter McAllister. He doesn't see Peter lock the door behind him, or when he peeps through the windows as if being stalked.

While standing in the middle of his study, facing the window with his hands locked on his hip, Evan's eyes see nothing in particular.

Peter enters the room and says, "What's the matter with you, Evan? Okay. I know you heard that I collapsed in the hospital yesterday, but I'm better now. Trust me." Evan Parker says nothing, refusing to even look at Peter until he says, "Do you hear me talking to you?"

As Evan slowly turns, his eyes come to rest upon the briefcase, the newspaper clippings, and an old photo of them with Coach Bridges. He spins around and decks Peter McAllister. The blow sends him to the floor. It is nothing more than simple reflex that allows the essentially weakened man to rise so quickly, but Evan is on him the moment he regains his feet. He lashes out again, punching Peter in the stomach with awesome force and deliberation.

"Who gave you the right, you son of a bitch?"

Peter wheels, sent to the floor by a vicious right cross. He hits the desk on the way down, spilling the briefcase from hell into his lap.

As Peter gasps, the room spins. "What the hell is the matter with you, Evan? Are you crazy?"

Parker reaches down and snatches Peter by the collar, looking directly into his old friend's eyes. Their noses are nearly touching as Peter stares into those livid eyes with his ass hovering just above the floor.

"Trust you?" Evan Parker growls. "Trust you? Who the fuck gave you the right, Peter?"

Peter struggles in Evan's grip. Blood is flowing, seeping into his mouth when he says, "Get the hell off of me damn it. You're nuts!"

"Why did you do it? Was it because, deep down inside, you don't think that people of color are as good as Whites? Is that what you really think deep down inside? Has our so-called friendship been a sham all along? You're a fucked up motherfucker, McAllister!"

With unmistakable hatred in his eyes, Evan slams Peter back into the desk, where he sits trembling. He can only wonder, while staring up at Evan Parker's six-foot frame towering over him with the rigidity of a steel beam. He has never seen Evan this angry.

"What the hell are you talking about, man?" Peter asks at a total loss, but it strikes home with painful clarity when he follows Evan's harsh gaze into his lap.

Peter grabs one of the books. The final page of which states, 'Gate is Closed' 2000. His eyes widen in total disbelief and his heart leaps the tracks of several beats. With his mouth working to form a silent explanation, Peter McAllister is forced to look up at Evan again.

Evan Parker is fuming. He wants to beat this man to death, craving it like nothing he's ever wanted so badly in his entire lifetime.

"Yeah. I know everything, Peter. I know why you have nightmares. Why you call Cecil's name in your fucking sleep. I know why you're so sick, too. It's called guilt!"

All that Peter's quivering lips manages are a couple of buts.

"But—my fucking ass. You had the coach murdered so he wouldn't expose this information!"

"But I didn't kill him, Evan. I swear it. I just... I..."

"You just what, made a phone call? Maybe you all figure that we don't deserve what this type of information will give us. Like the power over our own individual destinies. Is that it?"

Peter finds the strength and courage to finally stand. "Evan, I'm sorry, but I had no control over what happened to Cecil eleven years ago. I didn't think they would actually kill him, for God's sake!"

"That makes you either a liar or an idiot. You knew alright. It may not have been your finger on the detonator, but you made the call that set it in motion. That makes you and Barrette Holt just as culpable."

"No. It wasn't like that. I swear," Peter whimpers.

"Get out of my house, Peter. Get the hell out, before I really hurt you."

Reluctantly, Peter moves toward the door. He stops to ask, "What are you going to do, Evan?"

"Why, you got another phone call to make? Am I next because you think we're all just a bunch of animals and totally incapable of handling the truth?"

"This is going to cause a lot of trouble, Evan. Please don't do anything. Please."

"You've got that part right. It will cause a lot of trouble. And maybe Black people won't handle it very well, but that will only happen because you killed a good man to keep it a secret, vilifying his name and memory to the shame of his entire family."

For a split second, Peter considers grabbing the books and making a run for it. It is written in the dire straits of his desperate eyes, but Evan quickly uproots the idea.

"Don't even think about it. You and your friends are going to pay for what you've done. Do you hear me? Cecil Bridges treated you better than that dysfunctional fucker you had for a stepfather. He even secured your career, so it must have been pretty damn convenient to assume his position once he was out of the way. How could you live with yourself, Peter? How could you betray him after all he did for you?"

Peter is now in tears. While spittle flies from his mouth, bloody snot bubbles from his nostrils. When he tries to reach for Evan, he's austerely rejected. Whether it's due to dehydration, physical distress, or knowledge of the betrayal, Peter, somehow, seems diminished in Evan Parker's eyes. He is gaunt, thinner, and malnourished to the point of transparency. Much of what Evan Parker knew of Peter Q. McAllister is gone.

"Please, Evan, I'm begging you. Don't do this. You don't know what you're up against. Just take the money that they will offer you and keep quiet about this. Please!" He reaches for Evan again, but his hand is rudely knocked away.

Evan Parker's eyes are ice-cold when he says, "You disgust me, Peter. Your best bet is to cut a deal. Now get out before I wring your pitiful neck. Get the fuck out!" He shoves Peter toward the door.

Peter McAllister turns away, totally dejected. His once proud shoulders sag and convulse from the heartfelt tears that are truly motivated by the loss of a friend. Peter feels it now, as if a part of himself is missing in a mirror. He feels it now, like a person who doesn't know they are wounded until someone else screams in horror.

There's nothing he can say to dissuade him. Evan Parker has become Peter's worst enemy and he knows that he deserves the man's distaste. Parker's anger and hatred fills the room just as prevalently as the demons Peter has battled for the past eleven years.

When Peter's eyes find the stone walkway outside the front door, a question is put to him from the rear. "Why did you hire me for this particular job, Peter? Did you think that giving your poor, troubled friend a job would make up for what you did? Did you think that I was too stupid to ever discover the truth? Or did you, subconsciously, want me to find out? Which is it?"

Peter pauses on the steps. Those words cut him deeper than anything Evan has said since he entered the house. He looks down at his shaking hands and turns halfway, but he can no longer confront the contempt that marks Evan's face in stone. He says nothing more and simply drives away.

Peter's unable to face his wife, who's still in a hospital that he left without a doctor's release. His cowardly eyes wish only to shy away from all reproach and distaste, for they are now beings of gloom that show him no light, no good, no saving grace at the tunnel's end.

Evan fills a basin with cold water and ice cubes to soak his fist. While doing so, he calls South Carolina. When the phone rings at 6:31 in the afternoon, both father and son are relieved to hear one another's voice.

"Pop, it's me. How's Melissa? Did they arrive on time?'

"Thank God, Evan. Melissa is sleeping peacefully. As you can imagine, she's very tired and very worried about you. So am I."

"I'm okay. How's Maddy doing?"

"Well, that Maddy is a peach. She's a really nice and very caring woman. Melissa told me about what's been going on. Is it true, did you find anything of use?"

Evan sighs. "I'm afraid so. I tracked down Cecil's former assistant, a woman named Deedra Wilson. She was very tight-lipped. I believe she has been living in fear of her life for the past decade." Evan goes on to fill his father in, wanting Jarvis to know everything he's learned up to this point in this investigation.

At the end, Jarvis Parker says, "So they made up the story about Cecil's shady involvement with terrorists. I knew he wouldn't be involved in any plot to bomb Washington. They probably framed those poor foreigners as terrorists to make it look good. No one could be left alive to refute the allegations. Dogs, every one of them. What are you going to do now? I'm worried about you getting mixed up in this dangerous mess. Remember, they killed befotre, and they're probably willing to do it again. You have a wife and children to think about."

"I know, pop, but I have to see it through. We all know that the police will be a setback, so I'm going to Washington tomorrow to see President Gore. I believe he can be trusted," Evan says with conviction that alarms his father.

Jarvis sighs long and hard. "There has to be another way, Evan. You can't trust any of them. If you do this, please be careful. I'll see to it that your wife is safe here. Don't worry about her and stay sharp. Please be careful."

"I will, I promise. Tell Melissa that I'll call her later. Pop, you do know that I have to do this, don't you?"

"I know, Evan. I know."

Following the conversation with his father, Evan cleans up the mess he'd made while thrashing Peter McAllister. After rearranging things in his study, Evan goes upstairs where he stands before his bedroom window to absorb a colorful evening.

He allows his mind to wonder and breathe, but his thoughts creep to the farthest reaches where he never seeks to venture. Killing Peter is the hot subject of that tenacious devil on his right shoulder. A nasty flash of his bludgeoning death gets through. All in all, Evan Parker finds it hard to believe that he's thinking this way. He's no killer.

He is emotional and reactionary. His brown eyes wince as he pictures Cecil's death—burned alive—ripped to shreds while Allen Peterson was engulfed by flames. Suddenly, something moves in the shadows of the greenhouse!

Evan tentatively opens the window and looks over the backyard. Whatever he saw was both swift and human. Evan's heart jackknifes when he thinks of what he's done, realizing that it could have been a fatal mistake to confront Peter McAllister so soon. He kicks himself because something deep down inside of him wanted to believe that Peter would never make the call. His emotions have made him reckless.

Evan Parker's eyes and mind quickly sweep the bedroom. He grabs his garment bag on the scramble, vaulting downstairs to snatch his heavy briefcase before bolting for the car.

Parker drives into town with one eye on the mirror. Circling twice, doubling back until certain that he isn't being followed. He parks so that his license plate cannot be easily seen. Then he rents a room at the local Holiday Inn.

At Geddon Air Base, Kyle Parker and Alicia Markham are rolling around in his bed. He is laughing because she is tickling him, a weakness shared with his twin brother.

Alicia, wearing her white cotton panties and an athletic bra, straddles her man to keep him pinned down. Her fingers are laced with kryptonite and superman is powerless to defend himself against the assault. They made love earlier and this is the post-game cool down, a playful instance before they tear into each other again.

They have attended classes and briefings for most of the day. There are always pre-descent briefs in preparation for what the missileer call the Garden of Hades or Jonah's Belly.

The things they like to eat have already been stowed in coolers, even though the freezers below are well stocked. There are also more than enough MREs, or Meals Ready-to-Eat stowed below. Their gear will be inspected before they can enter the command facility, a rule that is never broken.

Alcohol or anything stronger than aspirin is not allowed below. If a team member is taking prescribed drugs, they'd need permission from the commanding officer before pulling time below. Those are the rules.

When both Kyle and Alicia began in their careers as missileer, there was little time for relationships. They were consonant professionals, given to drive and individual purpose. There was hardly time to date, but theirs became a mutual attraction that grew despite them.

As comrades in arms, they worked closely with one another and often competed, even when it wasn't required. Being competitive never became an obsession, but it did service the bridge of respect and trust beyond measure. Kyle and Alicia first met as soldiers. Then they became partners, which transcended into a trusting friendship and deeper companionship.

General Austin gave them his blessing to be wed before telling them that they'll be separated as a team. Neither relishes the idea, which they have come to expect. General Austin is convinced that overexposure will invite problems both in their personal lives and work ethic.

The officers will have to make adjustments, but it only means that they will be free to spend time together without problems. General Austin is not ignorant of newlyweds' need for quality time. They will be completely separated from each other for no more than two forty-eight-hour stretches in a seven day period. The only exception to this would be when they have to endure drills like the one they are about to engage, which will be their last.

The phone rings and Alicia answers while her free hand continues the assault on her betrothed.

"Jarvis? Is that you?" she asks. "Okay, he's right here. I'm fine, and you? Good. Here he is, dad. I just wanted to try it on for size." She giggles.

When Kyle takes the phone, grateful that the finger torture has ceased, Jarvis says something that causes his expression to change from a smile to a grimace. Being in sync with him, Alicia sits up and tries to read the situation.

Once abreast of things, Kyle calls Evan's home in Maryland, but no one answers. Soon, Alicia knows all that his father said. She suggests that he call Colonel Terrell to request an emergency leave, but Kyle's appeal is made with very poor timing. Colonel Terrell and his wife are having one of their increasingly silly marital disputes.

Terrell asks Kyle if he or anyone in his immediate family is dying. The truthful answer is negative, therefore, Terrell refuses the request. Alicia tries, expressing the fact that she is aware of extenuating circumstances concerning Captain Parker but can offer no specific information.

They cannot tell him what is really going on. The last thing Jarvis said was not to trust anyone with this information.

Colonel Terrell staunchly denies the request. He cites insufficient cause for another leave so close on the commencement of the stress exercise that is scheduled for the following day. In the foul mood that he is in, Terrell cautions them not to bother General Austin in any attempt to go over his head.

Kyle tries Evan's home and cell to no avail. Then he calls Jarvis to explain why he cannot get away. By the end of the conversation, a worried Melissa Parker awakens and the entire story is repeated. They can only pray for the best and wait for Evan's call, nothing more.

CHAPTER 26
THE DESCENT

Friday, April 7th. 0600 hours.

Distracted and edgy, Kyle and Alicia report for duty and descend into the Garden of Hades. Neither has slept very well after a night of seemingly endless discussion and worry.

Against his better judgment, Kyle makes another attempt to beg-off, but Colonel Terrell's patience has worn thin. In the end, Kyle and Alicia are forced to descend deep into the heart of Angel Mountain without further word from his father or Evan.

They secure the elevator by forcing the stainless-steel pylons into the locked position. All of the other perimeter security measures are implemented. The waiting begins, but in the mind of a twin, terrible images are yet to unfold.

═══╬╬═══

It isn't until after four in the morning that sleep begins to visit Evan Parker in drifts of twenty minutes or so, but finally...

The drums are now pulsating like never before, but this time, he does not recognize the people who are sitting around the fire with Kinzana and Insanyanga. Although a stiff wind is blowing, their robes, hair, and head-dresses are not disturbed by its fury. Only the sound of rustling trees and the tongues of dancing flames give indication that the wind is blowing at all. Coming from somewhere, maybe below, Evan Parker hears the sound of pounding surf.

This strange array of people is dressed in all manner of ceremonial garb. Some of them are clad in loincloth and naked above the waist; many of which are women. Encircling the fire, some are seated on plush, overstuffed pillows. Others have chosen to sit on the red clay floor of the circle itself.

As Evan looks at each of them, Kinzana beckons him to assume a place reserved. In the light of the fire, he looks down upon himself and sees the rippling muscles from younger years. He, too, is wearing only a loincloth about the waist. His brown flesh is moist with perspiration, suddenly cooled by a breeze that brings new sensations.

Kyle Parker is seated his opposite. Although he is smiling, tears are streaming from his eyes. Though the drums are pounding fiercely, Evan is unafraid when he sits at Kinzana's feet.

They are all drinking from a bowl when he first appears, or when they appear before him. Insanyanga, draped in a flowing white gown, now hands Evan that ancient piece of primitive pottery and admonishes him to drink. Only now does he realize a thirst.

A low, guttural hum begins about the circle as Kinzana prepares to speak, and the whites become the eyes of each man and woman. Only Kinzana remains standing with his hands outstretched.

The high priest's eyes are ablaze with the reflection of the fire and his voice is liquid mercury, flowing forth when he says, "You drank deeply from the cup of life in an attempt to quench a great thirst for freedom, my son. And now it is time that we embark upon this quest, this perilous journey that seems to be the sole purpose of our existence within this garden. Your courage will lend the bloody tide its meaning and direction, for one man's peril will represent that of an entire nation—even that of an entire world. Fear not *our destiny, for we may perish only once from this earth. And if that is the will of the Lord God Damballah, our souls will fly on silken wings above the heavens with He Who is All. You are destined to affect the surge of this black tide, which rises even now. It is so written that these two brothers are blessed of the twin gods, Marrassus and Dossa, who have multiplied our masses to numbers untold. Thou are blessed of Agoue'ta Roya, the master of the tides, for you are destined to bring light to that which is unlawfully hidden. Although truth is the basis of love, and light is the essence of life, blood is the requirement of death, my sons!"*

A Harpy Eagle peers at Evan Parker over Kinzana's left shoulder. Upon the wooden perch, where its yellow feet and iron talons dig deeply, this bird of prey stands four-feet tall. The back of its neck is covered with frills and a long, dark grey crest. Its head and neck are grey, and its proud, massive chest is a sort of a brownish-black. Its underbelly is an immaculate white. The bird's penetrating eyes blink incessantly at Evan Parker. Its cold, calculating stare causes him to shudder. It screeches and cranes its neck as if it's preparing to attack. Though it is night, its seven-foot wingspan easily raises its body to take flight. Its wings whip at the air as it climbs, rising out of sight. When it screeches again, a subtle rumble moves the earth.

"Your children will become living testaments of your efforts, undeniable statements of a truth that will no longer be denied or concealed. Stand fast in your convictions, for you are chosen!"

Lightning flashes, splitting a nearby tree to its roots. Violent thunder rumbles, impacting the air. As the wind howls like banshees across the swaying treetops, no one is moved, for such are signs of Damballah's awesome powers.

Kinzana decrees, *"We will soar through time and space to the constellations, but first, there will be a fire that will burn our souls free of these dying imperfections, releasing us to fly in the purest sense of creation. We will sit at the feet of Our Father and taste of the loveliest fruits, those which the inhabitants of this world are not yet worthy. Man will soon learn his lessons well, or they will fall like rotting grapes left too long in an unending noonday sun! Remember thy charge and hold fast thy convictions, for in our lifetimes there will be what glory fails to describe. First, however, my beautiful children, there will be a fire!"*

Lightning strokes the sky, touching the earth when Kinzana's eyes turn to whites. When the Juju man's hands fall upon Evan's and Kyle's heads, they quake with a charge of electric energy of indescribable essence.

Far below, Kyle Parker awakes from his nap…screaming.

Evan's eyes fly open at noon, just as those of Peter McAllister. One is at peace with himself, while the other is panicked by haunts beyond his explanation. Evan reaches for his watch. Peter reaches for his liquid tranquilizer, finding very little comfort in Jack Daniels' fix-all elixir.

Evan Parker calls his wife to reassure her as best he can, but it is quite a struggle. Again, there is the shedding of tears that will change nothing.

During the short trip to D.C., Veronica Sellars tells Evan more about the conference she wants to attend, which is only a few blocks from their hotel. This televised gathering is being held on the outskirts of what many consider to be a bad part of town, which serves a symbolic meaning in itself. Where else should one begin to mend a broken, neglected fence, other than where it is broken and neglected? There is even greater irony in that such teeming decay lies at the feet of the world's most powerful government.

Suitland, Maryland.

Since leaving Evan Parker's hostile gaze, Peter McAllister has not strayed from the walls of his home. He finally manages to call

Valerie, promising to see her soon because his place is at her side in sickness and health.

Peter McAllister spent the better part of the last evening boozing and popping pills, while staring at the telephone. By the early morning hours, his drunken mind insisted that it was indeed the phone that watched him. On several occasions, he reached for it with a sweaty, trembling hand that declined to do its duty. He removed the receiver from its cradle twice and even summoned the nerve to dial a few digits before slamming it down again. While talking to himself and wringing his hands raw, Peter paced for miles only to find that he could not live up to the responsibility.

Mercifully, he was finally able to drift off to sleep. At noon, Peter awakens to his own screams when the yellow eyes and iron talons of a huge bird of prey attacks his eyes. He retches in the trash bin and promptly resumes drinking, the only thing that helps him to sleep and forget his woeful dilemmas.

Although dreams seem to close in on Peter's eyelids every time they shut, he now snoozes in the black oblivion of many temporary comforts. Just as he had eleven years ago, Peter passes out on the couch while the world swirls about him. Four fitful hours later, he hears nothing of a dark figure that enters by the backdoor.

The intruder moves quietly through the gloom of the house where all the blinds are drawn, following the bellowing snore. He looms over Peter McAllister and could easily kill him without a sound. He observes the freshly bruised, swollen facial features, noticing the empty bottle. Smelling the vomit that festers in the small trash bin, he wonders how something so offensive hasn't eaten through the thin plastic liner. Peter's uninvited guest knocks the bottle to the floor, but the thud only causes him to mumble in his sleep. He picks it up and slams it into the mirror overlooking the mantle of the fireplace. Because the sound of shattering glass barely gets a rise out of McAllister, he's rudely snatched from the couch!

As if fighting off a mugger, Peter flails blindly until he's slapped to an even ruder awakening. His eyes gain focus and his heart fills with dark dread when confronted by the livid eyes of Vincent Sterne!

His ears begin to function, hearing Sterne's raised voice. Spittle flies from his venomous lips to form a temporary bridge between them. "Goddamn it," Sterne shouts. "You fucking lush, wake up!" Sterne slaps Peter's face much harder than is necessary, while holding him erect with the left hand. "Damn it, McAllister, get your shit together this instant, or I'll beat you straight!"

Sterne rears his hand to deliver another blow.

He does not strike when Peter shows signs of consciousness by raising his arms to ward it off. "I'm awake damn it. Don't hit me anymore, you fucking prick."

"Are you really up or are you lying down on the job, Mr. McAllister?" Vincent Sterne backs away from the stench of Peter's rancid breath.

"What the hell are you talking about?" Peter asks. He looks back to be sure that he will not miss the couch as he tries to sit.

Sterne stands over him and says, "Why haven't you informed us that Barrette Holt has gone around the fucking bend? Why didn't you tell me that the asset was losing his freaking mind? Answer me!"

Peter winces. "Please stop yelling. I was planning to go check on him, but my wife had to be hospitalized. We almost lost our baby!" Peter clasps his hands over his ears, seeing more anger and disgust in his boss's eyes than he ever wants to know. "Why? What did Barry tell you? I was really going to call you, but…"

"But fucking what? Tell me something, Peter. How exactly does a dead man tell anyone anything short of having an autopsy performed on him? Tell me that, you fucking idiot!"

"What the hell are you talking about?" Peter asks, hoping that his drunken ears have just run errant.

"That fucking freak blew his brains out in front of two cops. I had to find out from one of our guys in Indiana, and he saw it on the news for Christ sake!"

When Peter rises from his slouch, his head aches as if a hatchet has been planted down the center of his skull. "What? Barrette's dead?" His throat burns from acid reflux.

"Our friend is history, Mr. McAllister. Now, because of your incompetence, the network has been disturbed. Checks and balances, mister. You were supposed to keep one another in accord. Don't tell me that you had no indication that the man had gone stark, raving mad. His freaking house looks like something from a morbid Stephen King novel."

"I did not know, honest. Well, he did tell me that he felt that he was being watched or something like that."

"But you didn't think it was important, so you did not take him seriously. The man was covered in his own filth—as if he'd wallowed in it. Holt had six deadbolts on his bedroom door. His windows, and I mean every last one, were screwed shut. He littered his home with crosses, crucifixes, garlic, candles, and Bibles as if he was trying to ward off vampires," Sterne scolds as he opens a file.

"Look, look at it."

When the horrid photos are thrust before his eyes, Peter tries to stand, but his head swims and his knees buckle. Nausea sweeps over him like a mudslide. As he tries to speak, vomit rushes his tonsils. When he goes for the wastebasket, the smell already emanating from it makes him even sicker. The headache monster ravages his brain with its jagged teeth, causing his eyes to water and blur.

Sterne's disgust redoubles. He walks into the kitchen where he finds a cold pot of coffee and forces Peter to drink it, even though the liquid refuses to stay down. Each time he pukes it away, Sterne forces him to swallow more until the retching stops and all of the cold coffee is gone.

"Now these two photos should be self-explanatory, but I will set the stage for you. This is the floor of his bedroom. I call it the fucking Valley of the Dolls. Look at this shit. Take a good long look, motherfucker!" Sterne thrusts the photos of the mutilated toys before Peter's unbelieving eyes.

All of these emotionless eyes seem to suddenly take on hints of innocent terror when he sees what Holt had done to the rest of their bodies and heads; mouths and eyes taped, stapled and sown shut.

"My God. Barrette Holt did this? Jesus." Peter says in a near whisper.

"This is the mad menagerie of a very sick and tortured mind, Mr. McAllister. This kind of psychosis does not manifest over night without the use of some extremely powerful, mind altering psychedelics that sends you spiraling into a bad trip down the rabbit hole of no return. The words—it just happened all of a sudden—can never apply here."

Peter moans and covers his eyes, but Sterne yanks him by the hair to force his attention back to the stapled and taped mouths; back to those wide open, terrified, staring eyes.

All that Peter can say is, "God, Barrette. Jesus."

"And then there is this," Sterne says, forcefully.

This final photo sends a rippling reality up Peter's spine. There, on the wall above the headboard, decorated by a pattern of high-speed blood splatters, are the words, "Thank you, Peter. Now I am finally free."

Horrified, Peter says nothing.

"I sent a cleanup crew to Barrette's home and guess what they found. Guess! You don't have a clue, do you? They found absolutely nothing. We have sequestered his office and files, but that did not produce what we need to secure. Did he transfer on schedule or not?"

When Peter chokes, Sterne knows from experience that he's hiding something.

"What is it? What's happened?" He snatches Peter from the couch and drives him toward the nearest wall. "Give it up right now, damn it. Give it up!"

Sheepishly, Peter looks away to whisper, "He found out. He went to Indiana because I was at the hospital with my wife. I don't know why, but Barrette must have handed over everything."

Sterne shakes Peter. "Who found out? Talk damn it, or I'll bury your sorry ass right here!"

A lump rises in Peter's throat because the time is finally at hand. This is where his loyalties will be tested or tempered by self-preservation. His shoulders sag beneath the weight of Vincent Sterne's harsh glare. He inhales deeply, but exhales a pitiful whimper. "Deputy Director Evan Parker. He's got it all." His cowardly eyes now seek the floor.

"What? The hell you say." Sterne hurls Peter back on the couch where he cringes in the face of pure wrath. "How long has the gate been breached?"

"Last night. I went to his house and he had it. He figured it all out and then he beat the crap out of me," Peter explains. He does not have the courage to meet Sterne's gaze head-on.

Sterne takes a better look at the shiner on the side of Peter's face that he hadn't slapped to rouse him. "And you said absolutely nothing? You fucked up, McAllister," warns Sterne with his lips curled back and anger toned down to a snarling growl. He considers shooting Peter right here and now.

"What are you going to do? You're not going to kill him, are you?"

Sterne is consumed with rage when he barks, "Listen to me, you bum. You'd better hope that he goes to that bleeding heart in the White House instead of going directly to the press. If he goes to the media with this, you'd better be worried about what I'm going to do to you because you can become disappearing evidence just like everything else. You hear me? Disappeared."

Peter says, "But I...he's my friend."

"Mister, you have more buts than an ashtray. Just shut the fuck up and listen to me. Clean up this filth, yourself included. Put on your best suit and visit your wife in the hospital," Sterne orders. On the way there, someone will run into your car to explain the bruises. The police won't fuck with you, but you better not smell of liquor. Hit the shower and get dressed. Got it?"

"What?" Peter asks bewildered by the demand.

"I'll tell you why. You'd better be ready to smile as usual and deny everything, or you should at least be dressed for your own funeral." When Sterne pulls out his cell phone, Peter flinches. "I have to get started on damage control. Get your sorry ass in gear, you miserably disappointing fuck up, or I swear I'll do you right here." He walks by, slapping Peter for good measure. Sterne leaves by the backdoor.

Before Vincent Sterne travels three blocks, his phone rings and he knows that Evan Parker has gone to Washington. He also knows Evan Parker's hotel and room number. Sterne breathes a little easier. Yet, in his heart, he already knows that both Peter McAllister and Evan Parker will have to be eliminated. If worse comes to worst, that will undoubtedly be the case.

CHAPTER 27

THE POWER OF THREE

Friday. April 7, 2001. Washington, D.C. 5:00 p.m.

The Monarch Hotel is a grand place, built in the early 1900s with money that was old even then. Five hundred rooms and suites constitute most of its ten floors, taking up over half a city block on Main Street. Its well-kept grounds are bordered by an array of pampered flowers, trees, and shrubbery.

The building is surrounded on all sides by stainless-steel flag-poles that display the emblems of many foreign nations as its signature of welcome. The main entrances in front and back, are flanked on either side by two American flags. The rear entrance leads to a blooming garden where private dining areas are surrounded by soothing splashes of red, pink, yellow, and violet blossoms.

The hotel features a health spa, and a resident physician remains on call at all times. Two of the hotel's favorite features are its valet parking and two four star restaurant. All of the rooms on the second, fourth, seventh and tenth floors are large suites with two to three bedrooms. Each unit is equipped with plush carpeting, wet bars, queen and king sized beds. Many have hot tubs. The furniture has been constructed from the finest cherry oak, mahogany, and teakwood from India. Every unit opens onto private or semi-private balconies that are complete with stylish outdoor furnishings. Each balcony overlooks at least one of the stainless-steel flagpoles.

Over many years, there have been several upgrades, though keeping the unique qualities intact was a must. For visiting dignitaries, playboys and their playmates, the hotel's prices are quite lofty. However the Monarch caters to U.S. Government officials at most reasonable rates, assuring that the rooms are always full. When America entered World War 1 on April 6, 1917, Harold D. Monarch took his eldest son and daughter to the top floor and made it known that 'the Monarch family have and will forever remain American patriots, who must serve the cause of this great nation in any way necessary.'

Since the United States of America fought alongside its British, French, and Russian allies, things have never changed. The Monarch Hotel went from 300 rooms to 500 before the Second World War drew America into the fray, but Harold D. Monarch swore his children to an oath that nothing would change even during the harshest of times. And so it remains standing and thriving because it always has open arms for American Government officials coming into Washington, D.C.

Evan and Veronica's suite is on the second floor. After checking into suite 233, they will go their separate ways.

Veronica changes her clothes and does some sightseeing before going to the Winter McPherson Auditorium. In an area only ten blocks from the hotel that seems somewhat disconnected from the rest of the town, the auditorium is located on Fifth Street.

Veronica misses the opening of the program, which features prayers and two gospel selections by the McLaughlin New Direction Choir. Their inspirational songs are original and fitting to the occasion, serving to break what is left of the ice in a theater of nearly thirty thousand people.

The auditorium is packed. Therefore, Veronica has to stand in the rear until a kind gentleman gladly gives up his seat for a beautiful woman. Two speakers, Reverend Jesse Jackson and the much maligned Louis Farrakhan, exchange greetings and embrace as a physical display of their unity. This gesture is expected to be emulated by all. It is an act of sincerity and commitment. After the official greetings, an older, well-spoken woman named Maya Angelou delivers the itinerary for the evening. Now, the audience watches a short film presentation of interviews with children, teenagers, and adults whose lives are adversely affected by drugs, a lack of health insurance, racism, HIV, and gang violence.

Entrepreneurs of several nationalities, ethnicities, and religious backgrounds formally announce their company's endorsements to support a wide range of proposed programs with solid business models intact. African, Canadian, and British dignitaries in search of opportunity have also made endorsements. A large banquet for nearly three thousand RSVIP will follow the event, which is no small feat.

Both Jackson and Farrakhan deliver stirring speeches that captivate the audience and never let go. The subjects with which they deal are hardcore, lacking the sugarcoated clichés that often prove to be bandages where many sutures are badly needed. They are not just offering witty idealism or religiously anecdotal bric-a-brac. They have actual plans, which, with honest effort and conviction, may hold the solutions needed to curb the state of African American citizens. The ideas based on solid business platforms will even cause many congressional members to actually sit up and take note.

This is not a collaboration based on separatism, but on unity amongst African Americans. No matter what their religion, the basis is built on the hope of advancing the fate of young, uneducated, angry, misguided people. This is about the future and necessary changes. They're offering resolutions to reach down into the gutters of American society to enlighten and uplift all minorities by helping them to relocate a sense of self-esteem. Because their goal is to offer the people alternatives in life, they have been garnering resources for the creation of more college scholarships, job training for specific employment already in place and waiting to be filled, and minority-owned and integrated businesses meant to generate revenue.

All that Farrakhan and Jackson will propose is constructed on a national scale, to be powered by networking conglomerates. It is based upon, and can only hope to succeed in togetherness. This project was never about groveling for more government money, but creating opportunities for minorities and the systematic weaning of the welfare system, counteracting rising unemployment be creating it with a bevy of cooperative businesses.

The much-touted conference, The African American Solidarity Conference, is being picked up by several cable and satellite channels across the nation. Its founders hope to spark the process of change in the lives of millions.

Solidarity—true solidarity—is a noble concept, which has remained alien to the average Black citizen since the chained exodus of countless ancestries to these American shores. With great effort and the passage of time, it could eventually reach their hearts. Maybe not everyone, but certainly many, many more to come. Throughout this nation, elder generations sit attentively with their children and grandchildren to watch and pray together. Given the wild nature of the day's youth, it is indeed up to the older folks to see to their attendance. It is up to the older generations to hold them down, to sit them still just long enough to expose them to new ideas, new concepts of what actual adulthood entails and requires in a world that is quickly leaving them behind. It is up to the mothers, fathers, and grandparents to expose them, willing or not, to knowledge and the embrace of new hopes and dreams for the future.

New ground is being broken, but it's not based on blaming the White race for everything that's wrong in the world of African Americans. The time for that singular-minded and self-defeating way of thinking is also passé. However, Whites aren't completely exonerated because it simply wouldn't be Louis Farrakhan were such things never mentioned. His very carefully orchestrated words, however, are minor footnotes that never actually grow out of context, nor do they become the focus. Overall, their goals are based on Black Americans affecting their own destinies in coexistence with one another and White Americans. This seems to be a pleasant curveball for most, who expect the much-maligned Farrakhan to rake the blue-eyed, White devil over the coals once again.

Parents are admonished to pay more attention. They're advised and even challenged to assume more active roles in their children's mental, social, educational, financial, and sexual development; the missing fundamentals of a chain that can only become as strong as the weakest link. After all, the time for shying away from the subjects of taboo has also past.

Farrakhan and Jackson chose to speak of sex education. Even though abstinence until marriage is a basic component of both their religions, they do not feign to think that they could ever completely stop premarital intercourse. Instead, they admit the sex drive to be one of humankind's strongest impulses. They advise parents to speak on the subject with the children who are destined to bloom into a world that exploits sexuality in commercials, motion pictures, and even cartoons. In a time with the Human Immunodeficiency Virus running rampant, it would be much better for parents to bite the bullet, rather than ignore the dangers by leaning on that often most fatal statement: "Not my child."

Nothing hurts parents more than watching their children wither and die in agony from something that a simple talk may have prevented.

"Tonight, Ladies and Gentlemen, Sisters and Brothers," Jesse Jackson shouts, "we have gathered here to embark on a social and holy fellowship. We've come together in a communion of striving souls, which we seek to bind unbreakable for the future of our children in this great nation! We are here as Muslims, and we are here as Christians. By the Almighty's decree, no longer shall we remain separated by color lines, by faith or religious jurisdiction because most of all—I said most of all—we are here as citizens irrevocably woven into the very fabric of this growing nation and a worldwide society that requires our evolutionary growth. Americans, one and the same, we are all God's children! No matter what name you choose to cry out at the heights of joy— what name you cry out in the depths of darkness—what name you cry out from the belly of despair—we are all God's children! Where there is hope for one lost child, there lies a hope for us all. Amen—amen—and amen!"

At the close of this presentation, the energy in Jackson's and Farrakhan's voices electrify their audience. It seems predestined that things threaten to become a good, old fashioned, holy throw down. The people rise from their seats. Some of them clap their hands and stomp their thunderous feet. Many of them cry, "Thank you, Jesus!" Others shout, "Allah, be praised!"

As it is in almost all things good, there are some standing in the shadows, who find this a most disturbing prospect.

The White House. 1600 Pennsylvania Avenue.

Evan Parker's meeting with President Gore goes pretty much the same as Cecil's meeting with former President Bush, but with a few new twists. Evan Parker presents evidence of murders that have to be considered, along with a copy of the 1980-1990 census report to corroborate the allegations as well as a reasonable motive for assassination.

Evan Parker gives witness and agrees to testify in a court of law that Peter McAllister admitted to, somehow, being involved in the murder of Cecil Bridges. He demands that President Gore launch full-investigations into disturbing matters that cannot be ignored or placed on some list of things to do.

To his disappointment, President Gore goes through the same emotional twists and turns that George Bush once experienced. However, there is an overwhelming amount of evidence to accompany Evan Parker's theories. President Gore and the first female Vice President Eleanor Graff experience periods of denial, disbelief, and gripping shock in reaction to Evan's barrage of information. And now, he tops it all off with a real, live witness in Allen Peterson. Evan Parker strongly suggests that Peterson be given immediate protection, a personal promise he made to a suffering victim of the American Government itself.

Gore and Graff are convinced that, no matter how unsavory the dish, they have to partake of its essence. Presidents and most politicians, however, are fickle that way. They are eager to promise what is not bound by contract, but subject to swinging with the most powerful breeze that blows. Al Gore is very distraught by the time Evan Parker suggests that he start the investigation with Peter McAllister and George Bush senior. He points out that Barrette Holt has taken his own life, so Peter McAllister and George Bush are the most likely places to begin. And to hell with the former presidential status. If nothing is done, he promises to take his findings directly to the media.

Evan Parker implies that Cecil Bridges' obvious course of action in such a case would have been to immediately contact President Bush, his true reason for being in Washington eleven years ago. It certainly wasn't to engage in clandestine business affairs with ruthless terrorists. Evan suggests a probe into the source of the bogus information that tied Cecil Bridges to the dead terrorists because it could give further insight into who else had been involved in the cover-up.

Parker is assured of Gore's and Graff's immediate attention to this matter. Before leaving the Oval Office, Evan asks for Gore's personal assurance of his safety. Al Gore does not like the tone or the implication, but he gives it willingly. The American President dispatches personnel of the Secret Service to accompany Evan Parker to his hotel, where they are to stay and watch over him.

As Evan Parker leaves, a very distinguished looking gentleman rudely bumps into him with no apology. This person is obviously upset, and he seems to look right through Evan Parker at the point of contact. His face is somehow familiar, but Evan could not place it. Upon departure, Parker and his guardians never realize that they are being monitored.

Before receiving admittance to the Oval Office, Vincent Sterne is joined by two men because he feels that this is sure to be his greatest challenge. Both President Gore and Vice President Graff swallow hard. George Bush and Alabama's Senator Detrick Myrtle, the hardline opponent of the welfare system, affirmative action, and most things that will benefit those who are no longer the minority, flank CIA Director Sterne wearing dour expressions.

When they enter with the White House Chief of Staff, Gore and Graff share a glance. George Bush's presence drives together the unsubstantiated pieces of Evan Parker's ugly little puzzle. They both know all too well the Republican senator's usual, though publicly understated stances on things. In addition, apparently, Evan Parker's suggestion that they investigate the source of the eleven-year-old background story holds more merit than they wish to substantiate. It is Vincent Sterne's presence that clearly validates the motives and opportunity of Evan Parker's alleged shadow organization. His presence almost assures that everything was never as it seemed.

President Gore sits back in his chair and says, "I suppose we now know this is for real."

Vice President Eleanor Graff says, "President Bush, Senator Myrtle, it's pretty obvious by your sudden appearance that we have a major situation here." Like civilized people, they all shake hands before sitting down to let the games begin.

Because Vincent Sterne is allowed to speak first, he takes the better part of an hour to recount the events that led to this formidable meeting of allies. Sterne is a confident and prideful man, who does not completely shy away from the fact that sentient beings have been murdered and more to keep the secrets of the gate. He speaks with the conviction of one who truly believes their actions to be for the greater benefit of the United States, its government, and citizens. His arguments hold merit, undeniably, but in this case, their true motivations are simply the preservation of life for innocent White people and the status of control in the U.S. Government. Essentially, that is the unstated bottom line here.

The chariot is once again set ablaze. Sterne goes so far as to say that there could be even greater mayhem if President Gore exposes the fact that they had killed, implicating and disgracing the very office he now holds. He cleverly uses the cause as an effect. The first sin is used to abate the second, which were all done for the benefit of the country. There are times when Sterne's fervor borders on ranting and raving. However, when he finishes the speech that won over Bush and Quayle, as he suspected, this Democratic President is not completely convinced.

President Gore asks, "How can any of you sit here and justify your actions? You assassinated and then vilified an innocent man, while subjecting another to a life of fear and agony."

For the first time, Vincent Sterne's brilliant tools fail him. He grows more frustrated by every syllable from Gore's mouth.

With sweat upon his brow, George Bush intervenes. "Al, Mr. President, you must understand that none of us wanted this. The fact remains, however, there will be immeasurable consequences if you disclose this information for public recrimination. This country will be cast into ruins. We may even end up in a civil war that will hamper the nation's ability to defend itself from outside threats. Think about what you will be doing to America. When it is all said and done—believe you me—no one will love you for having been an overly moral man. You will become the scourge of this nation. You will be hated. Think, about it, man. Think carefully."

"Don't you think that we can absorb this, or is it that you're all just concerned about saving your own skins?" asks Vice President Graff.

The former president's eyes burn. "It wasn't easy for me to live with, but I had to. This is the greatest nation in the world and I love it that much. I will pray to God for forgiveness until the day I die, but if faced with that same grievous decision, I'd be forced to do it again in light of the negative economic and social ramifications," Bush confesses.

The sixty-three-year-old senator says, "Mr. President, what we've done protects this country from itself. How many kids do you have, Al? Well, I had six of my own. Four boys and two girls. My eldest daughter is alive and well, but my baby girl is dead after being raped and beaten by two Black men." Senator Myrtle glances at Eleanor Graff. "My youngest son is also dead. Killed when a Black gang attacked him and his friends for no reason. I know that I shouldn't blame an entire race for the actions of a few, but you tell me this one thing, Mr. President. You tell me that there won't be, exponentially, more of the same. Can you assure me that?"

Tears begin to stream from Detrick Myrtle's eyes, which remain glued to President Gore's even though he just lied about the true cause of his youngest son's death. The conviction of two Black males for the rape and murder of his youngest daughter was never based on DNA evidence but his status and influences with the District Attorney and a trial judge's willingness to please and appease said power.

President Gore says, "But we don't know that for sure. Those people trust us. How can you expect us to just turn our backs on this? Don't you realize that these numbers just don't add up? Are you telling me that there may be nearly four hundred million people in this country?"

Then, with deliberation, Sterne asks, "How can you turn your back on your own race? They voted for you, too, didn't they? What about their children?" This statement is an accusation of betrayal that is meant to hurt.

Gore sticks to his guns. "If we've been cramming that many people into a scheme that has been predicated for only two hundred and fifty million, then there's little wonder as to why we had such a hard time balancing the budget. I suppose you have handpicked number jockeys hard at work there, too. Where is the undisclosed portion of this nation's taxation going, gentlemen? What happens to that enormous resource? Or are you going to tell us that it simply doesn't exist—that it hasn't been diverted because these millions of people are lazy and don't want to work? They're all just sitting around, twittering their thumbs while waiting for a government handout. Is that what you would have us believe?"

Senator Myrtle inhales deeply to say, "Mr. President, you're not looking at the bigger picture."

President Gore adds, "What you've been doing in the name of the nation may very well have been a major factor in our economic decline. Politicians sing songs of rampant welfare policies on a daily basis, blaming everything on the people that we still refer to as 'THEM'. However, this could be our own fault—your fault. This nation depends on truth of fact, gentlemen. Those people out there are depending on us to give it to them damn it!"

This realm of conversation is Gore's and Graff's best vantage point, initiating a dialogue on the economic ramifications. Nevertheless, that avenue of discussion virtually goes unexplored. The money is out there. The question of appropriation or misappropriation, however, is ignored in the face of the bigger picture.

President Gore's single-minded focus on the subject is treated as an annoyance, rather than a question of illegalities and covertly funded projects that rest outside of normal parameters. Even though Al Gore's convictions are just, his faith in doing the right thing is already tarnished. His truer true colors are going to be forced to rise from what is destined to become the ashes of his staunch convictions.

Eleanor Graff walks away while entertaining thoughts that cause her to shudder. The Vice President is thinking about a senate committee hearing that she had attended. The subject at hand concerned allegations that the CIA had introduced crack cocaine into neighborhoods to destroy and control African Americans. She thought the entire idea to be ridiculous at the time, but no longer. In a way, that subject pushes her more into alignment with Sterne's belief that the census should remain secret. She recalls how much emotion those hearings generated, which essentially left the African American people with more questions and doubts than believable answers. All of those things will be rehashed, and she will be in the middle of it. Though silent, she returns to the conversation.

"We depend on you to make decisions that protect the entire nation's interests and safety, too. Mr. President, this is unfortunately the nature of political minefields and the very calling of this office to maneuver through them with temperance," says George Bush.

These three men are looking at Gore and Graff as if they are traitors. The leaders of American Government recognize and feel this very deeply. They're forced to imagine how it will feel coming from millions of their own kind.

Sterne says, "This worst case scenario has been put to the most advanced computer systems at our disposal. Even artificial intelligence backs up conclusions drawn by some of the most intelligent and philosophical minds in this nation, those who were faced with the Disclosure Hypothesis. The predicted outcome—chaos—utter and complete. That's what we've come here to discuss, Mr. President. Go right ahead, be self-righteous about this, but we will stand up like men and take responsibility for our actions. Lock us up, if that's what you truly want, but I guarantee you that we'll be the safest people in America. Can you live with the bloodshed? Can either of you live with your greatest contribution to the annals of history being an American slaughterhouse? Now is not the time for something like this to come out, Mr. President. We need time to prepare for the changes that will come. You cannot just shove this thing down everyone's throat and expect it to be received graciously. Wall Street may never recover, the effects on the worldwide financial market will leave it in shambles."

"How can we be expected to simply ignore this? There will be unfathomable consequences, either way. It isn't right to simply erase tens of millions of American citizens. That's not what this country is about," Gore says under the weight of their morbid glares. He is badly in need of an ally at this point.

"This revelation will undoubtedly cripple this government. You will cast us into a sea of red tape that will severely undermine the infrastructure of this nation. It will take decades to sort out!" Myrtle argues.

"How will I be doing these things, if you're the only components here?" asks Gore. "But you're just the primary components, aren't you? There is no way a handful of men could have pulled off this deception because there are far too many points of discovery between interacting government agencies. This is incredible. You must have your paws firmly rooted in every ruling committee and subcommittee from top to bottom, even the IRS. How many?"

Bush warns, "There's no need to go there, Mr. President. I once asked the same question, and believe me, you don't want to fight this uphill battle."

"He's right. There will be terrible consequences if you choose not to support us, Mr. President, and it will surely develop beyond your wildest imaginings," Sterne emphasizes. "If we can contain this situation as it now stands, and we're sure that we can, then there will never have been a problem. The blood ..." Sterne pauses to strategically clear his throat. "Excuse me, the ball is now in your court, Mr. President."

"But I...I don't know what to do here," is all President Gore can say as he searches for strength over his right shoulder. Unfortunately, Vice President Graff's eyes suggest acquiescence.

Tension fills the air. Gore realizes that he is out-manned and out-gunned. His second in command has just defected in the sacred name of national security.

After very stressful moments of inner debate, Al Gore asks, "Just what do you suggest I do?"

Like the others, Vincent Sterne is quite relieved. He says, "You don't have to do anything, Mr. President. I will personally offer Mr. Parker alternatives with special dispensation, of course. I'm certain that he can be convinced."

"And if he refuses, what then? What happens if his convictions are as strong as those of Cecil Bridges?" asks Gore.

Unflinchingly, Sterne answers, "He must be dealt with, one way or another. I'm afraid that's inevitable. If Evan Parker takes the money and signs an ironclad non-disclosure contract, then it will buy us the time we need to prepare for full disclosure in the future." His lie is quite transparent because, if Evan Parker can be bribed, they will never need to disclose the truth. They all know it.

Gore is repulsed. "You're going to kill him. But I gave Mr. Parker my personal guarantee that he will be protected from any hostile repercussions!"

"That is regrettable, Mr. President. However, you won't be implicated in any way, no matter what his decision should be," Sterne reassures.

Bush adds, "You're making the right choice, Mr. President. Believe me, you are."

Senator Myrtle says, "This is nasty business, Mr. President, but we will attend it. We've already broken a few rotten eggs, so an omelet is long past due. What sense would it make to toss it to the wind when the only alternative is to eat dirt and a slow death? Nothing of this discussion should be brought up publicly or privately. Not even your spouses are to know of it."

Gore is further repulsed by the comparison of human lives to rotten eggs. He stands and paces, seeing no need to ask his running mate's opinion since it's so clearly written in her expression, resounding so loudly in her silence. Gore bites his fingernails and rubs his chin, debating the vicious issue before him. He questions whether his conscience can handle partaking in a conspiracy that already involves murder and false documents, or possibly, another righteous killing. He knows that there is no plausible way for these men to reveal the truth without destroying themselves in the process. They may have been misguided, but what scares him most is that he can actually see their good intentions. This political nightmare should forever remain under the auspices of classified information. Like shards of bone jammed into his gums, he begins to understand George Bush's dilemma of eleven years ago.

President Al Gore has found himself in over his head. This entire situation has developed too quickly for him, so he eventually takes the backdoor. It's the easiest way out. He tells them that he wants to know nothing more. Like Pontius Pilot, Al Gore, a good and compassionate man decides to wash his hands clean, as if he actually can. He has sworn an oath to many people, but at this moment, he now knows exactly to whom his allegiances lie.

It is suggested that he goes on hiatus, which sounds like a very good idea to him. At the end of this meeting, Vincent Sterne holds a private conference with Vice President Graff that leaves her nervous. They want her to keep a close eye on Al Gore. If anything goes wrong, she is to report Al Gore's actions and wavering attitude, should they become direct contradictions of the unwritten pact that they forged this Friday evening.

CHAPTER 28

FEATHERED NAILS

The aftermath of a fatal accident is now clear, granting freedom to arteries of stagnant evening traffic around 8:30. This limousine ride to the airport is a somber occasion. Bush has already gone his own way.

Senator Myrtle squints, burping quietly into a fist. His banished ulcer threatens a spontaneous reawakening. He calmly asks, "Well, Vincent, have you gotten the cash together?"

Sterne says, "Yes. It'll be waiting for me when I return from the airport." He offers Myrtle an antacid tablet.

"Some of our more nervous associates, myself included, believe that we should consider offering Parker more money. Maybe even double. That should do the trick."

Sterne grimaces at the passing scenery, noting that a murky cloud formation resembles the head of a dog. "I can do that, but I'm afraid it won't do any good."

"What do you mean? Every man has his price," Senator Myrtle says. "You just have to dig a little deeper to find it for some."

"I'm saying that this is personal to Mr. Parker, and he won't take any amount of money. I'm almost certain of it. His financial status is completely useless to us because he doesn't need money."

"How can you be sure? You haven't spoken to the man yet, have you?'

The CIA Director sighs, venting his frustration. "No, but believe me, it's all very personal. Parker did a bang-up job on Peter McAllister. He was a mess when I got to him."

"I see," says Myrtle, who no longer fiddles with his pipe.

"No, Senator, maybe you don't see. It turns out that Parker and McAllister went to college together, and Cecil Bridges was both their coach and professor for at least their freshman year. Apparently, Cecil Bridges became and remained close with the Parker family, even after he moved to Maryland to assume his post as the Census Bureau Director. Mr. Parker won't take the money."

"Why in the hell would McAllister put himself into such a tenuous position?" Senator Myrtle asks. He hates surprises.

"He did it for the same reason that Barrette Holt killed himself. Pure, unadulterated guilt. On a subconscious level, McAllister may have been trying to make restitution, a silent confession of sorts. He has made a mess of things by failing to perform the job for which he's paid an extra two hundred-thousand a year."

"This is a most unfortunate turn of events." Myrtle purses his lips and draws a deep breath to ask, "Do you think he's crossed the threshold of usefulness?"

"It's pretty simple, really. If Mr. Parker accepts the cash, which I seriously doubt, he and Peter McAllister will live. If Parker refuses to play ball, they'll both evaporate. Peter may have to go in any event. He's just not the same man, and the strain has finally taken a toll, just like the others. That being said, I believe him to be a liability that we can ill afford," Sterne articulates with a lack of remorse.

Senator Myrtle arches his eyebrows, using a fingernail to remove an annoying sesame seed from his dentures. "Do whatever you think is best, Vincent. Try the money first, even if you don't think it'll work. God help us all."

Sterne clasps his hands together to crack his knuckles. "We may have to rethink this entire operation, removing the human element. Or recruiting our personnel only from the ranks of ex-military. We need people who will perform their duties without cracking under the strain and pressures of keeping classified information classified no matter what."

"That may be. Barrette Holt's disgraceful breakdown and suicide, and McAllister's falter offers undeniable proof that civilians aren't properly equipped to handle this beastly assignment for very long. They seem to have too short of a shelf life, posing a threat we can ill afford to risk again."

"I'll have to find out if Parker's and McAllister's wives know anything. If they do, they'll have to be eliminated as well." Sterne is deadly serious when it comes to their secrets. If anyone is man enough to handle this irritation, it's most certainly him.

"Of course. Still, this is deeply regrettable."

⚔⚔

9:21 p.m.

After abating his hunger at Simone's Palate, 1 of 2 restaurants on the first floor of the Monarch Hotel, Evan Parker tries to take a nap. The food differed from what he's accustomed to, but most people find themselves adaptable when facing an annoying growl in their stomachs. Truth is, he should have just stuck with a burger and fries.

The doorbell chimes to wake him from an uneasy rest. When he answers the door, he is faced with a man whose identification badge is ready for inspection. Evan soon realizes that CIA Director Sterne is the very man he had bumped into as he left the Oval Office.

When Sterne is allowed to enter, another man follows with two briefcases. The cases are placed on a coffee table.

"What's all this? I assume that President Gore sent you to begin the investigation, Mr. Sterne, but just how is this a matter for the CIA?"

Stern tells his man to wait in the hall. When they are alone, Vincent Sterne removes three counterfeit IDs from his breast pocket. One is a FBI badge, a Secret Service badge, and one that represents a member of the NSA. He states, "I could have pretended to be any one of these three gentlemen. So could my associate in the hall out there, but I won't insult your intelligence with pretense, Mr. Parker. I'm just going to cut to the chase because I really see no need for double-talk. If I have anything to say about it, there isn't going to be an investigation. This nation can't handle the consequences of what you're proposing, so I've been authorized to offer twenty million dollars for your silence. Simple." He opens one of the briefcases and backs away. "Twenty or even thirty, if it will do the trick."

This must have been the way it happened with Cecil Bridges years ago. He's reminded of Allen Peterson's warning, and that of his father. "Exactly who authorized you to do this?" Evan demands. His blood boils, bringing an unusual harshness to his dark brown eyes.

"That doesn't concern you, Mr. Parker. What does concern you is that you take this money and keep quiet about things."

"Or what, you'll murder me like Cecil Bridges?"

While looking Evan Parker directly in the eyes, Sterne says, "You don't know anything about anything, Mr. Parker. If you do what's smart, you can have the rest of your life to mull over issues of morality. However, you'll be rich enough to purchase a new conscience every time those thoughts enter your mind. And that, sir, is your best option. Believe me."

Evan is too angry to feel fear. "Keep your filthy money and get the hell out!" The presidentially assigned bodyguards become anxious in the hallway when they hear Evan's raised voice. Sterne's man assures them that everything will be all right.

"Before, things go unsaid, I'd like you to know that I created the Departments of African American and Latino affairs many years ago. It was never intended for this purpose, but I suppose you won't believe me no matter what I say. However, it wasn't until the second decade that the trend started taking form, and it seemed to bloom just because we had become aware. This phenomenon is beyond us now, so all we can do is hope for time to find the right way to disclose this to the people. Take the money and trust your government to find its way, young man."

Evan Parker looks at him with slanted, suspicious eyes. He knows this man to be a liar, and a meticulously calm liar at that.

"I know you're a proud man, and Bridges was your friend. I also know that this thing will have to play itself out, come what may," Sterne says thoughtfully. "If I figured that it would take more money, I'd gladly offer it. I have to respect you for having the guts it takes for a man to hold onto a losing hand on the very slim chance that your opponent may be bluffing. But I never bluff."

"Personal gain is not what this is all about for me, although, I suspect that's not the case with most of you," Parker growls. "Where does that kind of expendable cash come from, money you can just burn without care? Recently, I've been forced to give great thought to such things. I suppose it's somehow connected to all the poor Americans you're forcing to live in slums and ghettos. At least, this is my own theoretic interpretation. The patterns play out all too clearly for me to ignore. You've all been draining us dry, milking us like ignorant cattle. You've been taxing our small businesses into oblivion, watching our communities diminish into poverty and crime-ridden streets just to retain control."

"Being the statistician that you are, I figured you'd say something like that, but your decision is unwise. This world runs on money and financial stability, Mr. Parker. You are independently wealthy, I know. So why even bother working at the Census Bureau where you're only going to make a pittance by comparison? Maybe you are just a crusader. I imagine that small incident with a certain young sophomore didn't help matters much. How exactly did you get her to confess on paper before she died? I wonder what really happened on the rooftop that night, when you were so conveniently in the area. I congratulate you, Mr. Parker, because coming up smelling like a rose couldn't have been an easy task. Too bad for you, all of those moral and financial victories can be gone like a wisp, just like that." He snaps his finger.

Rage fills Evan's eyes. "You filthy son of a bitch."

Sterne plays his trump card by saying, "Before going all in, don't you think you should discuss this with your lovely wife first? I can only assume that Melissa is aware of the reason for your sudden trip to Washington. She may want to send your kids to an ivy league school someday, or she may get sick again during her pregnancy. Absolutely anything is possible. Anything at all."

There should be something to fear about Evan Parker, if Sterne doubts having the situation well in hand. His smug demeanor is highly conspicuous, Sterne is overly confident that past events insure, by their evidence, the obvious outcome of the recurring crisis. Tragedy has proven to be the next step beyond the refusal in this drama, and Sterne's wicked smile betrays him. That smile is a mistake.

Before Sterne knows it's coming, Evan lashes out with a blow to the jaw that sends him sprawling to the floor. Parker leaps on Sterne before he can recover, slamming his fist into the face of Cecil's killer, again. In this nasty instance, he has become one of those evil zombies from his childhood dreams. His mind is bent, and he is summoned to destroy all the White visitors to Makuunda.

Parker pins the much older man to the floor with a hand clenched around his throat, cutting off his breath. Meanwhile, his other fist is cocked and ready to deliver another blow.

"You murdered Cecil, and now you sons of bitches are threatening my wife. That was no less than a fucking threat, was it?" He squeezes with the clenched fist. "Come near me again, or within a thousand miles of my family, and I'll kill you myself. Get out of here before I send you to hell where you belong."

Someone is knocking on the door. Evan Parker hauls the gasping Sterne from the floor and shoves him toward the money. Their eyes are locked as Sterne wipes a trickle of blood from his chin. With this unspoken hatred between them, nothing more is said. As Sterne collects his bribe money and leaves, Evan Parker wisely stays close to him until he is out the door. Had he not done so, things might have turned out differently.

Even in the midst of danger, Evan has derived some measure of pleasure from busting Sterne's ass, but he won't be completely satisfied until this man has been duly punished. The blows he struck are a mere pittance of the revenge he seeks for Cecil Bridges, Allen Peterson, and all African American zombies.

It is inconceivable that President Gore has knowledge of this meeting. But in a case such as this, heated belligerence and naiveté often become the most fatal of flaws. This has to be Peter McAllister's doing. Who else would have alerted Sterne?

Evan Parker tries to contact President Gore about the attempted bribe and threats made by the CIA Director Sterne. Nevertheless, the White House Chief of Staff tells him that President Gore and Vice President Graff are involved in a top priority meeting. They are unavailable at this time, so he leaves an urgent message. Evan Parker is assured that someone will be in touch, and instructed to stay put until then.

After hanging up, Evan checks the hallway to be sure that his guardians are still at their posts. They ask if there's a problem.

He wants them to keep an eye out for Vincent Sterne, who is not to come near him again. Reassured by their presence, Evan Parker locks the door and takes his briefcase out onto the dimly lit balcony.

Veronica Sellars was napping in a long, hot bath when Sterne made his quick visit. She heard nothing of the fight in the sitting room as she relaxed to the tune of music. She removes the headphones and rises from the water. After dressing and lightly reapplying her makeup, Veronica lets her hair down. Her firm, young body is quite the deadly package in the white teddy that boasts a sheer crotch and laced bodice. It makes her look innocently nasty and she feels extremely sexy.

She stands just outside the door for an uncertain second before walking into Evan's bedroom with a chilled bottle of champagne and two crystal glasses. It's time to find out if she can have him.

Veronica's disappointed, until a subtle breeze comes from the open balcony doors. She tiptoes to the source of the fresh air and peers out. At first, she does not see Evan in the corner. When she finally lays eyes on him, her heart races and her skin grows hot. There is a briefly suffocating moment when she nearly backs away, but what she desires is much too strong to deny. That tenacious fire inside tells her that simple rejection could be the absolute worst of it.

Veronica walks onto the balcony in her stiletto heels and asks, "Evan, would you like some champagne?" She's smiling from ear to ear.

Without looking up, Evan said, "Sure, Veronica. Anything with liquor in it sounds good right about now, but I'm afraid I might need something a bit stronger."

Her voice comes as a purring whisper through those pouting red lips when she says, "I think I can supply that. Why don't you open it while I hold these very heavy glasses?"

"Sure. No..." he says, suddenly taken aback. "...problem." His voice expels slowly as his eyes crawl upward.

"Here you go. What's the matter, cat got your tongue, Mr. Parker?" Veronica's eyes are dancing, and her disarming smile is so incredibly innocent that the coyness of it is almost believable. Leaving the seat on feeble knees, Evan takes the bottle from Veronica's hand. At a temporary loss for words, his eyes scan Veronica's body in a moment that she savors. She is satisfied that her special effects are well chosen.

When Evan's voice finally returns, he stammers, "Ah that must have been some seminar." The statement sounds so lame that he wishes he'd kept his fumbling mouth shut. He pops the cork.

As he pours, she replies, "Oh, it was quite stimulating and it touched me deeply."

Evan Parker clears his throat as she moves closer to look up at him with those dreamy doe eyes. Having forgotten his woes, Evan feels as if he might wilt, but being limp is the least of his problems.

"What are you doing?" he asks.

Veronica tilts her head and caresses his chest through the half-buttoned shirt. "Well. I've been wondering if you would like to touch me just as deeply, Evan."

Growing even bolder, Veronica kisses him in a motion that seems to take a lifetime to unfold. His lips are moist and hot, but most of all they feel hungry. She wraps her free hand around his shoulder, stroking the back of his neck so softly that his nerve endings prickle and his skin becomes flush. She moans with the realization that Evan is kissing her back.

They're engulfed in Veronica's fragrance when she moves even closer. Her nipples frost, when Even's erection throbs in protest of its zippered harness. The temperature is now on the rise. Because Evan hasn't made love to his wife since she nearly lost their child, he is weak and vulnerable to Veronica Sellars' unyielding sensuality. He cannot deny the attraction as his arms pull her closer where fervent heat and passion brews. Both their hearts now mimic the drums in tumult.

She moans, grinding her fertile hips into him while gently plying with those feathered nails. He wants her, but when their lips part, she makes the mistake of softly kissing his left ear and nuzzling his neck. Evan's mind flashes an image of his wife, his pride and joy, who trusts him never to be nuzzled in that erogenous zone by anyone other than herself.

Veronica's breath is coming faster, nearly panting when he suddenly backs away to interrupt that first step to rapture.

Evan groans, "No, wait. Wait, Veronica." It is, undoubtedly, a pleading request.

Ms. Sellars is not surprised that he experiences a moment of guilt. It is expected, but that kiss told her that Evan could be convinced to cross over into her valley of temptation. The young woman is tenacious and not easily flustered, so she does not try to force the issue.

Veronica whispers, "What's the matter, Evan? Don't you want me as much as I've wanted you for months?" While her eyes bridge the brief space between them, her pouting lips invite him—dare him to say no.

Evan is unable to maintain the gaze, so he averts his eyes only to confront an enticing body that calls to be embraced and freed of its frenzied sexual energy. Eventually, he is forced to turn away completely.

"Veronica, I'm sorry, but we shouldn't do this. You know I'm married, and I really have to stay focused on my reasons for being here."

"Why do you have to contemplate when this is really about feeling? It is all I've been able to think about because you haunt my dreams, Evan," Veronica whispers. She lightly strokes his back with a long fingernail that sends a rippling sensation up his spine. She is good and really wants to show him just how so.

"I have to think because I love my wife very much, and it's been too long since we've been together in that way. I've got to stay focused because my reason for being in Washington is of the utmost importance. Please don't do this to me, Veronica." Evan leans on the concrete banister, contemplating the lighted pathways of the hotel's rear garden. His quivering arms symbolize the wavering of his will.

Veronica Sellars is not dissuaded; her confidence has only swollen. Slowly backing away from him, she purrs, "I'll be here. This feeling isn't going anywhere for either of us. So take your time, and please remember that there are absolutely no strings attached. I'd never make trouble for you or your marriage." She smiles coyly. "I only want one thing—to feel you inside of me just once before I die. Just once before I die, that's all I ask, Evan." His name rolls from her lovely lips like the gentle song of the morning surf, echoing to a dreamer's infinity.

Veronica retreats into the bedroom, pulling the balcony doors nearly closed. She sips from her glass and sets it on the nightstand, smiling as she crawls onto his bed like a prowling cat in need of a good stretch. There, Veronica lies on her right side. While supporting her feverish head with her right hand, she watches him through the glass doors. Her moist crotch is on fire and she's tempted to run a well-trained finger down there to douse the inferno but decides to wait for the real thing. Only therein, will she know true satisfaction. Absolutely nothing else will do.

Miss Sellars is almost certain that Evan won't be able to resist. Knowing that it's just a matter of time, she basks upon the bed in her most seductive pose, stroking the sheets and her long legs. Even if he does turn to face her with the intention of declining her invitation, he won't have the strength. She knows this beyond a shadow of a doubt.

Deep down, Evan Parker has already given in to the temptation, due his man-sized weaknesses. When he turns around, seeing her in his bed, his erection resurrects. Although his feet are still planted where he stands, he is being drawn to her as a doomed sailor is drawn to a siren. Her nipples are as hard as diamonds, pressing their invitations into her clinging teddy. Her sly little smile is oh so inviting.

The woman's eyes are alluring jewels, dancing in the dim light with the knowledge that she is finally going to have him. Her invisible feline's tail twitches lazily back and forth in a pensive stasis. Patiently, she waits for him to be a man; waiting.

Boom da-da doom, doom da-da boom! The drums are pulsating in the night as bloodshot eyes slowly turn to whites for there is danger in the air.

The door to the other suite slips open and a silent someone peers inside. Without a whisper of hinges, he slowly opens the door to sweep the room with those recondite eyes. With his weapon raised, he moves toward the target. The bathroom door is closed. The woman is alone and completely unaware. He enters crouched low in frigid focus, but telltale keys jingle only once in his pocket and she hears. The startled woman turns and screams when she sees the gun. The intruder fires the weapon three times. Its silencer reduces the noise to dull, metallic thuds. The sheets and walls are splattered with a fine, crimson mist.

Evan Parker flinches, certain that he has gone insane. He cannot believe that the woman he was about to fuck just got shot to bloody hell before his eyes. Paralyzed and badly shaken, Evan stands there until forced to recede into the shadows when Vincent Sterne storms the bathroom. A sudden wave of guilt makes Evan Parker realize that his prideful belligerence may have gotten Veronica killed.

With his pulse hammering in his ears, Parker shrinks into the corner where the building ends and the balcony begins. Afraid to breathe, thinking that it will be too loud, he's peering over the side when his cell phone rings on the table. A bullet whizzes past him, missing only because it is deflected by the glass Sterne obliterates.

Small caliber weapons are often subject to deflection, often lacking the power to stay on course upon hitting a thick pane of glass.

Sterne's reason for choosing the twenty-five caliber handgun has greatly to do with a silencer's effectiveness in muffling the sound. He would have preferred, however, something with more kick.

When Sterne's next shot nicks his arm, Evan has to jump! With no time for the sudden pain, he thinks about the flagpoles, knowing that Sterne is running toward the balcony. He calculates the nearest pole from memory and leaps without climbing onto the balcony's rim. Diving over the side, he knows that his brain could be splattered all over the rear garden of the Monarch Hotel. Ten feet, he falls. Sterne reaches the balcony doors, shattering glass as he kicks them open.

Twenty feet, he falls!

Slightly off target, Evan shifts his weight to avoid being impaled by a vertical, stainless-steel pole. He reaches out, bringing his arms together around the shaft, which grow hot instantly. He's pulled downward, twirling with the relentless force of gravity burning his skin from the friction. His fingers tangle with the small cable that hoists the flag skyward. Although it burns, Evan Parker forces his arms and legs to clamp down even harder to slow his approach to the concrete pillar directly below.

Sterne reaches the edge, expecting to see the target sprawled on the concrete path. To his shocking dismay, Evan Parker is alive and well at the bottom of the flagpole.

Parker tries to run, but he falls when his feet get caught up in the cable. He's sure that he broke a finger when it crashed into the brass cleat that secures the cable. Overhead, there's a sudden gust of cold, harsh wind. Sterne takes aim and fires at Evan, but he misses again as the man struggles to free himself. Once clear of the cable, a bullet punctures the ground where he had fallen. Another zings off the stainless just as he runs away.

Sterne curses as he empties his weapon without cutting another hair. He thinks about repeating Evan's swan dive, but he's not so young and nimble. He takes Evan's briefcase from the table and runs back into the room, dialing his cell phone as he goes. He is about to open the door when he hears someone pounding on it from the hallway. His fingers freeze on the doorknob. Sterne moves through the parlor and into Veronica's room on the opposite side of the suite, thankful that these old suites had two or three doors. He had picked the lock to the assistant's private entrance to get inside undetected, and that's where he is forced to retreat.

With the dexterity of a thief, he opens the door and slips into the hallway, mere yards from the elderly couple that heard Veronica's chilling scream and shattering glass. He quickly moves in the opposite direction, knowing that someone from security will be coming. With his gloved hand, he yanks down on the fire alarm.

Sterne rounds the corner just as the manager and a guard come barreling out of the elevator.

They pass by without any real notice. The concerned people at the door did not see Sterne exit down the hallway.

When he is clear, Sterne tells his operative to catch Parker coming out the back way. In less than five minutes, the hotel will be crawling with cops and reporters, so Parker has to be contained. As he leaves the elevator, Sterne orders more agents to blanket the area just in case Parker eludes Morgan.

Morgan rushes onto Capital Street, nearly ramming into a tour bus filled with grumpy old men and blue-haired old ladies. After the Crown Victoria straightens out, he speeds north to New York Avenue, where he hangs a screeching left. Evan Parker is on the other side. He flags down a cab after several failed attempts. Morgan spots him and advises Vincent Sterne.

When Evan dives into the front seat, the cabby, Ramón Reveres, says, "Hey, man, backseat riders only."

Evan shouts, "Drive. Just drive right now!" He takes a one-hundred dollar bill from his wallet and crams it into the cab driver's hand.

Reveres says, "You got it, chief. Where to?"

"I don't care. Just get the hell out of here!" As the cab pulls away from the curb, Evan looks back to see if he's been spotted.

"You in some kind of trouble? I don't haul contraband in my cab, brother."

"I'm not a drug dealer damn it. Oh shit!"

The cab driver asks, "What? What do you see back there? Who's after you? Look, I don't want no trouble."

Morgan has received instructions to kill Evan Parker and the cab driver, so he's in hot pursuit of the west bound taxi. While accelerating on New York Avenue, he checks his weapon and disengages the safety.

Evan shows the driver another bill and says, "This is yours, too, if you don't get us caught. See that gray car back there? They're trying to kill me and they'll kill you, too, if they think I told you anything so I suggest that you haul ass!"

The cabby thinks about stopping to put Evan on the curb. When he sees the deadly serious look and the bloodstained sleeve of Evan's white shirt, he floors it. He says, "Man, why me?" He turns onto Fourth Street, nearly running down the oblivious delinquents tossing a football back and forth.

Evan Parker shouts, "Can't you move this bucket any faster? He's catching up!" just as a bullet shatters the rear windshield.

Reveres swerves onto the sidewalk where he smashes a newspaper dispenser. Two people barely escaped the same fate by diving into a doorway.

"Shit, dude, this is for real. That fucker's really tryin' to waste you!"

Morgan fires at the cab, causing the trunk to fly up when the lock is shot out. At this moment, Vincent Sterne is being picked up. He's soon joined by twelve other cars that converge on Morgan's coordinates.

"Man, what did you do to piss that guy off?" asks Reveres as he weaves through the light traffic.

"I know something those bastards don't want made public. We're both dead men if you don't step on it."

"I thought this kind of loco shit only happens in the movies. Here, take this," the cabby says while reaching under the seat for his .357 Magnum. "It pulls to the right, so hold her steady."

Evan looks at the Smith & Wesson for a few seconds, weighing the improprieties of shooting a government employee.

"Take it, man. He's trying to shoot you, ain't he? Just bust a cap in his natural born ass!"

Another bullet ricochets off the cab, snapping Evan Parker from the malaise. He takes the gun, turns, kneeling in the seat to fire through the missing back window. He misses because the cab driver turned right on North Street. They sideswipe the brand new Lexus Coupe that sits at the traffic light. Morgan does the same.

They exchange gunfire until Evan runs out of ammunition. Morgan floods the piston cylinders of the Crown Victoria to catch up. Then he rams the cab in the side, trying to force them to crash. The engines roar as they race up North Street. Morgan slams a new clip into his Glock .45, shuffling one of thirteen shells into the empty chamber automatically. He's got them!

The cabby prays, "Hail Mary, full of grace…"

When Morgan squeezes the trigger, a bullet crashes through Reveres' window and smashes into his temple. The cabby dies instantly as a gaping crater opens up on the right side of his head to splatter Evan Parker with bloody grey matter. His foot remains on the gas pedal as he slumps on the steering wheel.

Evan desperately fights to gain control of the speeding car as it snatches to-and-fro. When he glances at the grinning Morgan, the world stands still. Every element of thought, time, and moving matter seems suspended.

Before squeezing the trigger, Morgan takes one last look forward as they approach the intersection at North and Fifth. Suddenly, he raises his hands to cover his eyes and screams. Evan instinctively plants his foot on the brakes. Morgan's car shoots by, crashing into the bus loaded with old people. His vehicle slams into the coach midway, exploding on impact.

The cab skids, scathing the rear end of the charter and is harshly deflected to the right. It bounces off of another car that slides to a sudden stop at the intersection, taking flight into a shop window where it comes to an abrupt stop.

Somehow, on wobbly legs, Evan crawls out of the wreckage. The rear wheels of the cab are suspended in midair, still spinning even though the engine has shut off in the crash. His nervous fingers gingerly survey his head where a gush of warm blood runs down his face.

Time is short. Evan bites down against the pain that comes when he applies pressure to the wound and makes his way out of the impromptu opening the cab created in its short flight. The sound of crunching glass beneath his anxious feet is almost sickening.

People are gawking through the opening at him, amazed that anyone has survived the wreck. When they help him out, the first thing Evan sees is the burning bus, where a few brave street heroes are hauling old people from the smoking wreckage.

His blind trust in President Gore has disappeared like the fleeting wind. If Gore is a party to the attempt on his life, then surely the police will be used to deliver him into the hands of the enemy. Sterne could not have returned to take him with Secret Servicemen present, so they had to have been dismissed. He's lucky to be alive, but that can change in the blink of an eye.

With pain racking his body, Evan stumbles away from the scene. After adrenaline-stoked blood clears his head, he runs as fast as he can, limping and holding his aching ribs.

Vincent Sterne and twelve of his agents soon arrive. With their weapons drawn, they head for the building where the steaming cab has come to rest. There is no immediate concern for the fate of Agent Samuel Morgan. The only thing they will find inside of the cab is the father of two small children with his brains smeared all over the interior.

Sterne grabs an onlooker and rudely asks if she saw a Black man leaving the scene. The frightened woman points north.

Blocks away from the scene, Evan runs into the Lambert Housing Projects, where many children are still playing without parental supervision. The cord is severed on the useless pay phone, and he wonders whom he would have called if it were intact.

People are watching him closely because it's obvious that this stranger is in trouble. Realizing that he's looking for even more trouble in this place, Evan Parker enters a building with the large letter 'D' painted on it. He bangs on doors, asking for help where none will come.

It is only a matter of time before he attracts the attention of those who might help him into an early grave. Most of the residents that hear Evan's cries for help, expect a scream that will soon be followed by a gunshot. That's usually how it works in the projects when strays have strayed from the beaten path.

When he hears sirens approaching, he wishes to disappear. Those playful children now scatter for the entrances of various buildings. Apparently, the cops were told that a wounded man left the scene of the accident before Sterne arrived.

Parker runs from the rear doors into bums' alley, a dismal place that wreaks of spilled beer and rancid urine. Here, homeless drunks huddle in the shadows. Many of which scamper, thinking that he's come to dispatch them. Parker bends over with his hands upon his knees, trying to catch his breath. Upon doing so, relentless pain stabs at his head and injured rib cage.

The derelicts, who realize that he isn't the man, begin to skulk toward him. This is an excellent place to get mugged, so he heads for the ten-foot fence. From the other side, Evan takes a look back and it becomes painfully clear as to why he has to expose the government's suppression of its census findings.

He heads for what looks like an abandoned building in the distance, crossing railroad tracks that are no longer in use. In the distance, Parker hears excited men shouting from the projects where people are being questioned because there is a blood trail.

From the shadows of old buildings whose ownership is in dispute, he watches official cars racing about in their frenzied search. A chopper is on the way, its blades beating the air in the distance. He takes a moment to lean against the graffiti marred walls. Evan Parker is in grave danger and very much alone. Once again, he wonders whom he would have called if that vandalized telephone had been operational.

Vincent Sterne is irate, angry at Evan Parker for trouncing him at the hotel. No man has ever stricken him as an adult and gotten away with it, a philosophy going back to his father's often brutal teachings. If young Vincent came home with a black eye and failed to convince his old man that the other boy was in much worse shape, he received his second whipping for the day.

Sterne is annoyed at Evan for being smart enough and daring enough to evade his bullets by leaping from the balcony. However, Sterne is even angrier at himself for the inability to displace his personal need for revenge. He should have allowed the competently disciplined Agent Morgan to take care of Evan Parker's elimination.

His pride had simply gotten in the way. Sterne contacts Chief of Police Emery Bolton, but they immediately engage in a jurisdictional dispute. Bolton refuses to call his men off, citing that murders in his town must be investigated. They argue for five curse-slinging minutes, but Sterne hangs up and calls President Gore. A few minutes later, the police will leave the hotel suite as well as the Lambert Housing Projects.

The cops are allowed to secure the scene of the accident, but they are denied the right to handle the bodies and automobiles. If that's allowed to happen, the police could end up with physical evidence that might prove that Agent Morgan's gun had killed the innocent cab driver.

Many of Sterne's D.C. based operatives have been mobilized to search for Evan Parker, but none of the agents involved in the manhunt are African American because of the obvious hazards. Those who have been activated for the search are instructed to shoot Parker on sight, unless he comes peacefully.

Shadow people are dispersed to every newspaper and broadcast network in Washington. Parker is to be given no chance to contact the media. Illegal wiretaps will be next in order, and the entire network comes to life with its nostrils sniffing at the wind.

Once he's seen to these things, Sterne calls Al Gore again and demands that he enact the Seven Veil Quarantine. Given little choice, Gore starts the process, but he will do so only after laying the blame for this mess at Sterne's feet. The frightened leader tells Sterne to clean it up, or he might turn up missing himself.

Threats usually prompt Vincent Sterne to strike first, something else that goes back to his father's teachings. He hates empty threats, especially when issued by spineless people who haven't the stomach for their own dirty work.

Evan backs into a darkened doorway, wincing at the sound of creaking boards and squeaking hinges. His head aches with each heart pounding breath. Surrounded by a menacing darkness, he peers through a crack at the outside world. He hopes that this will be a safe haven to catch his breath and think, but there is something very disturbing about the place. As he listens to the sirens around this dark refuge, he wonders why he smells burning wax.

When the wet hairs of Evan Parker's neck stand on end, he turns and the shadows move! Several loud clicks in the darkness will force him to relive that near fatal meeting with Barrette Holt. Obscure, silent figures are standing poised in the candlelight with several guns pointed in his direction. Evan Parker's breath freezes as he slowly raises his arms with the palms out so they can see that he's unarmed.

A hulking man ventures from the shadows so Evan can barely see his face. Although his skin is very dark, a long scar glistens beneath his right eye. The scar moves with the flaring nostrils of Douglas Johnson, who is better known as Gunner. He is the undisputed leader of this gang.

Gunner moves closer to shove his pistol into Evan's stomach. Now, Evan realizes that he may have injured his ribs more seriously than first thought.

The gang leader says, "Give me one reason why we shouldn't blow your ass away right now, Po-Po." Someone moves in on his flank and Evan thinks it's a White man with an Uzi. When he offers no answer, Gunner sadistically pokes him with the gun. "Time's runnin' out, cop!"

Evan Parker winces. His words come in a panting whisper as he says, "Wait. I'm not a cop, don't shoot. Please!"

A voice came from the darkness saying, "You sure look like a cop to me, nigga!"

Gunner says, "Well? Give me a reason to believe."

Evan Parker says, "I've already been shot once. If you kill me, brother, it will be the biggest mistake you've ever made."

"That sounds like a threat to me. You must be the man, 'cause they're the only people who would use sorry lines like that when the gun's in the other hand," Gunner growls.

"I'm not a cop. Man, I'm running from them and the CIA," Evan says. "Please, you've got to believe me. I need help."

Gunner pats him down, taking Evan's money and gold watch. He tosses the wallet over his left shoulder to what looks like a White man.

"I'm the Deputy Director of the Census Bureau in Maryland and right now, there are people trying to kill me."

"Why would anyone be interested in you?" the gang leader asks.

Evan looks at the person with his wallet and says, "I'll tell you, but not in front of him. Not with him pointing a gun at me."

Gunner laughs. "Him? What's the matter with him? You got something against Puerto Ricans? You some kind of racist?"

"Yeah. What's the matter with me? You think you better than Juan?" He pulls the slide on the Uzi and raises it to Evan's head, grinning.

Despite the cold muzzle's proximity with his brain, Evan blows a sigh of relief. "Man, I thought he was Caucasian. That's why I wouldn't say anything."

Gunner says, "You thought that yellow nigga was a cracker? Damn if that isn't an insultin' prospect." When he laughs, the others join him.

Evan actually manages a smile, but the laughter ends as abruptly as it started.

Gunner pokes the nine-millimeter into Evan's ribs, causing him to double over. They're definitely bruised, if not fractured. "Why, what did you do to White folks? And I don't want to hear no fairy-tales about the CIA and bullshit like that!"

Someone says, "Shhhh! Gunner, somebody is movin' round out there. It looks like at least five suits."

Gunner quietly bolts the sagging door and they all move further into the building. The candles are blown out as they listen to footsteps hurrying by. While the gang members retreat, someone gathers a tablecloth with a bag of white powder. It's quickly stashed in a cavity behind some loose bricks. Gasoline is squirted around the area to throw off any dogs. The bricks are repositioned.

Someone on the outside says, "We don't see him, but he couldn't have gotten much farther. He may have bound his wounds. We lost the blood trail, so we're going to run ahead to make sure before we search these abandoned buildings. You two take up positions over there and there in case he tries to double back. The boss wants his head, so take no chances."

When those men move on, Gunner says, "You better tell me what the hell is going on, boy. We don't need you bringin' us any of your trouble. I just as soon throw your sorry, black ass out the door. Maybe there's a reward for you, huh?"

"Please don't do that. They may take me in, but they'll kill you all on sight. They've already killed two people trying to get me. The only reward you'll get is a bullet in the back of the head, while tomorrow's headlines will read, gang members killed execution style," warns Parker. "I've got to get out of here."

"You some kind of spy or something? Why they want you so bad?" Juan whispers.

"I work for the Census Bureau. I came across some important information about Black people that they don't want known. Eleven years ago, right here in Washington, they killed the man who used to run the bureau. He was the first African American to find out what I now know. It's very dangerous shit for them."

"Man, what the hell are you talking about?" Gunner asks.

"There are almost twenty million more Blacks in this country than Whites. That's just counting the ones old enough to vote."

Gunner scoffs, "What? Man, you gotta be shittin' me."

"Says here that he's Evan Parker, the Deputy Director of Census," Juan read while looking at Evan's government identification card in a sliver of light. "Sounds crazy, but it looks like he might be legit, G."

Gunner says, "Well, I'll be damn, brother." When he takes the gun away, Evan lowers his fatigued arms to hold his aching ribs. "Is this shit true?"

"Yes, I swear to you that it's all true. I have proof of it. I came here to seek help from President Gore, but he must have sold me out in light of this overwhelming information."

"Well, what the hell did you expect him to do? He's White, ain't he? You must be crazy as hell to think that a cracker would help you. This government was built by crackers for crackers, my foolish friend. Where the fuck did you grow up?" the gang leader scolds.

"That may be true, but right now, I'm more concerned about being around to raise my twins."

There is a moment of silence as a chopper passes overhead. Then Juan whispers, "We gotta do somethin' soon. You know they're gonna go infrared on his ass."

"We better try to get you out of here. Taz, go get the rocket ready for launch," Gunner orders. "We will have to take you to some of our people until things calm down."

"Okay, just as long as I'm far away from here. Thanks, mister."

"Call me Gunner, Mr. Parker. Let's move.

They scamper through the dark rooms of the old textile mill, until they come to a gaping hole in a brick wall. On the other side is a bay area, which opens onto a dirt track leading to Logan Street. "Somebody has to run interference," Gunner says. Two of his fastest runners agree to risk getting shot in the back. They go back through the hole in the wall, and disappear. They split up, leaping from broken windows on either side of the room to run in different directions. One of them is spotted immediately. Shots ring out in the darkness.

Evan is surprised by their unquestioning loyalty and obedience. The others do not hesitate to jump into the hopped up 1990 Mustang GT Convertible. Taz starts the engine, horsing it for a moment before vacating the driver's seat. Thick smoke begins to fill the room as the engine chugs. When the doors are opened, the rest of them pile in.

Apparently, agents heard the car start with its belching pipes and rumbling V8. When Gunner rakes out of the stall, there is immediate gunfire!

Evan tries to make himself as small of a target as possible as bullets ricochet off the canary yellow paint, ripping through the canvas top.

Gunner veers left, nailing one of Sterne's agents. The man's body rolls up the hood and windshield, before slamming into the leading edge of the convertible's top. His body hits the frame so hard that the impact smashes one of the latches of the top before he is thrown to the ground behind the accelerating automobile.

As Gunner turns west onto Logan Street, Juan says, "You might as well drop the top, bruh. It ain't no good to us now, they already seen us."

Some time ago, they disengaged the safety mechanism, making it possible to drop the top in transit. As soon as the top is laid back, gunfire resumes, coming from cars this time. Four of the gang members return fire.

Juan sprays the windshield of the first Crown Victoria, pelting both agents. Their car runs into a parked vehicle and careens through the air. It flips over and smashes the top of another vehicle that's just joining the chase.

Evan hears one of the guys in the back seat gasping. Taz cries out, "Slick! Oh shit, he's dying. They got Slick!"

"Motherfuckers!" Juan shouts. "They gone pay for that shit!" He looks at Gunner and says, "Drive this puppy, yo!"

As they approach the intersection of Logan and Third Street, two cars slide to a stop in an attempt to block their path. Gunner is forced to take a hard left and fishtails into the side of the green Crown Victoria. He regains control and speeds south while his boys shoot both cars full of holes. One of them explodes when a bullet bores into the gas tank. The other automobile is engulfed in its flames. Its windshield, which should protect the men inside, shatters. One agent is blinded by flying glass as his screaming partner leaps from the car a screeching fireball, running to beat the flames. By the time he remembers to stop, drop, and roll, all of his hair has burned away.

Again, Gunner's path is blocked when the Mustang shoots toward the intersection at Third and North Streets. He's forced to slam on brakes, hanging a right this time. Oddly enough, they are heading west on North Street.

Guns blaze away as Juan and the others shoot out tires and cause hoods to fly up with Teflon coated bullets known in the streets as 'Cop Killers'. In the exchange, Juan is hit, but the bullet only grazes his upper arm. It will make a great battle scar, if they survive this.

Evan feels as if he's been traveling in one big circle. And in truth, he is. He knows that they will soon be boxed in if they can't evade Sterne's people in a hurry. The circle is getting tighter and tighter. This is surely little challenge for a spy network that usurps entire governments.

He picks up Slick's weapon, fully prepared to defend himself and newfound friends from those who intend to put a sudden end to all their lives. It is at this very moment that he realizes for the first time in his life that he is capable of killing.

"We ain't gonna make it!" Gunner shouts. "Fuck it!"

When Evan looks ahead, the intersection has been cutoff. There is no way to turn as they approach Fifth and North. They cannot stop or go back because they are being pursued from the rear. It seems hopeless.

A bright spotlight drenches them from the sky.

"Oh shit. We're gonna die, brotha," Juan shouts. He has a curiously wild look of exhilaration in his eyes. "But we ain't going alone!" He flips the empty magazine and resumes firing an AK47.

"Not if I can help it. Hold on," Gunner barks. At the last second, he turns right, shooting the gap by going up the curb between a lamppost and a building. The muscular convertible takes to the air and comes down in the middle of Fifth Street. It plows into a hedgerow on the other side, but Gunner holds it to the floor. The car emerges intact on the far side, though badly bruised. This is no Chevy, no fiberglass body here. He's proud of this stallion.

They evade the roadblock, but with all the gunfire, only Juan remains alive in the back seat. When the Mustang jumps the curb and plows through the hedges, three of the other bodies are ejected from the open roof. The man called Taz lands on an agent's hood. Another is impaled on the standing section of wrought iron fencing when they crash through the hedge bushes.

They emerge in a parking lot. Though it is steaming a bit, the car still responds to Gunner's attempt to find a way out. The agents are making their way inside! When Gunner sideswipes an agent's SUV, he loses control. The convertible shoots up the steps and stalls gracefully on its fractured rims and deflating tires.

When they stumble out of the car, Gunner instructs, "Run, Parker. The parking lot is full. Run to the building. It's your only chance!" He turns to face-off with another AK47 blazing. The world slows down with each ejected cartridge. Chop-chop-chopping.

Evan lost his gun in flight, so he runs while Gunner and Juan hold the hunters at bay. Sadly, it is their first and last stand for Black kind, but they die well. They die free. On the other side of the thick glass doors, Evan looks back just in time to see Gunner go down as he stands over Juan's bullet-riddled body. He expires in a hailstorm of bullets with his blood staining the air when the back of his shaved head explodes.

Only four agents are running up the steps now. Five more lay dead or severely wounded. Bullets crash into the plate glass doors, shattering them instantly.

Evan hears voices, but he sees no one. He pulls open the first set of doors, hoping to see people. Even White people will do. A crew of janitors are pushing brooms in the quiet auditorium. He limps down the long rows of empty seats to the immense stage, while they shout, "Hey, you can't come in here!"

When he reaches the other end of the large expanse, the doors he had just used are yanked open and vicious gunfire echoes behind him. Bullets plow into the backs of the front row seats. They slam into the wooden stage, pelting the drawn curtains as he runs on blindly.

Evan dashes behind the curtains, eyes desperately searching through a maze of stage equipment for an exit. He bolts down a dim corridor that seems to go on forever. It is filled with the smell of spaghetti. With his gas running out, Evan yanks another door open and collides with a table. Someone screams when he crashes to the floor. Parker is dizzy and spent as he holds his fractured ribs. He tries desperately to rise, crawling on his hands and knees, but the room swims away. Consciousness soon deserts him.

When two agents burst through the door with their guns in hand, they skid to a halt. Simple reflex causes one of them to pull the trigger, striking a screaming woman in the chest. The air rushes from his lungs.

When the second team comes through the adjacent doors, they too are struck dumb. They all look the way any person would when he or she discovers that they have stumbled into a minefield, or into a room crawling with snakes. They have definitely crashed the wrong party.

There are about four-hundred people still left in this banquet hall. Many of which are scowling men. In an all-out attempt to kill an unarmed man, Sterne's hunters have burst into a room predominantly filled with African Americans and lots of cameras. They have chased him down without even knowing why, only that Sterne wants it done. In doing so, the most inexperienced of them accidently shoots someone.

Each of the four have the same thought and realizes for the first time that they hadn't cared when they engaged in the mindless pursuit of Evan Parker. But in this fragile, pulse-pounding moment, they forget that they are in authority. They feel like the undersized hunters that have stumbled into the shadow of some huge mother beast, which now stands flexed to guard the offspring that has run to her massive underbelly. They swallow hard, slowly backing out of that room because Louis Farrakhan's bodyguards suddenly produced firearms of their own as the mad scramble for the exits ensue.

The drums...pounding! Boom da-da doom!

At 10:45 p.m. limousines, cars and buses begin to leave from every exit, refusing to be stopped or searched.

Littered remnants of the media fleet, who were present during the sudden appearance of the fugitive and the shooting will try to put together some theories as to the wounded man's identity. Luckily, Parker has found protective isolation. They will receive no satisfactory answers and those who seek him will offer no names, reserving the right to question exclusively.

When Vincent Sterne arrives, he stomps verbal mud holes into his men for allowing Parker to get this far. The four agents who nearly had him, will get together afterward and ask each other, "What did he expect us to do, kill everyone in the fucking room?"

It certainly seems that way.

The drums are pounding at the end of Kwani Drive, at the African Village in South Carolina, and all across the map. Now, they will not stop until Kinzana's fire. Blood calls for blood, souring the stomachs of all who partake. Every person involved in this drama, no matter the side, has to drink from the very bitter cup before them. Boom da-da doom! Boom da-da doom! Boom da-da doom!

CHAPTER 29

VEILED CREATION

The latter months of 1997 brought about shocking events that rocked the world of espionage. This was especially true for the United States. The FBI and the CIA were engrossed in a joint investigation into the activities of Simon Tedesco, a sort of free-lance spy. For over twenty years, he auctioned his information to discrete buyers who could afford his price. He used considerable influence to steal government secrets when he was not busy with industrial espionage in the private sector.

Simon Tedesco was within a hairbreadth of getting his hands on the blueprints for the U.S. Air Force's F-117 Stealth Fighter and the Stealth B-2 Bomber. He intended to sell this technology to the Soviets, the Chinese, or North Korea. What mattered most was that they come up with the two-hundred million-dollar price tag.

His covert activities were relatively safe until he went after the Stealth technology, but greed and arrogance ultimately exposed him. When the CIA got wind of Tedesco's activities, he was fever-ishly sought out. Because he proved to be such an elusive target, the FBI was asked to aid in the search for a man known in the world of espionage as the mythical Shadow Fawn.

Every attempt Tedesco made to get out of the country ended in miserable failures and narrow escapes. Because some of the best hackers in the world found the trapdoors to breach Tedesco's networks and security fallbacks, time was running out. They were hot on his heels.

In a last ditch effort to bargain for his freedom and immunity from prosecution, Tedesco finally contacted the Director of the CIA. While using a scrambled telephone relay, he offered all of the secrets he'd procured from the U.S. and nations abroad. Being the generous man that he was, Sterne offered Tedesco an unconditional surrender with absolutely no concessions. In fact, Simon Tedesco took from Sterne's voice that he was a dead man, no matter what. At best, he would be thrown into some cold, dark hole where he'd never again see the light of day.

Tedesco decided that if it was not possible to get away with his life or his sensitive material, then secrets they would no longer be. He uploaded his acquired information to various factions of the news media, hoping to cause enough havoc to squeeze between the tightening mesh of Sterne's net.

Although, these people never knew him other than just an ordinary guy, different names, of course, Tedesco had made many contacts over the years with bright, ambitious media personalities to whom he dispersed his inflammatory information. As the result, his misbegotten facts were printed in several newspapers. His taped confession, which displayed his fear of deadly reprisal from the CIA was a hot exclusive that traveled over the airways to cities throughout the nation and across the world.

Those who reported Simon Tedesco's disturbing memoirs, domestically, took insufficient consideration of the moral and anti-patriotic implications. As the result of irresponsible reporting, they had pushed the envelope on another world war. Those who named names caused the death of over twenty-three agents in North Korea, Asia, and in the Middle East. He had the false identities of spies and their assets working in even allied countries, such as Great Britain, and Germany. It was a very intense time as governments of the world argued and threatened payback and war.

When the dust settled, the U.S. Government handed down very stiff reprimands and strict sanctions to those it held responsible. It would seem that President Clinton and the Republicans in Congress finally came together to agree on something worthwhile. They came up with a bill that they named the Seven Veil Emergency Quarantine. Compliance was forced down the media's throat. When threatened with the loss of their rights and licenses to report the news because such things faced permanent default, they chose to swallow the bitter pill.

No judge or lawyer dared to champion the media's First Amendment Rights after such extreme damage had been done, so the rules were rewritten. The Supreme Court had given the bill its unanimous blessing.

The Seven Veil Quarantine passed into law in February of 1998. In the most extenuating circumstances, the U.S. President commands the repression of information that threatens national security. The government does not have to validate the enactment of the Veil when needed because it is actually deemed an executive order. In addition, the media is required by law to report contact with persons or materials that are sought out by the CIA, FBI, US Military, and the FCC. Any material that is subject to the bylaws of the Veil, is to be immediately turned over to authorities. The source of the data is not sacred. In effect, it means total cooperation or shutdown. The Right of Free Speech had found its own limitations.

Because of Evan Parker, President Al Gore lowers the Veil across the eyes of America. After all he believes there to be a very real threat to national security running loose in the streets. Not to mention the threat to his presidency.

The news world is suddenly primed with nervous anticipation. President Gore's officials gave no specifics, other than Evan Parker's name and photograph. This very stalwart warning goes out by wire and couriers, but it isn't made public knowledge because of obvious complications that will defeat the purpose.

Top executives in the media syndications are informed and strongly reminded of their contractual obligation. Naysayers once predicted this act to be the kind of thing they'll all come to regret someday. Knowing the true nature of breaking big stories, they all wonder who might dare to violate the power of forced silence.

This is the first time the federal statute is employed since the slaughter of those agents in 1997 and the bill's expeditious ratification in 1998. The Evan Parker story is obviously big news, but they are all reminded that foreign news agencies cannot be held to American standards. The temptation is staggering, regardless of the rules that prohibit any media investigation into persons or materials that have been quarantined.

The guilt of 1997 fades, but someone has to be the first to buck the system. Any media network being the first to do so stands to lose everything, or possibly, become the heroes of the media world. One way or the other, there is no middle ground and the risks are enormous. The rules also apply to the Black-owned media networks, as it should. But then, it is even more so in light of current events.

It only takes the snap of the President's and Vincent Sterne's fingers to mobilize hundreds of men and women in the field to stand guard over these potential gates of chaos. Damage control is in effect even before Evan Parker causes any damage, except for that which has already been dealt to Sterne's enormous pride.

If Evan Parker can't be found quickly, African American citizens are about to undergo intense harassment. Anyone proven to have abated Evan Parker's escape from Sterne's net will surely have done so at risk to life and limb.

South Carolina is watching the homes of relatives in a matter of minutes. Meanwhile, rental car agencies and all places of mass transit are cast beneath the speculative eyes of the CIA and the FBI. The Federal Bureau of Investigations is also ordered to only use White agents. All personnel of mixed African American descent are summarily excluded from the search to avoid the contamination of possible sympathizers

When Sterne first arrives at the Winter McPherson auditorium, it hits him hard. The lighted billboard, which formally announces the "United Council for African American Solidarity" causes his heart to stammer. When he gets out of his car, he chews asses from end to end. He barks like a rabid dog, tearing into his men with an abandon they'd never witnessed. This is obviously personal and getting worse by the second. The immediate concern is tracking down the people responsible for Evan Parker's escape, which are, undoubtedly, Louis Farrakhan and Jesse Jackson.

There is great danger in the air. Vincent Sterne knows that this dilemma can only end with death. One death or many. Evan Parker's name has turned to bile upon his lips. The drums! The drums!

Unfortunately, the news media has already gotten wind of the murder in suite 233 of the Monarch Hotel. Sterne's second mistake was that he hadn't positioned his people to sanitize the kill zone because he did not anticipate any problems. That was another fatal mistake of his vanity, his pride, and his ego. Parker decked him and Sterne allowed it to cloud his professionalism.

There's only one thing left to do. The media will be allowed to run a partially fabricated story about Evan Parker's murder of an assistant with whom he was having an affair. Though it only serves to peak the media's interest, this is supposed to be the extent of the deliberate leak. A gossip columnist is forwarded compromising photographs of Evan Parker with a beautiful, scantily clad woman on the balcony of his hotel. He was actually paid to run the suggestive story without threat of being sanctioned for it.

Because of the Veil's enactment, however, they will question even more. Why would such considerable resources be used against a man who was allegedly involved in a simple, everyday lover's quarrel that ended in the everyday murder of an overzealous mistress? This is very intriguing, indeed. Some would question how and why those particular photos were attained and publicized without swift punishment to follow an obvious breach of contract. Astute members of the media are smelling the carcass of a long dead rat, rotting within the walls of their journalistic confines.

When the late breaking news bulletins of the scandalous murder is allowed to air, Evan Parker becomes public enemy number one. Anyone he tries to contact will be forced to steer clear or turn him over to the authorities. Isolation is the key, but Sterne knows that he has his work cut out for him if Evan Parker is with the people he suspects. That is the worse part of this mess, so he has to bombard the media with the tip of the Parker iceberg in an attempt to discredit him in the eyes of American citizens. Containment and damage control.

This is extremely serious business for Sterne. He accepts the fact that he may have to destroy Jesse Jackson, that adulterous, preaching, part-time politician. He'd consider it a bonus to destroy Louis Farrakhan, whose following has been a thorn in the government's side since the days of Malcolm X and Martin Luther King. Farrakhan is constantly crying conspiracy and Evan Parker is their smoking gun; therefore, they are secretly considered fugitives as well. This will have to be done in the strictest confidence because of either man's ability to rally supporters.

Vincent Sterne has no qualms about kidnapping Mrs. Parker, if it comes down to it. There would have to be surveillance on her because she is an obvious point of contact. However, it seems conceivable that Melissa Parker might believe the newscasts about the affair and the murder. She might be angry and repulsed by her husband, revealing herself, but she could be compelled to make trouble if she is aware of her husband's real reason for coming to Washington. In any event, she would be under visual and audio surveillance. With one call, he makes it so.

CHAPTER 30

DAMAGE CONTROL

11:45 p.m.

From out of the darkness comes a twinge of pain, and murky voices are a low echo. It is raining hard...somewhere.

"This is not good. I don't know what this young man has done, but they want him bad enough to draw their weapons and shoot innocent people. Strange how they haven't mentioned the latter part," says Jesse Jackson as he changes television stations.

"What were we thinking, Brother Jackson? What could we possibly have been thinking to go from eating and having simple conversation to this?"

"I can't explain our reaction to it either. Those weren't policemen back there, and I've got a sneaking suspicion that there's more to this than what's being reported on television," Jesse Jackson confesses. "In their pursuit of this man, an innocent, unarmed Caucasian woman was fatally shot, but absolutely no one is talking about it. Not one of the journalist, who were present at the time of the shooting are airing it. Not one bit of film footage of that tragic event is being shown or discussed."

"Do you really think that they would use such extreme, and reckless force on a common lover's quarrel that ended in murder and the death of an innocent?" asks Louis Farrakhan.

"I don't know, but they looked like the FBI. If I'm not mistaken, they had murder in their own eyes," Jackson says. "What bothers me is the way they reacted when they saw all of us. If they were the FBI, nothing should have prevented them from taking this man into custody. They may have put their weapons away to defuse the situation, but they never would have backed out to regroup."

Louis Farrakhan says, "I see your point. Maybe it was the fact that they suddenly found out what it meant to be the minority. Still, I can't help wondering if we did the right thing. I'm sure that we haven't in the eyes of the law. However, they never identified themselves, so we reacted as if we were under attack. This frightened, injured man seemed like an innocent victim in everyone's eyes."

In many ways, they acted contrarily to instincts because Evan Parker is essentially a stranger. Hustling Parker from the scene when he begged for help and mentioned something that faded with his consciousness is ultimately inexplicable. Evan Parker's whispering words of conspiracy were mumbled and undone, which could have meant something dire, or maybe nothing at all.

"Before losing consciousness, he claimed that they were murderers. He said that he was an innocent man being setup. He claimed that he knew things."

Jesse Jackson clasps his hands about his left knee. He sits back with a sigh. "Well, let's agree right now that if it appears he really murdered that woman, we have to turn him over to the authorities. Otherwise, we stand to destroy everything we've just accomplished."

"That is acceptable. We must take comfort in the fact that this man will be delivered into the hands of the police unharmed. I pray for the woman who was shot in his stead. I was just informed that others were wounded or killed as they pursued this man into the auditorium."

Jesse Jackson says, "Let's get him up because now they're saying that he may be responsible for the death of several law enforcement agents and a cab driver. We may as well find out before getting in any deeper." He moves closer and lightly taps Evan on the cheeks. "Wake up, son. Can you hear me, Mr. Parker? You know, I feel as if I've seen this man before."

When Evan moans, Farrakhan taps on the glass partition. Though armed and poised for trouble, the bodyguard is to remain unseen. Now, Farrakhan turns off the television.

Evan opens his eyes and flinches as he struggles to focus. He is wild-eyed, panting in disoriented panic. For a moment, Jesse Jackson and Louis Farrakhan look like his pursuers because of their skin tone. When he puts his hands up to defend himself, they back away.

"Take it easy, Mr. Parker," Jackson says in a non-threatening manner. "We won't harm you, so please stay calm."

"Where am I?" Evan asks while looking about.

"You're in our limousine. You're safe with us, so try to relax," Farrakhan says.

"But how did I get away from them? I thought...I thought I was a dead man." When Evan rubs his bruised forehead, his ribs protest. Now, he touches the superficial bullet wound on his arm. All of his ailments resume their complaints. The minor head wound from the crash has stopped bleeding, but the drying blood stains his scalp and hair.

"We protected you, and got you out of the auditorium while you were still unconscious. Before you passed out, you said that they were assassins trying to murder you, among other peculiar things. Now, you owe us the truth of why those men are chasing you. We deserve an explanation, so please be honest with us, Mr. Parker."

Evan sits up with a groan, peering through the small rear window in search of his pursuers. On the heels of a long drink of water, he tells the men, whom he know to be among the most charismatic Black leaders of the day, his unimaginable story.

Time goes by with the sky dumping buckets of water on the world as lightning strokes the sky. Evan Parker's tale seems too fantastic to be a lie made up on the spur of the moment by a man with a head wound. There are far too many details from beginning to end.

He asks, "Just how did you know my name?"

"Turn on the television, Mr. Parker," Jesse Jackson says. Immediately, Evan Parker's name is mentioned in association with multiple homicides in the District of Columbia area. He is repulsed.

"My God. This can't be happening. My wife, what about my wife? I have to call her because she's in danger."

When he reaches for the phone, Farrakhan stays his hand. "That might not be advisable, sir. If what you're telling us is true, then there is no doubt in my mind that you may be subjecting her to greater danger by trying to make contact. This is no laughing matter to the network, and she is probably under surveillance by now," Farrakhan suggests.

"But she knows everything. These people probably have no idea that she's in South Carolina with my father, but they will soon. I have to call, don't you see?"

Jesse Jackson says, "There may be time then. Go ahead and make the call, but I wouldn't advise that you stay on the line very long. Is there a trustworthy person they can go to, somewhere off the grid?"

Evan thinks for a moment. "Kinzana," he says. "Yes. Kinzana." When a woman answers the phone, Evan says, "Aunt Thelma, is that you? I really need to speak to Melissa and my father. This is very important."

His eyes bulge when she says, "I'm sorry, Evan, but Melissa isn't here, nor is your father. Tell me what's going on, baby?"

"What? Where are they?"

She says, "They left for Maryland, Evan."

"Oh, God no. She didn't," he shouts. "She promised me."

Jackson and Farrakhan sit at attention, growing concern upon them.

"Your father tried to stop her, but she insists that her place is with you. She told us that she couldn't just sit around worrying about you, so she booked a flight back. They got lucky, and were able to catch a flight that left some time ago. We tried like the devil to convince her that she would be traveling too much, Evan. In the end, Jarvis couldn't stop Melissa, so he had to join her. Please don't worry, he'll keep her safe."

"I can't believe this. It's too dangerous there. How could my father let her go back?" Evan says.

"Melissa is a headstrong woman when she wants to be, just like your mother was. Nothing we said could have stopped her, so your father asked me to stay here in case you called. Evan, baby, what's going on? No one told me anything, but I know something is terribly wrong."

Thelma peeks outside, thinking that she heard something. A hungry, stray cat perches atop a metal trash can, preening itself.

"It's best that you not know, Aunt Thelma. I'm sorry, but it's for your own good. Please tell me, if you can, what time is their flight supposed to land?"

Upon Thelma's answer, he asks that she leave his father's home immediately. After hanging up, Evan is silent. His mind's eye is creating far away images of most unpleasant things.

Jackson asks, "What's the matter, Mr. Parker? Has something happened to your wife?"

"My wife and father are headed to our home in Maryland as we speak. God! This is a nightmare, and I have to stop it. What am I going to do? If anything happens to them because of this..." Evan's eyes pitch back and forth, as he seeks a solution. "I have to turn myself in. That maniac won't have any reason to harm them if I just turn myself in."

Farrakhan and Jackson look doubtfully at one another. Jackson warns, "That won't help, Mr. Parker. These are dangerous waters, and while turning yourself in is a noble gesture, it will not prevent your family from being in harm's way. You did say that both your father and wife know about this conspiracy."

"Yes, they do. So does the housekeeper, who's traveling with them," Evan says in a near whisper.

"Do you really have proof of what you're claiming?" asks Farrakhan. "I suppose we should have asked that question a long time ago, but it is nevertheless imperative."

"I made complete copies of everything, but for some reason, I left the originals well-hidden at my home. God, what am I going to do? I can't allow them to be slaughtered. My wife is pregnant with twins and I don't think that bastard will bat an eye if he has to hurt them to get to me. I have to go back to Suitland. This is my family we're talking about."

"Where are we, driver?" Jesse Jackson asks with his finger on the intercom. The driver tells him that they have been driving in circles. At the moment, they're on Twelfth Street, near the Southwest Freeway.

"Please, the Southwest will take us straight into Suitland. I know it's a lot to ask with you having saved my life once already, but my family is headed for danger. If you refuse to get in any deeper, I'll understand. I will, but I have no choice."

"Don't you think that the roads will be blocked by now?" Farrakhan asks.

"Maybe not, if they're still concentrating their efforts in the area I was last seen. Eventually, they may block the roads, but I have to take the chance."

There is a short pause before Jackson says, "Mr. Parker, I think I can speak for Minister Farrakhan when I say that we want to do everything we can to help you. Whatever we're going to do has to be done quickly and cautiously. Getting you and your family to safety is of the utmost importance. This situation has turned out to be much bigger than either of us could have imagined, therefore, we have to be extremely careful. I'll make a phone call and have someone meet us to exchange vehicles."

"Why?" Parker asks impatiently.

"Quite simply, this is a rented limousine. It's equipped with a tracking device in the event of theft or hijacking. They'll figure out that you're with us. Sooner or later, they'll track this car to find it abandoned somewhere in Washington," Mr. Farrakhan says.

"Mr. Parker, I believe that there's divine intervention here," says Jackson. "Trust in God, son, because it could only have been by his hand that we were guided to intercede on your behalf." He picks up the phone to make the call.

"What do you mean?" Evan asks.

Farrakhan fields the question while Jackson makes his call. "What he means is that it was either one hell of a coincidence that you happened to run into our banquet, or maybe you were sent to us. After all, we're all African American, and only Blacks are going to help you now. The thing is, we're now in as much danger as you. It is a willing sacrifice, if it will help the African American citizen to gain some footing in a country that was built on our blood, sweat, and tears. If all that you say is true, it must be our destiny."

"Destiny. You sound like Kinzana."

"Then your Kinzana must be very wise indeed," says Farrakhan.

Evan thinks back to the night around the fire. "Is this the storm Kinzana spoke of?" he asks himself.

With his important phone call completed, Jesse Jackson says, "There are a number of things that still bother me about this revelation. For instance, we deal with Black America every day, but you would never think that we outnumber Whites. What I mean to say is that if you take a walk in downtown anywhere at lunch or quitting time, who do you see? White people, hustling and bustling about their lives. Where are we, Mr. Parker?" He sits back, reflecting on his own question. "Where are our people?"

Farrakhan states, "Where else? They're in prison, Jesse. Probably many, many more than we're led to believe. Am I right, Mr. Parker?"

"That's a big part of it. Our people have been vanishing from the streets of America. They're being incorporated into the legal system one way or another. Also, I'm convinced that there are millions upon millions of us living in squalor and poverty, where they eventually end up in the underground of drugs and a variety of other crimes. That road leads to prison or the grave. So many are selling that poison to make the grade, or using it to forget their shortcomings in a field of very few choices to do otherwise because the Census determines where the money goes. The cycle is vicious indeed. There are other considerations that greatly contribute to the very answers you seek."

"I'm forced to agree, Mr. Parker," Jackson comments. "But what are these things you speak of?"

"One of the statistics, not usually monitored by the bureau states that a great number of those unaccounted for are made up of fraternal twins, triplets, quadruplets and more. That's fraternal twins, not identical twins. And I strongly believe that is why we haven't noticed it ourselves."

Farrakhan says, "That's absolutely amazing. In cities of millions, we didn't see ourselves as clearly as those who were watching."

From far away, but very much in tune with the day's situation, Evan says, "Our young people have no real heroes, other than the older kids whom they see making a few hundred dollars a day on the street corners. The older kid has probably dropped out of school for the same reason. It's continuous. It must be a stifling temptation in a country that would rather sell itself bit by bit to foreigners, rather than to cultivate a young Black mind that has something positive to offer to the world. It must seem so hopeless to them all—you know, getting an education in hopes of making a career. There's little wonder they choose street corners over classrooms filled with outdated books and poorly funded curriculums. My own home state of South Carolina is now dead last in national

SAT scores. Now that I think about it, the Census may have a direct bearing on that statistic. If there are more Blacks in public schools than Whites, why spend the needed funding to upgrade the school systems to provide teachers and students the tools necessary to compete. Let those, who can afford it, send their kids to private school for a better education."

Farrakhan glances at his counterpart and says to Evan, "Sounds as if you've given this a great deal of thought, young man. I can tell that it troubles you deeply."

"It's all I've thought about since making this discovery. The more I compared the data, the clearer the interpretations became. They translate into so much unnecessary suffering—minority suffering... lower-class suffering that nearly guarantees that at least nine out of ten will never make the middle-class. This is how I see it. With greater numbers comes greater strength, and with greater strength comes true hope and prosperity. We are blinded to our own overwhelming genealogy. We're also ignorant of our own monetary contributions to the nation's economic wealth. It's denied us, diverted to whatever cause these people deem necessary. And in more ways than one, it's probably being used against us. Ultimately, we've been excluded from the benefits of huge networks and fantastic technological advances. I don't feel that the overall African American population wants to be given handouts, just a chance to make it without barely making it," Evan says. "Those who've made themselves more equal than others must see our numerical advantage as a hopelessly terrifying threat so they milk us like cattle. They are taxing the hell out of the poor and middle class while the filthy rich are afforded tax breaks that are ultimately crippling this nation when we should all be prospering. They call themselves job creators, but they create those jobs overseas with cheaper labor whenever fair taxation is raised to question. They even import Asian work forces to do the jobs that our educational system can't seem to make us smart enough to do. When the question of a fair taxation of the rich is called to form, the lobbyist who pull the political strings in this country claim it will hurt the economy by hampering the job creators. Essentially, it's nothing more than a threat and a form of blackmail. These companies enjoy those tax breaks, and yet, the jobs are still outsourced."

His words cause the civil rights leaders to smile. In countless ways, the things that they preach and have alleged for decades are right on target. It fills them with a sense of pride and accomplishment.

"There are now people out there without homes, who have worked all of their lives, eating out of trash cans. I get so angry when I see politicians so willing to give billions in foreign aid. They give themselves raises while American citizens starve; Blacks, Whites, and all things in between. They preach about deficits and inflation, but they can attend thousand-dollar-a-plate functions. Such waste seems almost criminal to me. Sure, back in 1996 the Congress rejected a raise for themselves, but that was probably only because it was an election year. It was nothing more than a gesture, politics at its finest. They're trying to get rid of welfare, Medicare programs, while pushing for privatizing social security. These things are essential as far as sick, hungry children, and the elderly go. Can you understand what I'm getting at, gentlemen? We are being taxed into the ground without our interests being represented in the grand scheme of things."

"Go on, son. What are you driving at?" Farrakhan asks.

"They're trying to cure the disease by hurting innocent people who really depend on those programs, but what they've done by disavowing Black people could be the very reason for the sickness. Do you see it? I do. We've been taxed without representation. The money has been diverted, but they blame poor people and minorities for putting a strain on the economy. It can be no mere coincidence that we've been replaced as the largest minority, supposedly, by the Latinos. But I clearly see now that it's all just on paper. Only Peter McAllister could have thought up that one. It's ingenious, actually."

Jesse Jackson asks, "Will your reports prove what you are saying, Mr. Parker?"

"They're willing to kill me, aren't they?" Evan Parker asks rather harshly. "I still want to believe that most politicians start their political careers with good intentions. Then, when they get tired of fighting for the little people, they fend for themselves. There are a lot more people involved in the keeping of this secret than we will ever know. We should take everything they own. Throw them out on the mean streets to survive in the hell that they've created for the average person. Then we'd see if they will experience a growing and profound appreciation for what basic comfort and safety means. That's what the American people should do to our so-called governing bodies. Toss 'em in the mean streets without lobbyists and kickbacks to pad their miserable fall. No pensions to nurse while they rob this country blind right in front of our faces. Mixing in everyone else's wars because wars—up to a very specific point—produce more profit than healing the wounded souls of our countrymen." Evan Parker is fuming, consumed by passion never before realized. "We count, despite what they would have us believe. We matter."

"Careful, or you may be called a socialist," Farrakhan says.

"Or worse," Jackson adds.

"They take all of the money that African Americans inject into the American economy and give billions in tax breaks to large corporation and the rich. Is it any wonder why so many parents fail to push their children to do better than they did themselves? Changes have to be made so that we won't have to soil ourselves on the low road because it looks like the only way that's open to us. That's why this secret has to be exposed," Evan says with convictions that are set in iron.

"Amen, Mr. Parker. Amen," Jesse Jackson agrees.

"Finally, gentlemen, think long and hard about this little sleight of hand because it has been right in our faces all along. When the age for retirement was set at sixty-five, the average African American was lucky to die in their early to mid-fifties. Because that money never trickles down to their children and grandchildren, it pays for the next person to reach retirement. You work all of your life, paying taxes as a productive citizen, but you may not live long enough to retire while the average Caucasian lived to see age 75. Don't you see it now? As African Americans began to benefit from better education and health care, living longer lives, the numbers could never add up without revealing the true influence of the Census. Mark my words. In the years soon to come, there will be a crisis and overwhelming calls for reform, but they will never tell the truth as to why it is suddenly so necessary."

As if a light magically comes on, Jackson and Farrakhan are both stunned by its brilliance; by its hubris. Much of what they have seen with their own two eyes over the years, now makes too much sense. As long as these people remain in control, they can blame politically problematic issues on anything other than.

"Now my family is in jeopardy. So help me God, if anything happens to them, I'll kill President Gore myself. I swear it by all that is right and true. How could I have been so naïve? How can I so easily interpret all these things with but a glance at simple statistical information, and not realize that it has the potential to turn a good man into a silent villain?"

Silence descends between them as their eyes seek the tinted windows. The rain is much heavier and fierce lightning cracks the midnight sky. The limousine stops beneath an overpass where a black van waits in the gloom. It's time to change vehicles.

※※

Twenty-five minutes later, and many miles away from the overpass, the van stops at a roadblock. An FBI agent and State Trooper Book approach the vehicle. The rain is coming down in sheets, and the lightning repeats directly overhead to cause their necks to recede between their shoulders. This is the moment they have dreaded. The hearts of Farrakhan's personal bodyguards' are racing in their chests. Wallace opens his window, squinting as the water is blown into his face.

Agent Kirsch looks at the two Black men suspiciously while the trooper places a flashlight to the window to examine inside. Three coffins are in the back of this meat wagon.

The driver asks, "Has there been an accident or downed power lines ahead?"

The agent says nothing as he peers inside of the cab. Then he detects an odor that causes him to back away. He looks at State Trooper Book, who does not like the number of coffins. His eyes suggest that the fugitives could be hiding inside.

Agent Kirsch asks, "Where are you men headed in this nasty weather?"

The driver says, "Baltimore, sir. What's going on?"

"Why are you wearing those masks over your faces?"

The passenger says, "Are you kidding me? Don't you smell that shit back there?"

The driver looks at his companion and barks, "Will you shut up and let me handle this?" He turns back to Agent Kirsch. "These bodies have been exhumed. We're taking them to the Center for Disease Control in Baltimore. From what they told us, these three saps may have died of some pretty nasty little bug. They want to do an autopsy, and then they'll cremate the bodies if they find that it's not safe to plant them back in the ground. The first transport broke down, so we had to pile them in here."

Trooper Book joins them. He no longer cares because the rain has gotten into his collar to run down his neck. He shivers and says to Kirsch, "Satisfied? Let's get the hell out of this weather."

Much to the dismay of Farrakhan's bodyguards, Agent Kirsch demands, "Please step out of the vehicle and open the coffins." State Trooper Book rolls his eyes and groans.

"What?" says the driver. "Are you fucking crazy?"

"Do it now. I won't tell you again!"

"You heard the man, gentlemen. We're just doing our jobs, so let's get it over with."

"Man, fuck. I don't believe this shit!" the driver says. They both get out of the cab and go to the back of the van. "You people are sick. You're wet and miserable, so you'll stop at nothing to spread the joy. Thanks a lot."

When they open the door, the odor of decay blossoms in their nostrils. Trooper Book turns away and covers his mouth and nose with a handkerchief.

"Are you satisfied officer?" the passenger asks. "Can we get out of the rain now?"

Kirsch looks at the grimy coffins that have been worn by time in the ground, but they number at three. Kirsch says, "Open them up."

"What? Have you lost your mind?" the driver protests. "I'm not opening those things for you or your mother. Didn't you hear what I said about these three stiffs?"

The other bodyguard says, "You're nuts. Why do you think we're wearing respirators? We don't want to catch whatever killed them!"

"That's enough of your lip," Kirsch shouts. "Open them!"

State Trooper Book pulls Agent Kirsch aside to say, "Is this shit really necessary? It smells like a sewer in there."

Kirsch squints at the policemen through the driving rain. He says, "That first coffin has a gash in it. It could be an air hole. Don't you understand? The fugitives may be hiding inside of those coffins, so I have to check them out."

Book is disgusted, but he's been ordered to comply with Agent Kirsch's demands. He looks at the driver and says, "You heard him. Let's get this over with."

The hearts of the drums are beating like thunder and they mimic the rhythm in the bodyguards' souls.

As they drag the top coffin to the edge, the driver says, "This fool thinks that this is an air hole. For what? Dead motherfuckers don't breathe!" He grabs the crank and shoves it home. "This coffin was damaged by the bulldozer when they dug it up, jackass."

Agent Kirsch says, "What are you waiting for? Open it."

The defiant bodyguard backs away. "Hell no, you open it. Be my guest."

Kirsch draws his weapon and looks at Book, who says, "You want me to open that? No fucking way."

Kirsch yells, "Do as I say, or your refusal will be noted on your record."

Grudgingly, Book approaches the coffin and turns the crank to break the seal. The bodyguards ease their hands inside their soaked jackets, ready to disable these men if necessary. When the seal is broken, Book glances over his shoulder at Kirsch.

Kirsch moves in with his weapon pointed at the coffin. The lightning flashes with such intensity that it hurts their eyes. The immediate crash of thunder causes them all to flinch.

Book takes a deep breath and yanks the coffin open. As Kirsch points the weapon inside, Book groans and moves away. Both their stomachs roll as Kirsch stares down at the rotting, bloated corpse of an obese man. The body has been poorly preserved, which is evident by the boils that have developed on the flaccid skin.

When lightning flashes, the corpse shudders in their eyes. Kirsch flinches, nearly pulling the trigger on the worms that crawl from the corpse's nostrils and ears. The odor engulfs them both by the time they're forced to inhale.

"Oh God!" Book moans. He turns away completely, but Agent Kirsch heaves once on a dry run. Then the floodgates open to purge him of his most recent meal. As he retches, the nervous bodyguards look at one another, wondering if he will stop there.

When the retching is finally done, Agent Kirsch takes a long look at the other two coffins. He considers them for a moment and decides that he's had enough so he turns to the driver and says, "Thank you, gentlemen. I'm really sorry for the inconvenience. You...you...you can go."

The driver wants to laugh, but thinks better of it because he needs something from Agent Kirsch. He says, "Look, mister, you've already cost us time and now we're soaking wet, again. I have no idea who or what you're looking for, but I'd appreciate it if you would call ahead and make sure that we don't have to repeat this performance all the way to Baltimore."

Officer Book says, "Don't worry, gentlemen. There is one more checkpoint between here and Suitland, but that's it. I'll call ahead and tell them to leave you guys alone, unless my colleague here has objections." He glares at Agent Kirsch, ridicule in his eyes.

Kirsch averts his eyes and concedes, wordlessly. The bodyguard quickly reseals the coffin.

"Thank you, officer. I'm glad to see that there's at least one reasonable man in this bunch," the driver scoffs. Book laughs at the little barb, feeling that Agent Kirsch deserves derision for puking like a little schoolgirl.

Before they get back inside, Kirsch says, "Hey, wait a sec. What did they die of anyway?"

The driver scowls at him with disdain and says, "Something called Nymfuckulitis, and I'm quite certain that you now have it, too." Kirsch nods and backs away.

Moments later, the van turns onto a dirt road where the heavy coffin with the gash is dragged out. Jesse Jackson and Louis Farrakhan are extremely grateful when they're released from the cramped confines of the coffin they had to share. Evan, huffing hard on his oxygen mask, is just as happy to get out of that ungodly box.

All of the vehicle's doors are opened, and the inside is drenched with an aerosol disinfectant. With the rain crashing down and the lightning summoning a hurried departure from this place, they hasten words over the dead stranger that saved all their lives before leaving his coffin hidden in the woods.

The long ride through bad weather is tedious and filled with vigorous anxieties that accompany the anticipation of impending doom.

As they endure the final leg of the trip, Jackson and Farrakhan attempt to contact key Black officials. The first of which is the leader of the Congressional Black Caucus, but the electrical storm interferes with the cell towers and there is no time to stop. That's just as well because Sterne has ordered wiretaps on all African American officials, media personalities, and anyone associated with Jackson and Farrakhan.

Director Sterne is frantic and feverish in his pursuits. The effective time to apprehend Evan Parker and those who aided his escape is running critically short. Contamination seems now imminent, and he knows it with dark dread. His hopes rise when the Direct Limousine Service pinpoints their missing automobile in the northwest quadrant of Washington. When Sterne's men surround the vehicle with weapons at the ready, they're disappointed to find that the fugitives have abandoned it.

All access roads are riddled with checkpoints. The new subway system, train and bus stations, airports as well as rental car agencies, have been saturated with even more personnel from both branches of the CIA and the FBI. Evan Parker is proving to be a most difficult quarry.

Jesse Jackson's friend, the mortician who loaned them the van and coffins, has been given Evan Parker's credit card numbers. He's been instructed to purchase disposable cell phones to call the major airlines and other sources of mass transit with Evan Parker's credit card numbers to make reservations going to all ports anywhere.

As designed, Evan's false trail wastes precious manpower. Vincent Sterne's efforts are still concentrated in Washington.

Every time one of those annoying calls comes in to report another of Evan Parker's false footprints, no one reports his destination to be Suitland or South Carolina.

Director Sterne's best men have been dispatched to both locations. If the fugitives resist, his men are ordered to terminate without hesitation. If taken alive, the captives will be tortured until compelled to reveal the names of any and all persons Evan Parker has been inclined to tell his nasty little secret.

⇒⇥ ⇤⇐

Geddon Air Base. Hours earlier.

Captain Kyle Parker and Lieutenant Alicia Markham have just ended the equipment check. After the last item on the list is monitored and proves within acceptable parameters, Kyle's incessant pacing resumes. He's already contacted the commanding officer three times during the course of the day, and his requests to contact his father and brother have been met with merciless denial.

Colonel Terrell has lost patience, adamant against breaking protocol at Captain Parker's insistence.

The deprivation test is not to be breached for any reason, and this so-called emergency proves the importance of such programs. Just what will a missileer do if he is cutoff with such strong concerns for family members during and after a nuclear attack? That has always been the age-old question, what tests like these are designed to determine. A missileer's reaction to stress is the foremost item of this venue. Because of it, Kyle is being viewed like a test rat in a laboratory maze.

Alicia turns off the cameras connecting them to the topside command post and shuts down the audio link. Both mechanisms can be reactivated from topside, but no one is watching because it isn't necessary to intrude upon the officers at every moment during the first stages of an exercise. Closer observation will be required later, a more critical period as the deprivation couples with antici-pation of finally leaving the hole in the ground.

Alicia Markham pleads, "Please try to relax, Kyle. You're going to give yourself an ulcer." She leaves the panel and goes to him. Kyle stops pacing while she gives him a hug.

Captain Parker takes a deep breath and confesses, "I just can't stand not knowing what the hell is going on up there. It's killing me." The muscles of his bronzed jaw constrict and flex to reflect his tension.

She kisses him. While searching his face with her worried eyes, she says, "I know, Kyle. I can't stop thinking about it myself. Who would have thought?"

"This situation is beyond me. My brother is caught up in govern-ment conspiracies. Who knows what will happen? We, of all people, know just how wicked bureaucrats can be."

She squeezes him tight and suggests, "Let's try to think posi-tively. Speculation at this point will only drive you nuts, and me along with. We can turn on the TV. Maybe there's something to report on Evan's meeting with President Gore. Meanwhile, I'll fix us some chow. How does that sound?" She forces a smile.

"I'm not really hungry."

"But you've barely eaten anything since last night. You should eat, or don't you like my cooking? We are going to get married soon, so it's time you practice your lies about how really good it is."

Kyle smiles and relents. "Okay, but nothing too heavy. My stom-ach is full of butterflies."

"MREs then?"

He looks at her and says, "Hell no!"

Satisfied, Alicia turns toward the galley. Kyle turns on the tele-vision, thumbing the remote control. Alicia's about four-yards away when the remote hits the floor. She turns to see Kyle grimacing in pain as he grasps his right arm.

"Kyle, are you okay. What is it?"

"I don't know. I just had this sudden pain in my—oh fuck!" Kyle turns his palms to his face. For a moment, they are infernos. "My hands are burning!" Then he grabs the pinky finger of the left hand, which feels like someone just smashed it with an invisible sledgehammer. Kyle howls in pain.

"What's happening to you, Kyle?" She rushes to him, thinking that this is the strangest heart attack she's ever seen. Alicia expects Kyle Parker to clutch his chest before collapsing from the stress.

The painful sensations abate as quickly as they manifested. "I'm okay. The pain just came out of nowhere."

Kyle sits at the desk to the left of the instrument panel. He rubs his arm and checks his hands, which still seem a bit warm in the palms. He's fine, otherwise.

Alicia kneels next to Kyle and looks at his hands. "Are you sure you're okay? Has this ever happened before, Kyle? Should I call the medic?"

"No. It's gone."

Moments later, Alicia peeks from the galley. Kyle is still sitting, but his head suddenly snaps backward and he clutches his skull. He tries to suppress a horrid scream. As she approaches, he rises with one hand on his head, holding onto the desk with the other. When his dizziness clears, he clutched his ribs against a sudden agony that emerges there. After a moment of intense pain, he's okay again.

When Kyle sits, he looks up at his fiancée and says, "Evan. Something bad is happening to Evan."

"What do you mean?"

"I'm..." he says, "I think I'm experiencing his pain. He's hurt."

"But how can you know that? I'll call a medic. They better not refuse my request," Alicia says.

Upon making contact with the above ground post, Lieutenant Markham is instructed to connect Kyle to the command capsule's medical monitoring equipment. After she wraps the blood pressure cup around his right bicep, she sticks electrodes to his chest and temples. A blood oxygen sensor is clipped to his right forefinger. Then she turns on the machine. The information is relayed to a neurologist for evaluation. When she finds nothing wrong, both Kyle and Alicia are chewed out by Colonel Terrell, who promises that no more of their antics will be tolerated without consequences. He will listen to no explanations or excuses, and instructs the person on watch to ignore further requests unless the visual equipment shows a problem.

For Captain Parker and Lieutenant Markham, sleep is a rich man's commodity that teases them both to no end. Throughout their stay down below, it visits and runs fleetingly away from their straining eyes just as they close.

One tries to rest while the other watches. With the nervous energy charging the imagination, they both fight to shut down a mind's computer that will not go willingly. Yet, when they do manage to fade into temporary oblivion, they are beset upon by the pounding drums of dark, unearthly magic.

CHAPTER 31
CREATURES OF THE NIGHT

Suitland, Maryland.

B ecause the pilot had to circle the violent storm front to find a safer window to land, their flight arrived a little late. When the cab stops in the driveway, the fare is paid quickly. Three passengers get out on the run. Two of Sterne's men have followed them from the airport, shadowing the cab until certain of its destination. They veer away just blocks from Melissa's home, where they are not needed.

The rain is pouring from the sky. Wind gusts assure that Melissa, Jarvis, and Madeline get wet, despite umbrellas they purchased at the airport. In their eagerness to get into the house, they do not notice the pale faces of their watchers in the cars parked on the street.

Sterne has sent six of his most able stateside agents to the new Parker home, and each is an expert killer. One car is parked on the rear access road, which is used primarily by service vehicles. Another car is parked on Pine Street, which runs in front of the house. The third vehicle is on Cedar Street, parallel to the side of the house. Because the home is on a corner lot, it's easy to survey. There are two agents in each car, except for the one on Cedar.

Immediate contact is established by the team leader when the headlights of two vehicles are seen approaching the area. The yellow cab is expected. The other vehicle, a black van, leaves Pine Street and continues on Cedar.

Because the lone agent on Cedar Street completely focuses on the people entering the home, he doesn't notice that the van turns two blocks down. The heavy rain blankets the brake lights of the van, dulling their crimson nighttime glare.

Special Agent Anthony Perry, the senior operative, instructs the others to do nothing. He's been forewarned that the man in the cab with the women is not Evan Parker. Perry talks to his man on the inside with difficulty. Being in the basement shouldn't interfere with communication, even in the midst of such an intense electrical storm. Given the sophistication of their communication equipment, the storm's hindrance is a most unusual annoyance. It's the same interference that hinders Sterne's people from pinpointing the fugitives' cell phones.

Melissa climbs the stairs shouting her husband's name, but she receives no answer. It seems as though the louder she shouts, the claps of thunder reciprocate to taunt her. Jarvis Parker takes one look around the house and grabs a poker from the fireplace before joining Melissa upstairs.

Madeline looks about in the gloom and decides to turn on all of the downstairs lights. The house is a wreck. The floor of the kitchen is littered with pots and pans. Rice, flour, and sugar are everywhere. When Jarvis and Melissa come back downstairs, Maddy is staring down at a large footprint in the spill of flour. Her left hand absently reaches out to close the refrigerator door.

"My god," Jarvis says with disgust. "This is a mess. Those dirty bastards had no right to do this to your home."

Melissa walks out of the kitchen, so he follows her into the living room that Evan labored to perfect for her homecoming. The overturned furniture is ripped to shreds. Vases are broken, along with one of the lamps. Every drawer and closet stands ajar. Paper is strewn about the floor. Even the throw rugs have been disturbed, and upstairs is trashed much the same.

Madeline joins them there, worrying about Melissa's state of mind. She no longer doubts what she's gotten herself into by taking on the employ of the Parker family. Yet she's determined not to fold on them in this time of need.

As Maddy strokes Melissa's left shoulder, she senses the struggle to hold on. She can tell without seeing Melissa's face that she is fighting back both tears and panic.

Melissa Parker is overwhelmed by fear and disgust. She looks down at her stomach, caressing the safe harbor of her twins. The dam finally breaks to bring a flood of morbid tears. She whispers, "Where is my husband? Evan, where are you?" She slowly turns to Jarvis to cry upon his shoulder.

Madeline tries to call 911, but the line is as silent as a stillborn child drawn cold into the world.

Evan Parker is frantic as the van continues to circumvent the block. The driver maneuvers onto the access road without headlights.

As he peers through the small window, Evan says, "They're in the house already. There's no telling what could happen. I've got to get them out of there." When Evan bolts for the door, his two coffin mates are forced to restrain him for his own sake.

"Wait! You can't go barging in like that. You know that will get you killed, Mr. Parker," Louis Farrakhan warns.

Evan struggles. "Let me go damn it. I have to get my family out of there!"

"Slow down, son. Just slow down for a moment. Being hasty won't help them right now," Jesse Jackson pleads.

Evan snaps, "Just what the hell do you suggest, that I sit here while God only knows what is happening inside?"

"No. We're simply suggesting that you exercise extreme caution. If they take you now, all is lost," says Farrakhan. He looks forward and asks, "Does it look safe?"

The bodyguard on the passenger's side says, "Yes. But I'd better check out the car in front of us just in case."

Evan looks forward and says, "That doesn't belong there. I've never seen that car before. Hurry."

He takes his weapon from its holster before exiting the van, and walks cautiously toward the parked car.

Prepared to fire, the two agents crouch on the floorboard as Farrakhan's bodyguard approaches. They are wearing black, so he doesn't see them even when the lightning flashes directly overhead. After testing the locked door, the drenched bodyguard runs back to the van to report that he'd seen nothing amiss. Since he's already wet, Farrakhan tells him to accompany Evan Parker in the attempt to retrieve his family.

At this moment, Evan shrieks, "The lights just went out. The lights are out in my house!" They all look toward the home, but his is the only house in the area draped in darkness. Even the streetlights still burn brightly.

While looking directly into Evan Parker's urgent eyes, Farrakhan says, "Be very careful, Mr. Parker. Don't rush when you get out of the car, and please let my man go first. Listen to me, son. He was a Marine, so let him go first." He's given the weapon from the bodyguard's ankle holster.

"Okay. Now let me go."

When they get out in the driving rain, Evan follows the bodyguard in a low crouch as he crosses the lane. They have to climb over the rear fence because the gate is locked from the inside.

When they leap to the other side, they stay low against the hedge row, following it with painstakingly slow progression. They make several stops in the shadows along the side of the yard. Evan Parker has to fight the temptation to abandon all caution. His heart thuds in his ears and chest, growing more desperate with each step.

Special Agent Warner is one of Vincent Sterne's most competent operatives. Over Warner's eighteen year career in the CIA, he's assassinated more than twenty-five men and women, those who Sterne had tagged threats to covert CIA operations and enemies of the state. Many of Warner's targets had been American citizens. By the time Warner retired from Special Forces, he was a heartless man with no qualms about killing people when necessary. And it is always necessary when Vincent Sterne claims it to be. Warner's convictions are completely mechanical, forged within the coldest depths of humanity and a warped sense of American patriotism. Were he a Roman warrior when Czars reigned over empires full of enemies, he would have been Praetorian.

Tripping the circuit breaker cuts the power, casting the house in an utter darkness that is only interrupted by lightning. From the basement, Warner hears a woman cry out when darkness seizes them. It's Melissa, who's being comforted by Jarvis Parker in the living room.

Jarvis calls out to Maddy, who is trying to clean up the mess in the kitchen. She has to do something to keep her ragged mind busy. Jarvis heard her stumble, thinking the worst when a pot clanks against the refrigerator.

"Maddy, are you all right in there?"

"Yes, Mr. Parker. I'm coming," she says.

"No, just stay there. I'll see if I can get the power back on!"

Melissa tells him where to find the breaker box in the basement. After she sits on the couch he's righted, Jarvis searches for a candle holder on the mantle. In the end, he uses his lighter to find his way. As Jarvis passes the kitchen, he sticks the lighter in the doorway to make sure that Maddy is okay. After nearly falling, she stays put. He finds the basement door and slowly descends the stairs. The motionless air smells of cardboard boxes and the lingering of recently painted walls. Jarvis trips on the last step, tumbling into some boxes on the floor below.

When Maddy hears the crash, she shouts, "Jarvis, are you okay?"

"I'm fine, just getting clumsy in my old age. Don't worry!" he shouts back. He feels around for the lighter, which singes his fingers. Jarvis stands and dusts himself off, whispering a damn this or that. The hot striker scorches him as he thumbs to relight the refillable. It sparks once before relighting, but when Jarvis raises the lighter, he's looking into the cold blue eyes of a killer!

He gasps and tries to move, but Warner clamps a strong fist around the hand that holds the lighter. When Jarvis swings at him with the iron poker, Warner blocks the left-handed blow and issues a punch to the old man's unguarded face. Without hesitation, Warner drives the same fist into his stomach. When Jarvis bends over from the blow to his mid-section, Warner brings a knee up to his face to cause a sickening crunch!

All the women upstairs hear is the clatter of metal on the concrete floor. Warner is still gripping Jarvis by the wrist when he blows out the lighter's flame. He lets the old man's body fall to the floor.

"Jarvis, can you find it?" shouts Maddy, but there's no reply. She figures that he must be too far into the basement to hear her over the weather.

Silently, Agent Warner stalks up the stairs. He reaches into a pocket for the Garrote he uses to strangle unsuspecting victims, wrapping it around his gloved fists.

Agents Mercer and Wayne were peering out of the car's windshield when they saw Evan Parker and another man go over the back fence. Mercer advises Agent Perry of the situation. Perry tells them that one will have to go after Parker while the other agent secures the van.

The driver's attention is focused on the house, so he does not notice the two men slip out of the grey Pontiac. Mercer and Wayne slither into the nasty weather to rush the vehicle, taking the driver by complete surprise. They quickly drag him from the cab and stomp him to sleep. Then Mercer forces Louis Farrakhan and Jesse Jackson to lay face down in the mud where Wayne can keep them pinned down. Having been caught off-guard, they pray to their maker because they will probably be dead very soon. Mercer advances on Evan Parker from the rear.

With the stealth of a cat sneaking up on an unwary bird, Agent Warner maneuvers through the cooking utensils on the kitchen floor. The lightning flashes and he moves closer to the woman while her back is turned. Madeline's hands are clasped, head bowed. When Warner's shadow appears on the fridge, her eyes are shut as she prays. Grains of rice crunch beneath his feet, but Maddy turns too late. The scream has no chance to escape her lips. Her throat closes shut with a gurgle when Agent Warner deftly wraps the wire around her neck. Maddy struggles, feeling warm blood on her fingers as she tries to free herself, but she is powerless. Warner's muscles flex as he applies deadly pressure, listening for that satisfying pop!

The sound comes as the wire cuts through the cartilage of Madeline's throat, slicing her jugular vein to send her blood spurting over the counter tops and floor. She kicks pots and household cleaners as she convulses in her death throes. Her left hand was less than an inch from the handle of a knife that could saw through the head of a metal hammer. The already darkened world fades for the last time before her wide eyes.

After feeling her way through the darkness to reach the kitchen just as Maddy dies in his grasp, Melissa Parker screams. She runs down the hallway toward the back of the house, crashing and trampling things like a bull elephant gone rogue. Warner casually allows Maddy's lifeless body slump to the floor where blood and flour sticks to her face and open eyes.

When Evan hears his wife's shriek, he abandons all caution, taking to the run. The bodyguard is with him stride for stride through the deep puddles of water, until a silenced bullet explodes through his chest. He falls face first in the mud, sliding to an ungracious stop. Evan continues running, hearing bullets as they zip and ricochet all around his bobs and weaves.

Melissa sees someone approaching the greenhouse where she crouches in the shadows. She is surrounded, having no idea that it's her husband outside.

When Mercer stops to take aim at Evan, who's trying to get into the greenhouse, there's a bang! He looks down at his weapon, which should not have made such a loud sound because of the silencer. He hears another report and slumps to his knees. Now he realizes his fatal error of not putting a true-kill shot in the back of the bodyguard's head as he ran past him. Because Mercer abandoned his training, he will have to join the bodyguard in death.

Evan slams his body into the door, knocking it from its aluminum frame to crash on top of a mound of shattered glass. Ignoring the minor lacerations, he tries to stand. He pivots as someone comes at him from the shadows. Evan wheels, pointing the gun at his wife's face!

Melissa cries, "Evan, thank God you found me. There is a man right..."

They are both sent sprawling to the glass-strewn floor! Evan loses the gun and pulls a tray from the workbench, scattering his sainted evidence around them. Warner now stands over them with his weapon poised to kill. He smiles when he sees what could only be the documents he's been searching for. While Evan and Melissa Parker hold each other at Warner's feet, paralyzing fear seeps into their hearts. They're looking up into the smiling face of the man who's about to kill them.

The lightning flashes and wicked thunder claps on its heels. Warner's face is that of a devil with the killing fever when he says, "Mr. Parker, you've been a very naughty boy. You're the reason that I had to get off of my favorite piece of ass, just to get soaking wet in this nasty weather. Well, sir, you're all going to pay for that. However, your only chance to survive is telling me exactly who you've contacted!" He kicks the garbage bag containing the census reports. "If you refuse, I'm going to shoot your wife in the belly first. She'll suffer, but that won't kill her. Not right away. Oh dear, I see that she's with child, too. Now talk."

Evan tries to cover his wife when Warner levels the gun on her. "You son of a bitch!" he shouts.

"Suit yourself, Mr. Parker," Warner says as he fingers the safety.

Suddenly, there's a flash of angry lightning that seems much too close. Someone moves behind Warner! Evan's and Melissa's eyes grow even more when the blade of the machete gleams in the azure flashes of light. It comes down with authority, splitting Agent Warner's skull down its center to the bridge of his nose. It makes a sickening splatter when it's buried deep into the cerebrum, having first torn through hair, flesh, and bone to get to the grey matter beneath.

Warner's eyes cross and his gun discharges as the result of a rebellious reflex. The bullets barely miss Evan's head, shattering the glass wall behind them.

The storm rages on. Its furious wind rustles the leaves of potted plants, flinging debris and potting soil to sting their eyes. They're wordless in the presence of a new and unknown menace.

Kinzana stands over the body of Agent Warner with his eyes blazing so that lightning is not needed to see them. He looks as fearsome to Evan and Melissa as had Warner just one heart-stopping moment before.

⇒+ +⇐

Outside, Agent Perry is trying to make contact with his men. He's only able to reach Agent Wayne, who is still standing in the rain with a gun on the other three fugitives.

The lone Agent Turner is still sitting in his car on Cedar Street. His head is laid back on the support of the driver's seat. His hands are locked in an immortal clutch at his throat, which has been sliced open to the vertebra of his spine. His mouth and eyes are agape, but no image of the car's ceiling is sent to his brain from those unseeing organs. No sound emanates from his silent plead because he's already dead.

Agents Perry and Stratford are getting out of the Jeep Cherokee because they cannot raise the others. Something has gone wrong. The gunshots they heard moments ago means that someone else has a weapon.

When they get out in the torrential rain, Agent Stratford screams, but Perry can no longer see the tall man over the roof of the jeep. He draws his weapon, pointing it through the open door.

Stratford is convulsing on the street next to the vehicle. His bloody right hand gropes at the seat and floorboard, flailing and clutching. He issues a gurgling cry and then silence.

Perry turns around, searching for whomever has incapacitated his partner. When he turns toward the rear of the jeep, there is no one. He quickly pivots toward the front. This time, there is someone standing in the rain. He points the gun and reaches into the cab to snap on the headlights, which brings the lightning and a woman.

She is naked from the waist up. In the light of the high beams, she's holding a long machete that boasts a subtle hook at the tip. She does not threaten, holding it leisurely down at her side. Her eyes blaze insanely. Though it is raining very hard, Agent Perry can see that her entire body is painted with long stripes of medium and dark green. It looks as if she's made-up to mimic long leaves, stretching from the center of her back to her front. No stranger thing on earth has Perry ever seen. This woman gets down on her hands and knees, placing the machete between her bright white teeth.

"What the fuck? Don't you move, bitch!"

The camouflaged woman pays him no attention. She cat-walks, slowly switching her hips from side to side as if she's trying to seduce him. What a thing of deadly beauty.

The team leader feels himself sweating, despite the rain. He decides to kill her where she is. When he tightens his grip on the pistol, there comes a swiping sound that carries with it a sudden, merciless fury! Warner screams as a machete makes a smooth slice completely through his right ankle. The bones of his right leg jam into the unyielding pavement when his right foot is severed. It sends shockwaves through his soul and torturous pain blazing jet-fueled pathways to his brain.

Perry grabs the top of the jeep and shoots blindly at a woman who has suddenly disappeared. While holding his right leg aloft, Perry realizes that someone else has to be underneath the car. He points the weapon at the floorboard, but the blade swishes again, severing his left foot this time. All of his weight, every ounce of fat, bone, flesh, and blood drives his stumps into the unforgiving pavement. Vibrant pain seizes Perry, making him too weak to pull the trigger. The gun falls away, meeting him on the drenched street.

Perry screams, looking into the face of another painted lady, who's now crawling from under the car on her stomach. With those cold eyes locked with his, she is coming. He tries to scoot away, but slides into the other women. She is the first he'd seen, the one who distracted him. Perry is bleeding out as they watch. There is no need to hack him to his end; that has already been done. All that's left is the dying so they simply watch the life and the fight drain from his body.

Special Agent Perry's blood runs from the stumps, but quickly fades as it travels down the street with the churning rainwater. Bright crimson...pink...then nothing.

A few moment later, another blood-curdling scream is drowned out by thunder. It comes from the service alley where Agent Wayne now lies face down in a muddy, red puddle. His blood soon dilutes.

A black semi carefully maneuvers up the rear access and is soon gone. Only the mangled bodies of six CIA agents, one bodyguard, and a faithful housekeeper remain to hint at the events that have taken place in and around 666 Pine Street in Suitland, Maryland. Because the coming dawn will bring firefighters, policemen, and reporters, contamination is imminent. The drums!

At 7:04 a.m., the WBLE News helicopter circles 666 Pine Street, sending live pictures over the airwaves from the scene of a fire and an apparent massacre. The airborne reporter tells viewers that there are at least five bodies visible on the grounds surrounding the smoldering home. He explains that the fire is under control while the camera pans the charred remains of what used to be a two storied home with a basement. Firefighters are going through the burned out house in search of more casualties.

Sharon Masters, a sleek brunet, speaks into her microphone when the station switches from the helicopter to the ground unit. She begins by saying that there's a severed foot protruding from the tarp that's been placed over one of the two bodies on Pine Street.

There is a sudden disturbance, so she and her camera operator run around the corner to Cedar Street where someone has discovered another body in a parked automobile. The man's throat is sliced open to the bone, and there's arterial spray everywhere. It looks as if something flat penetrated his window. The female reporter speculates that if the window hadn't been so heavily tinted, it probably would have shattered from the murder weapon's impact. It is a gruesome sight.

The police charge in to sanitize the crime scene but the real damage comes when Sharon Masters, the ace reporter, gets a hunch. She walks over to the curb to question the spectator whose arms are folded with a judgmental pout on his face. She overheard him saying, "I knew it. I knew something like this was bound to happen."

She says, "Excuse me, sir. I'm Sharon Masters of WBLE News Channel Four. Can you shed some light on what happened here?"

The onlooker clears his throat and states, "Well, I'm Tom Waters, and I live over there in the gray house. There was a really bad storm last night, as you well know. Anyway, I got up at about six for my morning cup of coffee and smelled smoke. When I looked outside, it was the darndest thing. That house over there was blazing away, even with all that hard rain coming down. That's when I called the fire department." He politely tips his cap at the camera.

"You called the fire department, Mr. Waters?"

"Yes, ma'am, I sure did," says Waters with a sense of pride.

Sharon Masters can't help smiling because she seems to have the primary witness. "Then what happened?" she asks with rabid anticipation. The reporter senses that this interview will be great for her career.

"Well, Ms. Masters, the rain started to slack off, so I came outside. That's when I saw the two dead men by that truck over yonder." Waters points at Pine Street and the Jeep.

Sharon Masters is exuberant, but she assumes a professional façade. She can't afford to seem too happy about the slaughter on live television.

"You actually witnessed the bodies? Can you tell us what you saw, Mr. Waters?" The camera zooms in as she holds the microphone closer, laying for every word from his lips.

He clears his throat, again. "Well, I yelled to Martha, she's my wife, and I told her to call the police. Two men were lying on either side of that Jeep Cherokee deader than doornails. They were dressed in black, wearing ski masks on their heads like robbers. That's when I saw the guns with silencers laying alongside them. One of the guys had a big gash in his belly and his throat was slit, much like this guy over here in the parked car. The other guy had both his feet cut off. Both feet, mind you. It was a gruesome sight. While I was waiting for the police to arrive, I decided to look in the backyard, careful not to disturb anything. But that's where I saw a dead Black fella and another dead White guy, both lying face down. Apparently, they both had been shot in the back. I noticed the shattered glass walls of the greenhouse where I discovered yet another body, I didn't go inside to check for a pulse or anything. It was plain to see that his head had been split nearly in two. This is an awful tragedy, ma'am. Nothing like this has ever happened anywhere near this quiet neighborhood. And I guess that's basically what happened."

She smiles despite herself and asks, "So they were apparently murdered?'

"There's no doubt about it, ma'am. I knew when that slick looking guy moved into this neighborhood that there was going to be trouble, but I never imagined anything as horrific as this. It's probably all drug related."

Vincent Sterne is on his way. He curses into his phone, "Get that bitch off of the air right now. Damn it, I don't care if you have to shoot the fucking cameraman. Shut her down right now!"

Sharon Masters asks, "Do you happen to know who owns this property, Mr. Waters? His name?"

"It's a Black fellow. They just moved in here, not long ago. I never saw his wife, but I was told that he is married," says Mr. Waters. He turns to his wife, who moves closer, and asks, "Martha, do you remember that man's name?"

An agent of the FBI arrives. He is running to the area where the live interview is being conducted with neighbors, shouting for them to turn the camera off.

"Let me see. I believe his name was...Parker. Yes, that's it, Mr. Evan Parker," Martha Waters says. "Claims to be some kind of government employee, I highly doubt that now."

"There you have it. This is Sharon Masters of WBLE News Channel Four with an exclusive from the apparent scene of multiple murders in this quiet Forest Point neighborhood. We will be bringing you more information with the developing details of this

bizarre crime scene at the home of a man named Evan Parker..."
The viewing audience sees the sky, trees, and the feet of several
persons upon the pavement.

The top executives at the WBLE News station are revisiting a
communiqué delivered during the course of the night directly from
the office of President Al Gore. They don't know whether to have
massive heart attacks or to just crawl into a very deep hole somewhere because they could be in serious trouble.

Sterne is furious. The hackles on the neck of his driver bristle with
every cuss word that spews from his foul lips. There is an enormous
surge building in the car, and he cannot drive fast enough in the
shadow of Sterne's explosive overload. More heads are about to roll,
which will only serve as a small personal satisfaction. His net has
been breached for the third time since he tried to kill the Deputy
Director of the Bureau of Census. Evan Parker is loose out there;
loose out there somewhere.

By 10:00 o'clock, the media world will have its collective ears to
the ground. The live report does serious damage to containing the
significance of Sterne's investigation. They have been forbidden to
broadcast anything without clearance, now the public may know too
much. News men like Ted Copple and Tom Brokaw are practically
begging their executive administrators to launch investigations into
the matter of Evan Parker, whose alleged crimes have left a trail
of intrigue and bodies from Washington, D.C. to Suitland, where
some comparatively smaller news station got the drop on them all.

Although Sharon Masters has unintentionally broken President
Gore's Veil, she became the forerunner of the media world. She's
given others reason to renege on their agreement to eat from the
scraps of the government's public relations table.

The likes of Ted Koppel and Brokaw used sharp angles to
lobby that this is news the public needs to know, if Evan Parker,

a government employee, is as dangerous as he appears. They ask, "Whose crazy idea was it to agree to the Seven Veil Quarantine, anyway?" The media stallions now smell smoke and they're kicking in their stalls, wanting to run wild and free. Their instincts are only heightened by the President's muzzling.

Hungry news stations are attempting to buy the broadcast rights to Sharon Master's accidental news report simply because American citizens need to be informed of this particular menace to society.

Evan Parker looks even more maniacal in the public eyes, so Sterne allows a representative to embellish a bit. By the time they're done slandering Parker's name, he will be unwelcome wherever he goes. Vincent Sterne even hopes that some racist, dirt farmer with a gut full of beer and a shotgun full of buckshot will run into Parker. It's a lovely fantasy to have that man take it upon himself to rid the world of what he thinks to be a dangerous criminal element. This is a long shot, but it has happened many times before, and to more deserving scoundrels.

Before the noon news segment is done Evan Parker will be implicated in drug trafficking, espionage, rape, and multiple murders. He's public enemy number one now, even amongst Black folks.

It's a ruthless scheme, but to Sterne, such actions will surely be the lesser evil. He believes in the justification of such measures when he envisions political chaos and social upheaval. When he does manage to nap, his dreams are haunted by buildings burning to the ground, mere effigies of the social hierarchy he'd sworn to protect. Chaos, madness rule his dreaming subconscious, but soon, he'll find sleep impossible.

As the drums are summoned to a driving crescendo, deep within the heart of a mountain, Evan Parker's twin brother is helpless, afraid, and furious at the world. Doom da-da boom! Boom da-da doom!

CHAPTER 32
SHELTER US FROM EVIL

After Kinzana kills Agent Warner in the greenhouse, he and Evan search for Jarvis. While descending the darkened stairway, Evan endures the haunts of all the horror movies he loved to watch as a teenager. This is like sinking into one of those foul dungeons, each step resounding with doom. He cannot see the hand before his face. It is deadly silent and the air fills with despair. In this instance, Evan Parker is descending the ten thousand steps of hell.

After seeing what Agent Warner did to Madeline Perkins, there seems little hope of finding his father alive. Jarvis is lying in a heap near the bottom of the stairs. He is unconscious and his nose is broken, but he's still breathing.

They drag Jarvis from the basement, through the greenhouse and out the back gate to a black tractor-trailer. Melissa follows with the garbage bag containing Evan's evidence. When Melissa is helped into the trailer, she is startled. The two sets of hands helping from above belong to two strangely painted, bare breasted women. Once everyone is inside, the driver secures the doors and leaves the sleeping neighborhood. The heavy rain washes away all traces of the truck having been there.

The trailer has been converted into rather comfortable quarters, with three cots secured to the carpeted floor. A small television set and a radio sit on a metal stand that's been bolted down. A small, well-stocked refrigerator is next to it. Midway, against the walls, two couches face each other. The trailer is complemented with a sink and showerhead. The painted ladies use these to wash the paint from their bodies with a special aloe concoction. The air conditioner, which is mounted beneath the trailer, maintains a constant seventy-degree temperature, after the soaking wet passengers have changed into dry clothing. The trailer boasts a first aid kit, police scanners, video equipment and more.

No one speaks for a long time, except for Evan and Melissa while tending Jarvis's injuries. They clean his swollen nose of blood and secure it with tape while he fusses. Even complaints are welcome to the alternative. He protests the ice pack, although it will help with the swelling.

Lost in a moment following shocking and nearly fatal events, Farrakhan and Jackson are warm and dry, but they are quiet.

Melissa tends the wounds of her husband by first cinching his throbbing ribs. She cleans and bandages the cut on his head and arm. She immobilizes his swollen pinkie finger. Although it's never surfaced before, Melissa's nursing instincts have kicked in right on time.

Dressed in a robe, one of the painted women bandages the cuts and wraps the head of Farrakhan's unconscious bodyguard. He has obviously sustained a concussion, so he and Jarvis occupy two of the three cots.

With U.S. Government discretely placed in white letters on the cab doors and on the black trailer, they head south. Taking Interstate 97 toward Virginia, they hit Interstate 95 South on the way back to South Carolina.

Once they are settled and some of the nervous tension subsides, Evan Parker hugs and thanks Kinzana. There is an awkward silence between strangers, so Evan makes a proper introduction. Now comes the conversation.

"How did you know that we were in danger, Kinzana?" Evan asks.

The rocking of the trailer is taking an effect on Melissa Parker, but the nausea passes quickly.

She sits with her husband, thinking of some of the things she learned in a stress management class.

Kinzana smiles before answering Evan's question. "It was in the painting and in the toss of the bones, my son. It was in the prophecy, for many events of the future are known unto me."

Evan asks, "But how could you know? Why were you really there?" The others remain quiet, listening to this exchange.

"We were always with you, Evan. Did you not feel our eyes upon you?"

"You? It was you that I saw in the backyard."

"You would never have known, unless we allowed you a glimpse. There was danger in the air for you there. So yes, Evan, we were present when you left out of fear, remaining to await your eventual return." When Kinzana uses the remote to turn on the television, Evan's face appears on the screen.

As can be expected, Melissa is upset by the terrible allegations that are made against her husband. And though she has lived in their new home for only a few days, it hurts her to see the overhead view of its burned out husk.

She says, in a near whisper, "Those ruthless bastards burned it to the ground. How can such vile, cruel men work for the American Government? I'm sorry I didn't stay put like I promised, Evan. I'm so sorry." She buries her tears in her husband's clean shirt. "My fucking stubbornness almost got us all killed. Madeline's death is all my fault. I'm so sorry."

"Hush now. It's okay, baby," Evan says while caressing her hair.

As the news report recants the murder of Evan's assistant, Melissa Parker's mind reels toward the past and the alleged rape of his student. She forces the distaste away because she can ill afford the doubt.

Kinzana reaches for her heart by saying, "Hush, little mother. You could never again live there in peace. For one very important reason was it laid to wasted embers. Your would-be killers were extinguished themselves, so they did not start the fire, Melissa. Do you remember just how violent the storm had become when I first appeared in the greenhouse? The wind was howling like airborne wolves and the black sky was blue from the lightning. The rain was one steady flow of water from the sky, and the thunder drummed through our bodies into the ground. At that very moment, the fire was started when Damballah's lightning touched the roof. It was already ablaze, even when we went in search of my dear, hardheaded friend in the basement."

"Lightning?" Evan asks.

The image replays in Louis Farrakhan's mind. He had looked up just as the blue tendril danced across the top of the house. The bright blue glare coincided with the electrical tremor that caused his short hairs to stand on end.

"It happened while you bravely sought to sacrifice your life for that of your wife," Kinzana says.

Evan asks, "But why do you say that it had to be destroyed?"

Kinzana looks at the civil rights leaders. "It was destroyed because it leads a trail to the truth, telling the story within a story that must be revealed to the world. You see, even now the media casts you in a murderous light. They accuse him of killing those men, those who surely would have killed you and all to whom you've spoken in regard to your secret documents. To the television audience, you are a psychopath. You're a man capable of destroying your own dwelling, and slaughtering yet another woman, whom they'll undoubtedly assume to be Melissa." His eyes sparkle.

Evan is silent while the newscaster theorizes as to the identity of the woman found in the smoldering rubble. They speculate on the whereabouts of Mrs. Melissa Parker, the wife who is yet to be located by authorities. Evan's mouth falls open. He shivers, visibly.

Kinzana says, "Be strong, Evan. Your adversary is a cunning man, but he's also very desperate. You may be branded a renegade on a mad killing spree, and your name will become synonymous with outrage and hatred. Yet, sadly, that will not be exclusive of Blacks. Before finally seeing that you are indeed a component of good, they will only know you as a problem. Regrettably, there shall be much darkness before the light, my son. I know that there are many questions, but understanding will fall upon your brow with a quickness. You are all now facets of the black tide, each having missions to fulfill and destinies to realize. Trust in this, friends, for there is method to my madness. He who has created the timeless galaxies demands that we all cling to our convictions, for change is like the sweeping wind. To believe in your individual destinies is to understand that even death is not always the ultimate sacrifice, but that life can also be a burden for what you believe. Even if we all perish, it will not be so bad a thing, for it is what transpires before the moment of mortality that matters most. You will all see that this small gathering is not by coincidental circumstance."

The reporter switches to unrelated stories that prove to be equally bizarre. A snowstorm is bearing down on the African equatorial regions from the Atlantic to the Indian Ocean.

Police have no new leads in the investigation of the African Zulu Death Mask and other religious artifacts that were stolen from an exhibit in a New York City Museum. Outside of the museum, where the items were on display, a trespasser had burned a small campfire. Someone's shadow has been burned onto the outer wall of the building. It seems as if the silhouette has been airbrushed there by vandals. In a bizarre twist, the same shadow is also found on the inside of the same wall. The authorities are attempting to ascertain what was used to create the strange human silhouette, but it is quite

a mystery. When they examined the area more closely, the building material, both concrete and wood, seemed porous, crumbling
to the touch. No one can offer any plausible theories on how the
Zulu Death Mask was removed from the exhibit without setting off
the alarms, or even how it was taken from the building where there
appears to be no forced entry. All in all, however, there are a lot
more valuable things they could have stolen the curator informs.
What he doesn't know is that there are none more important.

Jarvis listens to the television as he lay motionless.

Throughout Kinzana's monologue, Jesse Jackson and Louis
Farrakhan share looks of skepticism. They wonder who this man
thinks himself to be, understanding little of what he speaks.

Evan looks down upon his wife, who has been swept away on the
wings of sleep. She hears some of the conversation before drifting
into a peaceful place. It seems that Kinzana's voice often holds that
effect on her. Even when his words are frightening, his hypnotic
inflections soothe her. And in this case, her exhaustion is an added
anesthetic. His accent is liquid mercury; Melissa Parker's ultimate
tranquilizer.

Though Jarvis Parker lay still, he is aware of the words of a
man he's learned not to doubt. Evan Parker, however, chooses to
remain in the middle of the road. His confusion is pacified because
Kinzana's singular insight has saved the life of his family, but he
remains doubtful, unsure of his station in things to come. Kinzana
is confident that Evan's lack of certainty will dwindle to mere reservations. His reservations will soon bloom into total commitment,
with only moments of falter. Evan Parker must now follow Kinzana
to the ends of the earth, regardless of the perilous circumstances,
for there will be precious few choices to do otherwise.

When Louis Farrakhan finally breaks his silence, he says,
"Mr. Kinzana, it would be wrong of us not to thank you for saving
our lives. And I do thank you, sir. What I want to know is just what
have you been talking about? Just who are you claiming to be?"

"I, Minister Farrakhan," Kinzana says with a wily smile, "...am but a humble emissary—the glue that binds the tide together. However, Evan Parker is the catalyst, like the moon's gravitational pull on the turbulent waters. Even now the black tide rises on the American shores."

Jesse Jackson says, "I don't understand any of this. You talk as if you're supposed to be some kind of prophet."

"Why do you seek to crush our resolve with so much doom and gloom? Who do you think you are, God?" Farrakhan asks with an obvious lack of respect.

Kinzana's hearty laughter resonates throughout the trailer, annulling the constant whine of the rotating tires. He knows above all things, that this clash is inevitable.

Jarvis croaks, "He's not God, but I wouldn't bet against him knowing God very well. Son, are you there?"

"Yes, pop. I'm here."

With subdued reproach in his voice, Jarvis Parker asks in a near whisper, "Minister Farrakhan ... Mr. Jackson, didn't that man just save us all when no one even called him for help. All of my life, I've been told to take what I hear with a grain of salt, but I learned not to doubt Kinzana's words. What he predicts isn't always going to be pleasant, but such is life. Is it not? Years ago, he told me exactly how my wife was going to die. I didn't want to believe him, and at the time, his words made absolutely no sense to me. But later on..."

"Pop, you need to rest," Evan admonishes out of concern for his health. He also wishes to change the subject, something that Jarvis understands.

The old man groans as he sits up on the cot. "Listen to me, Evan. I'm begging you. There has got to be a greater force at work, something more than the sum of the people gathered here at the very least. Kinzana is our friend. No matter what, he's always been there for our family. You know, many years ago, your mother and I attended one of his ceremonies out of a curiosity that seemed to drive us both. At the end of it, he told us that we'd have twin sons who would make us proud even in death. He told us those forty-some-odd years ago, that my children would go down in the annals of history. Well, here we are, Evan Parker, making history. I have always feared what Kinzana seems to know of the future, but I still trust him with my life. So should you, Evan. We have to listen to him no matter what happens, No matter how strange, or how vague his words may be, we have to listen now. I am asking this of you because I get the distinct feeling that nothing we want is as important as what God apparently wants of us. If you still haven't realized it yet, it's now snowing in Africa, son. From ocean to ocean, this time of year, it's actually snowing on the African Equator."

"I hear you, pop. I'll try," Evan says. The tape recording in his mind brings back words of a news report that has just escaped his attention. Kinzana's fireside prophecy seems to be coming true.

With his pride and his Muslim showing, Farrakhan says, "Surely, you don't believe that this man dictates what Allah does."

"That would make Kinzana God himself. However, gentlemen, I believe that he's working for the Lord, no matter what you call him in the dark of night. Kinzana deals in a strange reality, but it's some kind of reality, nonetheless. Listen to him, Evan, because what we have got to lose now seems to add up to a bit more than just our lives?"

As Evan Parker gazes down at his sleeping wife, he feels the subtle rise and fall of her breath. It seems so clear, what she now dreams. He turns to Kinzana to ask, "What do you suggest?"

"I am happy that your trust is in me, Evan. Know this, my young friend, no harm will ever befall your wife and unborn children. Those who have been commissioned to print those compromising photographs of you and the dead assistant will regret their part in besmirching your good nature and name. This venture is endowed by the highest of powers, and we must all face our fears. If the evil of this world and our sworn enemies are so strong that Damballah's will is superseded in this land, then I'm afraid that all may be lost for humanity itself."

"Photographs?" Evan asks. "What photographs?"

Kinzana hands Evan a copy of this morning copy of the gossip rag that the enemy paid to have distributed. He looks at his own image, standing on the balcony while opening a bottle of champagne as his alluring assistant gazes up at him in a white negligee. He places a fist into his mouth, biting down as he looks at his wife. The photo of the brief kiss nearly causes him to shriek.

Kinzana reaches for it, removing it from his grip. "Fear not, Evan. They will pay for this, too. It will never come to douse the light of love in Melissa's eyes."

"But, I swear to you nothing happened. I didn't initiate this," he says in a near whisper.

"I know. You have nothing to prove."

"What would you have me to do?"

"I want you to sit there and record your message to the world. Tell them what you would have them know of this great and terrible secret. Tell the world your truth, and let the chips fall where they may. There is a laptop with a printer to duplicate your evidence. I trust that these things will be of use to you. We also have a facsimile machine with phone directories for Great Britain, Canada, Germany and even Japan. There is an address for Nelson Mandela in South Africa, and Bishop Desmond Tutu in Johannesburg. Nothing will be traceable. I hope we have everything you will need. We even have access to the Internet, but it may be wiser to let it lie for the moment. Even with all that I've seen and done in this world, I still do not trust it. It has and will always be used for such wickedness. I suspect it may be faster, but what you refer to as low tech will be much safer. Use the video equipment only when there is utter silence. Even though this compartment is made to dampen the road noise, the enemy will employ every form of technology at their disposal to find us. Is that understood?"

Evan nods before laying Melissa against the couch. He raises her feet, using a blanket to keep her warm, and kisses her forehead. She murmurs, but remains asleep. He goes to the front of the trailer to survey Kinzana's impressive array of modern-day gadgetry.

"I never had a chance to tell you why they were after us, or what's contained in these papers. It would seem, however, that you already know." Evan receives no verbal response. "Kinzana, are we headed to the ends of the earth? Where are we going?"

"To South Carolina, and eventually, your father's house," is his reply.

"But that's madness. You know they'll be looking for me to show up. How can you ask me to take my family into an obvious trap?"

"I see that Melissa does not carry the journal I've bestowed upon her. Is it not at Jarvis' home?"

"I don't know. Is it important enough to risk our lives?" Evan asks.

Jarvis says, "It's on the kitchen table. But why?"

Kinzana is patient. "It was left there, perhaps, by mishap or for a reason. Apparently, that reason is so that we may return for it. You must be seen going into the home by your enemies. If they were to take possession of it, then they will surely find us. You must trust me on this because it contains my full name within its hallowed pages."

After some deliberation, Evan is silent. With the assistance of the two painted ladies, he goes about the business of using the machines. The women are actually quite attractive after they cleaned the junk from their faces and covered themselves with robes. They are also identical twins. While one studies medicine at the Medical University of South Carolina in Charleston, the other studies law at the University of South Carolina in Columbia. The painted ladies are natives of Nigeria, but they're betrayed by no accent because no one has heard them speak. Nor will they, unless absolutely necessary.

Farrakhan and Jackson are sitting with their heads together, while Kinzana goes to Evan. He whispers, "You are doing these things for mankind, not just Black kind. The first flowers to bloom in a world bereft of pain, Alana and Sonshal will be very proud of their father."

Evan's head whips about in astonishment, causing a momentary flare of pain. "How do you know what's in my dreams, Kinzana? Did Melissa tell you that?"

Kinzana smiles, patting him on the shoulder before walking away. He pauses, saying something to one of the young ladies who promptly leaves her station to serve them food and drink. Afterward, she will tend to the wounded bodyguard.

Following the bite to eat, Evan writes down what he will say in a brief video expose. Kinzana advises that the others get some rest. Now, he turns his attention to Louis Farrakhan and Jesse Jackson.

"You have many questions, I know. And I suspect that you may think me more than a little insane, perhaps? Here and now, I decree that you both shall enter a place of wonder where nothing is real, but every essence will bear tangible substance. Listen to the drums, for they shall speak to you. To your hearts."

As they scoff in silence, the truck leaves the road where Interstate 95 intersects with Highway 210. It soon eases to a stop at a large boat landing on the Potomac River. The driver buzzes the trailer and Kinzana rises. He says, "I must leave you for a moment. Please excuse me. This may be the moment of silence that you need to record your brief expose, Evan. We are far enough away from the road noise to do it safely, but the engine will be turned off most of all."

No one realizes that it's still raining, until the door is opened to the gloom. As they approach the water's edge, Kinzana disrobes and immerses himself in the choppy water with no fear of the lightning. The women join him as the rain continues to pelt their smooth, brown skin.

Shelara, the eldest of the twins by eleven-minutes, cups her hands to collect the cool water in her palms. Then she raises the fleshy cup above Kinzana's head as he spread his arms to regard the violent sky. She utters, "Blessed are the saints whom art called unto thee, Oh Lord. Blessed is our master, for he is the bringer of your commandments unto the unworthy inhabitants of this land."

Kinzana closes his eyes and opens his mouth to drink as she allows the water to trickle from her hands. She backs away, taking Kinzana's cane from her sister.

Aralesh, the younger of the two, takes her place before Kinzana. She scoops water into her palms and raises it above her master's head. "Blessed are those who have and shall obey thee even unto their own bodily destruction, Father. Blessed is Kinzana, for he is the master of thy grave calamities."

Kinzana opens his eyes as she releases the water upon his forehead. He does not blink as it runs from his brows and into his eyes.

They leave the water and Kinzana puts on his clothing. Now, Aralesh produces a small dagger. She gives it to Kinzana, who places it to his lips and forehead. Both women are allowed to kiss the blade before he uses it to draw their blood and his own.

The sisters plant his cane between them in the granite rocks for balance. Each raises her inside foot. Kneeling before the sisters, Kinzana places the tip of the blade to the arches of their feet and gently pricks them both. The wind rises to a howling chorus, hurling rain with its invisible fists. Neither woman utters a sound.

Kinzana stands and places the blade to the palm of his left hand to bring his own blood. He clenches his fist to force it forth. The women reach for his broad shoulders for better balance when they give him the cane. Their bleeding feet are not allowed to touch the worn stones upon which they stand.

Kinzana utters, "And so, children, let it be that we shall now shed blood." He upends his cane to slide the ivory serpents to the bottom of their feet and lathers it with their crimson flow.

With their blood intermingled, he grasped the serpents with his bleeding palm. With a gaze that suggests both pleasure and pain, Kinzana turns his eyes to the water's edge and lowers his staff into the turbulence.

With his eyes raised to the heavens, he says, "And there shall be signs, telling of something greater than man's agenda. No fish shall swim below thee. No waterfowl shall soar upon drinking in this place. And for seven years hence, this river shall run as black as the stones which mark the eastward gates of hell. Our blood shall seal this fate as they flee beneath our angry feet!"

Tendrils of lightning divide the sky to dance upon the Potomac River. In its brightness, the water boils where touched by serpents of Kinzana's cane. Like venom, black water begins to spread along the Potomac. Now they return to the trailer completely drenched, but each seems strangely exhilarated.

—⟨+⟩—

Seat Pleasant, Maryland.

Jim McCallum comes home to find his slovenly wife and child gone. Upon the dinner table, five large, pregnant cockroaches stand defiantly at the edge of a sweet pool of spilled milk. Jim looks at the bold pests with disgust. They suddenly disappear, as if they know his intent when he goes for a can of roach spray.

McCallum reaches down to pick up a bowl from the floor only to find a mound of soggy cereal beneath it. He drops the bowl on the table but refuses to clean up the mess. He considers righting the overturned chair only to leave it where it lay when he looks about the filthy apartment.

On his way to the refrigerator for a beer, he grumbles, "I swear to God, that nasty bitch should be living in the bilge of a fucking garbage scow."

After downing the first can with the door still open, he chucks the empty and opens another. Mr. McCallum sits on the couch and burps as he tosses a toy to the floor. As he points the remote control at the television, he notices the brand new DVD player perched on top with a red bow.

"What the hell?" he says, as the telephone rings. He snatches the phone from the hook as he inspects the gift that he knows he couldn't afford. "Hello," he says and slides the DVD in.

The altered voice of a stranger says, "Mr. McCallum? Good, you're finally home. By now, I'm sure you've noticed the new DVD. Play the disk I left so you'll know that I'm telling the truth. If you want to see your wife and child again, you will do exactly as I say."

Jim says, "If you and my sorry excuse for a woman feel like playing games with me, come on over so we can do this face-to-face. Then we can really play, motherfucker!"

Jim McCallum backs away when the brief video begins to play. There, on the screen, his wife is bound and gagged. She was lying on their living room floor when this footage was taken. The overturned chair is right behind her as she struggles and weeps. Jim's fat little son crawls to her, screaming at the top of his lungs. His mother is helpless. Then someone, other than the person with the camera, drives a boot into Vera McCallum's gut for effect.

Jim asks, "What the hell is this?"

The mysterious caller says, "As you can see, I'm quite serious. If you don't do exactly as I say, I'll kill them both. Do you understand?"

Without batting an eye, Jim McCallum says, "Go ahead, you'll be doing me a fucking favor. Do it, kill that miserable whore of a bitch right now. See if I care."

"This is no game, Mr. McCallum."

"Boy, have you got it all wrong. I could care less about either of them because I'm nearly certain that the kid isn't even mine, so do your best damage," he growls into the phone. There is the unmistakable silence of confusion on the other end.

After a short conference, the caller says, "Even if you really don't care about them, we can make it look as if you did it. Do as we say…"

Jim smiles as a wicked thought enters his mind, which crosses his lips when he says, "Tell me what you want done."

"That's better. You do remember Mr. Allen Peterson, the burn patient that you've been torturing? Does this ring a bell? Well, he told, Jimmy." Jim's heart races for a second. "It will mean your job and prison in all likelihood. However, if you were to eliminate Mr. Peterson, the problem goes away. As far as we're concerned, nothing would be finer," the caller says as if he is simply giving a friend a recipe for pea soup.

Jim reaches behind the DVD player for a grey case that was left there by the kidnapers. He opens it, removing a syringe that he holds up to the light. Jim McCallum says, "Okay. I'll do it, but you have to do something for me."

"You're in no position to make demands."

"Do it," Jim says.

"What did you say?"

"Do it," Jim repeats. "I never want to see that miserable bitch ever again. If you can make it look like an accident, we'll have a deal. What's it going to be, hotshot?" He smiles. "Bet you didn't see that one coming, did ya? Do it. We have a deal, and you better do it right."

CHAPTER 33

BREATH OF THE DRAGON

April 8th. 8:00 a.m.

Because three carpooling employees were lost to a fatal car accident, the shift rotation has drastically changed at Macedonia. Greta Sparks is making final rounds at the end of a grueling double shift. During the course of the night, she's quieted old people who fear sleep because that is when death usually comes. In the darkness, they feel most vulnerable to the grim reaper's persuasion.

The halls are always quiet in the morning before the elderly groan their way into a new day. All is calm until she opens the door of room 411 to find Allen Peterson dead. He seems to have died both in fear, and in ecstasy. The Crooked Politician's Nightmare died wearing a disturbing expression that suggests terror, by his eyes, but his mouth boasts the first genuine smile Greta Sparks has ever seen on his face. She closes his eyes and prays for a tortured soul that has been rescued from its mangled body by some kind of sweet death. Although a stroke is the probable cause, there will be no autopsy to reveal the puncture wound at the base of his skull. Having finally cracked the sky, Allen Peterson has found his peace.

Five hours later, Vera McCallum and her child were found dead inside the burnt husk of a vehicle over eighty miles away from her home. She apparently crashed into a tree at the bottom of a hill. Her purse and identification was ejected from the car, making the bodies easier to identify. Her husband was all broken up about the tragic loss.

⟫⟪

April 8th. 7:00 p.m. Winston County, Mississippi.

The bloody body of nineteen-year-old Willis Smalls is found lying in a ditch near a dumpster. It appears that he died of multiple stab wounds. His skull has been crushed with a blunt object that proves to be a discarded bat.

Less than twenty-four hours ago, Willis Smalls was exonerated of rape charges. The charges were made by his frightened, threatened girlfriend after being caught in bed with him. The young man narrowly escaped a bad scene by leaping from a window on that day, but the girl's father recognized him from the basketball team.

The young man's folks were poor, so he was counseled by a public defender that did not go out of her way because she felt him culpable. She was guilty of allowing her own experiences and gender to cloud her judgment, so Willis Smalls found himself standing before a stacked deck.

During a long overdue bond hearing, despite the shame it would bring her family, Willis' badly bruised Caucasian girlfriend showed up and relented her story before the judge. Despite the vicious thrashing that her proud, abusive father would administer afterward, Bonnie Jasper felt compelled by teenage love and teenage guilt to tell the truth.

Her behavior and sexual proclivity is considered to be intolerable in their community.

387

The homicide investigators are sure that Barney Jasper is responsible for the murder of Willis Smalls because of his daughter's soiled honor. No evidence to that effect will surface, however.

As a show of good faith, Barney Jasper is asked to come in for questioning. He does so of his own accord, but the inconvenience only lasts twenty minutes. He is guilty, but the law seems to be on his side. It does not sit well with the African American community.

Somewhere…

Somewhere between heaven and hell, the drums have been pounding throughout the day and they are unremitting long into the night.

This unfamiliar place is a freakish contradiction to all that is normal in their orderly lives. There are odors and sounds in the air to which Farrakhan and Jackson are unaccustomed as they stand on some windswept savanna. To the west of them, dry earth with sparse vegetation. To the sloping east, patchy woodlands are pasted against a backdrop of fitful clouds. To the north and south, are monstrous canyons with spires of rock formations that reach for the heavens.

"By forces that you cannot imagine, we have been drawn together for a dreaded event, which shall be remembered as Kuuta—the Blood Sacrifice!"

Thunder rumbles in the billowing clouds above.

"However, you have played your own roles in the separation of man from man. Oh no, gentlemen, you are not blameless in the realms of inhumanity. Our very own people are guilty of complacency amid quarrelsome division and senseless violence, and such are things that Damballah frowns upon. Burying our talents like the dead has been the nature of the dark man because we are creatures of passion, given to distraught emotions when our energy is devoid of direction. It disgraces us to adopt the popular excuses that shroud our shortcomings. However, because a dark seed struggles from within to change its direction in this land, Damballah chooses to rail down

upon those who would hold them back as if they be gods themselves. He is pleased that you two men have finally begun to see that the time for trivial pursuits and blame has passed."

Sidewinder rattlesnakes slither before them and stop, momentarily.

"At the end of this calamity, there will be no need to revisit that way of thinking because the dark child will no longer be forced to choose from the short list of other men. Working harder as a people pleases Damballah, but how do we settle conflicts with an adversary when we are at odds with our own? God wills that there be a time of human reunion or these events shall signify the end of all things to come!"

In the murky distance, upon the dark blue horizon of the west, rival troops of silverback guerrillas charge to the very edge of their territorial boundaries. In this territorial dispute, they face each other, thumping their chests and caterwauling threats. Suddenly, they clash. Blood and fur fly amidst a hail of furious blows. It is carnage, and yet quite natural.

"Look around you, holy men. See that our children are products of poisoned environments. These are environments that we as a people have not worked hard enough to improve, but they must stand as one now." While screeching its terrible threat, a Harpy Eagle glares at them over Kinzana's shoulder. *"Mr. Jackson, the hypocritical, preaching politician with appetites that you deny, was called by God before losing sight of his Holy Commandments, my very proud friend. Mr. Farrakhan, you are guilty of a doctrine that is too closely suited to discrimination, which is no better than the bigotry of the Whites because it is constructed on controversy and strife. Perhaps, even murder. Repent, for you've stirred the boiling pot with your own hands. Repent."*

They hear every word Kinzana speaks, but their unbelieving eyes remain glued to the primates' brutal struggle for dominance. It is so very savage this battle. Now Kinzana's smile seems to hold a measure of malice.

"Now, Damballah is pleased that two reeds, twisting in the winds of change have finally come together to bind for greater strength. For this reason alone, you are now chosen. Damballah is pleased that you have decided to walk away from the extremes in order that you might achieve something

positive and practical. Still, you must sacrifice your pride, which is useless in the capacity in which you both have chosen to exercise them. Even now, I can detect your disbelief and skepticism, but such things are merely residuals of what will soon be your former persona. You must look beyond yourselves because you have been selected to tame the blood lust and to calm the angered spirits that will soon rise to take hold of this nation if we survive."

As if the dance is choreographed by a fluted Indian snake charmer, the six sidewinders pair up and begin to entwine themselves. Their scales are raspy as they stand on their tails and reach for the sky. Although they are venomous, this strange display is a thing of beauty. The snakes soon return to their bellies to encircle the captive audience. Now they lie motionless on the red sand, watching them. Farrakhan and Jackson stare back at the snakes, making sure that none are sneaking up from behind.

"Mr. Jackson, you will help in the rebuilding of this country's political structure. And it is your charge, Mr. Farrakhan, to assist in the development of the Black nation's ability to coexist with our White brothers. You will quell the very hatred that your own following has helped to instill in the minds of Americans and Muslims abroad."

Black leather and matted fur lands on the ground just inches from Jesse Jackson's left foot. Jagged bones protrude the bleeding flesh. He is repulsed when he realizes that it is the severed hand of an unfortunate ape. The ground shakes, something roars as it charges at the strangers to this realm. A silverback pounds its broad chest and then thrashes the ground with yet another dismembered limb.

The beast stops short of the circle of snakes, slapping at them with the arm of one of its dead rivals. Its yellow teeth are borne and its ebony eyes glare at them with great malice. Advancing no further, it kicks up a cloud of dust that covers its sudden retreat. This gigantic animal seems to vanish into thin air.

As if none of these things are happening, Kinzana continues to speak. "Neither shall be easy tasks, but the importance will be immeasurable. In the face of the greatest temptation to use the advantage of numbers, you will commit yourselves to fairness and equality. You will obey this decree or you will perish in your disbelief and disobedience. Your Holy Bible and Koran will be useless and ineffectual in the creation of a new history. This is so because they are nothing but one-sided adaptations of the realities of the past, present, and especially of the future!"

Kinzana's eyes fall upon the two men whose pride will now rise as a danger to both.

Farrakhan shouts, "What are these parlor tricks and this line of bull you sell? If you think I will not lead my people to do to the White man what he's done to us, you are misled. Just who are you to tell me that my holy scripture is a lie?"

"This is blasphemy," Jesse Jackson warns. "You risk your mortal soul if you do not repent those words. You and your black magic are an abomination to our Lord and Savior Jesus Christ!"

Kinzana's eyes blaze, but the fury in them is a great contradiction to his laughter as he rocks back on his heels to consult the sky. The drums begin to throb with renewed intensity as Kinzana spreads his arms. When his eyes fall upon them again, they are whites. He now speaks in a voice that is distant, so distant that it seems as if his words were spoken in the past.

"The word of God was handed down in a time when mankind was not so widely dispersed throughout this world, but many chose to add and take away that which they fearfully disbelieved or woefully misunderstood, or could not use to their advantage. Throughout the annals of time, many have adopted such things as organized religion. Like Shakespeare, Clemens, and Poe, they are dramas of the imagination—merely misguided superstitions, sprinkled with but morsels of the truest of truths!"

Both Farrakhan and Jackson shout, "You lie!"

Their defiance finally angers Kinzana, who says, "Pray then to your Gods, for in this place you shall witness Damballah's power and grow to know it intimately. Pray for your miserable souls, for no mere man can save thee, Muslim. And your savior, Christian, was The Satan's own guise to prove that humanity has no worth to exist. Pray to them. Pray to them now, for every prayer to The Satan causes the God of gods a seething torment, which he will have no more!" When Kinzana thrusts a malignant finger toward them, the snakes coil and begin to rattle their tails in warning.

The wind rises swiftly, whistling through the nearby treetops. The fire licks its hungry tongues, but its flames do not die as sparks pop into the air to fly away. The sky boils with black clouds that toss and roil like reptiles in a pit, murmuring as if billions of lost souls are trapped in the air. The earth shakes as thunderclaps bang and vibrate the atmosphere, drawing nigh as if they are the approaching footsteps of God.

Electric tendrils stretch their scrawny fingers to illuminate the violent sky! Sand blows like tiny razors into their faces and across their skin. Then the ground splits open to consume the fire. A jagged crack in the earth zig-zags between Farrakhan and Jackson to end at Kinzana's feet. The two men try to shield their eyes from the stinging, airborne sand, stricken with ter-ror. Pain sears them to the quick and they scream in agony. They fall to the ground, grasping at their tormented bodies. They are retching, bleeding from their pores and every orifice.

The drums are pounding, but no beat is missed in their terrible pulses. Their eerie throbbing is never interrupted by the quaking of the earth or the lightning, which reaches into the belly of the earth to disintegrate the logs of the swallowed fire. Demonic spirits screech from the jagged gash, rising from the smoke to bite at their bodies as they scream and writhe.

Farrakhan and Jackson are suddenly seized and elevated to their feet by something foul, something that rises from the chasm. Its claws are graced with steel talons that bite into their flesh. Its black hairs are deeply embedded, bristling quills. Its eyes are as black as outer space—soulless, frigid, feeling absolutely nothing for these men. Its maw slowly opens to reveal yellowing daggers that drip with bile. Its tongue is a blade of fire, and its fetid breath causes them to gag when it seeks to taste them.

Their eyes lie. Their minds deny, for within their world dragons do not truly exist. Not for modern-day preachers.

And then…nothing.

Jackson and Farrakhan collapse to their knees, weakened by panic and terrors beyond their wildest imaginings. They have seen the hand of the true

God, and his anger prevails upon them both. His might has been hinted to make them believers, for this was no mere illusion.

The rainless storm subsides as quickly as it started, leaving the cracked earth to serve as a tangible reminder. And they will touch the jagged edges that formed before their very eyes, each fearing to look within its sulfurous depths.

Jesse Jackson and Louis Farrakhan know that there will be no second chances. When they look at each other, both have gone gray. Even their eyebrows have grayed, while Kinzana's short, night black hair has grown as white as snow. With their lessons taught, the drums cease. Silence becomes the night. Silence becomes the air.

Before he leaves, Kinzana takes a moment to stare down upon the cringing ministers, who have openly challenged his authority for the last time. Now, Kinzana walks away without another word.

April 8th. 9:00 p.m. Ferris, Maryland.

At the gruesome crime scene, someone shouts, "Turn that damn thing off. I can't hear myself think, for Christ sake. And make sure you're wearing gloves!"

The booming music stops abruptly to the delight of the homicide detective. Detective Jensen looks at the horrified neighbors watching from the park's perimeter. As he approaches this ugly scene, stomach acid threatens from within.

The bodies of four high school athletes were found shot to ribbons in a blue convertible. There are holes all over the blood-splattered vehicle, the image of which is burned into his mind by the forensic team's flashing bulbs as pictures are taken from all angles.

Detective Jensen recognizes these kids as three senior football players of Ferris High. The other was the dominate star of the basketball team. Three of the four kids had secured scholarships to different colleges, and the fourth was expected to follow suit because they were all very talented athletes.

When the photographer says, "There goes the neighborhood," Jensen glares at him with obvious disapproval.

Officer Cindy Collins notices when Jensen rubs his forehead as if he has a headache brewing, but she is about to make matters worse. She approaches and asks, "Hey, you okay?"

"Yeah, Cindy, I'm fine. I think I'm just tired of this job. Do you have any witnesses?"

"Negative, Detective Jensen, but we do have this." She gives him an evidence bag that contains a partially burnt letter addressed to Evan Parker at 666 Pine Street in Suitland, Maryland. When the acid level rises in his stomach and a tear falls from his eye, he knows that it's time to change professions.

⇥⇤ ⇥⇤

11:00 p.m. North Charleston, South Carolina.

When Louis Farrakhan and Jesse Jackson open their eyes, they are sweaty and panicked. They frantically search for truth in the dim lighting, and both men will reach for their hair upon seeing a gray circle on one another's head.

With his work long done, Evan Parker has returned to Melissa's side at one end of the couch. Kinzana is sitting on the other end, opposite of the two Black leaders. His eyes are still whites. His right fist is clenched about the ivory serpents' head of his cane. A trickle of blood is running down the white bone to the wood.

The truck had come to a stop while they slept. It has been parked on Legare Street, just three blocks from the home where Jarvis and Alvina Parker shared many wonderful years raising their family.

The painted ladies are once again naked from the waist up and fully camouflaged, preparing to strike out again.

When Kinzana's eyes roll downward in their sockets, he smiles directly at the Black leaders, knowing that they are filled with questions and consumed by fear. He now recognizes another nuance in their demeanor; total and complete awe. They will ask no burning questions at this moment.

At 11:45, there is a light tap on the side door. The two women have returned to speak to Kinzana privately while Farrakhan and Jackson watch with apprehension. After the women point out several places on handcrafted maps, Kinzana says, "Leave him. Yes, leave him. Are you quite certain that is everyone?" When the sisters nod to confirm, he says, "Make it so."

The painted ladies leave again, this time with camouflaged backpacks. Soon, a stolen taxi pulls up behind the trailer without lights and the engine is turned off. Now, Kinzana awakens Evan and Jarvis Parker.

Beneath the cover of a moonless, overcast sky, they crawl on their stomachs, moving through shadows and under bushes with deadly, catlike agility. In the vans, trucks, and cars, partners have exchanged many war stories and lies about their sexual conquests. No air conditioners are on in any of the vehicles, which would require that their engines be running. That will make the surveillance teams conspicuous in a predominately Black neighborhood, so they are forced to tolerate the heat and rising humidity of Charleston.

Funky gases are also exchanged between partners after consuming so many burritos and pizzas. The fumes, which are the products of fast food and nervous digestion, forces them all to want fresh air. At least one window is open on all the vehicles, but they have no idea that they are being stalked by human predators.

They are the night and the shadow, creeping forth unto their objectives. The two women have separated to work their way through all five of the two-man teams. The camouflage and their patience allow them to move within four to eleven-feet of the unsuspecting surveillance squads. With the cover of hedgerows, bushes, and naked darkness, they remove sections of bamboo from the backpacks. The foot and a half sections are assembled end to end like a wind-blowing instrument.

The sisters each have a package of gray powder, which is poured into the far end of the bamboo, where a piece of silk is affixed between the final pieces. A small amount of water is dripped onto the powder, causing it to turn into a gas. The near end is sealed. A small hole has been bored into the side of this first section about midway. The far ends of these pipes are deftly maneuvered close to the open windows. They blow the odorless gas into the vehicles without making a sound. Just as water will crawl along to saturate cotton, the gas floats and mingles in the stalled air just inches from the faces of the unsuspecting CIA agents.

At 1:15 a.m., there is another tap on the small door. One of the sisters says to Kinzana, "It is done, baba." After whispering her message, she is gone like a gust of wind.

He turns to the others to instruct, "It is time. You must remember to move quickly once you have entered the house, but first, you will allow the remaining agent to confirm your identities. Trust in these words, for I am afraid it is very necessary. Melissa, fear not for your husband."

Melissa says, "Evan, I'm not sure about this. What if there are more of them than we think? What if the man on top of the church has a rifle and decides to shoot on sight? I'm scared, baby." She weeps on his shoulder, holding him tight.

"I'll be careful, Melissa. I don't know why, but if Kinzana says that it's necessary, I suppose there has to be a good reason. He's gotten us through so far, so I feel we must continue to trust him. If they notice that journal, they may be able to track us to the village. We'll be okay, I promise." Evan Parker feels his heart racing despite his bravely spoken words.

Jarvis experiences momentary dizziness when he gains his feet. He steadies himself and takes his place at the door, feeling a little better with the passing seconds.

Jesse Jackson and Louis Farrakhan are shaking at this point. Each feels himself insane for going along with this crazy plan, which can have no sensible outcome. They will be tempting fate, but they also remember the extremely overwhelming dream that they had shared in every detail. They, too, gather at the small door.

The four men expect to see the painted ladies when they slip into the darkness, but the sisters are near Jarvis' property to serve as lookouts. They will run interference if any agents have escaped their attention.

The man who has ridden shotgun in the cab of the semi drives the taxi. His name is Nara, whose fraternal twin did most of the driving as they cautiously bobbed and weaved their way south.

Kinzana consoles Melissa Parker as the cab drives away. She cannot help feeling that she may have seen her husband alive for the last time.

As the cab approaches with its signal lights on, Special Agent Frampton's heart thumps in his chest. He keys his radio and says, "Look alive, ladies. We have visitors." He is looking through a pair of night vision glasses when the cab stops to let the four fugitives out. Frampton whispers, "Very sloppy of you, Mr. Parker. Very sloppy indeed." A disturbing thought suddenly occurs to him, so he calls on the radio, again. "We have positive IDs. That's Parker, his father, Jackson, and Farrakhan. What the fuck are you waiting for? Move in, take them now."

Frampton's heart thuds, but his anxieties are nothing compared to the hackle-raising tension that those four men experience while Jarvis unlocks his front door. They are all sweating and waiting for a bullet to take someone down.

Frampton grabs his rifle and readies for a shot. By the time his scope finds them, the last man slips inside and the door is shut. "Fuck! What the hell is going on?" he says to himself. Agent Frampton takes his phone from his pocket to call Sterne.

Once they get inside, Farrakhan and Jackson move cautiously to the windows to pull the blinds. Despite the pain, Evan sprints upstairs to the room he and Melissa always used during visits. He hastens to fill a shopping bag with a few things. He grabs Melissa's suitcase and runs to Jarvis' room.

Jarvis moves as quickly as he can to get to the basement. He slides the ceiling-to-floor shelves to the left, and enters the code for the door to the tunnel. This tunnel ends at his bomb shelter. The two civil rights leaders follow him closely. Jackson shouts for Evan to hurry.

When Evan yanks open his father's closet, his heart stops from the sudden shock of looking into the murdered eyes of his Aunt Thelma. Those dead orbs pierce Evan, as if they can see right through him. Like a rag doll, she has been propped up on his mother's collection of shoeboxes. Evan Parker's soul aches as she rolls into his arms. She's been shot in the head, and it looks as if she died trying to scream. For one terrible moment, Evan Parker can see through her eyes. He sinks to the floor with her stiffening body, holding and crying for the aunt he loves dearly.

Time is of the essence and though it hurts to do so, he has to leave her there. He gathers a few of Jarvis' things and remembers to get the journal on the way downstairs.

The CIA director answers the phone in a bad mood. "Sterne here, go!"

"Director Sterne, this is Frampton. The package has just arrived. All four boxes." Vincent Sterne smiles, despite himself. "But there seems to be a problem, sir. No one moved on them according to plan. I cannot raise any of my surveillance teams."

Vincent Sterne's smile crashes like an airplane out of fuel as he visualizes the scene at the Suitland house. It seems to be happening again.

He shouts, "What the hell happened? Listen to me. Do not hesitate, blow the fucking house now."

The journal is on the kitchen table. Evan scoops it up on the run and careens down the basement steps.

Agent Frampton's men have wired the entire house with explosives. Every unit is linked to the same detonator frequency. Frampton now holds the detonator in his hand and pulls the antenna to its length. He flips the arming switch. When a green light confirms that the explosives have been armed, he pushes the red button.

Boom da-da doom! Boom da-da doom! The drums are beaten furiously.

Jarvis Parker's house is obliterated. The explosion is so loud that it gives a sleeping neighbor a fatal heart attack.

Shards of glass and wood are sent slicing through the air. Shrapnel rips through the trees to pelt neighboring houses, shattering plate glass windows and flattening car tires in nearby driveways. The shockwave rocks the ground, felt blocks away. It is heard at much greater distances. The roof goes skyward, separating in all directions before scattering in the yard. Throughout an entire four-block radius, car alarms blare in driveways and along the curb where they are parked for the night.

"I don't think you have to worry about them anymore, Mr. Sterne. A gnat fly couldn't get through that!" brags the very special agent. Frampton expects a big pat on the back, but all he gets is a verbal kick in the pants.

"Stop your gloating," Vincent Sterne growls. "Get your ass in gear and see what happened to your unit. If they're dead, disappear. Move it!"

After hanging up on his man, Sterne makes other calls. One of which is to President Gore, who feels genuine remorse for having auctioned his soul to the devil. However, he is relieved that it is finally over. Sterne arranges to fly to South Carolina.

Evan closes the outer door in the basement, running down the tunnel when the blast occurs. He is fleet, which is lucky for him because there are explosives hidden in the basement. The force of the blast slams into the outer door, driving it into the tunnel, which quickly collapses.

Evan Parker charges out of the dust and slams the six-inch door to the shelter behind him just before the other door comes chasing after him. It hammers into the frame around the entrance of the bomb shelter, lodging diagonally.

Jackson and Farrakhan are speechless as the entire world moves around them. Jarvis hugs his son and cries, "Thank God. You barely made it out of there in time."

"Pop, we have to get out of here right now!"

Melissa's suitcase and Jarvis' things have been lost in the tunnel. The only things that Evan manages to salvage are a few articles of his own clothing and Kinzana's sainted journal.

They follow Jarvis Parker through the rows of distilled drinking water. Lighting is practically nonexistent until Jarvis flicks on a flashlight. The two men, who are completely alien to this place, notice the well-stocked shelves of canned and dry goods. They see boxes of clothing and bedding. Jarvis even has a full bathroom facility, as far as bomb shelters go. He's done his homework well enough to even install a ham radio and two generators.

When they reach the far end of the shelter, Jarvis detours to open a drawer where he keeps a pistol and ammunition. He unlocks a door to another tunnel that's dark and smells of trapped paint fumes gone stale.

Jarvis never opens this part of his bunker. The escape route that goes to the boundary of his property, ending beneath the stone ramp that Evan and Kyle Parker had lain upon just days ago. Because the ceiling is lower, they have to crouch as they hurry along the ascending passageway. Jarvis uses keys to unlock the last door. He peers out with his gun at the ready, but the door jams. They're trapped!

Jarvis and Evan are applying pressure when one of the painted assassins yanks at the debris blocking the door. Their hearts quicken when she suddenly appears, and Jarvis nearly blows her away. She stares at him, hissing her annoyance at having a gun pointed at her face by a shaking hand.

For the first time, she speaks directly to them in a whisper. "Hurry. We must leave this place. Follow me." They run amid the blaring car alarms, happy to fill their lungs with fresh air because the tunnel had begun to feel like a tomb for four.

When they reach the corner of the block, they pile into the trailer, which has been moved a bit closer. Its massive engine is idling, but that makes no difference because the world is already filled with the sound of sirens and car alarms. Small fires are rampant throughout the neighborhood, and the smell of smoke is building in the still air.

No neighbor sleeps. Many of them are busy trying to put out fires on their lawns or rooftops. No one seems to notice the dark figures running through the smoke to the getaway truck.

Melissa is sitting on the couch crying her eyes out, certain that the explosion claimed the life of her husband and father-in-law. There could be no greater joy for her than when Evan lunges back through the small door. Her knees are too weak to run into his arms as she wants to, but her eyes reach out to touch his soul from where she sits shaking.

Frampton does not hear the ambulance, fire trucks, or police sirens. His mind is consumed with what he sees in the first surveillance unit. He slowly circumvents the vehicle, peering through the windshield and side windows. His subordinates are staring into the great wide open with blank expressions on their faces. Their eyes lack any awareness, never blinking. Frampton could see their

Adam's apples moving up and down, so they're not dead or dying like the men in Suitland, Maryland. But they certainly look dead and they soon will be if Sterne gets no satisfactory answers.

"What the hell went wrong? Why the fuck didn't you follow my orders? Roberts? Paget?" His people continue to stare, wordlessly, so Frampton reaches inside and shakes Tina Paget. But when he turns the agent loose in frustration, she slides across the seat where her head comes to rest on her partner's left shoulder. Roberts doesn't even blink in protest. They can see everything, feel everything. The recently quiet neighborhood is now saturated with blaring chaos. And yet, they cannot move.

The bewildered Frampton looks around at the frightened, questioning faces of the confused neighbors. By this time, they have all heard the startling news about Jarvis Parker's renegade son, but most of them do not believe a word of it.

Frampton receives the same type of welcome from team two, but Agent Burch stares forth with a twelve-inch shard of wood protruding from his bleeding chest. He is slipping closer to the eternal breach with every blood-gushing heartbeat. This man is in excruciating pain, and his mind is panicked. Yet, he cannot move.

Amid the busy firemen, Frampton hits redial when he sees the news teams pulling up in their mobile units. Their presence means trouble, but at least Parker has been eliminated from the equation. However, it will be a bit more difficult to explain the drugged agents, who look as if they have all suddenly gone comatose. There are at least three different news channels hounding for a story, and controlling the hungry media is never easy. Sterne will know what to do, Frampton hopes.

CHAPTER 34

SANCTUARY

As the semi steams down Highway 17 South, toward Kinzana's village, Evan and Melissa quietly watch a news bulletin.

Carolyn Murray of News Channel Five in Charleston reports, "Hours ago, the bodies of four innocent teenagers were found murdered at a basketball court in Ferris, Maryland. Authorities say that there are no witnesses to the homicide, but they have found evidence that the fugitive and South Carolina native, Evan Parker, may have been involved in the killings. It now appears that Evan Parker, the recently named Deputy Director of the Census Bureau has somehow slipped through airport security and flown to North Charleston, South Carolina. As many of you know, there was an enormous explosion in the North Charleston area moments ago. Authorities suspect that Mr. Parker was responsible for the bombing of his own father's home."

The reporter informs the television audience that the mutilated body of another African American woman has been found in the rubble of the demolished home. Allegations have also been made by reliable sources, which link Evan Parker to an undisclosed militant group that may have supplied the high explosives. Evan Parker's psychotherapist has cited doctor/patient privileges and refuses to work with law enforcement agencies, even though his insight may help authorities to understand Parker's psychopathic tendencies."

"There will be updates throughout the night and during the six o'clock morning newscast. Sources say that the fugitive may have in his possession some form of nerve toxin, which authorities believe he has already used on federal agents. Charleston's Mayor Joe Riley and Mayor Hobbes of North Charleston have authorized a curfew because it is believed that Mr. Parker may be hiding in the area. Please be advised that this is a very serious situation. They have asked that you stay inside your homes, and lock the doors. This man is extremely dangerous, and he should not be approached. The police are asking that you call 911 immediately if you spot this man in the area. They are asking that you report any suspicious activity in your neighborhoods. You can help federal and local law enforcement by observing the mandatory curfew. If you are out on the road, and away from home, go to a friend's house or a hotel because there is simply no telling what the suspect is capable of next." She moves on to another story.

"My God in heaven," Evan spits, bitterly. "They'll blame me for bad weather next. They're even claiming that I have a shrink. Can you believe this fucking crap?"

Melissa watches as her husband paces in agitation. She says, on the verge of tears, "This isn't right. Why is that man doing this to you?"

Kinzana says, "Our Mr. Sterne is trying to cut him off from the rest of the country. Who would aid a man possessed of such demons?"

Jesse Jackson, who is still involved with the political world, considers the situation for a moment. Then he says, "He's right, I'm afraid. I believe President Gore has given the CIA free rein in the apprehension of your husband and anyone with him. We all know that means dead more than alive. More than likely, they are carrying phony identification to keep the CIA out of it in the media."

"But the media doesn't have a clue. Those vultures are making Evan sound like some rabid Rambo, running around raping old women and killing kids. How can this be? Don't they realize that they are liable?" she says. Evan sits with his wife in an attempt to quiet her fuming agitation.

"Well, I may be wrong, but I believe President Gore has now enacted the Seven Veil Quarantine. This executive order was created and forced into law just a few years ago. In fact, it was one of the few things that the Republicans and President Clinton readily agreed upon. In the interest of national security, the quarantine is designed to safeguard against impetuous and irresponsible media activities. In other words, we're talking about censoring media activities that pose any potential threats to national security. After the media world compromised secret operations abroad, the law was then forced down the throats of the news networks. You all must remember the tragic incident involving a man named Simon Tedesco in 1997. Many American intelligence agents were captured and killed because of the media's actions. Those still living are probably imprisoned by foreign countries for life. I was all for the law then, but I never imagined that it would be used in this manner."

Louis Farrakhan adds, "Politicians almost always find ways to turn something good into something bad. This is especially true of the Republican Party, but not exclusively, as we now see." Farrakhan's views have always seemed a bit twisted and strikingly harsh, but his words hold a measure of truth for them all.

"I tend to agree. In this case, it is a bipartisan conspiracy," Kinzana adds. "There are no party lines here, only race. Notice how a Black woman reports your misdeeds to those with whom you are most familiar. It is no coincidence that other Blacks are being used for the same purpose."

Jarvis shouts, "Those bastards murdered my sister for no reason. She didn't know anything, but they killed her anyway. And then they destroyed the house where my wife and I raised our children. Thelma was the sweetest person alive, and they shot her like a mad dog. Someone has to pay for this, and someone damn sure will."

"I know, pops," Evan says. "We'll find a way to make it right."

"All those precious memories, all the personal things that kept those memories alive in my mind with a simple glance or a touch, they're all gone now. My dear sister is dead, and everything is gone," Jarvis says. At the end of his statement, his voice trails off in a moment of guilt. He feels responsible for Thelma's death, angry at himself for uttering her name and the destruction of his property in the same breath because losing a home can't compare to losing a loving sister. Now the most bitter of his unused tears escape his aged eyes.

"Maybe it's time that I try to reach some of my political contacts. Maybe the NAACP can help," Jesse Jackson suggests.

"That's a good idea. And I'll try to reach my son," says Farrakhan.

Kinzana disagrees. "My friends, as soon as you contact anyone with influence, you will probably jeopardize us all. As you can see, the CIA has vast resources working to find you and Evan in their efforts to keep things quiet. It is no mere happenstance that your names haven't been mentioned on the news. They're expecting you to contact those who would have the credibility to propose something as incredible as this. By doing so, you place their lives in jeopardy, also. However, if you feel that you must try, then follow your conscience. But be warned, once that bridge has been crossed, there will be no going back for any of us."

What Kinzana said makes a great deal of sense. Neither wants to endanger others, much less themselves.

"But what else can we do while the media is being manipulated by the government? This is the very thing that the Bill of Rights was supposed to protect against," Jesse Jackson says.

"There is method to this madness, gentlemen. That is why I demanded that your cell phones be destroyed at the burning home in Suitland. If you will trust me, we will fulfill our destinies. But if you would rather go your own way, then so be it. No one is a prisoner here," Kinzana answers.

He is testing them and they know it.

Now the painted sisters emerge from the darkness at the unlighted end of the trailer. They are dressed in modest skirts, and their breasts are no longer visible. No one has really noticed their hazel eyes and sleek, black hair because of their initial appearance. They are quite beautiful women. For some strange reason, Melissa Parker experiences a momentary twinge of jealousy. Then, it is gone.

Aralesh says, "We believe in Kinzana."

Shelara declares, "And we think that you should trust in him as well."

"To stray from this path means certain death. Damballah requires obedience and faith. Nothing more, and certainly no less," Aralesh states.

Her sister says, "I am called Shelara and this is my twin sister Aralesh. To our great misfortune, we were born in the year 1970 during the Nigerian-Biafran civil war. We were infants of a small village whose civilian parents were murdered in a war that divided a nation. Our lives were saved by God when we were surely doomed to starvation and death. We have never known the names given to us by our birth parents and we never will, but such things no longer matter as long as we reside upon this earth."

Aralesh continues by saying, "We were trained as proud warriors whose names, combined, means 'two furies of one shadow'. We have been cared for, nurtured, trained and educated by our god-parents. Willingly and faithfully, we pledge our lives in the service of Damballah for it was only the God of all gods that whispered our desperate plight into the ear of Priestess Insanyanga, the seer of things unseen. By belief in her visions alone, Kinzana quickly directed his followers to quietly enter our ravaged nation to rescue us from what seemed a certain death."

Shelara says with conviction, "You may trust that every word from our lips are the unadorned truth. Fearing for our lives, our birth mother left us hidden in the bushes while fleeing the slaughter that still claimed her life. She sought to lead her captors away to protect her infant children from evil men who brutally raped and dismembered her body. Only days old, we were helpless, hungry, and blind still. But Damballah saw fit to spare our lives."

Enthralled by their incredible story, Melissa Parker asks, "How did you survive without shelter and sustenance?"

The twins look to one another and returned their serious gazes to Melissa to answer in unison, "The smell of her blood and our crying complaints drew all manner of predators towards us, including the Simba. However, instead of being eaten, we were suckled by a pride of lions and guarded by the great maned lord of the land, whose mighty roar still reverberates throughout our souls. When we were rescued by the men directed by Kinzana's influence with the gods, we had been licked clean by the lionesses of the pride and well fed. Surrounded by the carcasses of dead hyenas, baboons, and snakes that sought to consume us whole, our pride allowed us to be taken by those of our own kind without interference or harm. They must have been very brave men to do such a thing."

"My God, it's a miracle you survived," Melissa Parker utters in astonishment. She looks at Kinzana, who only smiles and nods to the viability of their life story.

The sisters go forward to package the remaining sets of Evan's evidence. They place the selected items in plain cardboard boxes addressed to the names on the list of suggestions they have all decided upon.

Evan takes a moment to wonder at how the painted ladies evolved from their hideous cocoons to become such beautiful, graceful butterflies. How very strange.

Kinzana assures, "Tonight, we will drink, we will feast, and we will pray. I will welcome you all to my home where all arrangements have been made to accommodate your arrival. You can rest there and the drums will not intrude upon your slumber."

Kinzana reaches to his right to place a hand on Jarvis' shoulder. He says, with a sincere measure of sadness, "And to you, my dear old friend, I am very sorry for the loss of your wonderful sister and your lovely home."

"I know you don't mean to hurt me, Kinzana, but why was it really necessary to go there?" Everyone, those who are awake, find this to be a reasonable question.

Kinzana's answer is, "More will be revealed to you as to the purpose. For now, I can tell you that, thus far, the media has been our enemy. I am more than certain that our Mr. CIA is aiming to make Evan public enemy number one. Someone who has been following the news, being abreast of all the deceptive charges accredited to his homicidal rampage, would probably shoot him on sight. This incident will serve to show just how desperately they are trying to kill you all. This and the home in Maryland are very public events that they cannot completely cover up. Only portions of the truth have been told to the media, and they must be licking their lips for more by now. When the truth is exposed by reputable sources, those who would have no reason to lie for your sakes, the people will put the facts together. As long as we stay one step ahead of them, we'll avoid being captured before the truth comes out. Every time there is a mess to clean up, the world sits up and pays attention to this drama. Mr. CIA's plans will soon blow up in his face. But there will be danger even then, for no White man in this country or its government will readily relent, unless they are of the truly enlightened."

The truck is slowing to a stop when Melissa asks, "But what is all this nonsense about Evan having nerve gas? Don't you think that's a bit far-fetched?"

Kinzana chuckles. He glances at the twin sisters and says, "My goddaughters made zombies of the assassins who watched Jarvis' home. However, by the time they know what has incapacitated them, the damage will have been done. That is, if they ever find out."

"Zombies? But how?" Evan asks.

"They will explain it to you, if you wish. I believe we have finally arrived. I feel the presence of my people."

Kinzana picks up the black cane, using the intertwined ivory snakes to scratch an annoying itch on his cheek.

There is a polite knock at the door. They have made it to Beaufort, South Carolina, where Insanyanga greets her husband and the others with teary eyes. Her tears mingle with Melissa Parker's as they embrace.

Farrakhan and Jackson marvel at the rather elaborate greeting. They are impressed with Kinzana's compound beyond expression because their visions of the place have been very stereotypical. As proof that they are learning to discard their doubts, both men experience a moment of shame.

The group is guided to an open courtyard near the end of the compound, where a beautiful garden is surrounded by woodlands. Tables of food and drink are theirs to test.

What seems to strike them all is the collection of people who gather to treat Kinzana with what could only be described as reverence. Some of these people adorn plumes, beads, and even animal skins as attire. Oddly, they are not all African American, or even of African descent.

The silence is broken when Kinzana takes his place at the far end of the garden. He beckons his companions to join him on either side. They are brought bowls and basins of water in which their hands and feet are washed by humble servants.

Women will bring tray after tray of unique delicacies the new-comers never experienced. They are encouraged to eat to their individual contentment. The appetites of the weary travelers are very much intact.

The drums thrum in the company of strange flutes and horn instruments. Three old men blow over the openings of hollow gourds, creating a sound reminiscent of soft drink bottles. It makes an eerie, whooping lament, but the sound is not unpleasant.

In the center of it all, burns a small fire. Younger men and women dance while others sing songs of merriment. The last song, however, is very sad. None of the guests recognize the lyrical language, but it is a sad thing to them all. This time, Insanyanga does not lead what's called "The Goodbye Song".

After everyone has eaten to their heart's content, there comes the quiet. The guests and other dignitaries of diverse races and African tribes listened to Kinzana's words and instruction. Then they are escorted to their private, comfortable sleeping quarters.

Melissa and Evan Parker talk for a very long time, and there are more than a few tears shed. Mostly, their hearts are at ease when an acceptance of the burden is somehow achieved. Layer by layer, Melissa Parker's stress washes away. They both decide that something more important than them is taking place here. After realizing there is very little they can do to change their places in this new history, they accept that they are a part of it all. To trust Kinzana is their only recourse, for he alone seems to have the answers and the power to see them through.

Evan Parker is saddened by what his honor requires of him. With tears in his eyes, he divulges the material that she may or may never have seen in the tabloids the government fiends have leaked to discredit him with his wife and those who are meant to never know the truth. His assistant Veronica, a lovely young woman stands before her husband with unmistakable desire pouring from her eyes on the balcony of the Monarch Hotel. The kiss gives Melissa Parker a prick to her heart, but she relieves his soul of guilt, worry, and self-condemnation.

She smiles at him, without a hint of malice or vengeance. She whispers, "I wondered how long it would take before you told me yourself. I heard the conversation you held with Kinzana, but I believed you when you claimed that this was not your idea. I pretended to sleep and soon slipped off into a place of peace because I have faith in my faithful husband, whom I shall never doubt as long as we live. I love you, Evan Parker, so let us never speak of this again. Put your heart and mind at rest." When all is said and done, sleep comes too easily for them all.

Before the rising sun, the painted ladies, dressed in business suits, will leave the compound to patronize several shipping companies far away from the Beaufort area. Postage for their deadly packages will be paid for same and next day express delivery with UPS, Federal Express, and even the United States Postal Service in Savannah, and Midland Georgia. In a way, the trail leads south.

As the drums pound deep within the belly of the earth, Captain Kyle Parker dreams that he opens the cabinet where he selects cards number two, nine, and eleven. He bends the red plastic covers until they snap at their perforated centers. Then he removes the authentication codes and fingers the keyboard to enter them into the computer. When Captain Parker awakens, he stays on his cot and stares up into infinite darkness. His madness is contagious and the drums vibrate throughout both their tormented dreams.

He will soon traverse the labyrinth to the missile silos. There, he will remove glistening black access panels to bypass circuitry as madness seeps into consciousness. This madness shreds Captain Kyle Parker from within to taint his moral fiber, urging him toward the unthinkable. The drums have provided the keys to vengeful destruction. This is insanity; utter madness.

CHAPTER 35
THE CONFESSIONAL

April 9, 2001. 7:00 a.m.

After enduring a night of constant cigarette smoke, Vincent Sterne's red eyes are irritated by the early morning light. He kicked the habit three years ago, but picked it up again without realizing it. Thanks to Evan Parker, he is quickly heading for two packs a day.

Having gotten very little sleep in the last few days, his disposition is consistent with that of a very bad pre-menstrual syndrome. His body aches, cursing him with messages of cramps that are coming from every muscle and creaking joint. He feels like long-dead, bloated fish. His extremely temperamental gut is a twisted knot. For the first time in his life, he is truly beginning to notice his age.

Vincent Sterne sails cuss words in his mind and often aloud as he walks through the wreckage of Jarvis Parker's demolished home. Adorned with dark glasses beneath a cap, an FBI embossed windbreaker and badge, he blends in well with everything around him but for the insufferable heat.

There's no sign of the people they are hunting. His men sift through the rubble with dogs in a futile search for anything that will suggest that there was more than one body and some good smelling chicken in the house when it exploded.

Much to his dismay, there is nothing more to find. Even a blast of that magnitude would have left some bits and pieces, as is proven by what's collected of Aunt Thelma. Parts of her are being found up to three houses away.

Finally, someone calls out from the gaping hole that used to be the basement. After moving a section of the roof that covers the partially collapsed tunnel, an agent finds the door to the bomb shelter. The outer door of the primary tunnel is dragged aside by a bulldozer.

The keypad has been obliterated and the wires fused, so a local welder is summoned to cut away the steel door of the bomb shelter. During this time, Sterne and his men wrestle with growing anticipation. Sterne has carefully balanced his network of people to fall into line, but most know nothing of what truly drives this frantic manhunt. Evan Parker is simply an elusive enemy of the state; someone that has to be apprehended.

The perimeter is secured of all media and onlookers. No outsiders can be allowed to see what they intend for the fugitives once the door is no longer a hindrance.

Melting, red-hot metal pops and drips on either side of the door as the welder works. Jarvis has done his homework well in building his nuclear haven. The door's core is made of solid lead and surrounded by thick tempered steel. The hinges are inside, making it necessary to cut the lock and hinges from the steel frame. The welder is nearly finished with the last incision, but he stops suddenly.

As Sterne and his men gather near the entrance with weapons drawn in their sweaty palms, the welder glances over his shoulder at their faces, which are obscured by gas masks. Now, he looks back at the door. The old man stands up and hands the torch to one of the agents and runs away without a word.

Hank Moseley realizes that he isn't being paid enough to expose the hiding place of a man who has killed people from Washington to South Carolina. Because the welder is an avid follower of the daily news, he is well aware of the inherent dangers of cornering Evan Parker. The man has to be psychotic if he is willing to blow up his father's house in an attempt to fake his own death. This welder is no fool. The gas masks and the intensity on their faces prove that he is seriously underpaid.

The agent looks at Sterne with the torch in one hand and his weapon in the other. Sterne's expression tells him that he has to finish the incision. So he does, after a moment of hesitation.

In the meantime, an agent named Paul Taper gains Sterne's attention by saying, "Director Sterne, with all due respect, I strongly suggest that you observe from the perimeter. We don't know who or what we'll find inside. For all we know, Parker may have rigged this area, too. We can't chance you getting hurt."

Sterne is livid. "Are you suggesting that I can't cut the mustard, Taper?"

A senior agent named Connors intercedes at this point. "That's not what he means and you know it, Vince."

Sterne spins around with every intention of tearing someone's head off, but he's met with the disarming smile of an old friend. He is the only Chief Operator with the tenure or the nerve to address Sterne so casually, though it is not normal for him to do so in the company of others.

Taper is dismissed and they walk away to speak freely. "That young pup was out of line," Sterne says, exercising restraint.

Jack Connors says, "You know he's right, Vince. Look at yourself, you're all wound up because you are too close to this thing. The big boss isn't tied to an office and a desk for no reason. You're supposed to direct, not get directly involved."

"That's right, I'm too close to let somebody foul up."

Connors smiles. "Listen, we'll handle it. If they are in there, where are they going? The kid was just looking out for you, and maybe trying to score a few brownie points while at it. But what does it matter? He's right. Besides, they have no idea that you blew up the damn house, so let us do our bit while you sit this one out."

"You have that look in your eyes, Jack," Sterne says. "What's the scuttlebutt?"

Looking Sterne squarely in the eyes, Jack Connors replies, "Well, I'll admit that I held a rather uncomfortable conversation with a few Senators who are more than a little worried about you, Vincent."

"I see," whispers Sterne, while looking over his glasses. "Are you getting ambitious, Jack? The big chair is whispering in your ear, is it?"

Jack Connors smiles at Vincent Sterne. "Not at all, Vincent. It takes a certain cerebral type to deal with bureaucrats and the like. I'm just a glorified foot soldier, more of a hands on sort of guy. You know that."

"Yes, I know."

With a sly smile building, Connors states, "But just because I don't want your job, doesn't mean that I'll sit back and resist the opportunity to tell you when you're fucking up. You've made mistakes, Vincent. Using and losing two wet squads without tasking satellites specifically for these ops were bad moves? Your eyes in the sky were shut because you wanted this all off the books. If you used your vast resources, they would never have eluded your net. We both know that underestimating the opponent puts even the strongest man at the disadvantage. Now you must admit, that's textbook Sterne 101."

Sterne looks Connors in the eyes to say, "I hate being lectured by a logical man."

"You know and I know, but these men don't have a clue what is at stake here. We also know that it's been a while since you've gotten your hands dirty. As you can well attest, it only feels good when it turns out right. That much has never changed, no matter where you are sitting when an op goes down. You're an important man, too important to go storming the bunker with the infantry. So let's concede that Agent Taper's assumptions are perfectly valid. If you ask me, Parker is long gone. He probably took the back door out of here just before the fireworks started. After all that's happened up until now, it would be one hell of a stroke of luck if they did get themselves trapped down there, huh?"

Both Connors and Sterne grin, slyly.

"Because I knew you would not disagree, I ordered retrospectives to scan all archival sat-observations. Every techy in the western hemisphere is either going blind searching endlessly through every second of telemetry footage of the last two relevant areas in question, or they are hacking into upper deck pods of our unwitting nosy neighbors. Twenty-four hours' worth of looking for something without knowing what that might be. They hate me for it, but I told them it's a direct order from you. So far, through the electrical interference of the storms and satellites looking in completely different directions, they haven't even seen this place go up. You really did a bang up job, son. Slipping rarely affords a soft landing, my old friend."

"Can't deny the mistakes I've made, but I haven't the time to take a bow. I'll wait up here. I hate it when you're right, Jack."

"Now ain't that a pregnant, whoring bitch?" Connors says as he climbs down to join the others at the door. Sterne remains above, watching pensively.

With the incision complete, the torch is turned off and discarded. After several tries with crowbars, the heavy door is forced inward. When it crashes to the bunker's floor, Agent Glass is the first to go in. Seven others follow on his heels with flashlights that slice through the blackness. They can see no one, but the shooting begins when something crashes in the darkness.

The startled men fire indiscriminately in the dark bunker. Perhaps Sterne's presence is to blame for the nervous reaction. Bottles of water shatter, their contents running like bloodstains across the floor. The ham radio is obliterated as canned goods ooze from bullet-inflicted wounds.

Agent Connors rips his mask away to see through the flashes of gunfire, detecting a faint whiff of gasoline in the air. He knows that they're about to blow themselves to hell. His heart races when a bullet ricochets off of a tank with a skull and crossbones on the side.

Connors shouts, "Cease fire. Cease fire!" He lowers his weapon and quickly reaches to his left, knocking Agent Glass' hands into the air because he's aiming in the direction of the huge gasoline tank. But Connors is too late. A bullet plows into the two-hundred gallon tank of instant death!

The explosion is merciless. Wrapped in crimson tongues of flames, two bodies are ejected through the doorway as the ground seizes. Jarvis Parker's escape door, still partially blocked by debris and slightly ajar, was not discovered by Sterne's men. When the gasoline ignites during their siege, fire and debris is forced through both doors, causing a vacuum in the center of the bunker that draws the flames back. The resulting back-draft explosion is so violent that it causes the ground to open up before Sterne's unbelieving eyes.

The two men that were ejected from the bomb shelter, though badly scorched, are the only lucky ones.

Despite all of the activity in the area and the cries of the injured men, silence fills the world.

Sterne's expression is one of abject depression, his eyes are downcast as he holds his breath. He's too stunned to issue words of supervision to the remaining agents. The closest thing he has to a real friend is dead, his body is badly broken and nearly incinerated. As Vincent Sterne looks down at Connors's mangled torso, a vision of Cecil Bridges dances in his head to make him shudder.

Moments later, Sterne is still deep in thought. His right foot aimlessly rearranges the small, loose pebbles of the street. A glimmer of pain stabs at his temple when his cell phone rings.

President Gore is sitting in the Oval Office with Vice President Graff. They are following reports from Charleston, waiting for Sterne to tell them the problem was eliminated from the equation by an earlier explosion that could only have been caused by one of his men. Gore knows nothing of this recent tragedy.

When Sterne's report turns out to be just the opposite of what they expect, shouting results on both ends of the connection. After President Gore hangs up on Director Sterne, he paces the office floor. Gore wrenches his hands and envisions himself swaying from a media-built scaffold in a public place.

Vice President Graff is equally concerned, but she contains her pacing within her seat. Although she appears to be calmer, she is just as frightened.

Gore has betrayed the American people, Blacks in particular; those who helped his campaign immensely. Somehow, he has immersed himself in a conspiracy to cover-up the truth, becoming a party to the commitment of murders and more. By allowing himself to be coerced from the path of truth and a lifelong pledge to be a good man, his hope of becoming the best leader this nation has ever elected is gone. Until he signed this contract in blood, that standard could have been achieved.

Capturing the White House had been a dream come true, but it has quickly turned into a nightmare. He is now imprisoned in a house of cards that's been hastily erected too near an open window, and there is a wicked, wicked storm brewing. Vincent Sterne is the only man who can reach that window. He prays that Sterne can close it in time, before the angry winds of change rise and scatter their building blocks all over this road of good intentions; that rocky road to personal hell.

Gore makes another call. Twenty minutes later, Counsel to the President Richard Denton, enters the Oval Office. After he is sworn to secrecy, which he finds insulting, Denton gets an earful of things he wishes he never heard. Denton's prospective is grim, and he can offer no acceptable solutions. He points out that which the President and Vice President are already painfully aware. Denton even comments on a future that is undoubtedly filled with guilt, if they actually get away with it. His outlook is very bleak.

Richard Denton thinks of resigning, considering the potential consequences. Such a move might be construed as a betrayal, where deadly repercussions may loom. He leaves, quietly under the guise of pressing legal issues elsewhere. Truthfully, though, he needed distance between himself and what he already sees as potentially catastrophic and unconstitutional activities.

Suitland, Maryland.

Valerie and Peter McAllister are just getting settled at home. He's hired a private nurse to monitor Valerie's condition because her doctor has ordered her to total bed rest. Peter makes a heated call to his home security company to rake the supervisor over the coals, accusing him of installing a faulty system. He demands an immediate upgrade.

After seeing to Valerie's stability and comfort, the nurse unpacks her personal belongings in the bedroom nearest to the patient.

When Peter rather thoughtlessly turns on the television, a local news broadcast is running a story about a mysterious oil slick on the Potomac River. Fishermen and recreational boaters are being warned to stay away until the Environmental Protection Agency and the Game and Wildlife Commission can determine the nature of the oil spill in hopes of neutralizing its effects. The Intracoastal

Waterway is closed from northwest of Washington, D.C., all the way to the southern region where the Potomac meets the Piscataway River. Baffled Officials are forced to report that they are yet to ascertain the cause of the apparent ecological disaster.

There seems to be floating fish and dead waterfowl every square foot of the way. The scientists investigating the dark water have no answers as to the cause of the phenomenon that now seems to deny even the laws of physics. They know that an oil spill is not the true nature of this dark water, which travels with and against the flow of the Potomac River. For the time being, an oil spill will have to be the official story.

Peter pays the half bath a visit, but the smell of his own bowel movement causes him to vomit in the sink while sitting on the toilet. Some kind of poison is coming out of him at both ends. While doing so, he recalls his late uncle Clement McAllister proclaiming that 'paying the Piper's Visit is a horrid experience of both bile ejecting and bowel expelling proportions.' He now knows exactly what his uncle meant before his liver failed.

After the Piper's Visit, Peter decides that he should smile more and assume the pretense of everything being okay. When he sees Valerie's expression, however, the phony smile disappears as if it never existed.

His wife is propped up on the overstuffed pillows with the remote control suspended in midair. While flipping through channels in search of something more pleasant than oil spills, she fumbled onto Evan Parker's face in full display on CNN. There she sits with her mouth agape, listening to things too impossible to believe.

Peter tries to take the remote, but she will not allow it. He tells her that she shouldn't watch because it is upsetting. Although sound advice, Peter's failure to defend his friend seems most conspicuous because he shows no disbelief in what's reported as one of the bloodiest, most bizarre manhunts in recent history. He obviously knows what's been going on, but never mentioned a word of it.

Valerie McAllister is a willful woman, who now senses the wrong of things and that Peter is somehow involved. That man on the television and his wife had visited her in the hospital just days ago. Her whispering nurses and doctor's casting hurried glances over their shoulders makes sense now. It isn't until she threatens to leave that Peter bares his soul, weeping like a scolded child in his wife's lap. He buries his face in her gown so she cannot look upon his bruised countenance as he finally confesses everything.

Valerie sits there, quietly stroking Peter's hair while she listens to his ugly declarations of shame. All those years of fitful sleep, nightmares, and mood swings fit together like pieces of a jigsaw puzzle that have been cut from the fabric of his suffocating guilt. She is rapt with anger, realizing the extremities of spousal disappointment while she weeps with him. Because of monstrous sins and mountainous lies, her beloved husband has become alien to her.

Cecil Bridges was murdered and defamed. Evan Parker, Peter's friend, has inherited the same bitter cup. Somehow, Peter has found the will to turn his back on what is happening to Evan and Melissa Parker, who could be dead already for all she knows. Though she loves Peter, who once swept her off of her feet with his silly antics and surprisingly romantic gestures, she will not condone or minimize his actions. Even his claim of having an accident to explain his battered face was a lie for her benefit.

She now looks down upon him with a heavy heart. "Why, Peter? Why? Haven't African Americans suffered enough in this country's past?" Valerie asks. "The monsters you're involved with have no right to decide the course of an entire race of people, an entire nation of people."

Peter finally looks up at her, but his sheepish eyes are quickly averted. "I thought we were doing the right thing, Val. They said it would save us all a lot of trouble." His answer is an obvious rationalization and they both feel it's a cowardly one at that.

"Trouble or change? Would it have saved everyone from tremendous troubles or colossal change, Peter? You had no right to play God with the destiny of millions. They have probably struggled enormously because of what has been going on here. You should have trusted in our ability to cope and deal with the knowledge in a positive way instead of casting lots with such rat bastards."

The sudden reversion of her Americanized accent to her British enunciations and axioms is like a hard left on a blind curve for them both, but she musters the strength to stay the course, holding to what she knows to be the undeniable truth.

"You don't understand. Sterne says that there will be rioting and worse," Peter argues. But his convictions are weak, sounding more like excuses than the hellfire and brimstone visions that once swayed him to do his part in Vincent Sterne's hush-hush operation.

Valerie remains calm while trying to reach through Peter's motley defenses.

"No, Peter. Don't you see? This wasn't about quelling the troubled waters to keep the peace because that peace has been maintained at the expense of one race and enjoyed solely by another. It is based on horrible lies and actual murders, heinous transgression even against mere children. There's no justification for it. Sterne and his friends aren't doing this country a service of protection. They're only seeking to protect the White American way in order to retain control of the government. It's all about power. In many ways, this is nothing more than slavery, but without visible shackles and chains. It is wrong, Peter. This is so very wrong for many reasons. South African Apartheid, American Apartheid, it's all the same. My God, can't you see that now, at least?"

"I know, Valerie," Peter whimpers. "But there's nothing I can do. What can I do?"

"I don't know, but you cannot just sit here and watch our friends being hunted down like animals and vilified by the press. Can you really live with that, Peter? They're trying to kill Evan and Melissa for God sake! I believe that you had no control over how they chose to deal with Cecil Bridges, but can you honestly say that you are powerless in this matter? Can you live with this for a lifetime, a lifetime all alone?"

Peter's head snaps to. His eyes plead for an assurance that she isn't talking about leaving him. However, he sees that Valerie means to carry out her soft-spoken threat. Her eyes are too sad and too meaningful for doubt.

He stands up and protests. Surely, she does not know what she is asking. Nor could she be aware of the dangerous consequences to them both, but Valerie understands. She means to leave her husband if he stands by and does nothing. She accepts that everything in their lives will have to change, and probably for the worse. Yet, she's not willing to sacrifice the lives of innocent people for the retention of personal comforts. For therein, she can find no peace.

Peter is vexed, walking away all twisted up inside like a child that has witnessed his mother's beating at the hands of father dearest. Children always seem to conclude, deep down inside, that the arguments in the dead of night are their fault. They know the ugliness of it even in their dreams, which are filled with terrible images that haunt them far into the daylight because things that live in bad dreams also live in the light. This kind of emotional vampire is impervious to the rising sun, but this child is a man, and he's guilty as charged. Such is the way of the day-walker, he who has finely tuned his talents for the work of evil men—they who have taught him to recognize the comfort of a place within the mind that is muted and blind to the truth or severity of their actions.

When Peter McAllister reaches the bottom step, he runs to the kitchen sink to vomit where he thinks he sees a maggot squirm.

⇒⊢ ⊣⇐

Angel Mountain.

Deep within the belly of the earth, a twin contemplates murder and mass destruction while his woman suffers at his side. There is hatred brewing in the heart of Captain Kyle Parker. His rage is a silent, brooding shadow that bodes deadly beyond all imagination. His vivid dreams are filled with the tumultuous drums, the relentless inspiration of his insanity. He is like molten lava and Angel Mountain is his volcano.

⟼⟻

Far away, behind prison walls, small flutes have been fashioned in wood shops and passed out to a few aspiring musicians with the sudden itch to perform. Before the day is done, many guards are stung by bees, or so they think.

Each time a thorn is shot from the flute, a guard yelps and slaps blindly at an unseen assailant. Each time there is a prisoner close enough to toss a bee at his feet. Obviously, the bee is to blame for the guard's sudden pain. Without further examination, most will stomp the culprit that has fallen at their feet to die.

These events are taking place all across America. Meanwhile, in Liebre Maximum Security Prison, Alunga Abuutu is beating his tiny drum in the darkness of solitary confinement. Something in the air is telling him that it nears his time for freedom!

⟼⟻

Charleston, South Carolina.

At 1:00 p.m., a well-dressed young woman walks into the Channel 5 office building in Charleston with a package addressed to Carolyn Murray. It's an ordinary cardboard box, which gives no hint of the monsters inside.

At NBC's Studio 3 in Washington, a cardboard box is delivered to Tom Brokaw. A similar package is given to Dan Rather at CBS Studios in New York. They have all been chosen because they are considered to be journalists of integrity. Though they are respected journalists, what they'll choose to do with the package of trouble remains to be seen.

━━┽ ┼━━

April 10, 2001. Winston County, Mississippi.

Led by a lawyer named Celia Brown, nearly two-hundred angry Blacks are marching on City Hall. Mrs. Brown has been asked by her neighbors to speak on behalf of Willis Smalls, the young man found murdered. She does not want the job, but feels it her duty to the Black community, which needs an educated voice of representation. The only African American attorney in Winston County has little choice but to recognize that these people have legitimate grievances and concerns. They deserve to be heard by Mayor Thomas and the police chief, who seem none too concerned about the innocent young man's murder. Because the obvious suspect has been allowed to walk in and out of the police station of his own accord insults the young man's family, friends, and fans.

Celia Brown fears that things could get violent and turn badly for the protestors if she does not give their energy some form of direction. As they march, she is flanked by Willis Smalls' sullen parents, who hold her hands all the way to the steps of City Hall.

The attorney has difficulty keeping the protestors in line. Willis Smalls was liked by many friends, making the task especially challenging with the younger, more aggressive protestors because they are so easily provoked. She does a good job of talking them back from the edge of bedlam and mindless violence. Such acts will not be conducive to their purpose or race relations, which is already heavily strained.

Belligerent people are standing behind the police officers along the sidewalks, taunting. They are watching for troublemakers, although that is what they consider the entire group to be. They chew and casually spit their tobacco anywhere they like, volunteering their services to local law enforcement just in case it becomes necessary to help keep the peace. They are all too eager to make that offer, which, strangely, has something to do with seeing that many colored people all at once.

Mrs. Brown speaks the mind of the people to the mayor and the head of police, who stand at the top of the steps. They never even consider walking down to the eye level of the people they would much rather look down upon. In the end, they both lie about a fictitious investigation into the murder of Willis Smalls to appease the people.

Nearly satisfied that something is being done, the disgruntled marchers will leave without further incident. Damballah, however, is not pleased. Their emissary is too nice to even raise her voice in the face of disrespect. She is too diplomatic, knowing that these men already consider the case of Willis Smalls' murder closed.

Something in Celia Brown has been tamed. By money, perhaps. Something in Celia Brown is weak and spineless. Something in her is too sheepish in the face of outright wrongdoing. Her cordially contrite correctness angers the God she does not recognize in the thunder overhead where the sky is perfectly clear. It wreaked havoc with each lying syllable from the mayor's mouth, and her willingness to accept it. Heat lightning scattered across the sky every single time the police chief spat tobacco before addressing them directly with that nonchalant attitude. She has bowed in the face of her God of unfair lawlessness, and she will reap its fury because she no longer hears the beating drums.

Da-da doom...doom...doom...resounds the drums with ferocity.

CHAPTER 36

THE HUMAN EQUATION

S omewhere deep within the fabric of the human psyche exists a black pit in which lies every person's undiscovered darkness. Those who readily seek out the clamor of such shadowy places are often consumed by what they find. There invariably exists a thing or situation for all, no matter how tame or docile, that can bring about a total loss of humanity where nothing, absolutely nothing is sacred.

Once shoved those final steps too far, the displacement of all reason gives life to the inner animal's rage. It's often instantaneous, a psychological break between morality and the violent release of distraught emotions. The subject is then given to behavior that is purely impulsive, driven by passion or deep-seated animosity.

Without this thing in the basement, however, human beings will not defend themselves in the presence of an adversary. There would be less passion for life. If it is possible to genetically remove this dark side, mankind would have no will or strength to live, nor fight.

There's an over-the-edge in every man and woman. Small dosages of its essence sustains them against the daily traumas. But when the pit dweller is unleashed, havoc often lies therein. The endless drums now appeal to that pit, beckoning its inhabitants to spill into the light. Mankind's dark nature is primal, vicious, and the drums are calling.

⚌ ⚌

At News Channel Five, Carolyn Murray watches and flips through pages, her eyes denying the things before her all the while. She reviews notes and recent footage of recorded newscasts from Washington, Maryland, and North Charleston, South Carolina. At the end of them all, she even looks at the broadcasts made by her. It all makes sense, but that is unacceptable because it would mean that she has also played a pivotal role in the conspiracy.

The news anchor has so eagerly judged Evan Parker. Her judgment was never based on his true merits, but on what was prepackaged and spoon-fed to her hungry, journalistic mind. She believed Parker to be guilty of all the brutality that has been laid at his feet, but now the door is open to new and highly disturbing possibilities.

Carolyn Murray never considered that there might be more or less truth in what she and others reported of the bloody trail that started in suite 233 of the stately Monarch Hotel. It was news, and all that mattered at the time. Evan Parker had become a commodity, and she has sold him out while keeping in stride. But her ignorance of the truth is an excuse she can neither use or find any measure of comfort.

Shortly after Carolyn Murray reads the letter she finds taped inside of the box, she leaves the studio. She walks past unfamiliar men and woman, who wear dark sunglasses even while indoors, noticing them noticing her. As Mrs. Murray approaches her car, she feels suspicious eyes upon her, recognizing that she must have known who those conspicuous people were all along. After ingesting the contents of the box, she's become so much more aware.

Somehow, they're suddenly more there, more tangible. Their motives are no longer meaningless to her.

While approaching the street, she notices the gentleman behind her. She senses that he's been assigned to watch her, to isolate her from the very contents of the box that sits on her passenger's seat.

When she pulls onto the street, he follows, but the street is as far as he gets because another car plows into him. As Carolyn Murray speeds away, she becomes very mindful of her makeup, which has begun to feel like a false skin. She is sweating worse than she had during her first live television appearance many years ago. Her palms are clammy, such that she is forced to grip the wheel tighter in the turns.

Twenty minutes later, Carolyn Murray parks on the Charleston Battery and walks past the cannons and monuments as the letter instructed. She takes a long look at the marble base of a statue that's engraved with a scene of the Civil War. It looks to her as if slaves were being made to haul munitions for the soldiers who were fighting to keep them slaves.

She crosses the street. While leaning on the rails of the old sea wall, she gazes out at the choppy waters of the Charleston Harbor, waiting in the afternoon heat. The warm breeze does nothing to soothe her anxieties. She can feel the perspiration running down her face and melting her perm.

She is thinking that there is such great irony in this historical site having been chosen for the meeting. Very important battles were fought from behind these sea walls. This is a place where the Civil War left many ghosts of the scarred dead.

Someone approaches from her blindside. His touch startles away her nostalgic reflections. He introduces himself as Nara and assures her safety. After a moment of doubt, Carolyn Murray decides to trust him so they walk a few blocks to a black semi. The truck moves away with her and two others riding in the rear.

Carolyn sits on one of the couches, afraid to speak; something not ordinarily in her nature. The circumstances are most unusual and somewhat intimidating. Shrouded in darkness, two men are sitting her opposite.

Now a familiar voice comes to her from the gloom to say, "You have nothing to fear from us, Mrs. Murray. We would like you to know that we're grateful for you meeting with us under these conditions. As was stated in the letter, security is of the utmost importance at this time."

"Who are you?" she asks.

"Perhaps you're familiar with us both, Sister Murray. We're certainly no strangers to the media world, until lately," says Farrakhan, who reaches to his left to turn on a lamp.

Carolyn Murray's breath catches in her throat. Her exhilaration is quickly tainted, and her journalistic horns rise instantaneously. A fountain of questions bubbles forth in her mind, and there is something oddly different about them. Her many questions, however, are abated to allow her distinguished hosts to speak. Now that Evan Parker's taped exposé seems to have sprung from the truth, this situation has grown dangerous because these men are also caught up in it. She will know all soon enough.

"Of course, you're curious about our place in this rather nasty affair," Farrakhan says.

"Yes, I am. So it really is you. Both of you."

"We will tell you everything, but you must first vow on your life that you will never betray us, no matter what happens. Tell no one how we're traveling. Otherwise, this interview is over," says Farrakhan. Both men lean forward, probing the woman's eyes for her true feelings.

Jackson says, "We realize that you're a news personality, Mrs. Murray, but you're an African American first and foremost. In the here and now, that particular fact is what matters most. To betray us will be to betray your own race, your faith, and yourself."

"I promise to reveal nothing. Please tell me what's going on here. Are Mr. Parker's unbelievable allegations concerning the census based on fact? Is he really innocent?" She produces a mini recorder, a small pad, and a pen.

Both men regard this woman with care. They turn toward each other, assured of her sincerity. The black semi pulls into the parking lot of Brittle Bank Park, along the Ashley River. Directly behind it is the headquarters of the Charleston Municipal Police Department. What better place to hide, other than right out in the open?

They tell her the story of Evan Parker, making no mention of Kaleem Kinzana or the stranger aspects of their journey. It's not necessary. Nor is it prudent.

At the end of this tale, the reporter is shaken, understandably. The story appeals to her heritage, angering her to no end. But in knowing the truth, she suddenly finds herself immersed in the quicksand that they have somehow navigated.

"This is unbelievable. I feel so ashamed for being a part of the CIA's plans. They used me against my own people, and I was so willing. My God, the terrible things I said about that man were all lies?"

Carolyn Murray has long thought of herself as a seasoned journalist. She reports gruesome details of heartrending human tragedies almost on a daily basis, but nothing has touched her so deeply. She feels dirty and abused, wondering if she has ever really examined the exploitation of tragic events for the sake of ratings. Until this moment, she wonders if she's ever really cared one way or another.

"The question is—what can you do about it?" asks Farrakhan. "Are you willing to help undo that which you've helped to create?"

She finally looks up from her wallow. "What can I possibly do? We are forbidden to investigate this matter, or to report anything that hasn't been approved by government officials. Has either of you heard of the Seven Veil Quarantine?"

"I advocated its creation, Mrs. Murray. Believe me when I say I'm full of regrets. Nonetheless, we appeal to you as a journalist and as a strong Black woman. You must try to do something," Jesse Jackson says.

Louis Farrakhan is more forceful when he asks, "Will you help us?" She flinches when he shouts.

"What do you expect me to do? My network stands to lose everything if they allow me to run this story. I certainly couldn't blurt it all out in the two seconds it'll take for them to pull the plug."

"Are you saying you won't even try to convince your executive producers to help us? Don't you realize what's at stake here, Mrs. Murray?" asks Farrakhan. "Just one minute ago it was all about your little pity party. But now it's not about you at all."

"You don't seem to realize that this will eventually get out and when people find out that you or your network refused to produce the truth, your sainted licenses will be worthless. You should tell them that because it will be a far better thing to befriend the Black race now, rather than turn their backs. Things will have to change in this country once and for all, and it does not matter if the government shuts you down or even threatens you with imprisonment because it will all have to change. Whatever may be taken away, will be restored tenfold. This, I believe without doubt."

"This is extortion!" she cries.

"No, young lady, this is reality. And reality dictates that you are either in, or forever cast out. If you choose the latter, you'll be known as a traitor and an enemy of your own people. Can't you see that you are now at the forefront of the kind of story journalists live for? Now that it stands before you for the taking, you would shy away for fear of losing something that pales in the light of what we all stand to gain. Would you prefer to see the Parkers and all of us dead by our own government's hand? How will you sleep at night knowing the truth? What will you feel while President Gore continues to run this country with his teeth full of lies? And how will you keep a straight face when the story of our murders comes across you teleprompter? Answer me!" demands Farrakhan.

Again, Carolyn flinches from his harsh words. She is lathered in the disappointment she now sees in their faces and hears in their voices. Knowing that Farrakhan comes from a staunch line of Muslims, she expects Jesse Jackson's cooler head to prevail. She expects Jackson to intercede, but he lays into her, also.

"He's right you know. You won't be able to live with yourself knowing that our time was running critically low when we came to you. I'm sorry, but if you will not at least try, we won't fail to mention you—if we survive this. Sister, if you knew the things we've seen and the things we have experienced thus far, you wouldn't bet against our survival because this thing is laced with such divine power that we are afraid to walk away from the responsibility even though it may mean death. There is a far better place waiting, Sister Murray. Best believe you me, there are also far, far worse!"

Jackson pushes the call button, buzzing the cab of the truck. They began to move a moment later.

The reporter is given two choices. She will risk the loss of all that she's worked for, or she will lose her African American identity.

Moments later, she is returned to Charleston's Civil War Battery by the stolen taxi cab that pulled up to the trailer at Brittle Bank Park. Ranna, who had stayed to watch her automobile, takes his place in the cab. Carolyn Murray watches two of the triplets drive away in the late afternoon sunlight. Though it is hot and storm clouds are moving in, she knows that it will not cool off any time soon.

When Mrs. Murray returns to the station at 4:00, she walks briskly across the parking lot with her box of troubles stuffed into the gym bag from her trunk. The package seems to weigh so much more. Upon entering the building, the cool air chills the sweat on her soaked silk blouse. She looks like hell.

Carolyn is joined in the elevator by a stranger whose eyes keep creeping to her bag. They exchange suspicious smiles. She feels his eyes crawling on her flesh, prompting her to ask, "You wouldn't be interested in any Girl Scout Cookies, would you?"

The operative replies, "Sure. What kind are they?" He smiles with his eyes on the parcel.

She opens it and says, "Well, let's see what's left. I hope you're a fan of chocolate. I have Macaroons...Chocolate Mint, perhaps?" Her heart thuds.

Satisfied by what he sees, he refuses to buy the stale box of cookies because he's allergic to chocolate. She exits the elevator alone, moving down the hall with haste after getting a three dollar donation.

An executive producer is holding a heated phone conversation when she enters and slams the bag down on his desk and says, "We have to talk right now."

Although this elderly gentleman isn't the type of man to take orders from his employees, her highly unusual behavior prompts him to cut short the joyless conversation. Markowitz excuses himself rather rudely and places the receiver on its cradle. He takes his seat, looking at the box as she removes it from the gray and white leather gym bag.

"Okay, Carolyn. I'm told that you missed the strategy meeting, and left the building without telling anyone. No beeper, no cell phone. I assume whatever's in this box is supposed to be an excuse, so tell me what's on your mind before I ship you off to the shower and makeup."

Before she speaks, Mrs. Murray locks the entrances to his office, including the door to the conference room. He notes the worried demeanor as she wrings her hands.

"What's wrong, Carolyn? Are you in some sort of trouble?"

Carolyn takes a seat, but decides that she'd rather pace instead, which annoys him to no end. She finally says, "Do you know who I just held a meeting with, Mr. Markowitz?"

He scratches behind his ear and scolds, "I'm really in no mood for guessing games, so I suggest you spill it. Five o'clock is not that far away."

"I just had a meeting with Jesse Jackson and Louis Farrakhan in the back of a tractor trailer." She places a hand across her lips after saying more than she should have. She takes a tape from the box and rewinds it in the VCR.

"Really? I thought that they were involved in some sort of joint venture in Washington." When it dawns on him that she might have gotten a good story, his journalistic horns begin to rise above the hairline. "Well, what's the scoop? What brings them here?"

"What I'm about to say may seem incredible to you, but our network has been used to report disinformation. We've been used to alienate an innocent man. What I've learned in the last few hours may change the entire world."

"What are you talking about?"

"You'll probably be very angry with me, but we have to help those people or we'll be guilty of murder. Just as culpable as the person who pulls the trigger," she says.

"Now wait just one minute. What the hell are you getting at? Spit it out."

"The fugitive—Evan Parker. That's what I'm talking about," she says as she presses the play button.

Markowitz leaves his seat. "Evan Parker? What the hell have you been up to, Carolyn?" He looks about as if he's just farted in a quiet roomful of people. "Are you crazy? You know that's a restricted matter. Are you trying to get us shutdown permanently?" He comes around the desk shaking a memo at her. "We discussed this when it was revealed that he was a native of Charleston."

"I think you should know that, in all likelihood, the man is innocent of all the charges against him," she says in retaliation.

"How can you know that, Carolyn? How can you possibly know that? What do Farrakhan and Jackson have to do with this?" he asks in a frantic whisper. His brow furrows when he thinks about the timing, recalling something about a gun battle involving a Washington street gang.

Evan's tape starts, so she lowers the volume on the television set. She whispers, "CIA Director Vincent Sterne is framing the Census Bureau Deputy Director Evan Parker to keep him isolated from the public until he's captured. They've already made three failed attempts to assassinate Mr. Parker and his family. While trying to murder him, quite a few innocents have already lost their lives. Mr. Parker's assistant was the first victim at the Monarch Hotel in Washington, murdered by Director Sterne himself. A cab driver, killed during the chase. The Parkers' housekeeper, Madeline Perkins, and one of Louis Farrakhan's bodyguards were next to die at the burned out home in Suitland, Maryland where CIA operatives were lying in wait. I strongly suspect that Mr. Parker had nothing to do with those young athletes found murdered while listening to music at a park in Ferris, where the authorities just happened to find a partially burned letter addressed to Evan Parker. Why would they even divulge this type of information in an ongoing investigation that is quarantined? They spoon-fed leaked photographs to a tabloid, implicating that Parker was having a love affair with the woman he allegedly murdered at his hotel, but no one was punished or shut down for reporting it. Essentially, Parker wasn't even newsworthy before the murders, so why would anyone be spying on him? Who does that? And then, they murdered his aunt before bombing his father's home in an attempt to take them all out at once. I've also been informed that his wife is pregnant, but they don't care as long as these people are silenced."

"But, I thought his wife was dead. Didn't he murder her in Maryland?" Markowitz asks.

"That was the housekeeper. The wife's alive. They want to silence Parker because of what he's discovered. These men don't want this information to become public knowledge because of incredible political, social, economic, and criminal implications that even suggests President George Bush's duplicity in an assassination eleven years ago. And that's not the most shocking aspect of this case. These people desperately need our help, Joel. I'm feeling somewhat responsible for Mr. Parker's infamy and so should you."

"Okay, just calm down. I'll look at your evidence, but I won't make any promises. In the meantime, you should get prepped. Don't mention a word of what you've told me about this."

She agrees.

"By the way, what is the most shocking aspect of this case? What could he possibly know that would warrant an attempt of his life?"

"Watch this expose, and you will know what it's all about."

"Okay, I promise to do just that. Now hit the showers. We'll discuss this later."

She's reluctant to leave, but decides to do as she is told, if only for the sake of normalcy. Before leaving his office, she warns, "This is extremely dangerous information to an undisclosed amount of government officials, Mr. Markowitz. If you speak a word of it to them, as they demand, we're both probably dead."

Their eyes lock for an instant, and then she is gone.

After taking a shower, Mrs. Murray goes about her daily routine. During her hasty hair and makeup session, she reviews her story lines, thanking God her co-anchor will be responsible for the Parker segment. There is nothing new on the fugitive's whereabouts.

There is no time to see Markowitz before the airing of The News at Five, so she says nothing.

Carolyn Murray is obviously not herself, tongue-tied on at least three occasions during the live broadcast. That's quite a lot in this game. During the commercial breaks, she is coached by set directors, and fawned over by makeup technicians. Her only excuse is that she doesn't feel well, even though sickness has rarely gotten in the way of her professionalism.

The real test comes as her co-anchor mentions Evan Parker. She is forced to show no emotion, a task that's as difficult as it is to keep her eyes off of the men standing in the shadows of the studio. At 5:32, when it's finally over, she leaves the set with no time for small talk or lectures.

Joel Markowitz sits behind his desk with the VCR's remote in one hand, while the other scrolls down the year 2000 Census. His mind is in a fog. He jumps when Carolyn Murray knocks on his unlocked door. He wishes it had been locked when she walks in and sees the denial in his eyes. Fear is just as prevalent.

"Lock it, please. My God, what have you done? This is…this is unbelievable," Markowitz whispers.

"Now do you see why we have to tell the truth, even if it means being sanctioned?" she asks with pleading in her eyes and voice.

Markowitz paces behind his desk. His hands are clasped behind his back when he says, "I'm sorry, Carolyn, but there's nothing I can do. I just can't. This shit carries much too much consequence."

"What? You must be joking!" she says reproachfully. Because she knew this man to be compassionate and reachable, she sought him out exclusively on this matter. Carolyn cannot believe what she is hearing.

"I wouldn't joke about something like this and you know it. Have you given any thought to how much trouble we'd be in? This entire network will be made to suffer, if we…"

She snaps, "If we what—become responsible journalists? Refusing to help those people makes us components of the machine that murders them. I can't live with that. How can you?"

"That's enough!" he says. "We can't do it. I'm sorry, but we just can't. All I can do is promise not to mention anything about your involvement in this matter."

She gathers the evidence and says, "Then I'll put it to you the same way it was so harshly put to me. We've been telling our audience that this man is a sick, murderous bastard because that's what we're supposed to believe. In light of the truth, however, we continue to do so out of utter cowardice. Even the lives of this couple's unborn twins are in danger and they're going to die because you won't get off of your ass to do something. Well, what do you think is going to happen to your precious programming when the entire African American race finds out that you decided to let innocent people die and heinous injustices to continue on a national level? Don't forget the old man who died of a heart attack last night when they blew up Jarvis Parker's home. Don't forget the dead, Joel. The dead assistant in Washington, the dead housekeeper, and bodyguard, the dead school kids in Ferris, Maryland. Don't forget the dead because their blood is already on our hands. This place, and your very life won't be worth spit. You disgust me, Joel. I quit." Her tears now run freely.

"You can't quit, you're under contract," Markowitz says. No sooner have the words come from his lips does he regret having said them.

As Carolyn reaches the door, she turns on him to say, "Shove that contract up yours, Joel. I'm African American, just like they are. And you—you're just a Jewish flunky with no fucking conscience. You've obviously forgotten what prejudice and people like President Gore and Vincent Sterne can do with corrupted power. Maybe Adolf Hitler should have wiped your entire ancestry from the face of the fucking earth because you've learned nothing from the holocaust and the denial of manifest destiny. You better remember this, Joel. This president's executive order does not hold sway over foreign journalist entities. When this thing gets out, and it will because it's gone much too far to be contained—I'll make certain that you won't go unnoticed. If those innocent people meet with a wrongful death, you'll hang with them. I won't rest until you are fully implicated in this conspiracy to keep my race down, so I suggest that you hire a lot more Black people with big, ass-kissing salaries or you better get rid of those you have right now. How could I

have been so wrong about you? You're nothing but a coward, Joel."
She walks out, slamming the door behind her.

Stalling passers bye go quickly about their business, resuming their tasks as if they heard nothing. No one knew exactly what the explosion was about, but they certainly heard the part about Hitler.

Carolyn Murray goes to her office to clear out her desk. She only throws things into the box that are of a more personal nature, such as pictures of her family. For a moment, she considers taking the plaques and degrees, but she leaves them on the walls. One plaque is embossed with the words: *Journalistic Integrity*. It cuts too deeply. She can stand being here no longer, so she takes nothing of a journalistic nature. Such items are now representative of a façade, and they will feel dirty to her touch.

The drums are pounding across the nation. They are calling to Legba, the God of the Gate.

Vincent Sterne is holding a heated conversation with Dr. Robert Houston and Dr. Timothy Blake, who are the heads of Pathology and Toxicology at the Medical University of South Carolina. While Sterne awaits his own experts to arrive, they've been unable to isolate the cause of the comatose-like condition of his agents. Sterne demands answers that they cannot supply, but both doctors promise to continue intensive studies into the phenomenon. Until the FBI forensics team arrives, Sterne is forced to rely on their expertise. He has no reason to be concerned about their involvement because the true nature of his urgency is never revealed.

Sterne has no idea that Dr. Blake is a voodooist with a degree in holistic applications. Blake provides substantial obstacles to the testing, so things will continue to go unsolved from a medical standpoint. The bones and his girlfriend told him to sabotage the research. While covering their eyes so they cannot identify him, he secretly feeds sugar cubes to Sterne's quarantined men so they'll slowly come out of their trances. When they regain control of their motor functions, they will provide no answers. Drastically, raising their blood sugar helps metabolize the unidentified variant of TTX or Tetrodotoxin, the substance that immobilizes their bodies.

━╪ ╪━

Studio Three. Washington, D.C.

At 8:00 p.m., Tom Brokaw sits at a conference table with his top executives. The mood is sullen as the pros and cons are tossed back and forth like hot potatoes. Clenching his teeth does nothing to quell the anxieties that these issues have brought before him. Brokaw's journalistic integrity is sorely tested, but he has no power to sway their unanimity against unlawfully disclosing the Parker exposé.

Although Brokaw is a White American male, his heart bleeds for Evan Parker, whom he knows is doomed to die. He makes arguments that tempt his executives with the prize of being the first in a monumental affair, never mind their distaste for the census revelation. His network could take the first step forward against the atrocities for which they will not go blameless if it ever gets out that they chose to ignore the truth.

Alas, his arguments fall on a collective of deaf ears. The parcel is turned over to authorities, even after Brokaw appeals to their avarice. For being law-abiding patriots, these men are still detained for questioning. They will have to sign a nondisclosure contract before walking away. They do not seem to suspect that they are still going to be considered loose ends that must be tied off in the near future. Even after doing what is considered the right thing, they feel watched. That feeling of being watched will eventually escalate into feeling a threat to their lives. After all, they did view the material in question. Therefore, these men are liabilities.

⊶⊷

Elsewhere, Peter Jennings finally accepts the fact that he can't win. Much of the same takes place in New York, where Dan Rather sheds the tears of the powerless. At 8:15, Ed Bradley, who enjoyed an esteemed journalistic career with Sixty Minutes, is found dead in an alley. He's the apparent victim of a robbery. The box he's been carrying has disappeared. At 8:25, the executive decision at the Black Entertainment Television Studio, better known as BET, is go and let the government be damned! Ten seconds into the broadcast, a horrible explosion rips through the studio to sever the uplink transmission. Fifteen people die at the scene. Nine others are seriously injured, but they will never recover to tell their stories. The explosion is blamed on a radical faction of a skinhead hate organization.

And the drums sing their terrible songs.

⊶⊷

At 9:00 p.m., in Columbia, South Carolina, a gun battle and high-speed chase involving Richland County Sheriffs and the State Police is in progress. They're chasing two well-armed men and a pregnant woman, believing one of them to be the fugitive Evan Parker.

The renegades manage to kill two officers, wounding at least two others during a successful getaway. Vincent Sterne pulls up stakes in Charleston and converges on Parker's last known location one hundred miles west. As a precaution, an agent remains at each of Charleston's major newspapers and broadcast studios. Sterne wants Parker boxed in and isolated. This is his break, and heaven help the person that allows the fugitives to escape. Again, Black officers are called off without explanation. When the three cocaine and heroin

443

dealers in the late model sedan are finally pinned down, they'll never know why they will die in such a violent firestorm even after trying to give themselves up.

At 10:00 p.m., in Charleston, Agent Robert Hanson is relieved to be alone while the almighty Vincent Sterne is off to the hunt. Forty-eight hours without sleep is playing havoc with Hanson's migraines. Amidst his stretching yawns, the forty-seven-year-old agent makes his own executive decision. In the absence of his slave-driving superiors, he needs sleep.

At the village in Beaufort, there is an elaborate feast. Dark music and songs now reverberate throughout the surrounding woodland area where the wild animals creep away with their tails tucked between their trembling hind legs.

The people dance in ceremony around a blazing fire in the garden. None of the most recent visitors to the village know the meaning of the songs, but they know that they're about heroic battles and death.

Despite herself, Insanyanga sits at the head of the festival and smiles down on the Parker family and friends. Painted men and women, naked from the waist up, perform exotic dances while crawling about the ground like predatory cats. Snake bearers brandish their poisonous pets, whose presence are always significant of Damballah's authority. Fearsome looking men of great power invoke Shanga, the mighty God of War, and Legba of the gate.

Something of awesome power is in this place of sacrifice, fire-walking, and dark enchantment. One by one, their eyes turn to whites as the sky darkens over the entire eastern seaboard from New York to the Florida Keys. Boom da-da doom! Doom da-da boom!

Now, Carolyn Murray sits alone in her empty home. She stares at the images of her two kids and estranged husband, regretting that her career has cost her so much. The phone rings to rip her from the jaws of self-pity. She runs to her car and drives away.

CHAPTER 37

BLOOD FOR BLOOD SPILLED

"Almighty Father, although I am empowered and bound to do thy bidding in these great and terrible things, I implore thee one last time to forgive these wayward children their many trespasses upon thy jurisdictions of life. Bequeath unto them thy grace and fathomless mercy for thine is the power and the glory to do so. I bid thee, Great Creator, Lord of Lords, show thy face to the masses that they may no longer live by faith alone but by thy mighty presence. I ask that this bitter cup be taken from my trembling hands, Great Damballah. Let not the Pit Dwellers rise up in the hearts of your children for there are many who love and believe in thine existence. Although they are lost and reeling in a land where The Satan has beguiled them unto debauchery and lasciviousness, show them mercy. Hear me, Dear God of All Things Great and Small. I beg of thee—take my life in their stead."

There is only a disheartening silence from above. As Kinzana lowers his eyes and outstretched hands to the ground, a great sadness causes him to weep at the base of the oaken tree where the sprawling roots suddenly begin to crackle and splinter. As he steps away from its mammoth trunk, a swirling funnel reaches down from the heavens as lightning curses the sky and thunder rumbles the earth. Kinzana falls upon his knees with his eyes cast to the earth. Suddenly, he feels a searing heat as dancing shadows intrude upon his clenched eyelids. Finally, there upon his trembling knees, Kaleem Kinzana dares to open his eyes among those sprawling limbs that have been set to fire. The massive, churning funnel encompasses Kinzana's private garden, and those who witness it cringe upon their fearful knees. They dare not look at it for this is the chariot of God.

The dour, yet sullen voice of The Almighty whispers, "Oh, son. My son, I know what I now ask of thee, for they are your children as well as my own. I know the agony of the father overwhelms thee, Kinzana, for there are great and terrible things to come. Let not thy heart be troubled. It is for the continuing existence of mankind that I now unleash my vehemence, for day by day it has grown into a furious wind that ravages my temperament from within. My love for them is killing me, and so I must release it or perish a God no longer everlasting. Hear me now so that thy heart no longer frets. So greatly have they fouled my garden with hate and sinful ways …so long have they unwittingly adopted and worshipped the doctrines of the Great Satan that my love for them is no longer enough to stay my mighty wrath. Just as this living wood splinters and shards, the deepest roots are rotten and corrupted. Therefore, Kinzana, I cannot continue to allow the tree to die. My love for them tarnishes, for even my own faith in the overall goodness of mankind withers and scatters like smoke and ash. I am grown weary and old, my son. Though timeless amongst the stars of the universe, I find myself wishing to away this world. And so, this thing I do, I do for love. Would you have me walk away from this place, leave them forevermore, my son?"

Kinzana pleads, "No, my Lord. Do not abandon us."

"Then let loose my fury so that mankind may learn a lesson written in his own blood, for he is doomed to perish upon the land that grows sick and depleted. It is a far, far better thing I ask of thee now, for I will not promise tomorrow otherwise. Stay this path, my son, and let them bleed into one cup until it is full. It, Kinzana, is the only way. They must now know the sting of the prick for I am an angry God faced with questions of their total destruction!"

The wind grows silent. The flames vanish. He is alone.

"Thy words are my bond. There is nothing more prevalent upon my heart, so I will seek to obey and please thee until my time ends upon the earth. Hear me, Great Spirit, for I am Kinzana, the resurrection and the keeper of thy chronicles. But in this great and terrible thing, I am become Thy Desolation!"

Kinzana's eyes blaze, as he quakes with some inner power. As he prays, he clutches his heart and raises the other hand to the sky as if in physical pain.

"Even now, the drums are calling to the abased elements of mankind. As thy wrath requires blood, so shall it be spilled until the sand of mankind's hour runs red. I denigrate my soul, invoking the death and darkness that now creep forth from the cellars of thy children's souls as the approaching hour of the Kuuta falls like the dark angel's shadow. I am troubled. I am trembling—but nevertheless undaunted, for I know that thy will shall be done on the earth as it is in heaven. I know that only by thy grace, shall I be cleansed of this most foul deed. I failed my calling once in forestalling the inevitable dark, but I will not fail thee again no matter the cost!"

Kinzana begins to weep in the secluded section of his garden. He kneels, leaning against the trunk of an ancient oak tree whose limbs are spread in a canopy that nearly touches the ground. This is his private place, intruded upon only by the pulsing drums and songs of death. Beads of sweat roll down Kinzana's face as he prays, his steady hands quaking with his efforts. The sky is black and thunder rolls across the horizon, but there will be no rain this night. He raises his hands and white eyes to the angry heavens to hiss, "Rise, for you are so commanded by the Almighty God of all gods. Rise!"

Boom da-da doom, doom da-da boom! Boom da-da doom, doom da-da boom!

⚔ ⚔

22:50 hours, Angel Mountain.

The warning lights begin to turn, irradiating the above ground command center with a brilliant vein of red. The horns of doom blare, waking the dead from their peaceful slumber. Condition Red Alpha has been initiated without warning or provocation.

Lieutenant Clancy falls out of his seat, dropping the novel that he's been reading with his feet perched on the console. He curses and quickly stows the book in a drawer before activating the strategic boards, trying to pin down what is sure to be a computer-generated malfunction or an unscheduled drill. To his dismay, he finds just the opposite. According to his readouts, Captain Kyle Parker and Lieutenant Markham have initiated the launch protocols. This should not be possible.

The base is shocked into life by blaring horns. Men and women leap from their beds, scared out of their wits. America must be under the threat of nuclear attack. Then, after a few panicked moments, they deduce it to be a designated test of Emergency Procedural Readiness. However, General Austin and Colonel Terrell know that neither has scheduled a drill.

Colonel Terrell charges into Central Command to demand an explanation from Lieutenant Clancy. As he stands at attention, Clancy states, "Colonel Terrell, sir. Captain Parker and Lieutenant Markham have somehow initiated launch protocols without authority."

"They what? How can that be?" spits Terrell. "They can't know the enable codes."

449

"It would seem so, sir. According to my readouts, the system is armed. I'm afraid that they have targeted domestic coordinates only. Friendly coordinates, sir."

"Are they nuts? Pinpoint target locations."

Clancy inquires with the touch of a key. "They're locked on to five targets within the continental U.S." he shouts. "NORAD, New York, Los Angeles, Dallas, and Washington, D.C."

"Are you certain?"

"Affirmative. Confirming—NORAD, New York City, Los Angeles, Dallas, and Washington. Sir, he plans to destroy the nation's capital."

General Austin shows up breathing hellfire and brimstone. Once briefed on the situation, he immediately calls the White House. Meanwhile, Colonel Terrell has the camera and com links switched on in the command capsule. He asks Clancy, "Have they started a countdown?"

Clancy says, "Sir, that's a negative, but they have linked the five missiles into a single digital sequence, and they've already keyed all of them. They can launch instantaneously."

"Fuck if they aren't serious!" Terrell says as he punches the audio button.

Kyle and Alicia are seated at the command console when the Colonel's voice comes to them. Looking at each other in the two-way monitors, Terrell notes the haggard features and bloodshot eyes. It seems they've both aged. Radiation poisoning, perhaps?

"Captain Parker, I'm ordering you to stand down. Comply immediately, or you both will face court martial for treason. Do you hear me, airman? Stand down now!"

The tone of Kyle Parker's voice strikes icy fear in the colonel's heart as he growls back with great deliberation, "I refuse to stand down, Colonel Terrell. You ignored my requests and now my family is dead because my personal needs were not important to any of you. I'm going to blow Washington to hell the same way those bastards did my father's home in South Carolina. You can't stop me, Colonel. I've removed both self-destruct mechanisms from each missile. You will have no control. The secondary guidance systems have also been disabled, so you won't be able to change their courses or trajectory. I will give you no time to evacuate Washington, and if you attempt to stop me by any other means, I will launch the other warheads and destroy their designated targets. Washington killed my family, sir, and now I'm going to kill it!" Captain Parker's bloodshot eyes burn holes in Colonel Terrell's mind.

Alicia Markham says nothing to the contrary, which suggests that she's committed. She seems dazed and detached from what is happening. Lieutenant Markham is ordered to take her sidearm and arrest Captain Parker, but she doesn't comply. She refuses to obey her commanding officer, glaring back at him with her own insane eyes.

"Wait, son. Whatever this concerns, I'm sure we can work it out without needless bloodshed. Please think about what you're doing. There's no reason to take such drastic action."

"There is nothing you can say to change our minds, Colonel. This entire country is founded on a lie, but I will at least avenge my father—even if innocent people must die. They will all pay because my brother was no murderer!" Kyle barks. "But now, I am. Parker out!"

"No, wait!" Terrell shouts, but Kyle turns off the monitor. "Shit, this is bad. What in blazes is he talking about?"

"I'm turning on the backup, sir. They won't know that we are monitoring," Clancy says as he keys the command.

"What the hell is going on here?" asks General Austin. "I want to know just how the hell he figured out the codes and their correct sequences."

"He says they came to him in a dream," Terrell answers.

"He said what? That's impossible."

Terrell faces General Austin to say, "I'm afraid he means to carry out his threats, General. Parker is ranting and raving about the government killing his brother and father in some explosion. I have no idea what he's referring to. I'm having Clancy pull up his file."

General Austin slams a fist into the wall next to the console just as the five target areas begin to blink. He says, "Fuck. This shit can't be happening. Scramble our fighter squadron. I want you to issue an immediate self-destruct order if they launch those missiles. Hopefully we won't end up glowing in the fucking dark!"

"I'm afraid we can't, General. He's disabled all above ground control mechanisms and their backups. Because the capsule is completely self-sufficient, we cannot cut the power. There's little that we can do to stop them at this point," Lieutenant Clancy informs.

General Austin and Colonel Terrell move away from the console to talk privately.

"This is unacceptable. We'll have to gas them," General Austin suggests quietly.

Terrell is biting his thumbnail. It's a disgusting habit that he recently adopted, and blames solely on his nerve-racking wife. "I agree. The Altrex-7 will immobilize them within three seconds of entering the air supply. They'll never know what hit them."

"Make it so, Colonel."

Terrell unlocks his office door, turning on the monitor to watch as the gas takes effect. He enters an access code into the computer, which opens a secret panel on the steel surface of his desk. He pushes the red button without hesitation and they watch in pensive silence, waiting for the officers to keel over.

Seconds later, General Austin shouts, "Damn it all to fucking hell, the son of a bitch has disabled the nerve toxin."

"I was afraid of this. Captain Parker has had TL-21 training, he knows nearly as much as the engineers do about the complete design of this nest. The senior officers have to achieve Tech-18 in case something goes wrong. Technical Level-21 obviously means that Parker knows too much." They return to the situation room where Clancy monitors the renegades.

"Markham looks as crazy as he does. I doubt that she can be reached just because she's gone this far. What the hell do we do now?"

"I suggest you have President Gore issue orders for the immediate evacuation of Washington and Maryland, General. I believe Parker has every intention of carrying out his threat."

"What good will it do? Most of those people won't clear the hot zone in time. Nevertheless, I suppose you're right," says General Austin. "What are they doing now?"

"They're sitting at the console with their fingers on the button, sir," Clancy answers. "Sir, is it possible that his brother is the same man who's been killing people? Isn't Parker the name of the fugitive that the FBI is searching for in South Carolina? I believe that man has been accused of blowing up his own father's house down in Charleston. Could that be what he's talking about?"

General Austin admits, "I haven't really been following the news, but that just may be his stressor."

Captain Parker's file confirms their fears. Terrell clasps his temples when Clancy's words finally click. It's suddenly clear, but he missed the signs because he and the wife are going through difficult changes.

General Austin says, "Patch me through to the Pentagon before it disappears from the map."

Kyle and Alicia stare at one another in complete silence. She wonders if she is doing the right thing, but her course is set. Where Kyle goes, so shall she.

Sweat rolls down his smooth, brown skin while he asks God to forgive what they are about to do. They're set to go on the count of three when she looks up at the television set on her side of the command console.

"Kyle, wait!"

She removes her finger from the switch and turns up the volume. CNN is running a simultaneous broadcast of News Channel Five's broadcast of Carolyn Murray's unprecedented report. The Veil has been broken!

Joel Markowitz relented his earlier stance. Carolyn Murray's scathing remarks drummed in his mind while he viewed again the tape she had accidentally left in his VCR. Mr. Markowitz was suddenly overwhelmed by a sense of shame for his indifference to Evan Parker's plight.

At sixty-three years of age, he's both old enough and young enough to remember the tattoos and torturous screams of endless nights. At the age of six in 1944 Auschwitz, he recalled visions of ghosts that lived somewhere between the heaven of death and the hell of life. No Moses had come, only the ovens of ashen gray stood tall amongst his people. There were mammoth graves and odors of decay assaulting shrunken nostrils and sunken eyes that wondered how long before the end.

At age six, he wondered when he would no longer be required to help heave others over the banks of huge craters, but to be thrown himself amongst the relics of his endangered race. If he was an unlucky child, he would have found the end of the world inside of an oven while still alive.

Carolyn Murray's impassioned plea forced Markowitz to count his blessings, having reached a ripe old age with health, energy, strength, and mental capacities still intact beyond that of his many peers. If his long life after such a painful childhood serves any purpose at all, he's forced to see this as his more than journalistic duty.

There is nothing cosmic about his removal of those blue scars that turned into black serial numbers upon the skin. Yet, the scars of the holocaust are still tattooed within the straining muscles of his heart. These same scars had been stamped upon the hearts of his mother and father, who did not survive the camp. Had he gotten so old that he'd forgotten these things? The question, as well as the answer, causes him a burdensome, unnavigable shame.

⟖ ⟗

Now Captain Parker watches as the reporter tells the world of his brother's innocence from a studio where all doors of access are securely locked and chained. For twenty minutes, she tells her audience of Cecil Bridges' murder and the defamation of his good name eleven years ago following a visit to the White House. The very same now becomes Evan Parker's inheritance.

She paints a horrible picture of four murdered teenagers. Their deaths used to further influence the public's hatred and revulsion for a man who has been portrayed as a homicidal maniac and a rapist of old women. Carolyn Murray produces indisputable theories about the reported period of the quadruple homicide in Ferris, Maryland in comparison to the explosion at Jarvis Parker's home in Charleston. She contends that there is no way Evan Parker could have been in both places without the use of an airline. To have used such a method of travel, would surely have rendered Parker into the hands of authorities, who are still canvassing all major modes of transit.

With sincere tears welling in her eyes, she tells the story of how two powerful civil rights leaders got involved with Evan Parker, subsequently finding themselves in the path of danger. She now explains that Jesse Jackson and Louis Farrakhan's accidental involvement has been suppressed because of the obvious repercussions. She illuminates the ambiguities surrounding the death of the Washington gang members who bravely risked their lives and died to get Parker to safety, the undisclosed details of an innocent bystander's fatal shooting at the hand of CIA assassins bent on the single-minded mission to capture or kill their elusive target.

Finally, President Al Gore is named as a premier component in all the events that have transpired in the past few days. He was informed of the census falsification by Evan Parker, who was then offered a bribe of twenty-million dollars. The bribe was offered to assure that the world would never know that there are presently nineteen-million more African Americans than Whites in the United States of America—nineteen-million, six hundred and seventy thousand. When the Deputy Director of the Census Bureau refused the money, Central Intelligence Agency Director Vincent Sterne himself attempted to assassinate Parker and his assistant.

The murderous horrors of 1990 and Cecil Bridges began anew in suite 233 of the Monarch Hotel in Washington. Because of the government's twisted use of their own laws, most of the evidence of their treacherous brutality has already been publicly documented. The interpretations of these events were deliberately jaded from the beginning and this entire nation saw everything when they were seeing nothing at all.

Carolyn Murray tells the world that Evan Parker and his family are believed to still be alive somewhere, but his sister and her two children haven't been found as of yet. The screen goes blank.

While waiting for Agent Hanson to answer the phone, Sterne bites down on his lower lip until it bleeds. When Hanson wakes up and answers, he's blasted and ordered to blow the tower. Though News Channel Five's transmitting tower is destroyed, it's too late. The damage is irrevocably done.

Moments later, across the Atlantic, the BBC airs the tape of Evan Parker's exposé to rock the eastern hemisphere back upon its heels. Hostile Muslim nations cheer at the sudden fall of one country so great. Cries of vindication ring out along the desert dunes, however, there will be much more to come.

Quite a few networks chose to pick up the story, but in New York and Washington, the execs who had refused to lend a helping hand were vexed beyond expression. They had the ball and chose to drop it. Choosing to join the bandwagon after the fact, might only incense the Black people of this nation, but only if the truth comes out. In the end, however, Rather, Brokaw, and Jennings are finally given the go-ahead.

⋙⋘

Beaufort, South Carolina.

The mask was carved from a single piece of mahogany long, long ago. Its brownish-red face is smooth to the touch. Three diagonal grooves are etched upon both cheeks. Strips of a leopard's skin are embedded into the wood near the outer rim and beneath both eyeholes. The matted, black and white feathers of some ancient bird that walks the earth no longer, frames its outer symmetry. The mouth is a perfect circle. It is simple, yet foreboding. Four sharpened pegs protrude from the inner surface of the mask so that the flesh of any potential wearer must be pierced at the hairline and both cheeks. The mask is old, nearly as old as sand. It hasn't been worn by a human being in centuries, but it still smells of death.

Kaleem Kinzana is sweating profusely. While his hands tremble, he wets his lips, regarding the pegs before forcing the mask into place.

Kinzana is rocked! His head screams from searing agony as his eyes seek the dark canopy above. He hears the minions of death shrieking in triumph. The cries of the damned surround him with his own name. As the bloody sweat of his forehead trickles into his eyes, he clasps his ears and screams in unbelievable agony. Kinzana arches and convulses before crashing to the ground on his back, where he's enveloped by total darkness that speaks in frantic whispers. By minutes or maybe hours, time is lost to him.

The brightest star in heaven sheds light upon this area when a rift opens in the clouds above. From a surrounding sea of deep, dark blue it shines through the canopy of the mighty oak tree like a gentle whisper. Finally, he stirs and struggles to rise.

Kinzana stumbles into the firelight at the center of the festivities wearing the South African Death Mask recently stolen from the art exhibit in New York. Men and women alike draw their breaths to a trembling stop as they fall beneath his fearful gaze. The drums will cease for a moment of reverent silence.

Kinzana's bloody garment is soaking wet from perspiration. His voice is a harsh whisper through a gravel filter when he says, "Damballah's black tide is arisen. Now fly to the throats of your enemy—fly to the throats of your brothers. Rise!" The drums throb again to vibrate the earth.

Now Kinzana rips the mask from his tormented flesh and casts it into the fire, where it will not burn. He raises his hands, which now bleed from woundless fountains, once more to a murky sky. His short hair has grown pure white and his eyes are bleached orbs.

Dark is the sky. Lightning now creases it for miles to see. The wind howls, and thunder... there is so much thunder.

⊱✦⊰

New York.

Reverend Braxton's eyes burn before the television set in the church. He slowly turns his head toward the sound of Slash's voice, which comes from a bullhorn through the walls of his office. The preacher's jaw flexes. His teeth grind, squeaking in his head.

They are out there in the park with their leather jackets, shaven heads and spiked hairdos. The right of free speech gives them the gall to stand in the heart of a ghetto under police supervision to accuse Blacks of being killers and bastardized mongrels. With the blessings of City Hall's Permit of Assembly, they blame Affirmative Action for their having been replaced on the job by African Americans or denied employment because of skin color. But much deeper and closer to the truth, such things are probably due to arriving with a slovenly appearance, and the lack of preparation or qualifications.

The preacher's eyes fall upon the baseball bat that always sits next to the door of his office. Before Reverend Braxton realizes it, he lays claim to the aluminum haft. With screaming rage upon his lips, Reverend Braxton, a devout Christian, leads the charge. He becomes Samson and the bat is the jawbone of an ass. Enraged, they suddenly pour from the desecrated walls like ants. The angry inhabitants of the Polo Grounds surge across the street, converging on the park to drown Slash Messer and all who feign supremacy.

Across America, the prison doors are open, and death begins to stain the earth. Most of the White prisoners are slaughtered with no compassion or expedience because therein, they are the minority.

Deep in the heart of his solitary confinement, Alunga Abuutu's eyes are just as white as Kinzana's. As Alunga pounds his giant drum, the power to kill becomes every man!

The guards, mindless under the influence of the thorn-borne drug, walk about aimlessly until their lives are snuffed out.

Warden Carson of Liebre Prison is severely beaten. He is then gang raped, and torn to shreds! His screams mingle with many others before being drowned out by the sounds of unchaste rage. He, too, is forever silenced, but the last thing that he sees is the smile of Alunga Abuutu. Nelson Ammatha has opened the doors of bedlam.

As he raises the warden's severed head to the sky, Alunga hisses, "Rise, for Damballah wills it so! Rise and fill our master's cup with blood until his great thirst has been sated. Rise!"

All across America, the drums are pulsing a singular monotone that invokes a lust for blood in every African American. Young and old, they take to the streets in droves. Riots of this nation's past will hold no comparison to the devastation they now inflict. Only this time, they are not restricted to underdeveloped localities. They go to the White man's neighborhoods and business districts to kill…to rape…to pillage…to burn!

The greatest of ironies is that it has taken the actions of a handful of people to bring the Black nation together, when it required an entire network to keep them apart. It has been given a common enemy, and all that he possesses becomes theirs to destroy!

Doom da-da boom! Boom da-da doom! Doom da-da boom! Kwani Drive is vibrant. Animal sacrifices are frequent events, as it is at all the African villages throughout the nation. Blood is drank and flies through the air to stain maps of the no longer United States of America.

The sky grows black from the Atlantic Ocean to the Rocky Mountains, and thunder rolls a chorus in the castrated night as California quakes, threatening to fall into the sea.

The drums have opened the basement. Even grandmothers take to the streets with baseball bats and kitchen knives. They are old enough to remember Jim Crow and the death of a martyr, the birth of the equality lies.

"Rise and smite thy enemy to the ground. Soil this earth with his flesh beaten dead! Rise, black tide. Rise!"

Captain Kyle Parker stays his hand. He weeps in Alicia's arms, having heard that his family is still among the living. He has lived in such fear that Evan's pursuers caught up with them in South Carolina. He had consigned himself to the fact that they have been blown to bits in his father's home, certain that this particular detail has been suppressed. However, he will not relinquish his power. The blast doors remain shut on the heart of Angel Mountain because some darker instinct warns that his brother is still in danger. And what of his sister, where is Talia and her kids?

$$\Longleftarrow\!\!\!+\ +\!\!\!\Longrightarrow$$

April 10, 2001.

Death rules the night. They have risen from the slums and ghettos of New York to the hills of California to annihilate. They wreck and ruin, raping pristine cities of beauty. America is burning, but President Gore refuses to be interviewed. No press conference is called, even though the media is camped on the steps of the nation's capital demanding another truth.

Upon learning of Captain Parker's threat, the president still refuses to take safe harbor in the sky aboard Air Force One. He sits in the Oval Office under heavy guard to watch the terrible events, which are unfolding like a fiery flower before his eyes. His nightmare—his worst nightmare—is alive!

In Washington alone, there are no hospital beds left unoccupied. By morning there are already more than forty-five thousand dead, and many more have been maimed in the capital. The city is drowning in the endless blare of sirens, heralding even more tragic casualties of this human drama.

Tipper Gore and her children have been sent away. The same goes for the family members of Vice President Graff, who also stays behind on the sinking ship. They sit in the Oval Office together, sweating and talking about the inevitable.

"Al, you have to initiate the evacuation of Washington and Maryland, even if no one listens to you. And we have to leave this place," Eleanor Graff pleads.

There is a knock at the door and the bodyguard announces the Secretary of Defense Marquis Slater, and the Chairman of the Joint Chiefs of Staff General Bradford Smith. Their somber faces are creased with worry lines. None of the usual pleasantries are exchanged because serious matters are to be discussed.

Slater begins by saying, "Mr. President, I'm afraid that you must do two very distasteful things." Gore remains by the window, wordlessly looking out at nothing in particular. "You must issue a mandatory emergency evacuation of the capital, and at least five hundred miles of surrounding terrain. And I'm afraid you have little choice but to declare Martial Law."

"That's exactly what I've been telling him, gentlemen," says Graff. She doesn't want them to press because Gore seems so fragile, but pushing is the only way to reach him.

"At any given moment, Captain Parker and Lieutenant Markham can snap..."

There is another knock at the door. When Vincent Sterne walks in, both Slater and Smith go frigid.

"What's going on here, gentlemen?" Sterne asks with a straight face.

With spitting resentment, Slater says, "Oh, you mean you don't know? The illustrious Mr. Sterne has found that he doesn't know everything. Now what do you think about that, General Smith?"

"I find it hard to digest, and I find it equally hard to stomach his all-omnipotent presence!" Smith snips.

Sterne says, "Please stow the sarcasm and tell me what's going on. Mr. President?"

Al Gore remains at the bulletproof window. He says, "They want me to place the nation under Martial Law." His voice is very distant at this point. His lips and eyes twitch, but the others do not see it.

Sterne looks at his adversaries. "Well, in light of the situation, I think it's a good idea. Don't you agree?" His logical statement does nothing to appease Smith and Slater, as he hopes.

"They want me to order the immediate evacuation of Washington and Maryland," says Gore. As an afterthought, he adds, "Parts of Pennsylvania, and the Virginias."

"What? Why is that necessary?" asks Sterne, looking at Eleanor Graff.

Graff says, "There is an armed nuclear missile aimed at Washington at this very moment. The Black missileer says that he's going to blow the capital to hell. If you are aware of the Angel Mountain facility, then you're also aware that he can do it."

"A Black soldier?" Sterne repeats as he turns on Slater and Smith. "Just how the hell did you assholes manage to let that happen?"

"You're blaming us, you fucking maggot?" General Smith shouts as he advances with every intention of decking Sterne. "This program was perfectly safe and perfectly secretive until you tried to murder Captain Parker's twin brother, you prick!" Smith is a large man and very firm for his age. He cocks his right fist back to strike out while Sterne is in a temporary state of shock, but Slater stops him. Slater feels that it will do no good, though coveting the idea of dealing Vincent Sterne some hurt himself.

In the absence of Smith's fist, Sterne's mind issues its own slap. He realizes yet another mistake he has made in totally dismissing Captain Parker from the equation when his people reported the whereabouts of the other family members. He knows where the sister can be found because he plans to use her as his coveted ace card. When he first found out that Kyle Parker was on duty and isolated, he neglected to find out just what those duties were.

"But. But…" stammers Sterne, taking a disgustingly inadequate passage from Peter McAllister.

"But what, Vince? You didn't know that you were framing the brother of a man who works with the deadliest nuclear devices on the face of the planet?" shouts the Secretary of Defense. "We have no idea how he figured out the enable codes and the proper sequences to use them. But one thing is very clear. It was you who gave him the determination to do the fucking impossible!"

"What you did not know yesterday, the Soviets, the Chinese, and the rest of the world will know today because of your bungling. I don't think you or President Gore fully realize the worldwide implications of what has and will take place because you sought to play fucking God!" shouts Smith.

In retaliation, Sterne says, "You talk about playing God as if the practice is alien to you, but you two are the creators of this monstrous program of mass destruction!"

Eleanor Graff watches this exchange quietly.

"This is true, but only in times of war are those monsters to be unleashed, and not on our own citizens. This kind of incident was unforeseeable, never expected to happen because our people are staunch patriots of this nation," Slater states with growing hostility. "They would rather die than cause it harm, but when insidious motherfuckers like you are added to the human equation, there is no telling what will happen." He suddenly tears after Sterne in a sudden fit of rage.

The two men struggle and exchange blows, before being separated by Graff and Smith. When they finally agree to keep their tempers in check, they're out of breath anyway. However, it is noticed that during the brief struggle, Sterne reached for his empty holster. What would he have done if he hadn't relinquish his weapon upon arrival?

Vice President Graff says, "If you two are finished with this testosterone fiesta, we need answers. I suggest you leave your balls and bullshit at the door!"

With morbid tears streaming down his pallid face, a forgotten President Gore speaks from a distant world of private horrors. His voice is weak when he says, "It's all over, gone straight to hell. I have no one to blame but myself because I betrayed the American people when I should have been much stronger. I should have faced the problem that may not have been as insurmountable as it is right now." He whimpers, sniveling to himself. "I thought I could help to make this country a better place, stronger, more unified. Instead, I became a part of the problem that plagues us. So many people are suffering out there because of me and now, they want my blood, too. May God forgive us. The American people certainly won't."

Gore knows that the gathering crowd, with their graphic posters and venomous criticisms of administrative injustices are right. He is a traitor, and the only thing keeping them from his throat are the tanks and armed military personnel. Those soldiers are now authorized to fire upon anyone attempting to break the barricades they'd erected during the night of violence and senseless destruction.

"Mr. President, you must issue those orders. I'm sure we can come up with some disinformation about crazed terrorists running loose with chemical weapons to cover our asses. But then again, we all know that the CIA keeps such rabble off our shores because they reserve that sainted title for themselves!" Slater clasps his hands to regain his composure, but it's achieved with great difficulty. "In light of that, however, General Smith and I are not willing to toy with the lives of millions of American citizens to protect the secrecy of our program." Slater points an accusing finger at Sterne.

"That's not to say that we aren't putting together a plan to extract our subordinate officers from the underground command capsule by force. Captain Parker has decided to take no action since finding out that his family is still alive, but he refuses to relinquish control. Angel Mountain has a great many obstacles to overcome, but our experts are formulating a plan to breach the defenses that we no longer control from above ground. It will take some time, but we'll find a way to get a crack squad down there to take Parker and Markham out. We've little choice one way or another," says General Smith. Then he adds, "It's a shame that it might come to that because these officers have exhibited exemplary professionalism and intellect throughout their military careers. We cannot guarantee success, and he's given us strong warning that he'll execute his plans if anyone tries to move against him—or if his family members are harmed in any way!" He glares at Sterne. "You got that?"

"Just as we are willing to kill two, otherwise, sterling officers to protect this nation, you must be willing to expose yourself and this program by issuing those commands. The damage has already been done, Mr. President, so please make the call." Slater strongly suggests by slamming his fist on the top of Gore's desk.

President Gore flinches at the noise, nearly allowing a helpless yelp to escape his twisted lips.

All eyes are on him until he nods his head in affirmation. Graff hops to it. She goes to her own office to get the ball rolling for President Gore, who is barely able to make executive decisions. Much less, execute them.

Both Smith and Slater thank Al Gore, before leaving to motivate the far-reaching resources of the armed forces. However, they know with dread that their task will be difficult because they are receiving reports of widespread insubordination among Black military men and women. The behavior is spreading to military bases abroad, which could eventually mean brothers-in-arms against brothers-in-arms on aircrafts, carriers, submarines and virtually every aspect of the American armed services.

When they make this point to Al Gore, Sterne suggests something most unsettling. With some reluctance, both men are forced to agree that Sterne's insane idea holds merit if there is going to be anything left of this country when the dust finally settles. If ever it is to settle.

Sterne leaves the White House. He is most anxious to speak to Agent Eddings and Barker, who may hold the key to Evan Parker's silence and Kyle Parker's relinquishing the nuclear controls on Angel Mountain. His agents should have reported in hours ago.

The immediate evacuation of the nation's capital, Maryland, parts of Pennsylvania and the Virginias are ordered. Also, among the executive orders of the day, Martial Law is declared nationwide. However, he then orders the immediate internment of Blacks that will cause more rage. Congress, excluding the members of the

Congressional Black Caucus, will not fight them given the state of emergency. There are certainly not enough Blacks to initiate an effective protest.

Black politicians are already up in arms, of course. Hours after the orders are given, the most powerful and vocal will find themselves in a bind.

CHAPTER 38

GUILTY

It is an ugly thing, but factual beyond all denial. Even God himself must marvel at the passionate display of savagery by beings that are essentially forged in his image, by his own hands.

The escaped prisoners are drunk with the freedom of rage, running rampant throughout the streets of America. As they issue punishment, they take anything and anyone they want.

Terrified Americans are cringing behind locked doors with whatever means of protection they can find. Whole families find themselves barricaded and huddling together in basements, hiding from the crazed people who would break into their homes and sanctuaries. Calling the police is useless because their cups are running over with mayhem. It proves to be the greatest exercise in futility.

There are visions of looting and murder on every street. By the time President Gore's executive orders are made public, the death toll is in the millions and there seems to be no end in sight for an estimate that will continue to rise.

The rich and those with access to airports, gather their children and valuables, making their way through the glass-strewn streets in hopes of flying to safety. Mexico, Canada, and Central America will get rich. These countries are reaping great benefits by accepting those who could afford to pay for comfort, fleeing a nation in just the first days of complete turmoil.

The world watches as this great nation descends into darkness tinged with widespread bloodshed. Still, the drums continue to vibrate the earth, calling to the hostile thing in the basement.

When the terrorist plot to detonate dirty bombs in D.C. is announced, there begins an unruly exodus from Washington and surrounding areas. Every means of escape backlogs. The highways of the nation's capital are jammed with frenzied, panicked people, who had to first build up the courage to leave the relative safety of their homes to brave the danger in the streets. Being blown up or irradiated by a nuclear bomb is certainly motivation enough, but the roads are clogged with accidents that are reciprocated by more accidents.

Wrecked cars and buses are heaved into ditches and over the sides of bridges by desperate people who could care less about skin color, as long as their combined strength clears the roads. Often, immediately after these brief moments of human togetherness, the bickering and bad feelings resume. Amid the suffocating gas fumes, they wave angry fists at one another, shooting entire flocks of birds along with their verbal insults.

People of all races are struggling to get away from their home-towns, but the violence follows and greets them wherever they seek refuge within the continental U.S. The danger is there, wherever angry Black people reside.

Entire families lay dead along the roadsides; the victims of hate and haste. Some of them have just insulted the wrong people, and others are killed without provocation. The movement of traffic is painfully slow on any road or bridge that leads away from Washington. Hardly anyone stops to help the frightened children whose foul-mouthed parents lay dead or dying on the curb or in ditches.

Though regular Army and National Guard units are positioned to oversee the exodus, they are scant in most places where ugly circumstances and hot tempers flare. Every now and then, an angel of mercy emerges from the honking, tire-screeching motorcade to save the child of a dead stranger.

Those who fail to gain the attention of altruistic motorists, are truly orphaned in a world filled with choking exhaust fumes. Fearful people with no room in their hearts for extra burdens ignore them because, in such anxious, chaotic times, humanity almost always goes lacking.

Madness rules as the inner cities burn. Everywhere, exhausted firefighters are shouting, "To hell with it all!" Their jobs mean nothing in their attempts to rescue themselves and family members from the Black horde. "Let it burn!" they're forced to cry. "Just fucking let it burn!"

The looters, who are too busy stealing the television sets that they should be watching, never really understand why so much traffic is on the roads. Nor do they care. The only thing that truly matters is exacting their revenge on the White people who pushed this Negro race those final steps too far. And they rage on, running down the backed up streets, shooting anything that looks Caucasian. Their bullets shatter windows without provocation or discrimination of age. The Kuuta, the blood lust that began long before the African Zulus or oceangoing slavers, consumes them.

"Kill them all!" rings out amongst the insane warriors of America. It is infectious and spreading like staphylococci in an open wound.

Two-thirds of Winston County, Mississippi has been burned down by six in the evening. Its White, mostly racist, citizens are also up in arms. Before Martial Law was declared, the police department and civilian Whites took it upon themselves to defend the town by shooting any looters, or anyone simply running away from them.

At the Saint Bethel A.M.E. Church, Attorney Celia Brown gathers as many of the Black townspeople she can, totaling about eighty. There is also a Caucasian family of three at the church, the Yankee outcast members of this congregation.

Celia Brown has convinced these people that dealing with the news by reciprocating violently is wrong and anti-productive. She can do almost nothing with the younger generations, but she is able to convince some families with small children and elderly to stay in the church. They feel this to be the best place to ride out the storm, but this entire mess came down with racial tension at its peak in Farm Town, USA.

The wounded continue to file into the church, having been assaulted on their way to their homes or to the businesses they meant to protect. Some have had their fill of inflicting pain in that feverish state of madness that sweeps this country like the plague. Many called it quits only after receiving a measure of pain themselves. All are welcome at Saint Bethel.

At 7:00 p.m., the doors of the church are forced open by twenty men, who are led by none other than Terry Black and Barney Jasper.

Jasper has taken a bullet in the leg, limping in noticeable pain. It is little more than a flesh wound that he's tied up with a greasy rag, but it certainly adds fuel to his fire. These intruders are armed with killing in their hearts.

The seventy-year-old preacher offers strong protest to their intrusion, but he's ignored until the sound of his voice annoys someone who knocks him senseless.

Black and Jasper slap a few people around for good measure, stepping on the broken or shot up limbs of others. Since they squeal like pigs, they are going to be treated as such. The ninety-nine people, who'd taken refuge in the church are herded into the back of filthy swine trucks. As the church dwellers are taken away, black smoke belches from this house of God that gave them insufficient refuge.

They're taken to Jasper's pig farm and forced to stand in a vacated pen where pigs recently wallowed. The smell of feces and urine is simply overpowering.

"Turn on the sprinklers, boys!" orders Jasper. Four trucks are pulled close to the sides of the corral. These are the sort of vehicles with tanks on the back, which are driven down the rows of vegetables to administer liquefied fertilizers and pesticides. But in this case, when the sprinkler valves are opened, it is gasoline, diesel fuel, and kerosene that saturate the helpless people who stand calf-deep in the muck and mire. They plead and beg for mercy with their eyes burning and their lungs convulsing from the fumes.

Celia Brown admonishes Black and Jasper to reconsider. For shooting off her mouth, as children watch, she's dragged from the holding pen and molested by three men. The young ones learn the true depths of inhumanity while their eyes sting and their tiny hearts race. The other men just laugh as the lawyer is beaten and degraded.

When Celia Brown stops screaming, they find very little pleasure in her. The woman is hoisted over the aluminum railing by her hands and feet like a sack of manure. She lands on her back in the soft, shitty mud. When the other captives began to pull the woman from her imprint, her body makes a disgusting sucking sound.

When the sprinklers are turned on again to wet down these terrified people, several of them try to escape by climbing over the railing. They are battered with fists and the butts of heavy guns to keep them contained. All the while, these men laugh and spit chewing tobacco at people they consider to be no better than flies for the squashing.

One man lies dying of an acute asthma attack. Because no one can help him, he prays as the light fades on his heaving lungs.

Local reporter Erica Winger and her camera operator are watching helplessly from a nearby stand of trees. They are following a story that should be recorded for posterity, but they are sickened by what they're witnessing here.

Terry Black shouts, "Now, you will all know what it's like to fuck with us true Americans. If it wasn't for that nigger lawyer in Atlanta six years ago, we'd have an American President who'd know how to deal with you lowlifes!" He looks at his men and says, "Get them trucks away from here, boys. I think it's time to have ourselves a great big ole barbeque. That'll cut their numbers some. These here pigs won't be breedin' no time soon!"

A young man bolts through the mud, leaping for the top of the corral where he's flanked and greeted with the butt of a rifle. He hears those tobacco-chewing maniacs shouting, "Su-u-u we-e! Here pig, pig, pig!"

The young man does not intend to die this way, so he produces his brother's switchblade and slices a nice chunk out of the man on the railing, the very same person who'd clobbered him. The fumes are as thick in the air as the young man's hatred for them all. The trucks are still nearby when the man who's been stabbed draws his sidearm.

In unison, Black and Jasper shout, "No!" He pulls the trigger. The blast from the gun snuffs out the teenager's life, but it also ignites the air! The flames light up the night, destroying both races. Every single person.

The drums are pounding and they are to be obeyed. Rada! Conga! Boom da-da doom! Doom da-da Boom!

"Rise and destroy, dark children. Let this land burn an inferno far into the coming nights! Rise and destroy, for Damballah wills it so."

High overhead, and filled to capacity, a Boeing 747 soars toward Mexico. Passengers with window seats have to put up with those who leaned over them to peek at the world far below. They can see fires burning brightly in the night over Austin, Texas.

The passengers, who don't care to look, turn their attention to the broadcast of an interview taped at 6:00 p.m.

Dan Rather, who's flown to Suitland, Maryland to meet with the notorious Peter McAllister at the WBLE News studio facility, conducts the interview.

The camera crew starts the broadcast once the two men are finally settled. The well-known journalist faces the camera with a list of questions in his lap, anxious to get to the bottom of things. Peter McAllister is a ball of jangled nerves. His throat is as dry as a billion grains of desert sand.

"Good evening, ladies and gentlemen of our television audience. I'm Dan Rather, coming to you from the affiliated WBLE News facility in Suitland, Maryland. Tonight, Mr. Peter McAllister, who is presently the Director of the Bureau of Census here in Maryland, now joins me."

Rather clears his throat.

"At this very moment, as all of you must be painfully aware, mass violence and rioting is taking place throughout our great nation. The upsetting phenomenon began immediately following a rather earthshaking revelation that was bravely, though, unlawfully brought to our attention by a journalist named Carolyn Murray of Live Five News in Charleston, South Carolina. While disobeying the U.S. Government's news quarantine, Mrs. Murray enlightened us of alleged government sanctioned murders that date back to 1990 and the George Bush Administration. Apparently, this all started eleven years ago with someone named Cecil Bridges, who was then the Director of the Bureau of Census. It was recently reported that in August of 1990 Mr. Bridges made a startling discovery. Certain people, those who felt that his findings should never become public knowledge, were ultimately responsible for Mr. Bridges' horrific murder. Now, eleven years later, this hidden truth has been uncovered once again. This time we have a new American President, with the same CIA Director Vincent Sterne in office, who is named as an original conspirator in this matter. Cecil Bridges' discovery eleven years ago has now managed to resurface and uproot our well-organized lives and system of government. Yet again, in April of 2001, another African American, a man named Evan Parker, has uncovered the unbelievable data. Mr. Evan Parker, whose whereabouts are presently unknown, is the Deputy Director of the Census Bureau. That secret, frankly, although the numbers changed substantially over the past decade, is that African Americans now outnumber Whites by nineteen to twenty million in these United States of America. If true, these statistics must be mindboggling to the average citizen because it certainly takes this journalist by total and complete surprise."

Dan Rather looks at his notes as his heart races.

"Tonight, America is faced with a crisis beyond anything in the history of the nation. Our streets are now in utter chaos, and we now have it on very good authority that a Captain Kyle Parker of the United States Air Force is holding the nation's capital hostage. For those of you who haven't figured it out, Captain Parker is the twin brother of Evan Parker, whom I just mentioned. As we speak, Captain Parker is presently deep underground in a relatively new nuclear missile launch facility with his finger on the button. How did these staggering events come about? Is it conceivable that this entire mess is the result of a mistake or an elaborate hoax? Well, we hope to shed some light on these matters when we return with Census Director Peter McAllister, one person who can answer these questions. We'll be back in a moment, so please stay tuned. You won't want to miss this." He purses his lips, thoughtfully.

During a short commercial break, there are some adjustments made to offset a few programming problems. Dan Rather's makeup is touched up, but Peter McAllister is left as is. No reasonable amount of pancake makeup will make him look livelier because he looks dead already.

Moreover, Peter McAllister is the picture of a man who now stares into the face of God. The producers want him kept that way because it is so much more realistic.

With the technical difficulties overcome, the interview continues. With the hot lights beaming down and that black well of professional silence surrounding them, Dan Rather says, "Thank you all for staying with us. Mr. McAllister, can you tell us if there is any truth to the accusations by Evan Parker? He's made very strong, frankly, damning allegations about you, CIA Director Vincent Sterne, and even against former President George Bush, former Vice President Dan Quayle and current President Al Gore."

The camera zooms in on the sunken eyes and gray, toneless skin of Peter McAllister. Peter looks at the cool glass of water on the table between them, which perspires to spite his extreme thirst. He can almost hear his own sandpapered Adam's apple scraping his esophagus while it works up and down to force a very hard word from his mouth. He reaches for it.

"Mr. McAllister? Are all or any of Evan Parker's allegations true, sir? Are there actually more African Americans than Caucasians living in these United States of America?"

Peter drinks deeply of the cold water. Then he says, "Yes, sir. I'm afraid it's all...it's all... true!" His eyes bulge and he gags, "Oh God. Oh my God!" Peter McAllister begins to convulse. The glass falls from his hands, shattering on the hardwood floor of the set. When he grabs at his throat, his tongue sticks out between teeth that clamp down until it is nearly severed.

When he gags again, blood flies from his mouth with the froth of asphyxiation. His eyes continue to bulge, displaying the most life they have shown in days. His feet are kicking in front of him, vibrating on the floor before Dan Rather's unbelieving eyes. Then, as suddenly as it started, it is over.

In front of millions, Peter McAllister dies a gruesome, agonizing death. While he expires before the startled camera operators, a silent figure slips away unseen.

The drums at the end of Kwani Drive continue to pulse beneath white eyes. Sweat runs from their pores like blood.

Valerie's nurse drags her to the car and rushes her back to the hospital. This time, she is spotting heavily and the cramp in her belly causes her to wail. She has just witnessed the death of her husband, a man who was trying to rectify his wrongs at her urging.

Boom da-da doom! "Rise and bring blood that will stain this land crimson. Rise!"

All across the nation, the night is filled with screams and gunfire. Black National guardsmen, regular army personnel and police officers, are refusing to fire on other African Americans. They are themselves interned or shot in the field.

Across the nation, at least two million Blacks, peaceful or violent, young and old, are dragged from the streets to be taken to impromptu holding facilities. Some are taken to football stadiums, basketball coliseums and even barbed wired fields for livestock where heavily armed military personnel can control them. The threat of violence is continual. Many of these makeshift, poorly thought out concentration camps are simply overrun by seething mobs. Many will die during the revolt against the powers that hold them captive, but as it is all across the country, many more Whites are dying horrible deaths. Kinzana's black tide rages as an unstoppable force in the throes the Kuuta.

An estimated 32 million strong, angry people are surging against their restraints, smashing walls and burning entire cities to bring death and destruction. Following Peter McAllister's televised death, instigated by those who are still trying to conceal the truth, millions more pour into the streets.

The darkness screams, bleeding into the light of day. That thing in the basement, even though it thrives in the dead of night, fears not the coming of dawn. They are possessed by it; driven by it. The country is shrouded by an overcast sky, while the entire world watches and confronts the shadow of racial transgressions.

CHAPTER 39
DEAD EYES

The horrifying events of these dark days in American history play havoc with nearly every man, woman, and child. Few are unscathed by an angry race's immoral reaction to those first to offend. It becomes more than just the reciprocation of the original sin. It is more than an eye for an eye, for an eye—squared.

Families are slaughtered in more ways than one. Countless men and women, those who braved the great Black-White barrier in the name of love, now find themselves hating the spouse that they have sworn to uphold and honor. They painfully discover that they haven't fully erased basic prejudices that exist between the races, although married to exactly that.

Teary-eyed children watch their parents debating, arguing over issues of race when their marital vows and their offspring should continue to be testaments of their love, respect, and trust; an extremely colorless commitment. After the flames of anger subside, some of these torn fences will eventually mend while others will be irrevocably damaged.

The children, all children are slated to suffer because they might not make the same grownup mistakes. Thus, entering the

479

same grownup hell. The young, impressionable soul is hardly so hardened that it cannot be guided to new attitudes. They learn from their environments, the ones their parents do or do not perpetuate. Shamefully, though, parents so often impress their more negative idiosyncrasies upon the minds they're supposed to mold. Rather than instilling in them that race or color holds no real consequence because all people are essentially the same, they impart the negative more readily.

No matter what color the child, they always notice how mom's fingers fiddle anxiously for door locks when that person walks too near her automobile. They watch cartoons on television in which the bad guy is always of a darker color than the rest of the animated characters. They learn racism in many forms and fashions, however innocently taught.

⤜⥏ ⥑⥐⤛

Sightless eyes stare up at the cloudy sky of America, seeing night nor day. As chaos sweeps through the streets, there is the ever-present noise of humans running amok. They bang on automobiles as trash cans fly through plate glass windows. Everywhere the power is still intact, the sound of blaring alarms go ignored. All of these are very human noises, but the most prevalent of them all are the roars of triumph and the screams of an agonizing demise.

Droves of African Americans submit to some unknown demon, which commands that they rise from their hovels to kill and demolish. From the lowest of heroin junkies to the most eloquent Blacks, they give in to the need for bloody restitution. They seek to avenge all that White society has claimed to be nonexistent. They are the black tide arisen.

Death walks in masses to tear things down and to burn. Seems all the world is filled with angry people shouting obscenities while partaking in acts exponentially more obscene. The bloodlust reigns over their hearts and souls to motivate participation in acts of mindless violence, things they may never have been prone to in their everyday lives.

Good people and bad are moving across this land like giant amoebas, advancing in singular cohesion to loot, crush, and mangle. Even rival street gangs, with bloody histories between them, join forces to make THEM pay!

Within these terrible sounds are ensconced something even deeper and darker, something from the steamy floors and canopies of the thickest jungles. It is primal. It appeals to the Black nation from the basements of their beings, and the appeal forces forth a dark fantasy in them all that might have been bred away over many more centuries of civility or subservience.

The Rada and the Conga drums join together as two parts of a whole, summoning that wicked fantasy in every Black soul to kill a White man. Many will disagree, but it holds true for nearly every individual that has truly known the meaning of prejudice. From the whitest Black man to the darkest Black woman, there has been at least one instance in their lives when the thought of killing was there, even if only for one hot nanosecond. It was there like the flicker of a lighter in a pitch-black room. It dwells deep down there. It is mindless, seething, violent and very...very deep.

Dead eyes are staring at the steady onrush of feet, hundreds of thousands. Millions. Dead eyes, watching the greatest movement in human history. The ancient Romans would quake at being made the brunt of such a flood of belligerent people, those whose time have finally come.

From the pristine towers of the big cities to the backwater communities and farmland, people are dying horribly. Their screams and cries echo through the night like banshees giving up the ghost.

They lay precariously on the hoods or inside the cabs of burning cars that will explode to toss them into the air in shattered pieces. They are spread to the four winds by wood chippers, hung, dismembered, and disemboweled. The pain of the dead is over. For to die quickly is a final mercy such that only the Angel of Death can provide because they are being shot, bludgeoned, and ran over repeatedly by vehicles that feel no pity for the crunch of fused, mangled human bones.

Clinging pools of blood now paint the streets with human footprints. Dead people, are everywhere with their eyes popping from their sockets. Gray matter, filled with precious memories, oozes from ears that will never hear what tramples their bodies into pulp.

People are drowned and strangled. They are set on fire with gasoline while their mad audience watches them to their screaming end. They cook like rabbits on a spit while their legs dance with the devil, and their hands slap at the heedless flames. Screaming and blood. Oh, there is so much blood.

Foolish people are caught on the streets and swallowed up like plankton by herds of ravenous whales. Women and men just fall dead from heart failure and massive strokes when caught stark naked and defenseless in the direct path of a sudden, seething mob.

Remaining indoors is no guarantee of safety, however. Locked doors and barking dogs are insufficient deterrents to those who will not be stopped.

After the Kuuta, it will take years to retrieve the bodies from sweltering homes, which will wreak of the swollen, bubbling flesh of extinct inhabitants. Doors will be forced open to release hordes of fat flies that will have mated exponentially in that lowly species' kind of heaven. They will be freed to fly in search of new odors of decay, while maggots dig deeper into putrid masses of what used to be human, seeking to the very marrow of their bones. They will eat and breed to darken the American sky.

Military effectiveness is severely hampered. Someone has been double-dealing the numbers there, too. Esprit de corps: a spirit of devotion to the common goals of a group. This term fails its credo for the men and women trained to defend this country with their lives, but it's given greater meaning for the Negro race.

Fierce battles are waging between brothers in arms. Insubordination and outright attacks on other officers land many soldiers of color in the stockade. Many are shot in the field because they balk against orders to fire upon other African Americans, even those who are obviously engaged in wrongdoing. A firing barrage at an oncoming crowd is bitter business. Even with hundreds dead, the resilient tide surges forward. Like the Vietcong that used the weapons of those who'd fallen before them, they continue to advance, taking the bodies of those who have expired to shield themselves from the bullets and shrapnel.

Many soldiers die trying to hold positions that eventually lose all importance to them. The smart leaders will order their men to fall back, but they are often too late in reaching the decision to do so. The more gung ho military sorts, readily sacrifice freckled faced soldiers that cry for them to relent the order to stand and fight.

Of course, there are deserters, many of which are shot in the back while abandoning their posts. Some manage to escape, only to be killed when they run into another group of angry people. All of these reasons predicate and proliferate the miserable failure of Martial Law amidst an all-out rebellion.

This country bleeds a river under the tumult of the drums of doom for mad marauders stalk mercilessly, consuming the enemy as the hungry panther stalks its prey.

Vultures circle the sky by day. They walk the streets by night with their covetous wings spread to pluck at the eyes of men, the rarest delicacy on earth. Highest on the food chain, man is the only animal to actually bury its dead away from the spying eyes of the carrion lords of the sky. But in this hour, mankind lies a feast before their rapacious wings.

The drums, the drums. Doom da-da boom, boom da-da doom!

For two days, the south Florida coastline has been battered by forty knot winds. The National Weather Service is keeping a close eye on Hurricane Sade.

The severe tropical storm is upgraded to a Category-5 hurricane only hours after its Caribbean conception. Its force is immense, thrusting its weight around with one-hundred and eighty mile an hour winds. She is hungry to make landfall, scraping the Florida coastline from Miami to Daytona before threatening to suddenly stall over the Atlantic.

To the relief of many, Sade's fury begins to subside as her eye shifts due east, away from Daytona. Because of this welcomed surprise, many residents stay in their homes, breathing easier in a world already filled with carnage. The wind and rain seems to be godsends.

In the depth of night, whilst sleeping people dream of crooked business deals, drug transactions, and infidelity, Hurricane Sade revives her strength. Her violent winds are flung at diminutive Saint Augustine, Florida, one of the nation's oldest cities. This is the land of Ponce and the Bridge of Lions. Having always rested below sea level, unlucky tourists and disgruntled residents often claim that merely pissing in the streets during high tide will cause flooding.

One of the oldest cities in America is a tiny dot on the map where compassionless judges lock Blacks behind bars with impunity. This is St. Augustine, where police officers get away with murder. They steal from the very drug dealers that they have essentially created within a boa's constriction of unemployment.

This is the place in many African Americans' nightmares, where their lives have turned for the worst. This little tourist's town is a place where the rich get richer, but deeper down, the poor and the desperate are milked like goats and recycled by the incumbent system for small minds.

Now judged by God, St. Augustine is remanded to the wrath of hurricane Sade. The oldest, continuous city in America is gutted in the sleeping hours, transported bit by bit to somewhere else. Along with its weak-minded inhabitants, utterly and completely, it is laid to waste.

"There will be signs. Now let them rise, for this is not punishment enough! This is not punishment enough!" Boom da-da doom, boom da-da doom! Boom da-da doom, da-da doom, da-da doom!

CHAPTER 40

SZINJA SZIN: THE DESTROYER

H er smooth, brown skin is sticky. The air conditioner seems to offer no immediate relief. Her brown eyes are sworn to their duty, though torn between the desolate highway before her and the rearview mirror.

As with many cases of road paranoia, drivers find that even the most familiar stretches of highway are prone to sudden movement. This is especially true for they who cannot ignore the vehicle behind them. It often happens to drug dealers, schizophrenics, drunk drivers, and potential victims.

The road noise grows louder and the course more treacherous. Evan Parker's only sister yanks at the wheel to get back in her lane doing sixty-five miles per hour. Her heart roars at a much faster pace as she snatches her breath from the air. Her children have awakened, knowing instinctively that her anxiety escalates because they are inhaling her fear.

The driver of the beige van looks at his intense partner and says, "It's definitely a bust. She's aware of us. Can you tell me why this is true?"

"It's pretty obvious that she's been warned, Eddie. Phone records show that she received one five-minute call from Jarvis Parker day before yesterday, and her routine changed dramatically since we started this surveillance."

"We'll have to reign her in soon, so advise Sterne of the situation before we move in."

Talia's son has been watching her from the rear passenger's seat. The angle of the mirror allows him to see his mother's eyes. It is gnawing at his ten-year-old curiosity, so he quietly removes his seatbelt. When his twin sister sees what he's about to do, she takes hold to stop him. Intent upon disobeying their mother's demand, he simply has to see what she cannot resist in the rearview mirror.

The young man is startled when his mother shrieks, "Shaquile, sit down right now!" Though she is distressed beyond a ten-year-old's comprehension, Talia Parker regrets the harshness with which she's spoken. Her voice softens considerably when she says, "Please, baby, don't look back. Do as mommy says. Please." She swerves again.

"No, sir. She doesn't appear to be heading to South Carolina, and she hasn't been able to contact anyone there since her last call from the father's phone. We believe that the target was forewarned before we took our posts, and she's now attempting to disappear. Even before the rioting began, the subject refused to go to work. Her kids weren't allowed to attend school or go outside to play. Since the rioting started, her hospital has been packed with casualties, but she refused to go in even when offered a police escort. We believe that she's going to ground." There is a short pause as instructions are given. "Will do. We will make contact once we've reached the safe house in Macon, Georgia. Barker out." Agent Barker scratches that nagging itch on the nape of his neck and groans. He looks in his mirror at the two trailing sets of headlights.

His impatient partner asks, "What is it? What?"

"Nothing. I just can't shake the feeling that we're the ones being watched."

With obvious irritation, Agent Eddings says, "That again." He's aware that the CIA's resources are stretched to its limits, but he still resents being partnered with someone who hasn't been proven in the field. "What did he say?"

Barker looks at his senior partner, dubiously. He says nothing before pulling the mask downward to cover his stubbly face.

With his face also concealed, Eddings floors it, but yanks his right foot from the accelerator when another car suddenly appears and passes them in the fast lane. "Christ!" Eddings shouts.

The windows of the beige van are heavily tinted, making visibility difficult for persons within and without, but Eddings swears that someone is staring directly at him as the southbound sedan passes. He shakes the feeling as soon as those alien taillights disappear as it takes the off-ramp. His partner's paranoia is beginning to affect him, too.

Talia Parker whimpers. She presses on the gas pedal and asks if the children are still wearing their seatbelts. They are, but her son has re-engaged his belt improperly by failing to push until it clicks, as he's been taught.

"Damn, she's running. The terrain looks rough ahead, so you better push the button," Eddings suggests.

They're at eighty miles per hour and still climbing.

Barker palms the small remote control unit, pointing at the car. He says, "Well, Dr. Parker, you're about to have sudden engine failure."

When Baker presses the button. Eddings slows just enough to be right alongside the speeding Volvo when it suddenly decelerates. Instead of being corralled between the beige van and the roadside ditch, with a burning car blocking the outer lane, Dr. Talia Parker speeds away.

"Shit on toast. Nothing happened." Barker quickly opens the back of the unit and dumps the batteries. Once they are replaced, he tries to kill her engine again.

"What the fuck?" Eddings shouts. The subject's car slips into the fast lane with only inches between their bumpers.

Dr. Talia Parker is soon forced back into the outer lane because of the scattered obstacles ahead. They are weaving through a littered maze of debris, which is the direct result of deadly highway clashes between the warring races. It would seem that the rioting has also touched this desolate place in Nowhere, Georgia.

Eddings is beginning to sweat beneath the mask. Far ahead, there is an open stretch, with many more cars burning in the outside lane. He is determined to overtake Talia Parker before she escapes the convenient barricade. He shouts, "Use the backup to blow the tires, Paul."

"But she's going too fast for that," Barker protests. "It'll kill them."

Eddings flexes his jaw and clenches the steering wheel so tightly with his gloved hands that they creak. His cold eyes berate his rookie partner.

With her children screaming, "They're coming, mommy. They're right behind us!"

Talia prays, no longer doubting who they are. She lays claim to the pistol Jarvis had bought for her protection. He had also seen to it that she learned how to use it properly.

"Hold on. I'm here," she reassures. "I won't let anyone hurt you. I promise."

Her son cries, "Are the bad men after us because of what Uncle Evan did?" Her heart seizes. She was under the impression that she had shielded her children from those vicious lies. She was forced to take naps from time to time, which is a child's favorite time to watch television.

"None of that stuff is true, Shaquile. You know your Uncle Evan would never hurt anyone. Those were all lies, baby. Now hold on, and put your heads in your laps for me."

With her lane quickly coming to an end, the Chevy's supercharged engine guzzles fuel to overtake one of Sweden's best. As the children obediently fold their arms and bend forward, there is a clatter. Reesha's breath catches as she looks at her brother with panic

With his weapon pointed directly at his partner's head, Eddings says, "Sterne said 'dead or alive.' She can't be allowed to escape, and she'll never slow down. Now do it, or die in her fucking place, rookie."

"When did you talk to Sterne about that?"

"Do it!"

The Volvo's front tires explode at ninety-eight miles per hour. The car barrels left, then right, shooting toward an unforgiving ditch as Reesha Parker reaches for her unprotected brother. Directly ahead, another burning vehicle rushes to greet them!

"Jesus. She's going to hit it," Barker cries.

Talia Parker's scream freezes with her heart as she fights the rebellious wheel. Suddenly, they are airborne.

Flying debris from the blown tires slam into the windshield of the pursuing van, cracking it dead center. The van pitches and yaws back and forth on two wheels, threatening to flip the second he over commits to either side. The smoking tires squeal as the moaning suspension seems to sheer itself in two.

When the Volvo plummets, it comes down over a small pond that runs beneath the highway.

Reesha holds onto her brother with grownup ferocity as the car hydroplanes for what seems a millennium. It nose-dives into an embankment, twisting metal while shattering plastic and glass. It plows through soft mud, stopping mere inches from a tree.

Eddings regains control and stops. He backs up as fast as he can without repeating the near tragic performance.

Truly, this is a lonely stretch of highway. No other living cars are approaching from the rear, however, it is quite clear that storming violence has already graced this place. Paul Barker is morose, but he has just been given a sample of what insubordination will bring.

He's back on track, regardless of personal feelings. Whatever they are about to do is going to be done for America.

Amidst the ticking and pinging of mangled steel, steam rises from the crumpled hood while Talia's head slowly clears from impact with the air bag. Reesha cries for her twin, begging him to wake up. Her small arms ache from straining against the inertia that undoubtedly would have thrown him through the front windshield.

Reesha's stomach aches where the seatbelt grew taut, but her brother is in much worse shape. His head and shoulders are slumped on the rear floor, but his legs are between the front seats, pointing toward the windshield.

Talia wipes the blood from her busted forehead. Reesha's pleas remind her of the two most important people in the world. Brilliant pain fires through her leg when she tries to move, causing her to groan in insuppressible agony. Her vision hazes for an instant.

She struggles free of her restraint, only to find her son's legs where they do not belong. She squeezes his legs and quickly crawls into the backseat. This worried mother tries to calm her frightened daughter while calling his name. Before she dares to move him, her knowledgeable hands go about checking Shaquile's neck, spine, and limbs for broken bones. Although this frazzled woman is standing on the brink of total panic, her medical instincts take over. She believes her unconscious son has sustained a simple concussion. His nose is bleeding and the swelling suggests that it's broken.

It pleases them just to hear him moan Reesha's name. Talia Parker's heartfelt tears mingle with the blood and sweat on her cheeks. Through the muddy rear window and the surrounding darkness, Reesha discerns the bright red taillights of their determined pursuers. She whispers, "Mommy, they're coming back."

The gun is lost and Talia has to get her children to safety. She forces the front seats forward and drags her son from the broken window because the doors refuse to open. Her right leg shrieks when something snaps under her son's weight, but still she limps into the dark woods at the murky water's edge. Trampling through fennels and ferns, they run deeper into uncertainty.

Eddings tosses Barker a headset and they take to the chase. With their night vision goggles in place, they probe into the mire where the smell of stagnant mud prevails.

Talia has limped as far as she can. When her swelling leg rebels, torturous signals of pain rush to her head and she finally crashes to the ground. With her brave daughter tugging away at her brother's arms, Talia crawls on.

Reesha's young lungs are filled with discord, burning for her physical turmoil to cease. Her heart is pounding like thunder, but still she pulls on while begging God for strength.

Finally overcome by the exhaustion of the past few days and the pain of the crash-landing, Dr. Talia Parker collapses. With her face lying upon a molding collection of damp leaves, she weeps when a stranger's voice proclaims, "I see them. That way."

When Eddings and Barker first saw the subjects fleeing from the wreckage, they were amazed anyone survived the crash.

Nearly defeated, Talia Parker looks at her son. Now she looks at her daughter and begs, "You have to run, Reesha. Run as fast as you can and stay away from the water." Her lips tremble as her eyes rain tears of futility.

"No, mommy. Come on. Please hurry, they're coming for us. We have to go," Reesha cries.

"I can't, Reesha," her mother whimpers. "Mommy can't make it any farther. My leg is broken so you have to be brave. Now run, Reesha. Run!"

Reesha Parker reluctantly places her brother's hand on the ground. She does this with such gentleness that her mother believes that she will never leave their side. Both their eyes are begging the other to relent.

Reesha Parker takes off for the heart of her fate. In the darkest place she's ever known, the child runs, almost certain that she will never see her family again.

She hears her mother thrashing about and screaming, "No. You can't have them!" as she attacks Eddings.

As instructed, Barker goes after the girl child. He is afraid of what his partner will do to a crazed woman, who is only fighting to protect her children. His doubts fade when the woman's scream precedes a blow that resounds in his ears.

Reesha Parker hears him coming, but her little legs have begun to fail. With her heart pumping away, she rounds a tree on tiptoe. There, some woodland creature has hollowed a large gash, but she braves the black void with monstrous fear burning inside her body.

Her heat signature disappears. By the time Agent Barker picks himself up from whence he's fallen among rasping leaves and thorny vines that rip at his flesh, she is gone. He now moves cautiously, still huffing and puffing to catch his breath. Listening for crackling branches or splashing water that might betray Reesha Parker's whereabouts, he grasps his knees. There is too much water about, and his own swampland fears of a childlike nature begin to creep into mind.

At last disheartened, he consigns himself to the fact that he's lost her. In a very subtle way, he's glad for Reesha's escape. In another way, he fears for her and himself. The woods have grown so quiet that the sound of his own breathing becomes all that echoes in the world, until an angry raccoon hisses and chatters.

Reesha looks up into the hollow, seeing the glowing green eyes of something maniacal. She screams and bolts from its musky den. When Barker overtakes her, she fights valiantly, kicking and biting. The battle is lost in the end.

Moments later, Barker and Reesha meet Eddings at her unconscious mother's limp form. The CIA operative was forced to hurt the woman, leaving her there in a heap while he carried her son to the van. He is certain that Dr. Parker will be there when he returns.

Talia is just beginning to come around when Eddings scoffs, "So you did catch her. I must admit I had my doubts for a moment."

Barker allows the child to tend her mother. He says, "Just cut the crap. I made a mistake earlier, but it's over now. So let's try to get through transport without drawing our weapons, shall we?"

"Whatever you say, partner. Glad to see you came to your senses."

Barker stops with his back turned. He suddenly wheels, drawing his weapon and thumbing the safety in a single motion. Eddings freezes. With his right hand caught amid draw, he says, "Now wait kid. Don't..."

Barkers says, "Shut the fuck up. How's it feel, partner. Huh? How the fuck does it feel?" He spits with disgust. "If you ever draw down on me again, I swear I'll kill you." He puts the weapon back on the safe position and slides it into the holster, satisfied by the expression on the senior partner's face.

Eddings smiles wryly, though his eyes are wary. "Jesus, rookie, I didn't think you had it in you. My mistake. We're cool."

Eddings hauls his bound captive to her feet, but he's soon forced to carry her up the steep embankment. She's too weak and groggy to climb.

While reaching for the rear doors of the van, Eddings complains, "I'm sick and tired of driving, so I guess it's your turn, killer." When he opens the door to discover that the boy has escaped the cage, blasphemous thoughts race through his mind and pour from his lips.

With no regard for her pain, Eddings shoves Talia Parker to the heavily padded floor and spins around to search the flickering shadows for Shaquile.

"That isn't necessary. The woman obviously has a bum leg," scolds Barker.

When Reesha willingly climbs into the cage, she is surprised and happy that her brother has gotten away.

"Shut up," Eddings spits as he slams the windowless, padded doors. "Haven't you noticed that the kid is gone?"

Barker looks hastily at the doors. "What? How can that be? There are no latches inside. How could he have gotten out?"

As Eddings' steely eyes search the surrounding gloom, he reaches for his weapon. "So that means he had help from the outside. I guess you might have been right about being watched?"

"What?" asks the confused Barker.

"We're not alone, kid, so ready your sidearm," Eddings whispers. "And make sure you keep the business end of that thing pointed away from me."

They are startled by a whooping lament coming from the road-side, behind a smoldering vehicle they passed during the chase. With their weapons drawn, they move toward the SUV. As they approach, the breeze shifts without warning, causing the smoke to burn their eyes. The smell of burning rubber is profound.

They part, electing to round the overturned vehicle from opposite ends. With weapons pointed into the firelight of the ejected rear seat, their hearts freeze.

Two members of the African Maasai are leaping into the air. Their toes barely leave the ground as they spring up and down. Their red tunics seem to drip blood in the erratic light. They are clutching long spears, while whooping that fearsome lament with their eyes intent upon the wounded boy.

"What the fuck is this?" Barker says.

An old man with long silver hair, kneels before the child. He is caressing Shaquile with a lush, green branch while chanting something ominous.

"Maluwa makinaway. Maluka makinaway makinaway makinawa," the old man repeats in his native tongue.

"What is this?" Eddings demands. "Who the hell are you people?" Much to his distaste, they are ignored while the two men continue to bounce and make that irritating noise. Vincent Sterne's men move closer.

"Goddamn it. Who are you people, and what are you doing to that kid?" Barker asks with growing hostility. Strangely, though, he wonders if it is out of some twisted sense of trying to protect young Shaquile. What great irony.

The old man places a palm to his mouth as if he is eating something very hot. He blows smoke upon the green leaves of the branch. When the mist clears, the branch is dead and leafless. It crumbles into dust before the disbelieving agents' eyes, and they do grow to fear.

The old man places both his hands upon the crumbled, grey dust and rubs it into the boy's bare chest. He continues to chant words that they cannot understand. Shaquile Parker stirs, moaning for his sister to hold onto him. Apparently, he's locked within that moment before being knocked unconscious.

The old man feels a certain degree of sadness for this young man. His feelings, however, are not only motivated by the child's injury, but because he knows that the boy will never be the same again. He will probably always have some measure of hatred for White people, unless he is taught to forgive them.

Eddings says, "If you two don't stop making that racket, I'm going to shoot some fucking body!" The old man waves a hand and the others are quiet. "What the hell did you just do?" Eddings barks. "Is this some kind of voodoo crap? Who are you?"

The old man stands, wearily. He looks deeply into Special Agent Barker's eyes and sniffs the air, tasting his fear in the shifting breeze. His lips wrinkle into a snarl.

"If I have to ask who you are again, it won't be so nicely done," Eddings threatens. "Who are you and why have you been following us?"

"I," the old man hisses with contempt, "...am your every nightmare come to living, breathing flesh. My name is Szinja Szin. And tonight, I am the destroyer. We are their guardians, so I took the boy because you have no righteous claim to him, little man."

Eddings growls the challenge, "Want to bet, old man? You have no idea who we are and there's nothing you can do to prevent us from taking him."

Szinja Szin smiles wryly and says, "Oh yes, I know who you are. You're both the spawn of demons, walking inside the husks of dead men." His eyes blaze with the dying fire that suddenly leaps to life. The surrounding air grows dense and suffocating as thunder rattles the cloudy firmament. At this moment, what seems like a billion fireflies spring into the air on either side of the road. They rise, brightening the air before descending again as one body and mind. It is a wondrous thing of singular beauty, but it is also a thing to fear.

"What the hell is going on here, Eddings?" Barker's eyes are darting back and forth between Eddings and the three intruders, waiting for the senior agent to give him instructions.

Szinja Szin glances at Barker with a sense of remorse. He says, "It is such a pity that you fear him more than you fear your own immorality. When his kind would harm one so young and inno-cent, how can it be justified by a desire for leverage? It is also a pity that you fear him more than me."

Barker looks at Eddings because this frail looking old man speaks with such confidence and total disregard of their superior weaponry. Barker's instincts are now telling him that there must be more to it. They have to be the watchers, the reason for that nagging itch on the nape of his neck. He isn't prepared for such things, but he is sworn to duty.

The old man laughs. He slowly raises his arms, and with them, the gnashing wind cries out once and falls dead silent. As if encom-passed by an electric vacuum, his silver mane begins to dance upon invisible webs, climbing slowly and moving of its own accord. The firefly cloud dances in the air, surging toward the CIA agents and retreating suddenly. Again and again, they surge.

Some dark warlock is rising from deep within the ancient's soul, and he wants these men dealt with before the resurrection is complete.

Predatory cats, not indigenous to this region, begin to roar within the surrounding woods. The warning cries of hundreds of Howler monkeys grow louder with each passing second.

With sweat cascading from his brows, Eddings orders, "Fire!"

The Maasai warriors move swiftly between their master and the men with guns. Refusing to cower in an instance that is sure to turn fatal, they brandish their spears in defense of one so young and another most ancient.

Doubtfully, Barker looks to his left at his partner, who does not hesitate to squeeze the trigger. A single shot rings out, killing the man who stands before Eddings. That, however, is the first and only shot.

Agent Barker screams when fire pierces his right hand where a long, wooden dart has buried itself into his yielding flesh. And then another and another flies through the air, striking both men. Their backs and chests are riddled, and their legs and arms grow numb swiftly. Their knees buckle as their weapons clatter to make the unmistakable sound of metal striking stone.

Some strange paralysis overcomes Sterne's men. Barker and Eddings struggle mightily as painted men now emerge from the surrounding shadows.

Szinja Szin's face appears with the others in a circle above, as they lay helplessly, but aware upon their backs. His eyes are those of a wild animal and his teeth are exposed. Within their minds, the old man whispers, "If you are left here this way, the poison will slowly consume you both."

Barker begins to wheeze, fighting for air as his lungs struggle to fulfill his desire to breathe. He tries to speak, wanting to repent. He wishes to beg for mercy, but his lips merely twist to mock his efforts. The painted men begin to bounce, whooping that terrible sound again.

"However, we do not allow wounded animals to suffer. You can no longer speak. But believe me when I say...you can scream," the old man says. His laughter echoes in the darkness. He and the others turn away, gathering the fallen comrade before carrying the boy to his mother.

A billion fireflies surge toward Eddings and Barker, hovering and dancing above their paralyzed bodies. Suddenly, their fluorescent green glow turns crimson in the sky. Once the child is carried beyond the torched car, their screaming begins.

Young Reesha and her mother listen to the muffled cries of horror from their cage. They cringe together when the door opens without warning. They weep as Shaquile, while being held aloft in the arms of yet another stranger, reaches for their trembling hands.

Like a drifting fog bank before the invading wind, they are suddenly gone. Vincent Sterne's pawns are fled into the great wide open. Among the growing piles of human bodies, his men are added to the discard in the name of national security.

CHAPTER 41
THE COWARD'S WAY

On April 11, 2001 at 9:00 p.m., the word 'Impeach!' repeats across the land and throughout the pressroom with phenomenal rabidity. It resounds from the walls and ceiling, passing readily from the gnashing teeth and barbed tongues of the highly opinionated masses.

Few, other than Vice President Graff and Vincent Sterne, who's also heavily sought by the media, have seen President Gore. Gore wisely shuns the congressional representatives that have flooded the phone lines with unanswered calls since the unauthorized disclosure.

Only the brave, the uninformed, the helpless, the belligerent, and the journalistic of mind voluntarily remain in Washington. It is a matter of not caring, fearing, or knowing that Captain Kyle Parker's and Lieutenant Markham's sweaty fingers control the fate of this nation's capital.

The story about a terrorist's plot to detonate dirty bombs in Washington blows up in their faces when it was debunked by a damaging inside leak. The falsehoods, first reported by Dan Rather, were stamped by exclamation of Peter McAllister's painful death on national television. It all serves to raise serious doubts in this troubled administration.

This press conference is not the dignified, subdued forum the people of this country are used to seeing. The news hounds are shouting, "Where exactly is Evan Parker?"

With great hostility and suspicion, they ask, "Is Evan Parker alive, or dead and buried already?"

Another news correspondent yells, "What about his pregnant wife and aging father?"

Someone else shouts, "Where are Evan Parker's sister, Dr. Talia Parker, who is presumed missing along with her two children?"

They want to know, "Was Vice President Eleanor Graff also party to decisions made after the census discrepancy came to light?"

Everyone asks, "Can all of this be the result of some kind of elaborate hoax?"

When President Gore walks into the hall, there is bedlam. With the shouting of collectively incoherent questions, the gathering of reporters now holds with the consistency of a lynch mob. They sweat and strain against each other as if they have been starved for weeks before being offered a load of government cheese. A wall of nervous Secret Service personnel are positioned before the podium to prevent this ardent mob of reporters from getting too close.

Michael Baldwin, Al Gore's press secretary, shouts into the microphone, "Ladies and gentlemen of the press, please come to order. President Gore will not speak until you have come to order so please be quiet, or you will be asked to leave."

Though her place is at her running mate's side, Vice President Eleanor Graff is not present, at Gore's request. She is anxious, watching the press conference from her office while keeping an ear to the sky. Vincent Sterne is seated next to her, glancing constantly at the locked door.

They have made their bed with the devil, and they will either survive with him or they will all burn together. Normally, they would be forced to fly aboard Air Force One where it is safer when there is a nuclear threat. At the very least, they would be tucked away down in the bunker beneath the White House. The refusal to stick to longstanding safety measures is simply baffling to the Chief of Staff and those charged with protecting the highest executives in government.

President Gore's slightly wrinkled clothing suggests that he's had no care to change or shave during the last few grueling days. His face is pale and bristly.

Al Gore is focused on something distant when he takes the podium. His eyes are the reflection of utter sadness and dejection. He has not slept since the beginning of his windswept fall from grace, for this is a fall far greater than that of Nixon and Clinton.

Far from the White House, Gore's wife watches her disheveled husband with great empathy. She fears for him because he will not allow her to share this enormous pain. She resents being sent away, but his position is firm. His family is to remain isolated. The first lady weeps and utters a prayer for her beloved husband, hoping that he finds some miraculous way to make things right. She alone appreciates what enormous pressure he must have suffered to take such drastic actions and to make such terrible mistakes, abandoning his true self. The man she knows him to be inside, would never have allowed such villainy to continue. But this grievous situation proves only that he is no saint.

President Gore clears his throat several times, fiddling with the microphones with shaking, sweaty hands. Upon these hands, he now sees much blood. His raspy voice cracks when he finally says, "Today, I am here to confess my sins to America."

Both Graff and Sterne grimace.

"I have undermined the trust bestowed upon me by the American people, without which, no one can function in the full-capacity of this office." Tears flow from his extremely red eyes as his lips quiver to their next stanza. "I took the easy way out of my dilemmas, allowing a terrible abuse of power to continue and escalate beyond my wildest imaginings. It is my deepest regret to admit to you all that I am guilty of the allegations made by Evan Parker, to whom I must now offer my humble apologies after allowing him to be vilified and hunted down like a common criminal. I am so very sorry, sir. Please know that I'm deeply ashamed of actions that grate against my true nature."

When President Gore's eyes droop, several reporters raise their hands for better leverage to launch their nasty questions. Michael Baldwin flings the warning finger of dismissal into the air and shakes his head as a strong indication that Gore is not finished, so they have to take their seats with nail-biting anticipation.

"I let down the African American race, who were very instrumental in my gaining of this office. You believed me to be a better man than I've now proven to be. In these last few days, I have come to realize that I was never worthy of the esteemed office that I hold. I must now resign my post as the President of the United States of America because I alone am responsible for my one terrible, terribly wrong decisions." Gore grows silent at the podium.

The questions rain down on him from those who demand answers in detail, but they will receive none.

"Where is CIA Director Vincent Sterne?" many shout.

"Did Vice President Graff have anything to do with this? Why isn't she here as a show of support, Mr. President? Is it because she disagrees with what you've done?"

They are ignored by Gore, but not by Baldwin. Two reporters are escorted from the room, but one of them has done Sterne's bidding by slipping in that nasty little insinuation.

"Did you give the order to have Peter McAllister assassinated on national television?" someone shouts on the way out. "What's happening to this country is all your fault. This is all your fault!"

A moment later, Gore continues. "I pray that Mr. Parker and his family members are unharmed. To you, Mr. Parker, and to all African Americans, I offer my deepest apology. I find that words are grossly inadequate to express how I feel about my hasty decisions. Is it any wonder that they are so angry? We've killed to keep their proud race down since the beginning of slavery and far beyond. I'm begging forgiveness by all Americans for my atrocious transgressions against an otherwise beautiful and spiritual people. I'm asking my wife and family to forgive me for what I've done to us. Finally, I ask that you will all someday forgive my cowardice."

While bursting into pitiful tears, Gore pulls a concealed weapon from his belt and places it to his head! This weapon, supposedly given in the spirit of self-preservation, is a recent gift from Vincent Sterne. The mob gasps as the secret service personnel lurch into action. Doom da-da boom!

Vice President Graff is shocked. Her unbelieving eyes have swollen to relay the full-intensity of this gruesome scene to her brain. She is caught up in a sudden wave of nausea. She feels so alone.

Vincent Sterne smiles. His lips curl for the first time in what seems like decades. As of yet, no one has answered the questions of Eleanor Graff's knowledge of Evan Parker's meeting with President Gore. No news station reported it. Nor had Parker's taped exposé shed light on the fact that Graff was just as deeply involved as her predecessor.

Sterne presses his chapped lips to her ears, holding the trembling woman firmly until he finishes whispering instructions that he will not repeat. He intends to disappear before Graff becomes the immediate center of attention, but the phone rings before he leaves. The Secretary of Defense is calling with urgent news.

At noon of April 12, 2001, Eleanor Graff sits behind the desk of power. At this time, she is the highest government executive of these United States of America, such as it is. Because of the ragged state of the union, members of Congress who could be found have chosen to forego the formalities. She is sworn into office in great haste, without an in-depth investigation into the census scandal.

The chair feels good, even though Al Gore had to blow his brains out for her to get here. Before she assumed her distinguished place in history, Graff had taken precious time to console Tipper Gore over the phone. In earnest, Graff's mind and heart have been elsewhere. It prompts amazement at her own lack of genuine compassion, though not completely repulsed by the fact. She figures that she is merely numb from the death of a close friend, that it will probably hit her later. However, when she does allow herself to examine her emotional response to Gore's suicide, she is forced to recognize that there's still unfinished business to tend. It's running free out there among the raging masses, a threat that still has to be contained and discredited.

Power corrupts only that which is corruptible. This is true of many who begin the political trek with genuinely good intent, before finding out that the machine will roll on with or without their cooperation. With power comes change, more often than not.

President Eleanor Graff gazes into the camera, fighting back the emotions for the world's benefit. Her eyes water, while her lips quiver with convincing sadness. If ambition and survival require that she become an actress upon this political stage, then she is going for an Academy Award.

"My esteemed citizens of the United States of America, it is with the greatest regret and sadness that I must report that President Al Gore has died. At 10:15 last night, President Gore was pronounced dead of a self-inflicted gunshot wound to the head. I cannot tell you his reason in regard to the census matter. I only know that he was a good friend, and someone whom I am proud to have known. I cannot explain his reasons for taking such drastic measures, except, maybe, that he was afraid of changes and subject to making very human mistakes."

She takes a moment to wipe away her tears, which aren't entirely insincere at this point because flashes of the events from the recent past are flooding her mind's eye.

"Again, I apologize for all of the needless pain and suffering that America has endured because of bad decisions made in haste and desperation. It is not my wish to minimize the seriousness of the situation when I say that it is now spilled milk. What's done is done. My job now is to right those wrongs for the sake of our nation. Because of my love for this country, I have accepted the duties and responsibilities of the President of the United States with a very heavy heart. I will serve the American people to the best of my abilities. Of this, you have my solemn oath."

President Graff takes another short passion break, weeping outwardly because she cannot appear to be hard and uncaring. At another time and in a different situation, showing such emotion would be highly inadvisable. But in light of all that transpires, she can ill-afford to appear as the unfeeling bitch in charge. Neither can she afford to show weakness by completely falling apart in the face of overwhelming adversity. President Graff has been coached well, but she always knew that she has to show a balanced response to the situation.

With her composure regained, she decrees, "As my first duty to the American public, I pledge to do all that is within my power to bring this great nation back to a state of unity. I was present during Mr. Evan Parker's initial meeting with President Gore as he revealed his very shocking findings. I was there when President Gore assured Mr. Parker of his personal safety. However, I swear to you by all that is righteous and true that I had no idea or inclination in any of the events that followed because I was attending other matters of state. To you, Mr. Parker, wherever you may be at this moment, I must say that I was rather emphatically informed that you were mentally ill. I was told that every shred of evidence you presented to us had been cooked up by your twisted imagination. I am sorry that I was so naive because I would have done everything in my power to put a stop to your defamation. This is a travesty, and the greatest tragedy in the history of our great nation. I now feel obligated to do everything I can to restore faith in the American system of government and justice."

She pauses again, clasping her hands together, gaining strength and momentum from the darkening well of her soul.

"First and foremost, I must admonish the people involved in rioting and other crimes of passion to stop this immediately! I am asking that you not continue to judge the entire American body by the actions of a few fingers. There has been more than enough undue violence and needless bloodshed. Mr. Parker, I realize that mere words are small by comparison to the recent events of your life because this betrayal was monstrously conceived and propagated. Please trust in me as I now extend my hands to you and yours so that you may come in from the cold. Come to Washington and verify all of your findings because I feel that only then will we begin the process of healing. I pray that you can hear me, and that you will accept my invitation. Sir, you have my word that you will be safe as you walk up the steps of the Capital Building where I will meet with you personally. I have chosen the Capital Building because we must address these matters with the utmost expediency. I'm requesting that the Congress be convened for an emergency session to that end. We must quickly find a way to deal with this revelation and the subsequent problems we now face. I am referring to a future of new beginnings and the hope that we will realize only in togetherness."

Graff extends her hands, displaying her open palms like the hooves of the Trojan Horse.

"Call me at the number at the bottom of the screen. I will then see to it that you are allowed to speak to your brother, Captain Kyle Parker, in an effort to assure that he knows that you are unharmed so that he may relent his threat to harm the nation he has sworn to protect. If we are to convene the National Congress here in Washington, we must secure their safety. Also, I will provide your safe transport to the capital. On the other hand, if you wish, no one needs to know how you may choose to arrive. Please come. Let us, hand-in-hand, put an end to the suffering and pain. It is time to let the healing begin but you and I must lead by example. May God bless and keep you safe. Thank you."

The presidential seal replaces Graff's red eyes. Somewhere out there, amidst the chaos, Vincent Sterne smiles and says, "Good girl."

The seismographic readings go off the scales. Black ink mars the graph paper to its outer edges. Pitches and valleys are coming together as a cryptic message to those who understand that this is indeed the big one. Terrified seismologists pray to the unknown God as the San Andreas Fault buckles and heaves without warning to the people out there.

Pipelines are obliterated. Natural gas lines are erupting beneath the streets of San Fernando to Los Angeles. Large-scale explosions undermine quaking buildings and highways as massive pillars of rock and ore pierce the earth, reaching for the sky.

When pristine buildings topple to the ground, glass explodes outward to seek out whatever life there is to extinguish. Nearly one-hundred miles becomes the epicenter, a magnitude never before experienced by the west coast. The land seizes and yawns, tearing itself from the continental United States with the dramatic shift of the tectonic plates. Los Angeles, what doesn't fall victim to the Pacific Ocean, becomes an island—Angel Island. The Isle of Angels.

At this very moment, Kinzana emerges from his prayer in the garden. His entire being shivers as he whispers, "It is time we walk through this valley of death."

He stumbles away from the mighty oak tree in the midday heat, tired and drained. He's sweated so profusely in the last forty-eight hours of fasting that a considerable weight loss is evident. Nevertheless, he is still the strongest man on earth. The drums have seen to it, and they are yet to cease their dark rhythm. Boom da-da doom, boom da-da doom, boom da-da doom, da-da doom, da-da doom!

CHAPTER 42
THE VALLEY OF DEATH

For the first time in five months, Evan and Melissa Parker make love. Though his heavily bandaged ribs scream in their traces, there is no thought of frailty. Such worries are displaced by the need for intimacy, the release of powerful emotions that are multiplied by the recent activities of the hungry inner animal. Their love is hot and passionate, and every ounce is drawn from the other. Rest comes only after their sexual needs are sated; five months' worth of boiling lust, finally unchained. It is something powerful.

While resting comfortably in one another's arms, they dream together, smiling in unison at the antics of Alana and Sonshal. If this dream holds any measure of the future, they will be such sweet children with curly, jet-black hair. Their dimpled smiles warm their parents' hearts, and their eyes dance with a fire that could brighten the most desolate of landscapes. For them both, it is a precious gift.

While Kinzana stands quietly in the doorway, his white eyes slowly descend so that he looks down upon them with both joy and sadness.

Evan and Melissa soon awaken to the whisperings of Insanyanga, which become a part of their fading dream. Her voice flows to them like the scent of sweet honeysuckle on the faintest slip of a spring breeze. It is time to rise. They will share a festive breakfast and say goodbye.

When Evan Parker watches the compelling speech of the new president, he is moved to tears. Except for Kinzana, the other fugitives also show strong emotions.

Kinzana and Evan are going to travel back to Washington in the black truck, which has been fitted with a different U.S. Government transponder. This particular signal is only relegated to non-sensitive material. So, essentially, the means of finding these fugitives has always been within the reach of their deadly pursuers.

They will be accompanied only by the drivers and four painted bodyguards. Kinzana has convinced the others that they shouldn't put all of their eggs in one basket, if Eleanor Graff's impassioned plea for peace and justice is a mere ploy. Evan Parker is strongly advised not to use the number to contact his brother because they will surely trace the call. He finally agrees, knowing his brother will do nothing until he is certain of their safety.

With the noonday meal eaten, Kinzana and Evan now stand on bamboo mats in the center of the garden. The drums are interrupted as the two men stand naked and uninhibited for a ritualistic bathing. Four painted women, who are only wearing scant G-strings to cover their sex, bathe them from head to toe.

Melissa sits next to Insanyanga and watches with great pride in her man. With no hint of jealousy or insecurity, both women hold their heads high while their faithful husbands are fawned over by younger, firmer bodies.

Evan and Kinzana are dried with ostrich feathers and dressed with clothing of their own choosing. For Evan Parker, a pair of black slacks, a modest tie and a white shirt are sufficiently comfortable.

Kinzana adorns a long, white robe with a startlingly realistic image of a male lion embossed on the front. This king of beasts' gaze is intensely penetrating. Its eerie breath is subtly hidden within Kinzana's fluent movement, making it seem almost alive and about to pounce.

Kinzana walks away from the others to contemplate the smoldering fire at the center of the garden. Soon joined by his wife, he considers the Death Mask, which still rests intact with feathers and all amid the smoldering ashes. This concerns him greatly, but only Insanyanga would understand his reasons for distress. The future is still in the hands of man.

A group of fearsome warriors wearing loincloths and plumed headdresses are assembling around the trailer of the truck.

Eleanor Graff has extended the hand of peace and friendship. It is strongly believed that only Evan Parker's presence in Washington will be medicine enough to quell the violence in the streets.

Although the rioting Black nation doesn't know him for stirring speeches that address racial inequality, they are killing in his name and that of Cecil Bridges. Parker has never ridden in a parade or waved to his adoring public, but they have risen to smite those who sought to turn them against one of their own as a means of conquer. Unfortunately—most unfortunately—the innocent are suffering as well as the guilty. It seems Evan's duty to ask that his people bury the crimson hatchet, putting an end to this virulent aggression.

As they stand in the doorway of the trailer, those fearsome warriors begin to chant something ominous, pounding their spears against their shields and stomping their sandaled feet in unison.

Abatu Abuutu and his escaped brother, Alunga Abuutu, enter the center of the semicircle. Because he is weak, Abatu holds Alunga about the waistline so that he may proudly stand among the others. Now, Nimjara Kinzara and Princess Tuloni follow.

Suddenly, blaring horns shatter the quiet as two cars skid to a dust-raising stop. Immediately, the warriors take defensive stances, prepared to fight to the death. From the cloud of dust, the voices of excited children cry, "Aunt Melissa!"

Reesha comes through the haze, running into Melissa's arms. Meanwhile, under his own power, young Shaquile limps into view with a smile. Moments later, their mother comes into view with the assistance of crutches. One of her legs is carefully splinted, but she needs access to a doctor and an x-ray machine to have it reset and properly immobilized. It will be no problem. Her great pain is obvious, so someone produces a wooden wheelchair and helps her to sit.

Talia Parker looks drained and skittish, despite having been rescued. Her fear only begins to subside when her brother and sister-in-law hurry over to embrace. Jarvis Parker falls to his knees before the daughter he feared lost. They are all swept away in a moment of overwhelming relief and joy which lasts not long enough.

The twins hug their Uncle Evan with enthusiasm. Together, in a very grownup gesture, they wipe the tears from Evan's strong cheeks. Their smiles cause his eyes to water again.

Melissa and Jarvis will have to explain the rest of the drama to Talia Parker because Evan rejoins Kinzana at the trailer.

Szinja Szin slowly enters the semicircle, taking his place at the forefront. His silver hair is matted and his skin is pale, for he has expended great energy in saving Talia's son. Kinzana's eyes meet with Szinja Szin's as he smiles upon him. They reach for each other's shoulders, sharing no words, but it would seem much is said as they place their foreheads together.

The reunited five of the inner circle look reverently at Evan Parker and Kaleem Kinzana as they now stand in the doorway. As they slowly raise their fists, the warriors begin to shout, "Juju. Juju! He is the lion, master of this black tide. Juju. Juju. He is the blood which flows through us all!"

⌐╫ ╫⌐

Geddon Air Base.

President Graff is holding a conference call with Secretary of Defense Slater, General Austin, General Smith, and Colonel Terrell. These anxious men are seated around the conference table in General Austin's office, participating in a White House call with very grim attitudes. They choose to appear hopeful for Graff's sake.

"Just tell me what the hell is happening out there," President Eleanor Graff demands.

"Well, Madam President, we believe that we've formulated a plan to seize control of the missile installation," Slater says. "I will allow Colonel Terrell to explain it in detail."

He glances at his seniors and clears his throat. "Colonel Terrell here, Madam President. Ma'am, we feel that this is the only way to extract the officers from the command capsule, but there is the inherent danger that they will launch those missiles if we're detected."

"Then it sounds risky, Colonel. Go on."

"It's the only way, since you insist that we reclaim the facility instead of waiting to hear from Captain Parker's brother," Colonel Terrell states, feeling that he has to interject the latter choice once more. The others feel the same way, but no one expected Colonel Terrell to actually say what they were all thinking. They are happy that this conference call is audible only.

Choosing to ignore his statement, Graff asks, "What's your plan, Colonel?"

"We have been in the midst of thunder squalls all day, Madam President. They come and go, but the weather is bound to change its pattern soon. We will have a small window of opportunity when the next front moves through, which should be shortly, according to Weather Control."

"Yes. Yes, please get on with it," Graff says impatiently. "And, gentlemen, I know that this must be quite a gender shock for you all so why don't we just dispense with all the formalities and pretend like we're all just a bunch of good old boys?"

Colonel Terrell looks at General Austin with his lips wrinkling at the right corner. These are trying times for them all, but Austin's eyes admonish Terrell to keep his opinions in check like a good soldier.

"We plan to knock out a certain grid of the command capsule's above ground laser defense system. It'll show up as a simple malfunction due to the severe weather. We will be tapped into the surveillance system, feeding poor visibility footage of storm activity into a constant loop. If they are watching television, we will stream severe weather warnings for the immediate area to add authenticity. Now, here's where the tricky part comes in. Most missile installations have a guard station at the underground entrance. This installation, however, has been completely automated with highly sophisticated sensors and DEWs, which stands for Directed Energy Weapons. This facility was essentially bored out of solid rock, so there is no easy way inside. We can't risk sending anyone through the missile silos themselves because of the obvious dangers. It would also be quite impossible to do so without warning Captain Parker because the hardened silos are lined with a sensor net."

"So far, this doesn't look very encouraging," President Graff says with growing hostility.

"However, there's a weak spot, if it can be called that, which is close enough to the elevator's shaft to get at. During the next break in the weather, we intend to target this area with a mobile DEW, an ETM-11 Laser cannon. Once we're inside, great care must be taken to avoid setting off the sensors. It can be done, however."

After explaining the basic components of their plan, Colonel Terrell looks at General Austin. He is hoping that one of the others will take up the cross of conclusion by stating the most bitter detail of the briefing. There are no volunteers, so General Austin flicks a finger that urges the Colonel on.

"As I'm sure you are aware, once we're inside, Captain Parker and Lieutenant Markham will have to be put down. I'm afraid there's no alternative to that end if you insist that we proceed, Madam President. That's our plan."

"So if they don't launch when you knock out the laser defense systems, then the chance of you getting inside undetected is pretty fair?" President Graff surmises.

"It is, Madam President," Secretary of Defense Slater answers.

"Well, I suppose it's worth the risk. Thank you for the enlightenment, Colonel. I'm sure that your men will do just fine."

"The special task force has been flown in and briefed. The ETM-11 Laser, also called the E-11, has been prepped at White Sands. It should arrive soon," General Austin says.

"Just make it happen, General Austin. Get those maniacs' fingers off of the switch by any means necessary. Your plan had better work because I will be sitting on the hot seat here. Speaking of which, there's one more thing. I'm sure that you must have some idea of how critical our timing is, so while I'm tending the affairs of state, I'd like you gentlemen to liaise with Vincent Sterne. And I mean every goddamn move you make! Is that clear? There's a lot more to this entire mess than you men may realize. Vincent Sterne, may God bless his poor, misguided soul, was only acting in the best interest of national security, and with President Gore's initiatives. Therefore, he has just as much at stake here as any of us. Sterne will keep me abreast of the situation with your frequent reports. If you do as I ask without question, gentlemen, we may be able to salvage this nation. Good-bye and good luck." The connection is severed.

No one likes the idea of reporting their activities to Vincent Sterne, but they have little choice to do otherwise. To offend the newest power in the Oval Office would surely be to risk whatever remains of their futures.

As long as Sterne isn't here to interfere or breathe down their necks, it makes no real difference. Kyle Parker and Alicia Markham have to be killed, regardless. That alone insures that they will not launch their nuclear ordinance, so extreme force is warranted.

Even the most powerful tranquilizers, which has already been discussed and dismissed, have been known to fail where madness or other chemical substances reign in the body and mind.

Before anything is done, however, they'll make one final attempt to contact Carolyn Murray, the woman who first broke the story that sent this nation into a tailspin. They hope to convince her to reveal the whereabouts of Evan and Jarvis Parker, or to get a message to them at the very least.

She is not compliant because she does not know.

The F-15 and F-17A fighter jets take to the air from Langley Air Base to east of the Rockies, forming a barrier in the sky. These brave pilots have been sent on a suicidal mission in their attempt to shoot down the missiles if Parker manages to launch.

At twenty thousand feet, the cloud cover is heavy, blanketing the falling sun. There will be very little chance to intercept the missiles if they are allowed to reach the clouds. Dead men and women fly through the air, circling and refueling in midair. Infinite fear pulses their feverish temples.

Kyle and Alicia are together on the cot nearest to the control panel. They hold one another while exchanging spur-of-the-moment marital vows. Neither notices the slight flicker of surveillance monitors when the feedback of the stormy footage is introduced.

The lovers accept that they will face court-martials once this thing is finally over. They know that they may have to spend the remainder of their lives behind bars, never to see each other again.

In light of all that's happened, they can only cling to the small hope that the American people might be made to understand their motives. Freedom, after what could only be considered as an act of high treason, remains the remotest chance for them. If that is not to be the case, they will always be married in their hearts. They are bound together in mind and spirit, vowing to never love another soul.

Their second alternative involves a double suicide, but neither is cowardly. Although they are not the most religious couple in the world, they feel without doubt that suicide is an unacceptable sin that will damn their souls. Their path has been democratically chosen, knowing the seriousness of their actions long before the threat was made or the steps taken to assure the ability to carry them out.

Kyle and Alicia are given hope when a news report claims that Evan Parker, who opts to make his way to Washington incognito, has accepted Eleanor Graff's invitation. As a safety precaution, a third party far to the west, made contact with Evan Parker's social security number and birthdate in hand. No one knows how Parker will arrive at the nation's capital. They only know that he's on the way, and is expected to admonish fellow African Americans to end the violence.

Eleanor Graff publicly denounces what she considers to be the illegal and immoral internment of Blacks, promising that it will be discontinued as soon as the killing and burning ends. As any shrewd politician would, she explains that these people are not prisoners but American citizens under the protection of the United States Military. Keeping them segregated is for their own protection.

Kyle and Alicia look upward as the earth rumbles above them. Two Apache helicopters have zeroed in on the defense grid's concealed relay. Heavy guns knock out a relay junction, nullifying the deadly laser cannons that would activate upon detection of any ground-based assault.

No longer churned by the spinning rotors, the dust-ridden precipitation soon settles. Colonel Terrell remembers to breathe, then uses the radio to tell the leader of Tiger-3 to move in.

Caterpillars are brought in to quickly haul tons of dirt away. They alternate, gouging at the earth until they come to stone. Their final act is to smooth a path for the truck that carries the laser, which is affixed to a retractable arm. After the transport vehicle safely arrives at the rock face, the four man unit moves with swift efficiency.

The ETM-11 Laser is lowered by the mechanical arm and locked into position about four yards from the target area. When it is only partially powered, the squad places goggles over their eyes to watch the lime-green beam eat through hardened concrete and then the solid rock to the shaft. This will take some time.

Once through the rock, Colonel Joseph McGruder barks orders at his men, who pry smoking stone wedges away to reveal the black metal below.

The blueprints are consulted and the ETM-11 is repositioned so it can go to work on the thick metal wall of the elevator shaft. Before doing so, Joiner tap-welds two horseshoe shaped pieces of iron to the shaft. As the laser cuts along Joiner's chalk outline, the cannon throbs. It's creating an energy field that causes their skin to tingle and hair to stand on end.

McGruder immediately decides that he can't risk using the cannon beyond the exterior of the shaft's wall because of its pulsating hum. Therefore, the incision will only have to be two feet wide and four feet high to allow them access in the least amount of time.

Once the weapon's work is done, heavy packing grease is pumped into the incision to quiet the friction. Now, a steel cable is run through the loops to yank the cutaway free with a winch.

Colonel McGruder uses the time to double-check the working conditions of three heavy-duty chain foils.

⊨⊣ ⊢⊨

Highway 17 North.

Evan and Kinzana are watching the news, appalled by the helicopter's footage that shows hundreds of burnt bodies strewn across the ground in some obscure town in southern Mississippi.

They also witness the combined strength of enraged Black rioters ripping away steel bars of a New York pawn and gun shop where weapons and ammunition are passed through smashed windows as if they are merely toys.

They see people shot dead in cold blood, while buildings burn unchecked. However, the most heartrending of these images are of abandoned children along the roadside, desperately clinging to Mr. Bear or Barbie for comfort. Their faces and clothing are filthy and torn. The tracks of their tears are easily traced down their soiled cheeks.

Many of those frightened children weep at the side of their dead parents, waiting for them to wake up and take them to their favorite fast-food restaurant for something to eat. Some are filmed while tugging at limp arms and hands that used to hug them or patted them on the head in warm, proud moments. During such instances, these children will even settle for a spanking.

Some of them stare blankly into the cameras with eyes that seem totally devoid of emotions or understanding. They are lost, and terribly alone. Some are afraid beyond physical conveyance after being pile-driven into shock. Every crimson brushstroke of this human drama seems to sink deeper into the abysmal as the bloody tide surges. The death toll has risen to an estimated twelve million. Twelve million people. Black, White, and all things between are now dead.

Chicago.

There is a heated argument in the hallway, but none of the terrified hostages will move to listen at the door because they are afraid for their lives. The queen of talk show hosts trembles in a far corner with close friends. Together, they pray for God's mercy and prepare to die, as they have been told they will. Two gunshots ring out, causing all eighteen people in the studio to shriek or shudder. The locked door slides open to give their murderers entrance.

Blue Eyes, which is what the hostages have begun to call the tall blonde in desperate whispers, walks casually across the room with a warm weapon in his hand. His steely gaze is affixed on the cringing woman in the corner. She's all alone now, suddenly abandoned by those who huddled with her only moments before.

Her breath stops with the overpowering odor of freshly discharged gunpowder. A new surge of sweat saturates her blue, silk blouse as her eyes slowly crawl up the long creased legs of his dark gray slacks to the gun. In a final gesture of prideful defiance, she forces herself to look her killer in the eyes, suspecting that she is indeed about to die.

Upon further inspection of this man, if what she sees can be trusted, it would seem that Blue Eyes is saddened. Though it is not a certainty, it's the first real indication of emotion he's shown since his men prevented the staff from willfully breaking a strict federal statute.

He stands over the woman with his weapon tapping at his side, looking down at her newly formed stream of tears. In this moment, there are no heroes willing to die for her because her zeal has delivered them all into this deadly situation.

She has provided her television audience with mammoth portions of heart-wrenching stories of human drama. She has also doled out helpings of heartwarming showcases of reunited lovers and broken families. She often surprised her viewers with fun-time forums. On occasion, she exposed the criminal activities of common and some not-so-common people, and she has generously given millions away.

Unwilling to concede her fate, ratings had finally begun to slip over the last seasons of broadcast, the probable result of talk and reality show overkill, but Evan Parker's exposé was just the ticket to revive her slumping television career. That, however, wasn't the sole reason for Oprah Winfrey's pursuit of the tabooed subject. To break it would surely have catapulted her into the history books, not only as the host of a show that has striven on human disparagement, but as a visionary who'd thrown herself from the cliff's edge to bring the truth to those who needed to know it.

Oprah Winfrey's passionate coercion is suddenly lost on those once faithful co-workers and staff members who look at her from across the room, waiting for her death to signify the eventuality of their own. Lost somewhere between terror, anger, and pity, they wait for the sound of death to ring out once again.

In the depths of silence, she glances about and knows that she's truly alone. No one will speak for her, so she cries, "Go ahead. Just get it over with, but please spare them. These people have families and they were just doing their jobs. It's all my fault, so just get it over with. I hope God damns you to hell!"

Blue Eyes raises his weapon with tears streaming down his bold cheeks. She cringes, shutting her eyes to pray in silence. Her heart rate climbs to a nearly fatal rhythm. Instead of pulling the trigger, he smiles somewhat, turning the weapon around to give her.

The agent has killed one of his own to save these people. Blind faith in Vincent Sterne's method has never been stronger than his conscience. The order of their deaths had gone far beyond the often obscured realms of his job description.

Agent Cross helps her to her feet. After he is sure that he won't be shot with the gun, he surrenders it and himself freely. He and the other unit members offer their sincerest apologies to the hostages after two days of unlawful detention that only lasted as long because of Agent Cross's moral dilemma.

Moments later, the bedraggled and disheveled Oprah Winfrey forces a teary smile from her quivering lips. She tells the world what has taken place at her studio, of what nearly became of them all. She thanks God for Agent Cross having been a man of some integrity, turning his foul act of unwarranted aggression into one of instant heroism.

Oprah Winfrey's storied reign will continue because she's a true believer in the redemptive qualities of mankind. She will go on helping and healing the broken fences of society because the black tide phenomenon will give birth to an entirely new world of discussion.

CHAPTER 43
TEN-THOUSAND DESERT SUNS

Z iggy Marley, the son of the legendary Bob Marley, pledges that his newly acquired Jamaican Jamz radio station will play the original version of his father's song "Get Up Stand Up" for twenty-four hours, with few commercial interventions. Jamaican dignitaries are pleading with Marley not to follow through with his pledge because they fear it will be viewed by the American ally as an incitement to escalate the violence. Yet, young Marley is resolute. He laughs at their assumptions.

For twenty-four hours, the words, *'Get up. Stand up. Fight for all your rights'*, rings out across the turbulent, blue waters. The song calls to something powerful in the belly of the black uprising, feeding a fire that is yet to be doused by any soothing words or actions.

"Don't give up the fight. Don't give up the fight. GET UP—STAND UP!" is driven into the air. The words resurrect a fearsome fire that was nearly bred away by welfare pigeonholes and stored away in open graves of a once majestic race's self-hatred and self-destruction.

So softly stated are those words, but they take on new meaning many generations beyond the song's original conception. So softly stated are they that the meaning surpasses the clichés of militant recriminations. Bob Marley's wailing lyrics hold power over all those who hear and feel its prophetically ominous presence. Deeper still, its subtle drums are still drums—calling... calling to the thing in the basement.

⟨⟩

There is a brightness about this moment which seems so out of place in the late night hour as Evan Parker slowly ascends the steps. He is sweating from every pore. Someone stands at the top. Her bleeding hands are outstretched in a greeting, while her labored smile prompts those cheating, blue eyes to squint painfully. Evan Parker's heartbeat grows louder with each step. A warm wind blows garbage about his reluctant feet while bringing a crescendo of those phantom drums from some distant horizon.

There is subtle movement, so he looks to the left to face a stranger that watches him. There are splotches of red, blue, yellow and green on his clothing and skin. Though dressed as a soldier, his camouflaged uniform and skin boasts the colors of rainbows, and Evan shudders at the sight of this vaguely familiar creature. The soldier's black eyes reflect no light as he shouts profanity at Evan. And then, he...

The truck swerves, barely missing the wounded woman standing in the middle of the highway, staring into a ditch. She doesn't seem to realize that she came within mere inches of joining whatever or whomever lies dead in the gutter.

When Evan Parker awakens from the disturbing dream, Kinzana's eyes are fixed on him. Several moments will pass before either man speaks. After watching frame after frame of human grief and despair, Evan seeks answers. He will find, however, no significant measure of comfort therein.

"This is so awful, so hideous, I cannot find adequate words to express how I feel."

Although they are isolated in the trailer of the speeding truck, its walls are insufficient barriers when the tires slow down just enough to allow the sounds of human slaughter to permeate their moving sanctuary.

The northbound lanes are littered with debris, but mostly clear of moving traffic. Few want to travel in that direction.

"Such images are made to break the heart, but nothing that now lies before our eyes is unique or individual," Kinzana says. "This kind of violence has been present throughout the annals of time. That is before and during human time. But on this day, is it not the underdog that bites, rips and tears the flesh of the oppressor? It is a battle that all of humanity suffers, but this time, he fights a war that he is destined to win."

Evan looks at Kinzana in disbelief. "Win? You think this is about winning or losing. Have you absolutely no compassion for the people who are dying and suffering in the streets of America?"

Kinzana regards Evan very carefully. He absorbs a deep breath before saying, "I am not without feelings, my young friend. I have experienced such enormous pain at the hands of mankind that it would take more than an entire lifetime to convey unto you. I feel the anguish of every wasted acreage of land that burns in the South American and African rain forests—fertile land which burns so that resorts can be built for the enjoyment of the idle rich. I feel the agonizing death of the fish, whose gills are so saturated with filth and toxins they cannot breathe. Birds that cannot fly because their God-given wings are weighed down by spilled oil. Every time an invisible man tinkers in our native land by instigating wars between peaceful tribes, and each time a village falls prey to deadly covert medical experiments, I weep! Oh yes, Evan. I am very connected to this world and its inhabitants, those who create their own means of destruction and degradation each and every passing day. If you were to take the sum of man's inhumanity toward other men from the beginning of human time, you would see what is taking place all around us as nothing by comparison. But for man to witness and to feel it all at once, and in this dreadful manner, will insure that he stands up to take note of his neglected responsibilities. Our Father is weary with his wayward children, Evan Parker. You must see that some of our brothers have gone much too far in their willful ways. Thusly, God demands a parcel of blood and will accept nothing less. I know this because he has spoken these very words as I pled and begged for a different path. He spoke these words to me, directly, as I asked that he take this bitter cup from my trembling hands. However, I failed to curve his ire. Just as his prophetic words came from my own lips days ago, he repeated the same to my heart. It is either this, or the total annihilation of all mankind."

"This is insane," Evan says.

Kinzana's voice and eyes grow deeper and darker when he proclaims, "And there is nothing to do about what God commands except obedience. Take heart, my friend, Damballah's cup is nearly full and his thirst is nearly quenched. For this, I am so very thankful. Please do not view me as a heartless, unfeeling automaton. I have found no measures of joy in this, other than the fact that I was able to save your family from those who truly enjoy killing the innocent."

Evan wrings his hands and looks away. "But all of this is happening because of me. I can't help wondering if I did the right thing. Is it really worth it all?"

"Take not the burden that you've already borne to multiply it with needless guilt, my son. I am just as responsible, if not more, in this great and terrible thing. You are the symbol to which future generations will come to admire as a man of true conviction. I speak of a conviction that has not been abandoned in the presence of your personal threat. Damballah himself decrees that the world must see and feel to truly learn because lessons of mere words and ideology have been proven to have very short-lived meaning. In this particular moment of darkness, the tide surges to change the shorelines.

It will be tangible evidence, which must be forever remembered. And remembered by all. The whole of mankind will not be so quick to forget what has happened here. Change will be effected the world over, for it appears that our species must constantly peer into the maw of darkness until the light of day can be truly experienced. At the end of a perilous winter, the warmth of the sun must be felt as well as seen, which are both matters of man's faith and faithfulness. It is regrettable, but nonetheless true. Mankind will remember long after the tears have dried on the faces of his children or the burial of a multitude, for the Angel of Death will leave his shadow upon the land for all the world to see and repent. His ominous shadow will transcend the oceans, marking each continent with distinctive talismans of impending doom. Many will die abroad, but because of this, many more will live. Believe me, Evan, if humankind is to continue upon the earth, these are very necessary things. Such is true if only for the fact that Damballah wills it so. And as always, his superior will shall be done."

Kinzana opens an ageless bottle of cognac and pours for two. For a split second, Evan thinks he hears a voice escape the bottle as the cork is removed, which is simply madness. His eyes wonder to the four circular scabs that have formed over the wounds of Kinzana's forehead and cheeks.

"I am sorry for having doubts, Kinzana. It's just that, unlike yourself, I cannot see what the future holds. I keep trying to imagine, but I haven't a clue. It makes me afraid for myself and for my family. For all that is happening, I feel such responsibility."

Kinzana gives Evan a glass. He smiles and says, "You are blameless in all that has transpired, and in all that is yet to manifest."

"Are you sure about that?"

"I'm as sure as I am that the sun shall only rise on the morrow following three days of total and inexplicable darkness, as if God has extinguished the sun. I'm as sure as I am that somewhere, tonight, a child shall not be born and many will perish in their mother's wombs. All that I have said unto you is a certainty, but I shall fear nothing, for I am now doubtless wherein my own life or death lies. I also know what defines true hell for the soul of a disobedient servant, for I am liquid, Evan, and I am sand. You and I are connected unto the highest power, my son. You must continue to have faith."

Silence falls between them as they enter North Carolina, heading north on I-95. Nelson Mandela tearfully puts the sins of the American Government into prospective. From Johannesburg, he now witnesses the things his own countrymen would have done if F. W. de Klerk had not succumb to the wailing drums—what might have happened had de Klerk not relented the transgressions of his all-White government against the natural citizens of South Africa. The carnage that has overtaken the American shores surely would have been the result in his native land if some acceptable measure of change had not finally come to the land of apartheid. They were all overwhelmed by Kinzana's influences, which makes them, in a way, rational men. The American, however, is a different sort.

⊯ ⊯

Suitland, Maryland.

Valerie McAllister sleeps, uneasily, in her hospital bed, squinting and moaning while her head tosses to-and-fro on her sweat-soaked pillow. Her husband is suffering in her dreams.

"Oh, Peter," she moans. "Oh, baby."

Her door slides open for a fraction of a second as a sleek, dark figure slips into the shadows.

A woman dressed in black stands over Valerie's bed, watching for a moment before removing a small knife from her sash. Then she takes a small, thick leaf from her pocket and places it on the pillow. The stranger places a hand over Valerie McAllister's mouth to prevent her from crying out, which she is sure to attempt.

Valerie wakes, struggling to scream. However, she stops when a keen blade glistens in the sparse light.

The dark woman smiles at Valerie as she places the leaf to her lips. Valerie does not understand what this intruder wants until she places it to her own lips and pretends to eat it. She offers the pungent leaf to Valerie again, forcing it between her trembling lips to make sure she chews and swallows. Valerie obeys out of fear. The woman gives her a glass of water to wash it down.

Once Valerie McAllister swallows the bitter leaf, the woman touches her swollen stomach, causing the pregnant woman to protest. Though silently stated, it is a protest nonetheless.

The stranger brandishes the knife and Valerie ceases all movement. The woman caresses her swollen stomach again and whispers, "You must trust me, wise mother, for I was sent to rescue this ailing child and you. Take it." Now, she offers Valerie the knife to show that she means no harm to the child that doctors fear will be lost.

The woman begins to convulse while speaking in a language Valerie McAllister has never heard. As she watches those blazing eyes in the dim light of the window, she thinks about plunging the knife into the intruder's throat. She cannot, realizing that the pain is going away.

This person is a frightful sight as her eyes roll back until the whites are visible. Her feverish touch causes Valerie's skin to tingle.

"Fear not, wise mother, for your seed will be brought forth unto the light with life and limb intact. There shall be no children born alive unto this barren world until you and the other blessed one have brought them forth from thy wombs to suckle at your rounded teats. They shall share the sweet milk of life together for all to see, for they shall be firstborn among us."

The woman backs away with no further explanation and leaves. Valerie holds herself and weeps until two African American orderlies come in and roll her away because she has to leave this place. No one notices in the mayhem. No one cares, the hospital is being evacuated.

⟞⟝ ⟞⟝

Washington, District of Columbia.

Even with all that has transpired, nearly 50,000 people are crowding the courtyard of the Capitol Building. Though pensive, and somewhat polarized, they are daring no attempts to cross the line of men who protect its steps. National Guardsmen and regular army personnel are deployed to fend off any onslaught the crazies might launch at any given moment. Armed soldiers line the steps on both sides up to the doors, while others are firmly rooted before the bottom steps with their weapons at the ready. Tanks and armored personnel carriers line the streets, while military and government aircraft rule the immediate sky.

Inside, President Graff wrestles with mounting anticipation, hoping that the entire situation will just go away. Meanwhile, Vincent Sterne presses his headset to listen to what General Bradford Smith has to report from Angel Mountain.

While Persons and Macklin cut through the two-foot thick metal, Joiner tap welds his horseshoes into place. He places a heavy bar on the elevator tracks, about four-feet above the cutout. The chain foil is secured in the center of the bar. Packing grease melts from the jagged metal surface, filling every crevasse so that little friction hinders its removal.

Colonel McGruder reports that they are nearly through the first horizontal barricade, thirty-yards down into the shaft. Joiner tightens the slack in the chains to keep the circular cutout from falling to the next level. The noise would surely warn the renegade officers, so these are very necessary steps.

When the incision is complete, Joiner flips the directional mechanism on the chain foil to the down position. He pumps the crank to allow the circular section of metal to slide down slowly, making the opening for them to descend further.

⊨⊨

African Village. Beaufort, South Carolina.

Melissa Parker sits next to Jarvis while she leans back into the arms of Evan's godmother.

Insanyanga is rocking her back and forth, humming as if she is trying to quiet a sleepy child.

They are watching as things unfold.

Melissa suspends her reading to listen to the words of a weeping Desmond Tutu, who recants the issue of White oppression of Blacks in United States history. Being the man of the cloth that he is, Tutu appeals to African Americans to put an end to the bloodshed so that something positive can be achieved in the name of God and humanity. Tutu's ears are deaf to the pounding crescendo, but his eyes and heart are open to the future. He will not be punished as was Celia Brown. He is not taking money to say these words.

Looking down at the abridged journal, Insanyanga says to Melissa, "Come, child, it is time that I show you all of them." They leave the others without explanation.

⊨⊨

Spain.

Far across the Atlantic, the earth begins to yawn. Screaming people are running away from the extended wedding reception of Juan Carlos and his new bride, Regina.

The festive occasion is meant to last well into the hours of the next morning, but Juan's superstitious grandmother has warned him of something terrible in the air because their champion bulls have been restless all day. For no apparent reason, many have stampeded the electrified fencing. They were goring each other with their horns and costing the family a small fortune, so they had to be separated and the horns capped.

From the stately hills surrounding the Carlos ranch and farms, comes the howl of wolves. Their cries are haunting reverberations. It sounds as if they have gone mad with pain, and their plea to God is soon joined by their domesticated cousins.

Before the wedding ceremony, Juan's grandmother told him that these are very bad omens. Juan considered the interpretation to be jaded by her dislike for his bride-to-be, whose motives his grandmother does not trust.

With that conversation long past them, while lying in her ancient bed, the old woman prays furiously. She clings to her rosary beads as if they are the keys to heaven when the ground cracks open and allows lava to flow from its jagged seams.

Where they did not exist before, volcanic eruptions heave smoldering ash high into the air to set the quaking land on fire. The fires do not last, however, because the entire Spanish peninsula falls victim to an angry ocean that easily swallows over thirty-million people without pity!

Africa now stands alone. Her northernmost shores are dwarfed beneath the violent tidal surges that follow the making of a Spanish void. The Mediterranean Sea rises with the tsunami of the Atlantic Ocean, swelling to drown Israel and Northwestern Saudi Arabia in its marriage with the Red Sea. Many die and many more suffered under what they can only explain as God's wrath for centuries of unsolicited bloodshed.

Later, as the raging waters subside, airplane pilots spot something black on the battered North Moroccan coast near the

Algerian border. It glistens as they pass overhead and circle lower for a better look.

They first think it to be a whale beached by the tidal waves. As they lose altitude, it looks like some sort of black stone. From the sky, it looks to be a black diamond, roughly shaped like a slice of pie. It fills them with inexplicable terror. This is the first of three to leave its hiding place. Only the first of three. Three of seven.

I-95. Virginia.

Darkness fell hours ago. Now, Evan ventures a question. "Kinzana, can you tell me what will happen when we reach Washington?"

"We will change history, Evan. Whatever happens, good or bad, will force everyone upon the face of the earth to look deeply into their own hearts. Many will cringe from the evil that they may see there."

"But how can you be so sure that what is taking place in America will change anything abroad?" Evan sips the cognac, which is better than anything he has ever tasted.

"Because there will be signs to tell them that this is not an isolated event, but that its effects transcend man's understanding. Mankind spits out what tastes bad upon his tongue, wanting to forget the terrible experience more often than not. Like a child, he savors the sweet and seeks to retain its sensation. Perched between these two extremes, like day and night, there is twilight and there is dawn. Therein lies the bittersweet, the taste that clings like a magnet to man's palate, and he will remember despite himself. Death and war are bittersweet, Evan Parker. Whether in defeat or victory, it is bittersweet."

Alabama.

Detrick Myrtle slumps in a recliner before the television set, holding the remote in the left hand, while palming a stale glass of Southern Comfort between his portly legs with the right. His tired eyes pop open to search the gloomy shadows of his large study, but there is no one.

A thought reaches his weary mind, so he thumbs the remote in search of news. Strangely, there is nothing relative to his dilemma. The one time when his expensive satellite is needed, it offers nothing to soothe his dire curiosity. Even CNN lets him down in the midst of the nation's greatest crisis. It is strange, but he's sure to find some kind of update soon, if Sterne does not call first. After his fruitless search through many useless broadcasts, he pauses to watch an interesting documentary on the Discovery Channel.

Arched mandibles are raised to the air as the sentries disperse their chemical signals into the subtle breeze. During its journey through the army ants' territorial valley, something delicious pauses to graze on a blade of grass, never knowing that it is being stalked by ruthless hunters.

Detrick's eyes wilt as the caterpillar wiggles and humps through the attacking mob. The worm's milky flesh disappears beneath a dark red cloud that soon separates to show only a stain where something died a terribly agonizing death.

His head sways to the side as the television camera backs away from the scene of the vicious slaughter, rising from the valley to pan across the majestic horizon of some wondrous land.

A warm breeze ruffles his graying hair as a wildebeest mewls before falling to its massive side. Its weakened legs kick at the air as it struggles to rise from the bed of merciless marauders. A living shadow moves swiftly across the ground to engulf this huge beast, and the tiny assassins tear its thick hide away. Living leather is stripped to expose the succulent meat, which is soon laid open to the bone.

As the red stain begins to flow across the sand, Detrick Myrtle screams himself awake to find that he has been whisked to the crest of some foreign hilltop.

Myrtle looks down into the valley of the ants, which are now coming toward him. The senator discovers that he cannot get out of the recliner as they march upward, growing in size with every step they take toward him. The senator's heart pounds like the drums when they are finally upon him. He shuts his bloodshot eyes and yelps, but a sudden silence engulfs him like the blackness of death. There is no longer the sound of the marching feet shaking the earth. No more falling trees, no...

When Myrtle opens his eyes, an African man blows a cloud of dust into his face from an open palm. It burns the senator's eyes and skin. His drink spills in his lap as he suddenly convulses. He struggles but cannot move his hands to brush the powdery agitation away.

Soon, Myrtle can only look at his immediate surroundings by moving his eyes. Zulu warriors, whose eyes burn holes into his aching soul, suddenly encompass him. They are shrieking and rattling their spares against their shields, chanting something most ominous.

The tallest warrior among them comes forth and smiles at Senator Myrtle. His crimson grin is a threat beyond all mistaken intents. His eyes tell the story of Detrick Myrtle's immediate future. And when the old man's nonverbal question echoes, "Who are you? Where am I?" the tall man laughs at him.

The wind rises quickly as the warrior brandishes a gleaming machete. Now, he whispers an answer into Myrtle's aching mind. "We are your ants, master. And this is Isandlwana, Africa where the earth is stained with the blood of our ancestry and your own. You were warned to beware the coming of another dawn of the Zulus." Two of the others rip Senator Myrtle's shirt open to reveal his tingling, pink flesh. He cannot resist as the tall warrior says, "And we have come here to taste you, master. It is our honor to eat of one so fat and salty." Without warning, the machete is driven into the senator's chest! Myrtle feels every sensation as it slices skin and crashes through his bones. He cannot move to stop what is happening.

Kelvin L. Singleton

Senator Myrtle watches as the warrior reaches into the newly torn cavity and removes his heart, which is still beating before his eyes. Blood gushes from its superior vena cava as the warrior raises it to his whooping army. He tosses the organ into the air, splitting it clean through with the inverted blade of the machete. Both halves fall neatly into his open palm, still beating. He then tosses one-half of it over his shoulder, causing a ruckus among the hungry warriors. Now he tears into the remainder with his razor sharp teeth. Myrtle screams in agony.

Senator Myrtle's eyes are wide open when his wife and body-guards come rushing in to find him dead.

⟞⟝ ⟞⟝

Steaming geysers spew boiling sediments into the hazy sky...somewhere. The earth rumbles as if yawning itself awake after a very deep slumber. The ground quakes from its growing pains and returns to its peaceful trance. The land is alive with thick, green foliage that carpets the earth as far as the eyes can see.

The sky is energetic. Great winged birds of prey soar upon wind currents high above in a beautiful ocean of air. Both mammoth and minute, strange animals are going about the business of foraging, preening, or hunting. The air is saturated with their calls of contentment, fear, and hunger.

Something soaring on leathery wings, stalls in the sky before plummeting toward the green depths of a vast lake teeming with life. With wings compressed to its side, it slips effortlessly beneath the surface near the shore, barely disturbing the water with a gush of white froth.

Seconds later, its triangular head breaks the dull mirror with a fish in its powerful jaws. With the sound of snapping bones, the fish ceases to struggle. Instead of taking to the air from the water, the creature swims to the shore. There, its meal is quickly devoured beneath covetous wings. Leaving only the blood of the fish to mark its passing, it turns toward a short path that leads to a rocky crag.

Climbing straight up, with its head pointed skyward, the beast negoti- ates the cliff with the greatest confidence in its iron talons. When it nears the crest, it freezes and maneuvers its crowned head to survey the sky before its powerful legs force its body from the perch. With a scream that rattles the air, it spreads its wings and swiftly rises on invisible tethers of air. It circles the lake, soaring higher to search the water once again.

The clouds are themselves individual rainbows. They are heavy with life-giving precipitation and airborne ash that captures dazzling hues betwixt the color spectrum's extremes.

Kinzana sweeps the air with his right hand, wielding his cane as he proclaims, "Once, long ago, I stood upon this very precipice and marveled at its deadly beauty as you now do, Evan Parker. Is it not wondrous, this place?"

Evan is speechless, standing on the brink. His eyes inhale this prehistoric scenery as his lungs refuse their appointed duty. His heart races. His pulse grows loud in his ears as he clutches his chest and sinks to his quivering knees.

Kinzana looks upon Evan Parker with an omniscient understanding of his awe, so he places a comforting hand on Evan's head. "Fear not this vision, son. This is the absent piece of the puzzle that you wished to see, some- thing in which to believe. This is the land of Kilimanjaro, before Damballah's angry fists split the world into continents. This is the very cradle of life, Evan Parker, whose jungles conceal the true Garden of Eden."

Evan clasps Kinzana's robe and begs, "Take me away, Kinzana. Take me away from this place."

Kinzana smiles upon Evan, taking his best friend's eldest son by the shoulders to raise him to his feet. "Open your eyes, my son. A man should greet the answers to his greatest questions in life with his eyes, ears, and heart open. He should do so while standing to face them when they are finally revealed unto him. You have nothing to fear."

Evan opens his eyes and shudders. "Why have you brought me to this terrible place?" As if it protests his trepidation, the earth trembles beneath them. In the distance, Evan hears thunder, or the beating of drums.

Kinzana points to the giant in the sky and says, "Behold the predator above. She is a most skillful hunter of the sweltering air where no thing claims power over her talons and wings. See how she hovers. You can almost feel the wind of her wings as they pound the air to keep her aloft."

Evan watches with unbelieving eyes, then follows Kinzana's finger as he points at a wall of stone.

"She has young to feed. Can you hear their cries of hunger emanating from the cave in the face of that cliff? They depend upon her strength to feed and protect them from all that will devour them, but they also depend upon her wisdom and experience to survive the infinite hazards of life."

Evan hears her young calling out in the darkness. "Why are we here?" he questions, humbly. His eyes now seek the beast of the air, a bird he first thought to be a pelican.

"It has always been about life, this place. It has always been about this world's creation and the continuing evolution of life, Evan Parker. She is a mother, walking the sky to find her much-needed thing. She searches day by day for that which provides the sustenance of life for her children, whom she would defend with her very own being even though there are bigger, fiercer beasts in this land. Damballah simply chooses to present her to you in this manner for the sake of illustration."

It pleases Kinzana to see a new appreciation for the winged animal in Evan's eyes. He smiles, but it is somewhat saddened by his thoughts.

"Her name is Sierizaa, and she was once an archangel of the third legion. She was not struck down and made to crawl upon her belly when the war of souls had finally ended in heaven. Her only desire was to create and to raise children of her own, as human women do. She was once charged with the greatest responsibility of all, which was simply to serve the creator. But her insult to Damballah was that it seemed not enough, so this is both his punishment and mercy."

"She was devolved for her sin of a malcontent," Evan summarizes.

"In a manner of speaking. It is true what they say about emulation being the highest compliment, but such things are only of Damballah's jurisdiction. And ultimately, after all, it is what she desires. She will fill her gullet with

fish, and then she will disgorge most of it to quell the burning hunger of her seed. Listen to her triumphant cry when she spots her quarry, for it is with great pride that she performs her daily duties. Watch now, as she gracefully plummets from the clouds like a bolt of lightning."

When the beast shrieks, the echo touches the distant horizon as it folds its wings and dives without fear.

"If a man—any man—takes it upon himself to devolve another by curtailing bloodlines, then he curtails the symmetrical essence, beauty, and creativity of his entire species by limiting its potential for growth and evolution."

It splits the water seamlessly, disappearing momentarily as it had before.

"But what has one to do with the other?" Evan asks. "What has all this to do with our present situation?"

"Playing God is very serious business because there is always something bigger and more powerful amongst those who know no boundaries of morality."

Evan searches the water for the mother, which surfaces with yet another trophy in her jaws. Now he notices something streaking toward her. Its silver scales magnify the low light to shimmer beneath the surface, and Evan knows that she also senses the danger. Her wings unfold in a moment of panic, flapping at the air, but she could not raise herself from the water.

A sudden flash of razor sharp teeth rise from the depths to take hold of her vulnerable body. She screeches in agony, biting at her attacker as she's mauled from below. Her frightened eyes seek the sky as her tongue calls out for the last time. She is brutally thrashed about with a fury that seems cruel and unnecessary. As her snout disappears beneath the froth, a fountain of blood gushes skyward and she is gone forever.

Evan winces, shuddering when the brutal scene instantly replays in his mind's eye. Then a morbid sound of realization comes to his ears; it is pitiful and all-consuming. The offspring have heard the sound of their mother's horrible death, seeming to sense their own impending doom. Evan's heart sinks as their harsh cries dwindle to whimpers. There is a moment of silence as utterly dark as that cave.

"If the parent is destroyed, or if their very existence is simply denied by those who would claim godhood over their destiny, how then can their children survive the hardships of life without destroying one another?"

"Most will not," Evan whispers.

Kinzana points at the distant cave and says, "Because Damballah has instilled a measure of self-preservation in all living things, they may yet survive the day. However, such survival comes at a terrible price—what you call fratricide. In the end, it all comes down to genocide."

As if his eyes have been thrust into that dark habitat, Evan watches as the larger orphan pounces upon his sibling with a hungry fury that knows no mercy. He hears the runt scream as its soft, yellow underbelly is exposed and ripped open by its larger brother. His stumpy wings thrash upon the dirt nest, flailing until the sudden loss of blood dictates the inevitable end.

Evan Parker is repulsed by the fact that the larger of the two does not wait until the other dies to consume what will probably be the first of its last meals. Evan shuts his eyes to thwart the violent image. He clasps his ears, hoping to exorcize the sound of the feeding frenzy as the helpless pterodactyl lay upon its back, squawking a weakened protest at the threshold of extinction. Thankfully, it falls silent.

"There is no greater purpose in this garden than to expand and to become superior to what we are, for to evolve by adaptation is the very essence of our being. And no man has the right to hinder the manifest destiny of another, lest he will be judged harshly." Kinzana smiles and spreads his arms over the landscape. "Our world is a place of awesome wonder, filled with many joys and sorrows. This garden is filled with diverse cultures and ideals. We're all sentient beings who've been given minds of our own so that we may indulge a lifetime of discovery—tasting what one may never have known to be edible or palatable—doing what one has never thought to be done. As explorers, we may learn from others, as well as teach, for we are all equals under the laws of heaven."

Heartfelt tears have begun to stream from both their eyes.

Kinzana turns to Evan Parker and continues. "We are made as travelers and exchangers of ideas and art, each collectively and individually the masters of our own forms of beauty. It is man who estranges man from a distant brother, separating the world not only by geographical borders but also by magnifying cultural prejudice. The greatest hope and aspiration of the endangered future is that our children recognize, address, and corrects this all-encompassing issue."

Evan Parker thinks of the orphaned birds. He thinks of the rioting in the streets of America. He is awash with guilt. He stretches forth an open palm in the direction of the dark cave to say, "But this...this is..."

"Because you will have counted for something in this world, your children can never be discounted by anyone. What then of every man, woman, and child, who deserve—with or without fame or fortune—no less than the same? If a man tosses a bone between two starving dogs, would it not be the norm for them to fight to the death? If that is so, then it must also be true that any number of those survivors will turn away from that bone to eat the dead opponent. After all, therein lies more meat. Here lays that very same bone when another mad-starved animal is drawn into the pit of starved ghettos. What is often mistaken as personal choice is often predicated by malicious subterfuge. And that same man stands there and watches it all again and again, knowing the result because he has made it so. If the evolution of our species is to reach its ultimate destiny, those hidden masters must be removed from their ability to nurture this fratricidal cannibalism. But that in itself is not enough because the dogs will eventually have to learn to share the bones. They must learn to trust one another enough to work together, which will be an even greater task of the adventure before them. Is this not what you see when you interpret your numbers and facts, Evan Parker? Is this not what you see?"

Evan kneels before Kinzana, digging his fingers into the stony earth as he weeps openly and Kinzana soon joins him there. He embraces Evan and concludes, "Life is teeming with Damballah's extremely meaningful metaphors, Evan Parker. This is true, whether it existed in an era that you have always known as prehistory, or whether it is in our here and now. Regrettably so, as our Almighty God is God Almighty, the many are at times made to suffer for the sins of the few because the many have allowed it by *proxy. And as our Almighty God is an angry God, a patient God, whose patience has run out, his undeniable will shall be done upon the earth as it is in heaven." The wind rises and becomes frigid. Lightning walks the air to liquefy the skyward spectrum before dancing upon the choppy water.*

The sudden sound of sirens causes him to leap from his seat. When the trailer lurches over a nasty bump in the road, he stumbles and falls to his knees at Kinzana's sandaled feet. He takes a very deep breath and shivers, afraid to look up. Upon regaining his seat, Evan holds himself as if he's freezing. The ensuing silence is profoundly deep and so bitterly cold.

Status report: "We're in the stretch, Mr. Sterne. The team has gotten to the final barricade without detection. It's only a matter of time before they are in the compound. There is an air duct just above the elevator, which allows it to move freely in what would otherwise be a vacuum. They will use the air duct to get inside the command capsule. Once inside, they won't be able to physically remove the officers because there are locked sets of bars about ten and twenty-yards from the command console, so our men plan to take them out from the twenty-yard barrier," General Smith advises with a heavy heart.

"How long will that take?" asks Sterne, impatiently.

"We can't be exact, but it will be within ninety-minutes at the outside, if nothing goes wrong."

"Good. Just make sure that nothing does go wrong because our asses will be in a sling if your maniac officers are given the opportunity to launch those missiles!"

"I have to ask. Where are you, and just what are you planning to do, Mr. Sterne?" asks Secretary of Defense Slater.

"See if your guys can't move a little faster. I want a minute-by-minute report once the final barricade has been breached. As to your first question, where I am is none of your business. As to your second, I'm going to try to save this country from its worst enemy. Sterne, out!"

No one likes what Vincent Sterne said. They just know he's up to something potentially dangerous. They feel that Evan Parker's safety insures that Kyle Parker will eventually relinquish control of the missile site. They debate whether or not they should report any further progress.

—∣+∣—

Beaufort, South Carolina.

Boom da-da doom! Boom da-da doom! Boom da-da doom! Boom da-da doom!

After the guardian opens the creaking door to the darkened stairwell, he is dismissed by Insanyanga. She lights a large candle and beckons Melissa Parker to follow as she slowly descends the steps. The air is chilled but dry, and the room smells heavily of wax.

They leave the bottom step to stand upon a red clay floor surrounded by burning candles. When Melissa's eyes finally adjust, she sees the journals that Kinzana spoke of. She is surrounded by her legacy. They are old and dusty but well preserved by the waxy air. All along the shelved walls, Kinzana's ancient text awaits. In the center of the floor, the very last of the chronicles sits alone on a stone podium. Melissa takes it, as instructed, but she's not so anxious to open its unabridged pages.

—∣+∣—

Washington, DC.

A member of the Secret Service walks into House Speaker Pinckney's office where he and President Eleanor Graff have been talking and watching the news for what seems like hours.

She says, "Madam President, he's here. At least, that's what we've been told."

Pinckney stands immediately and says, "Well, I suppose we should greet the man. Madam President, are you coming?"

President Graff seems preoccupied. "Oh, yes," she finally says. "Go on. I'll join you in a moment." Pinckney turns to leave but stops in mid-stride. Graff looks at him with a slight annoyance when she asks, "What is it?"

The congressman faces President Graff once more and asks the Virginian as only another Virginian can ask, "I'm curious as to why you chose to meet Parker here at the Capitol Building instead of at the White House."

Graff's skin becomes flush and her eyes squint from the sudden flash of anger she now fights to contain. She thinks twice about lashing out at the Speaker of the House, forcing herself to smile instead.

She says, "Because we'll start immediate deliberations into this matter with all the congressional leaders we've been able to assemble. This windswept matter has to be defused as quickly as possible. Frankly, I'm surprised that you'd ask such an asinine question. Are you satisfied?"

Pinckney raises a brow and boldly ventures, "Just making certain that you aren't thinking of doing something inadvisable, Madam President. We are all operating under quite a strain. It's true without a doubt that, in situations such as these, our judgments are often slanted and askew. And that, dear lady, is to say the very least."

Through clenched teeth, Graff scolds, "Well, I think you just tried to say much more than the very least, Speaker Pinckney." Nothing more is said between them. Once she's left alone, President Graff contacts Sterne. However, he has no time to talk, only advising that she put on her game face.

Speaker Pinckney takes his aid by the arm in the hall. In a whisper, he tells her to follow him. His course and his hasty steps puzzle the young woman as they head for the helicopter pad. He is sweating bullets when he finally answers her frantic questions. As the chopper takes to the air, he says, "She's up to something. I pray that I'm wrong, but that bitch is up to something deadly. I can smell that sly old fox' hole from a mile away. Trust me on that." He taps the pilot on the right shoulder and orders, "If you've already gotten clearance, get us the hell out of here. There's no time to waste. Leave this area as quickly as you can. Is that understood, pilot? If you want to live to see your children again, you better haul ass!"

Accompanied by an official motorcade, the black semi slowly inches its way through the crowded streets until they can go no farther. With his safety assured, Evan and Kinzana transfer into an SUV, which transports them the rest of the way. When they arrive, the people become lively. Many of these spectators are Black, but most of them are angry Whites.

As Evan Parker leaves the vehicle, the crowd advances on him. Some want to shake his hands and wish him well. For the most part, however, they want to lynch him.

The camera lights assault his pupils as his eyes fight to adjust to the brightness. Meanwhile, some people threw things at him. They called him a lying bastard and a murderer, blaming him for all the terrible things that have taken place in the last few days. The guardsmen are forced to protect him, even though many of them feel the same contempt for Evan Parker.

Realizing that Speaker Pinckney has abandoned her, President Graff has no choice but to stand alone. She sweats profusely while standing at the top of the steps with her welcoming arms outstretched. Her smile is more like a grimace of pain, and her nervous knees quiver to her distaste.

Sterne marvels while gazing down from above with binoculars. It never occurred to him that Parker could be traveling in a tractor-trailer disguised as an older model government transport. Soon, none of that will matter.

The pulsing drums, are a relentless frenzy felt deeply within the bowels of the earth. Tiger-3 is in the compound, edging along a corridor that gives them little cover from detection. They can see Captain Parker and Lieutenant Markham at the control console in their steel, high-backed chairs. Their eyes are intent upon the small television monitors at either side of the console.

The four men of Tiger-3 can hear the crowd noise of the scene at the steps of the Capital Building. They inch forward with their laser sights turned on, but Colonel McGruder hangs back so he won't be heard whispering into his headset.

Kinzana's eyes are whites as he descends from the SUV, but no one pays him any attention. He's practically invisible because all eyes are on Evan Parker.

Two snipers are poised with their scopes trained on Evan. A clear shot is impossible with the crowd straining against the raised rifles of the guardsmen that protect Parker from those who would destroy him. Sterne's men, however, are going to have unexpected visits from very strange women and men who've been painted to mimic things that crawl only in the solemn darkness of nightmares. The would-be assassins die suddenly and painfully. Their blood splatters the walls that conceal their treacherous intents. Their screams are never heard over the noise of the mob below.

Evan's progress up the steps is painfully slow. His injured arm and ribs ache from the weight of the evidence he carries.

Vincent Sterne notices Kinzana. Though he doesn't recognize this man, Sterne is certain that Kinzana is the missing piece of the puzzle; the unknown variable that has plagued his search for Parker with failure after miserable failure. He wants Evan Parker's companion identified because it may lead to the whereabouts of the others.

Sterne barks into his headset, "What are you waiting for? Take them out, now. It must be now!" Seconds later, Sterne speaks into his walkie-talkie, telling his snipers to wait for his signal.

⊨╬ ╬⊨

Sergeants Joiner, Macklin, and Persons trained their laser sights on the backs of the two officers. They have no clear shot at either of them. Because the raised metal of their headrests are made of titanium, there is no opportunity for a shot at the base of their skulls. That would be an instant kill shot, shutting down all motor responses by severing the brain stem and obliterating the medulla oblongata. The drums are pounding!

Colonel McGruder uses hand signals to tell his men to target the deltoid muscles, the only feasible shot. Once the targets move in reaction, they'll be exposed. They have to do as instructed. None of them want this thing for fellow soldiers, but these two have to be taken down hard because they are a threat to millions.

Meanwhile, Evan Parker is halfway to President Graff, whose heart is a runaway jackhammer on a slanted street. Thunder rumbles in the distance, and a subtle wind begins to blow, bringing to Evan's flaring nostrils the smell of smoke from the burning city. Despite the noise, the world goes quiet for him.

President Eleanor Graff is standing there, questioning what she is about to do. Was it not Vincent Sterne, who had gotten her into this mess in the first place? Wouldn't it be easier to hand him over to that mob, instead of Parker?

Alicia Markham, who is slouching in her seat from exhaustion, looks to her fiancée with great relief. She says, "He's made it, Kyle. Your brother has made it safely. Thank God." She manages a smile.

When he returns the gesture, his face contorts because of the alien, red beam on her shoulder. It dawns on him too late. The shooting begins!

They are both hit by a single shot, which punctures the deltoid muscles of the shoulders! Upon exiting their bodies, the bullets slam into the upper deck of the console.

Alicia screams. Out of simple reflex, they both stand up. As they do, they are riddled with bullets that readily bore into their bodies and exploded through their chests to make them jitter.

Both Kyle and Alicia fall forward on the console. He is on his knees while she falls back into her chair. Both their faces lay on the blinking buttons of the horizontal panel as the echoes of gunfire resounds throughout the catacombs.

Colonel McGruder is satisfied they're dead, as suggested by their open eyes. He barks, "Go. Go. Go!"

His men leap into action, breaking out a thermite charge to disable the lock on the bars that separates them from the console. After it is frozen with liquid hydrogen, a small explosive charge will be detonated to complete the process.

When McGruder reports that the targets have been neutralized, maudlin cheers resound from the above ground command center. There are also cheers in the air where sweating pilots still soar on the razor's edge until told to stand down.

Forcefully, Sterne whispers, "Take him, now! Don't worry about collateral damage, just take Parker out. Now damn it!"

When there are no flashes from his men's rifles and no sudden burst of blood and flesh from Evan Parker's unprotected cranium, Sterne's eyes leave the skyline to peer at the silent walkie-talkie. He is awestricken. Then he looks up at Evan Parker, who is only three steps from the top. He tosses the hand-held radio down in disgust, breaking the ranks of men positioned on both sides to quickly advance up the steps of the Capitol Building.

Dressed as a Full Bird Colonel, Sterne pulls the Glock .45 from its holster and fires three lethal shots into Evan's back. The bullets hit their mark, sending him flying into the outstretched arms of President Graff, who never expected him to get this close! For a moment that seems an eternity, they are both engulfed in a white cloud of flying debris and smoke. When their eyes meet, Evan knows that he's been deceived.

The crowd moans with screams echoing throughout, but the drums still pound relentlessly.

Melissa Parker whimpers as Kinzana's Bible falls from her numb hands. She collapses in Jarvis' arms, who is struck dumb. Insanyanga wails with her.

The heavy book lies upon its spine at their feet, open to the last pages. A map of the United States is hand-scrawled on the page next to last. It begins to bleed where Washington, D.C. is approximated!

The television monitor reports that Evan Parker has just been shot by a man wearing a soldier's uniform. There is chaos, utter bedlam. No members of the Secret Service detail or military moves against Vincent Sterne. They stand frozen, staring at a man who might even be considered a hero among the ranks.

Vincent Sterne turns away from the crowd below and places the gun to his head. Earlier, during a fitful nap, he dreamed that he would go the way of President Gore. He is exceedingly proud to do this terrible thing for the sake of his beloved country. By doing so, he will be leaving President Eleanor Graff behind to clean up the legacy of his work by refuting relics of the truth by any means necessary. He has already decided that he doesn't want to live in a country that is being run by a woman. Once they ease their way into the White House, they'll be like roaches, and he'd never be rid of them. Even so, he salutes the new Commander in Chief. But much to Sterne's surprised dismay, nothing happens when he pulls the trigger.

Boom da-da doom, da-da doom, da-da doom!

From across a sea of rippled time and space, they stare into one another's dying eyes. Both are shedding their last tears, tears that mingle with blood before dripping to the stainless steel console upon which their heads lay. Evan Parker has been shot dead, they hear the news through all of the pain.

Alicia mouths, "One." Her eyes close against the pain. "Two." Her eyes open as his free hand meets her own in the center of the bloody console. The drums resonate a fever! Pounding into the burning night, they now drive the final spike into the heart of desolation. With white eyes, they both mouth, "Three."

With his left hand and with her right, they simultaneously depress the final buttons, which are marked *EMBARK*.

McGruder shouts, "No!" as he runs toward the two officers they thought dead. He fires his weapon at them repeatedly, but he is too late.

Gabriel one through five are shocked into life! The horns of doom begin to blare. For a moment, they are drowned out by the rumble of those angry angels of death, for they've been commanded to leave their sleeping places. Each is accompanied by the children of Michael, the Avenging Angel. The silo hatches fly open and five nuclear missiles explode into the dark, cloudy sky with their deadly escorts in tow. Angel Mountain roars, protesting the simultaneous birthing of her artificially inseminated spawn. The cylinder channels of the silos belch white plumes of smoke as the initial boosters force the quintuplets toward heaven and their destinies!

Liquid nitrogen is flushed from the vents at the silo openings to dampen their heat signatures, giving the lethal birds cover in their only detectable moment.

The four men of Tiger-3 look to one another first, then at the two dead officers whose fingers are locked in a bloody mesh. Their eyes are permanently affixed beneath the blinking lights of the Armageddon console. Now, in unison, the men of this strike force raise their eyes to the darkness that's become the sky inside of the capsule. This darkness is constantly interrupted by red flashes. It's as if a sword of blood is slashing into the dark flesh that is truly, at this point, the belly of Jonah's whale.

Sergeant Persons kneels on the floor. He clasps his trembling hands together and prays to his God for the people who will soon die because Tiger-3 was unsuccessful in its mission. He's joined by Macklin and then Joiner, who, for the first time in his life, hopes that there exists a God above to welcome the souls of the damned. Death has a way of making true believers of all, even when it is the end of others that is witnessed. Joiner knows that it is dying time. They all do.

McGruder begins to shout into the microphone at the men in the above ground command center. "Missiles away. We've got multiple launches. Destruct and disarming mechanisms have been rendered inoperable. I repeat. Self-destruct and disarming mechanisms have been destroyed. For God sake, someone answer me!"

Vincent Sterne looks at his weapon while many people remain in a frozen gaze far below. He knows that his gun was fully loaded, so he quickly shuffles a shell out of the breech, thinking that the last expended shell must have failed to eject. He places the gun to his temple, and again there is nothing but a click. He looks up at Eleanor Graff, who is still stunned.

Sterne's eyes become saucers and a grunt escapes his throat as Kinzana's blade finds its mark in the center of his back! Sterne falls to the steps below with his head facing the bottom and his legs parted above him.

He lies paralyzed but alive. A widening band of his blood slowly crawls down the steps, parting like blooming tributaries of newly forming rivers. Separated veins of deep red ink creep toward the bottom where they will surely rejoin in the depths of hell.

Some kind of madness touches Sterne's soul when Kinzana's white eyes appear in his line of sight. Vincent Sterne screams for the first time since he was last beaten by his father. He remembers every blow his old man prevailed upon him beneath a sudden nighttime rainbow. His loving father was angry because his disappointing son, the high school football quarterback and track star, had allowed a Negro whelp to keep him from crossing the goal line for a winning score on a naked bootleg. They were one-on-one in the mud and rain with time running out, but his boy lost the battle for the biggest six points of his high school football career.

Sterne remembers the look in his father's livid eyes. He remembers that, for an instant, his father transformed into a demon with three rows of teeth. His red and yellow, catlike eyes seemed to burn holes straight through to Vincent's soul. The demon's words, "Never fail me again," resounds in his mind like echoes in a bottomless mine shaft.

Kinzana growls, "You will not die so quickly, Mr. CIA. It is for you to witness the final stroke of the brush, the final wave of this black tide. You have already foreseen the potential of your foolish thinking. You have willingly entered into contract with destruction when peaceful resolution stood at the door, and now you will see the end result of your villainy." He raises his hands to the sky and says, "Rise now. Come, Black Death, and claim that which is yours to destroy. Only you will cleanse and close this bloody wound by scorching this parchment of earth where no man may freely walk for three-hundred years. Rise!"

The crowd is wordless and motionless, until the horns begin to blare. The final warning is now upon them as they run to-and-fro. They scream as if tormented by evil phantoms, knowing with painful finality that they have made the greatest mistake of their lives in being here. Suddenly, it is not so important that they shake Evan Parker's hands, or call him a filthy liar to his face. It is no longer imperative to be on the spot with microphones and cameras. They have abandoned all hopes of getting a career-boosting photograph or an exclusive angle to the biggest story of American history because they are all doomed to become exclamation points of that story.

The bloody blade, done with its butchery, falls from Kinzana's hand and clatters to the steps below. With a host of weaponry trained on him, he calmly walks up the steps to kneel before Evan Parker, who lies trembling in a pool of blood at President Graff's feet.

Kinzana looks into President Graff's eyes with a cold stare that freezes her heart and loosens her bladder. He snarls at her and says, "As Eve once tainted the garden, so have thee in her stead, Madam President. You sought to bloody the future that still lay—still lay—in your hands until this treachery was done to a man worthy of life! What now comes was never within my power to control or predict, for it has been relegated to the powers that were only your own. Even God Almighty left you choices that he could never make for you, and you have failed us all to misery."

Now he picks Evan up from the stone slab. Draping an arm around his waist, Kinzana holds Evan in an honorable standing position. With tears streaming from his penetrating white eyes, he proclaims, "You will greet the fire with me as a man, my son. Together, we will stand and see it all—this flowering of ten-thousand desert suns. Death comes but once for you, and we will be cleansed by its purifying fire. Into its brilliance, we shall flee to seek out the very center of the most beautiful of heavenly blooms."

Blood spurts from Evan Parker's mouth and nostrils as he fights to stay alive. The world flickers before his tearful eyes as he sputters, "Oh God, it hurts."

Although pain shreds his body as he convulses in Kinzana's arms, his thoughts seek the memory of Melissa's face for comfort.

Even with the stunned Secret Service personnels' urgings, President Graff, the ruler of nothing, cannot force her feet to move. Her lying hands are still outstretched and bloody from catching Evan Parker. Her mouth lies open, and her muted tongue is but a welcoming mat for flies. There are no more moving speeches as she stands on the steps of glory and urinates on herself.

The drums continue to pulse in the night. They have conjured wicked beasts from the basement, as per the charge of the Kuuta, admonishing those deadly things to rise and let blood flow across this land.

Having thought the crisis over, the fighter pilots find themselves woefully out of position. They are caught off guard when the missiles climb at supersonic speeds.

Because Kyle Parker has disengaged the system that makes it impossible for the rockets to fire on friendly transponder signals and commercial aircrafts, Michael immediately ejects seven Saber rockets that will send millions of dollars in aircrafts crashing to the ground without firing so much as a single shot.

West toward California and NORAD, north to New York, and south to Texas they fly, but these missiles are not armed. They have been set to fall harmlessly into the sea or crash in unpopulated areas. However, the missile that hunts a nation's capital carries within its glistening, ebony shell the power of ten-thousand desert suns.

The horns continue to blare. Those accepting the futility of flight, fall to their quivering knees. Praying together, Blacks and Whites now consign themselves to their fate and their God. The sky vibrates as Gabriel begins to plunge. Evan looks to his godfather and asks, "Who are you, Kinzana? Who in God's name...are you?"

Kinzana caresses Evan's bloody cheek and smiles with tears rolling down his iron cheeks. He kindly cradles Evan's face and says, "In another era, I might have been known as the resurrection of Adam. I am Adam of the garden, and we are going home, my son."

Night becomes day. Glass melts. Flesh evaporates. Bones crumble into dust, and concrete burns with the release of a billion stars. Doom da-da boom, doom da-da boom, doom da-da boom, da-da boom, da-da boom! And there was...a fire!

EPILOGUE

For seventy-two hours, time stands still. There are three terrifying days of total and complete darkness, as if the earth has been abandoned by the sun. The temperature plummets across the globe.

No machinery powered by fuel or electricity works as designed. To the seven continents, there comes inexplicable calamities. Rivers bleed red and black ink that climb against the currents. Earthquakes rock the land, shredding whole countries in half. Volcanoes erupt to drown cities in molten lava. Tidal surges sweep entire cities, townships, and villages away. After many a mountain crumble into dust, no children but for three, will be born unto this world for seven long years.

"Remember these words and deeds, for they are most profoundly written to serve as proof undeniable, my children. We are never to revisit the ways inimically abandoned. Remember that we are strong in numbers, but greater still in brotherhood. Our sense of inalienable pursuits and destiny has grown much more ambitiously toward peace and harmony. Yet, equally, we will tow the lines of responsibility to keep the peace which is now required of Damballah's will. Make no mistake in that the Black Tide can again be resurrected to raze humanity to the ground. Remember the past, children, so that it shall not become thy future. Heed this warning, for once, there was a great and terrible thing unleashed."

Three small children are sitting upon pillows with their legs folded beneath them while they listen intently to the story as the mother of the twins reads on. There are two boys and a girl. Two of them are darker, and the other is of ivory skin.

Their mothers have taken turns reading verses to them, and Melissa Parker's final words, before closing the book are, "And there was…a fire!"

The eyes of the enchanted young ones gleam and sparkle as they clap for the exhilarating story.

Melissa Parker and Valerie McAllister smile for the sake of their totally biased children. The kids rain hugs and kisses on them before going to bed to dream the things that happy children dream. They will not see the tears born deep within their mothers' souls.

Jarvis smiles at Insanyanga as they rock back and forth in their chairs. She sees their tears, through her own.

Although the year to date is April 12, 2009, and the world is ever changing, the question remains for you all: Are these the great and terrible events of an unforgettable past, or are they the unthinkable elements of a future to beware?

The End.

Made in the USA
Columbia, SC
18 June 2025

59547041R00311